BARE

The Journ

By C. A. Shilton

Sheila

In memory of mum and dad, and my sister Jill

Grateful thanks to Roger and Ann Dixon, Maureen Scollan and Elisabeth Skoda.

Cover design by Rachael Gracie Carver

Copse Corner Books 2013

Prologue
Toulon 1779.

The young woman on the straw mattress dozed fitfully, exhausted, but kept from proper sleep by the damp, pervasive chill. The light was dim, the tiny window set high in the north wall. Only at sunset might a gleam of sun creep in to brighten the gloom. In the opposite corner, her baby slept soundly.

The cell door creaked open, but she was too tired to open her eyes. Footsteps approached. She heard André's rough voice.

'The bitch has pupped then.'

'Yes Monsieur,' answered the Priest. 'A boy. Strong, he should live.'

'More's the pity. Another heathen gypsy brat.'

'No indeed, Monsieur André, the Commandant has insisted on the boy being raised as a Christian. He's already been baptised.'

'As what?'

'Nicu Javert.'

André grunted. 'Gypsy names! I'm sorry father, but so far as I'm concerned he's still a worthless gypsy bastard whose only future is the gutter.'

The footsteps receded and the cell door scraped closed. Silence returned. The last rays of the setting sun penetrated the window, streaking the makeshift cradle with red and black and casting the grim shadow of the bars across the sleeping baby's face.

PART ONE

The Pup

Chapter 1
Toulon 1788

Javert sat on the low cliff, gazing out across the ocean. Everything was still, with the curious hush that early evening sometimes brings. The fierce heat of the day was waning, giving way to a pleasant warmth; the sun on his face felt good.

Presently a whisper of wind drifted off the sea, stirring the leaves and lifting Javert's thick dark hair. As if the breeze had brought the picture to life, a boat appeared on the horizon, moving slowly. Javert became alert at the same time, sitting forward and squinting against the glare of the low sun. A small galley, heading out of Marseilles. Given the lack of wind they were probably using oars, almost certainly pulled by convicts. The Priest had told him that most of them would die at those oars.

Javert turned his head away, looking to the east where the Tour Royale - the prison garrison of Toulon - stood perched on the very edge of the cliff. Softened and mellowed by the golden evening light, it looked peaceful and tranquil. But that was a lie! He had been born in the garrison, had lived there all his nine years. There was no peace within those walls.

'Well, well, look here; if it isn't the little *gitan* bastard.'

Javert's stomach spasmed. He knew that sneering, threatening voice; hated it more than any other, except perhaps Monsieur André's. He scrambled to his feet and turned to face the newcomers. The four of them had crept silently down the grassy slope and were now strung out across the path. Bibet, the undisputed leader, was the son of the garrison commander - a beefy looking boy with narrow eyes and a sneering mouth. Around him stood his followers. The Beguin brothers – identical twins – were built like a pair of bullocks and were just as stupid. Ferrier was small, but wiry and quick moving, with pointed, rat-like features that gave added meaning to his nickname of *Furet*.

Javert's heart was thumping fast and unevenly. He was tall and strong for his nine years, but against the four of them he had no chance. He glanced left and right along the cliff, desperately seeking a way of escape, but there was none. He

11

was standing near the end of a jutting peninsula, with the sea behind him and to either side. Bibet was grinning malevolently, a *Lupari* toying with a trapped wolf. These wolf hunters were in no hurry, their prey was well and truly cornered.

'What were you doing, little *gitan*? Looking for papa, were you? Think you'll see him rowing by on his little boat, chained up like he deserves?' He spat on the ground in front of him. 'You're just scum, Javert. Go on, say it! Admit you're scum and maybe we'll let you go.'

'Why should I?' Javert retorted. 'I'm as good as you!'

Bibet snorted. 'You? As good as me? Your papa was a convict, your mamma's a gypsy whore and you're a bastard.'

'My mother's not a whore!'

Bibet looked at Javert's clenched fists, and his expression became even more malicious.

'Of course she's a whore – a stinking gypsy whore. Did she tell you your fortune today? I can tell it you. You're going to get a good kicking, little bastard. Then you're going to fall in the pigpen, with the other swine. You're going to get your face rubbed in the pig shit. I owe you for this.' He pointed to his left eye, still purple and swollen from their last encounter when Bibet had attacked with only Ferrier in support – a mistake he would not make again.

They were beginning to close in, but cautiously; experience had taught them that this wolf had sharp teeth. Bibet would never come in first, and Ferrier was also hanging well back; he had been hurt in their last encounter and now the ferret-faced little coward was hesitating. Javert could see just one chance, if only he could move quickly enough.

Unexpectedly, he exploded into action, showing the speed and suddenness they had learned to respect. His foot lashed out, the vicious kick catching Ferrier squarely on his kneecap. The boy screamed in agony. Before he even had time to clasp at his injured knee, Javert had thrown him to the ground and was racing away across the uneven turf.

It was almost a mile back to the garrison and his way was blocked by the cattle pen; the cows already clustered together around the gate as they awaited milking. Javert hurled himself at the gate, scrambling upwards. He threw his right leg over, straddling the gate; he was almost clear. Then he felt a hand close on his left ankle and his leg was yanked back, throwing him impossibly off balance. He catapulted forward and fell heavily, barking his shin painfully on the top of the gate and landing face downward in the hard mud of the field. He tried to scramble up and run on, but a heavy body landed on top of him, then another.

A boot thudded into his back, then his side - Bibet, for a certainty. He lashed out blindly with his foot and heard a howl as it connected somewhere. Then the boot thudded into his chest and he doubled up in agony, gasping helplessly for breath. The pain from his chest spread to his entire body. Time seemed suspended. He still couldn't speak, but he could see with surprising clarity: the sun-baked mud with the overlapping imprints of the cows' hooves; the other boys' muddy boots gathered around him; his own hand lying in the dirt, fingers clenched in agony.

There was a sound of sobbing and sniffing as Ferrier caught up with the other boys, then Bibet's voice.

'Pick him up quick while he's still out. Come on Ferrier, stop snivelling and grab hold of his arm. Hurry up, before he starts fighting.'

Javert felt himself lifted, one boy on each limb. Still holding him face downward they began to carry him across the field, his face bumping and scraping painfully. The hard mud turned to grass, dotted with huge thistles and liberally garnished with cowpats.   The procession halted when they came to the pig pen, and three of the boys held on to him whilst the fourth opened the gate. His breath was coming back now and he began to struggle spasmodically, well aware it was useless. They carried him across the pen to the filth and deep mud around the trough, where they dumped him face down, two still holding his arms whilst another straddled his back. With a shame that was worse than his fear, he could feel tears streaming uncontrollably down his face. Bibet grabbed his hair.

'Come on *gitan*, let's see you eat pig shit!'

Desperately Javert tried to keep his head up out of the dirt, but Bibet pushed his head down until his face was deep in the mud. He felt the cold ooze seeping into his nose and ears. He squeezed his eyes shut and clamped his mouth tight, but he still hadn't recovered from being thoroughly winded and his instinct to breathe was too strong. He began to choke and heave as he tried to take in air, but inhaled only the vile, stinking mud; mud that had been trampled by pigs, fouled by pigs. His struggles were weaker now, consciousness ebbing.

'Bibet - Bibet! That's enough!' Ferrier's voice sounded very far away.

'Don't be so soft, he's only a bloody *gitan.*'

'Bibet, let him go, for God's sake! He's going to drown! Bibet, come on.'

Suddenly the weight was gone from Javert's back. He lifted his face from the clinging, cloying morass, retching violently as he voided the worst of the slimy mud. Groping about with his hands, he crawled around until he felt the hard coldness of the water trough. He hauled himself up, swilling his face and head again and again in the fetid, muddy water until he could force open his smarting eyes. He pulled himself upright and looked around. All was still and silent, his tormenters had gone.

The pigs were nosing at him in curiosity. Pigs could be vicious sometimes; he needed to get out of their pen. He stumbled away from the trough, hauled open the gate and limped into the field beyond, collapsing on the clean grass. The stagnant water from the trough had done little to clean him; his clothes and skin were caked with stinking, viscous mud, his black hair coated with green slime. However, there was nothing he could do about it out here. In winter a stream cut its way through the cliffs close by the fortress, but at this time of year there wasn't even a trickle of water; just a gully across the field, with hard, rutted mud to show where the water had once flowed.

He pulled himself to his feet, still shaking with reaction. His mouth tasted of the pig droppings he had swallowed and his throat felt sore, like rough sandpaper. Every movement hurt; his back was on fire and pain stabbed at his ribs when he breathed. For a moment he gazed towards the garrison, which stood in isolation half a mile distant. He had no choice; however miserable his life there, it was the only home he had. Slowly, he began to limp towards the hated prison.

It was late evening when Javert reached the garrison. To the seaward side its walls dropped directly into the ocean, steep and formidable. The landward side was protected by a narrow moat, and Javert hobbled slowly over the cobbled walkway and across the wooden bridge that led to the gates. The heat still lingered inside the fortress and the odours were strong, the putrid stink of sewage and refuse overwhelming the more appetizing scents of food cooking. Javert limped past the stables, unthinkingly skirting the steaming piles of horse dung. Two men were crossing the square, both resplendent in the blue and red uniform of the *Marechaussee* – the mounted police of rural France – who were currently billeted within Toulon garrison. Javert stopped abruptly and took a quick step towards the stables, meaning to hide there, but he was too late. The older of the two men called to him sharply. 'You boy. Come here!'

Javert hesitated, then obediently limped across to the man. Monsieur André was a lieutenant in the *Marechaussee*. Now approaching middle age, he was built like a huge bear and had the same unpredictable temper, together with a total lack of humour or tolerance. His iron-grey hair was clipped close, showing the skull beneath. He grunted in disgust as he glared down at Javert.

'Look at him, Philippe, look at the state of him. You're filthy boy - you're worse than those convicts over there.' He jerked a massive thumb towards the prison. 'How did you get yourself into such a mess?'

Javert stared down at the ground, making no reply; there was nothing to say. The younger man intervened.

'Leave him to me, Monsieur, I'll get him cleaned up.'

André grunted again, gave Javert another glare of disapproval, then stalked away. Philippe looked down at the boy's bent head.

'Well, young Javert, how *did* you get into that state? Bibet and his lot, I suppose. I saw them come in about half an hour ago and I thought young Bibet looked pleased with himself.' His tone sharpened at the boy's continued silence. 'Come on Javert, talk to me!'

15

Javert raised his head and looked back at him, his expression unfathomable. He couldn't share what he felt, even with Philippe. And the new uniform was yet another barrier; Philippe was no longer just an older boy, he was a young adult. One of "them."

Philippe sighed, realising he was wasting his time.

'All right, come with me.'

He turned and strode away towards his billet, Javert trailing in his wake.

Chapter 2

Javert trotted across the courtyard towards the lodging he shared with his mother. His shirt and trousers, borrowed from Philippe, were rolled up at wrists and ankles, the trousers pulled in and secured at the waist by a worn leather belt. He carried his own filthy clothes in a canvas knapsack, also borrowed from Philippe. Their lodging was in a small courtyard deep inside the garrison, surrounded by high walls, crowding close. In summer, the sun brightened the courtyard and warmed the cobblestones for about two hours in the middle of the day. In winter, there was no sun.

As he approached he could hear the sound of violent coughing. The boy frowned, his mother must be back early from her work. He had hoped to have time to deal with his dirty clothes before she arrived home, now she would ask him for an explanation. The sound of her coughing did not disturb him, as long as he could remember his mother had suffered from a hacking cough, though it had certainly worsened recently.

He ran down the steep steps to their door, which as usual stood open; in the absence of windows the only light came from the open door. The room was damp as well as dark, set as it was low down in the thick stone on the same level as the nearby dungeons. Immediately opposite the door stood a large basket, filled with a miscellany of clothes. Part of his mother's job was to do washing for the police officers and guards who were billeted at the garrison. Javert looked at the still full basket in some surprise. His mother wasn't home early from work, she hadn't been to work.

He sidled over to the basket and stowed his dirty clothes behind it. He expected to be challenged and asked for an explanation, but surprisingly his mother said nothing. She lay on the bed in the far corner of the room, as far as possible from the draught of the door. She was wasted and gaunt, and her sallow complexion gave her thin face an unhealthy waxen tinge. Although she was still under thirty years old, she looked at least sixty. Her hair was still black, but that only accentuated

17

the pallor of her face, making her look like an old woman who had dyed her hair in an effort to hold on to her vanished youth.

She raised her head and smiled at him, but did not get up. He walked across to the bed.

'Mother. Mother, do you want me to get tea ready?'

She looked at him, her dark eyes enormous in her wasted face.

'No, I can do it.'

She swung her legs off the high bed and stood upright. Almost immediately her legs buckled under her and she collapsed to the floor, coughing helplessly. The boy ran to her and tried to pick her up, but she pushed him back and continued coughing in deep, tearing spasms, the rag that did duty for a handkerchief pressed to her mouth.

At last the attack passed and she leant her head back in exhaustion, resting it on the bed behind her. A hectic flush mottled her cheeks. The rag she held and the front of her bodice were liberally streaked with red.

For the second time that day, Javert felt a rush of fear, but this fear was worse – far worse. It was a nameless dread, or rather, he did not dare to give it a name. He was used to his mother's cough, but she had never collapsed before and he had never seen her cough up blood. Once again, he bent over and wrapped his arms round her. This time, she let him lift her up and help her back onto the bed. Exhausted as she was, she could help him very little, but the boy was strong for his age and she was light - much too light. He suddenly realised how thin and fragile she had become and again he felt that stab of fear.

'Mother, I'll fetch help. Wait here - I'll find the doctor.'

She started to shake her head, then sighed and leaned back against the thin pillow. Javert raced up the steps and across the tiny courtyard. There was a doctor in the garrison, whose working quarters were in the prison side. However, Javert was uncertain as to whether the doctor would come at his request; like the remainder of the garrison he had little time for the young outcast. So Javert ran back to Philippe's billet.

Philippe was in the washroom, stripped to the waist. He had just sluiced himself down, and water dripped from his

18

plastered hair and glistened on the dark curling fuzz on his chest. He looked at Javert in smiling surprise, but sobered as he saw the boy's expression.

'What's wrong?' he demanded sharply.

'My mother! She's ill - collapsed. She can't even stand. And she's coughing blood. She needs the doctor, but I don't know if he'll come for me.'

Philippe reached for the towel and dried himself quickly, rubbing the excess water off his hair. He grabbed his shirt and pulled it on, then put his arm round the boy's shoulders.

'Come on.'

They hurried side by side across the courtyard. Near the stables they passed Bibet, still with the Beguin twins. Bibet looked at Javert sideways, but made no comment in the presence of Philippe. Javert ignored them, he had more important things on his mind.

The doctor was just locking up his room, having finished work for the day. They hurried up to him, Philippe slightly in the lead.

'Doctor, can you spare time to come and look at this boy's mother? It sounds as if she's in a bad way. Total collapse, coughing a lot of blood.'

The doctor shook his head.

'Monsieur Philippe, there's nothing I can do for the woman. She's been to see me twice in the last month and I've given her what medicine she could afford, but it's too late for her. The woman's almost dead of consumption - I'm only amazed that she's lasted this long.' He looked at Javert, who was standing back respectfully, leaving Philippe to do the talking. 'I'm sorry boy, but I have a living to make. There's no point in my wasting my time visiting a dying woman who can't pay.'

Philippe regarded the doctor thoughtfully.

'I'll pay your fee for the visit,' he said quietly.

The doctor shrugged his shoulders.

'You've more money than sense, young Philippe. All right, I'll come, but there's precious little I can do, I'll tell you that much for nothing.' He turned to Javert. 'You boy, go and find the Priest. He'll be more use than I am now.'

Javert looked at him wide-eyed, then nodded and raced away across the compound to the little chapel. There was nobody visible, but he could hear the low murmur of voices from the confessional. The Priest was there all right. Javert sat down on a bench to wait.

After a few minutes, a uniformed officer emerged from the confessional. Javert's heart gave a painful jolt as he recognised Monsieur André. André glared down at him.

'What the devil are you doing here?'

Behind André, Father Vincent emerged. He was a middle aged man who had spent the past ten years of his life at the garrison, working mostly amongst the convicts. He looked tired and careworn, exhausted by the hopeless task of trying to care for the souls of the human wrecks in his charge.

'Well boy, what do you want?'

Javert ducked his head in respect before raising his eyes to meet those of the man. Like all the boys, he was in awe of the Priest.

'Excuse me Father, but the doctor asked me to come. It's my mother. She's very ill, and he said I was to fetch you to her.'

André grunted in contempt. 'And why should your mother want a Priest, eh? She's not even a Christian.'

The Priest nodded. 'That's true, but at least she had this boy baptised and raised in the faith.' He looked at Javert thoughtfully. 'You say the doctor asked for me, boy? Not your mother?'

'The doctor, Father.'

'I see. All right, I'll come. Maybe her immortal soul can still be saved. You go back now, I'll follow. Go on, I'll only be a few minutes behind you.'

Javert met the doctor at the top of the steps leading to his home. He was obviously just leaving, but stopped when he saw Javert.

'Where's the Priest, boy? Did you find him?'

Javert nodded.

'Yes Monsieur, he's following.' He looked down the steps, towards the room he shared with his mother. 'My mother - how is she?'

The doctor shook his head.

'Nothing I can do there, you'd best go in and see her while you can. She's been asking for you.'

He walked away as Javert ran down the steps. Young as he was, he had encountered death before, and he understood the meaning of the doctor's comments. The fear he felt was no longer nameless, he was beginning to face up to what he had refused to admit before, even to himself. His mother was dying, if she wasn't already dead. Beyond that he did not think. What would happen to him, what he would do when she was gone, were questions he dare not yet ask himself.

She was still alive, but it seemed to him that her condition had worsened even in the few minutes he had been absent. Her eyes glinted and wandered, bright with fever; her skin looked strangely transparent. She could no longer lift her head from the pillow, but she had heard his step on the stairway and held her hand out towards him. He ran over to the bed and took her hand in both of his. Her skin felt hot and dry, the shrivelled flesh loose on the bone.

She moved her head slightly to look at the boy, who was gripping her hand so tightly it hurt. His expression was frightened and confused. She whispered to him weakly.

'There's so much I wanted to tell you, but it's too late – there's no time. Stay here. No matter how difficult it gets, stay here in the garrison until you're grown. Promise me.'

She paused, seeming exhausted by the effort of talking, then tried again, her whisper becoming increasingly thready and weak.

'Stay and live here, stay on the right side of the law. Your father –' She paused again. The boy's grip on her hand tightened even more.

'Mother, please, tell me about my father. You never have. What did he do? Where is he now?'

His mother stared at the ceiling, her eyes losing focus. She was still breathing, but her senses were slipping away from her. Perhaps she was thinking about his father. She had told Javert very little about him, only that he had been taken away to the galleys before Javert was born.

'Javert.'

He started as a hand fell on his shoulder. Behind him stood Philippe, with the Priest. Javert released his mother's hand and stepped back, the Priest taking his place by the bed. The woman roused herself and looked at him. Weakly she lifted her hand, laying it on the Priest's arm.

'Father, promise me you'll help my son. Please - '

The Priest took her hand, laying it firmly back on the bed. He didn't respond directly to her plea; instead he lifted the cross, holding it within her line of vision.

'My daughter, do you now acknowledge our Lord Jesus Christ?'

Their eyes met above the cross and a message seemed to pass between the Priest and the dying woman. She nodded weakly. The Priest turned and glanced meaningfully at Philippe, who put his arm round Javert's shoulders.

'Come on, leave the Priest with your mother. It'll only be a few minutes, then you can come back.'

It was over fifteen minutes before the Priest emerged. He shook his head in response to Philippe's raised eyebrows.

'She hasn't gone yet, but she doesn't have long. But praise the Lord, she will die in the faith.' He nodded towards Javert. 'You'd best go back in boy, she's asking for you.'

Javert walked hesitantly back down the steps. Philippe and the Priest followed him, but stayed discreetly by the door. His mother was lying very still, staring into space with a far-away expression on her face. When he approached her she dragged her mind back to the present, groping at her neck.

'Medallion. Take the medallion - '

The boy fumbled at the chain, unfamiliar with the fastening and clumsy with grief and fear. His vision was misted by the tears that were now streaming down his cheeks. At last he succeeded in undoing the clasp. He tried to put the medallion into her hand, but she pushed it back at him.

'Take it - keep it. Remember - '

She paused and coughed slightly. There was a curious rattling sound in her throat as she let out her breath in a long sigh. Her open eyes still seemed to be looking into his, but their stare had become fixed, unblinking.

Philippe and the Priest approached and the Priest bent over the woman on the bed. Then he looked up and shook his head. Philippe put his arm round Javert, pulling him close.

'I'll take him with me for tonight,' he offered.

The Priest looked doubtful, then nodded.

'All right. We have to arrange the funeral, and I promised the boy's mother I'd make sure he was looked after. But there's nothing we can do tonight, I'll talk to the Commander in the morning.'

The funeral was held late the following day, attended only by Javert and Philippe. There was no money to pay for the service; she received a pauper's funeral, and was buried in an unmarked grave in the corner of the cemetery reserved for the convicts.

Following the burial, Javert was taken to the Commander's office. In addition to the Commander, Philippe, Monsieur André and Father Vincent were present. The Commander glanced distastefully at Javert, then looked round at the assembled company.

'You all know my views regarding this boy and his mother. If I had my way he'd leave now and take his chance with the other vagabonds and riff-raff. However, Father Vincent promised the boy's mother that he would be looked after and he is duty bound to keep that promise. So before we start to look elsewhere, is there anyone here who will take this boy?'

Philippe's arm tightened round Javert's shoulders.

'I'll take him, Monsieur.'

Javert's face lit in sudden delight. He looked hopefully at the Commander, but his hope was destined to be short-lived. The Commander spoke to Philippe sharply.

'You're hardly more than a boy yourself, and you're only just learning your job. It's out of the question.'

'I agree,' said the Priest firmly. 'You're too young for such a responsibility. This boy is going to need strong guidance and training. There's bad blood there, from both his parents.'

Javert's head drooped again and Philippe's arm tightened in sympathy. There was a silence, then André stepped forward.

'I'll take the boy. I'll see he makes himself useful. He'll learn right from wrong, if I have to beat it into him.'

Javert shrank involuntarily back against Philippe, his stomach churning in fear at the thought of spending his life under André's domination. He knew that Andre's threat was no idle one; he was an austere, harsh man, known for his rigid beliefs and his lack of humour.

The Commander nodded, looking pleased.

'Thank you, Monsieur André. That's very charitable of you.'

He walked over to Javert and pulled him away from Philippe, his fingers deliberately biting deep into the boy's arm.

'All right boy, you decide. Monsieur André has offered to keep you - nobody else wants you. With your background that's hardly surprising, it's a pity you were ever born. So make up your mind once and for all.'

He pointed towards the main gate.

'You can leave here now and follow your parents' path, or you can stay here and be brought up among respectable people - which is more than you deserve. Make your choice. You do as you're told, or you get out.'

Javert looked up at him, then down at the floor. He resisted the impulse to pull away from the hard fingers that were grinding into his arm. His mother's words echoed in his mind - she had told him to stay here, no matter what. He looked over at André, who was standing in front of the archway that led to the Commander's private quarters, his looming bulk almost filling the small space. Javert felt terrified at the thought of his future with André, but what else could he do? Where else could he go?

He raised his eyes to meet the Commander's fierce stare.

'I'll stay with Monsieur André, Monsieur.' The words were no more than a whisper.

The Commander glared down at him, then pushed him towards André. André flipped the medallion that hung around the boy's neck.

'What's this?'

Javert's hand closed defensively around the medallion.

'My mother gave it to me, just before she died. She wanted me to keep it.'

For a moment man and boy stared at each other - one large and fierce, the other small and frightened, but holding determinedly to the medallion. Then Father Vincent intervened.

'It was his mother's dying wish, Monsieur. I think we should respect that.'

André nodded slowly.

'Of course Father, of course we'll respect her dying wish. Now boy, you listen to me. Your father was a convict and a murderer. Your mother was a gypsy and a whore.'

'She wasn't a whore,' muttered Javert.

André's fist caught him on the side of the head, almost knocking him to the floor.

'Don't you back-chat me, boy. Of course she was a whore - how else do you think she got the money to send you to school? Not just by washing clothes, I'll tell you that. You should be ashamed of what she was. Remember that. Every time you look at that medallion, remember that!'

The words pierced Javert like a dagger - a stiletto thrust that caused little visible damage, but left a deep wound that would be slow to heal.

André released him, then stalked to the door. Javert, his expression now still and unfathomable, looked back once at Philippe, squared his shoulders and walked across to André. He opened the door politely for him, then followed his new guardian out into the night.

Chapter 3

The first weeks with André were the darkest period of Javert's life, as he tried to come to terms with his grief at his mother's death and to living under Monsieur André's rigid regime. Unlike most of the officers in the garrison, André was fanatical about smartness. His horse must be perfectly groomed, saddle and bridle gleaming and spotless. His uniform must be likewise immaculate. He made no allowances for Javert's youth and inexperience and his blows were both frequent and heavy. A neglected scuff on one of his boots would lead to a hard cuff round the head.

A month after his mother's death, Javert was in the stables, grooming André's horse and ensuring his saddle and bridle were in perfect order. As he left the stall, the light reflected off something at his feet; small, round and shiny. He picked it up and carried it into the daylight to examine it better. He was holding a gold coin, a Louis d'Or! For a moment he gazed at the object in awe – Javert had never had any money - then he thrust it into his pocket and hurried across to the officers' quarters. He had already learnt not to keep his guardian waiting.

André was already there. Javert was surprised to see that he was kindling a fire in the brazier - it was early August and the day was a hot one. André looked up at Javert's entrance, then walked over and examined the boots that the boy had cleaned earlier. After a moment he gave a non-committal grunt, then set them down next to his bed. Javert breathed a silent sigh of relief, evidently the boots had passed muster. He sat cross-legged on his own pallet as his guardian picked up several documents from the table, walked over to the brazier and began to feed the paper into the flames, piece by piece. Presumably, that was the reason for the fire. Javert watched him idly for a moment; then remembered his new coin. He took it from his pocket and gazed at it, enjoying its warm heaviness and the muted glow of the gold.

'What's that?'

Javert jumped and looked up, to find André staring at him across the room. Javert thrust the coin back into his pocket.

'Nothing, Monsieur.'

André put down the document he was holding and walked over to Javert, who stood up and backed instinctively away. André held out his hand, saying nothing. After a few seconds, Javert put his hand into his pocket, brought out the coin, and reluctantly handed it to his guardian. André's eyes narrowed as he looked at the gold in his hand, then he raised his eyes to Javert.

'Where did you get this?'

His voice was quiet, but deadly. Javert stared back at him, afraid but uncomprehending.

'Found it, Monsieur. In the stables.'

'When?'

'Just now, Monsieur – after I'd finished grooming Ceres.'

André stared at him coldly, then walked away and tossed the coin into the brazier. For a few minutes he continued to feed the documents to the fire. Then he picked up the fire tongs, groped in the red-hot ashes, and turned back to Javert.

'Come here.'

Obediently, Javert walked across the room to him. André grabbed him by the arm and jerked him closer.

'Right boy - I'll teach you not to steal.'

Javert looked at him in confusion. 'But I didn't, Monsieur, I didn't steal it. I found it, I swear I did. It was in the stables – just lying there in the straw.'

'And how do you think it got there?

'Well, I suppose …' Javert's voice tailed off. Andre's fingers bit into his arm.

'Well? I'm waiting for an answer boy.'

'I suppose – I suppose someone dropped it there. Monsieur, I didn't mean to steal, I swear I didn't. I never thought …'

'You should have given it to me, straight away. You're a little thief, boy, do you hear? Well, that's no more than I expected, but I promise you, I'll soon cure you of it.'

Holding Javert easily in the crook of his arm, he pulled the tongs from the brazier. Javert suddenly realised that he had used the tongs to remove the coin from the fire; there it lay between the ends of the pincers, glowing with heat. Before Javert realised what he was going to do, André had grabbed his hand, prised open the fingers and dropped the coin onto Javert's palm. Then he closed the hand tightly round the coin, forcing palm and fingers hard against the almost red hot metal.

Javert screamed uncontrollably. He fought to open his hand, to tear free, but André held him tightly, keeping his hand mercilessly closed. After a few seconds he let go. For a moment the hot coin stuck to Javert's hand, then it fell to the floor, taking some of the skin with it and leaving an agonising burn on his palm and the tips of his fingers. André grabbed him by the hair, forcing his head up.

'Better learn fast, boy. Next time it'll be white hot and you won't let it go so quickly. And you can stop that noise or I'll give you something else to snivel about.'

He let Javert go, walked over to the table and began to study another document, leaving the boy huddled on the ground cradling his burnt hand. He couldn't control the tears of pain that were running down his cheeks, but only a whimper escaped him. Monsieur André was not given to idle threats.

As time went on, Javert became used to his guardian's ways and learnt to avoid the worst of his wrath. André was harsh and unfeeling, but he was not capricious. So long as Javert avoided argument or back-chat and did his work thoroughly and well, he could usually keep out of trouble. He even found some unexpected compensations for living under André's guardianship. He was better fed; despite the fact that there were serious food shortages throughout France, the officers in the garrison did not go short. Also, he was no longer subjected to abuse by the other boys, none of whom cared to risk André's anger. Javert was still ostracised, but they left him alone.

October brought a new development. Javert was cleaning André's boots under his guardian's watchful eye, when there was a knock on the door.

'Yes?' growled André.

The door opened to admit Philippe. Javert's eyes widened in surprise and pleasure. Philippe had never before visited André's quarters; the two men did not socialise and their relationship was strictly a professional one.

'You sent for me, Monsieur?' Philippe's tone was a little doubtful, André rarely invited his colleagues to his quarters.

'Yes.' He looked Philippe up and down, and his tone sharpened. 'Look at yourself, man. Your boots are filthy and you look as though you've not shaved in a week.'

Philippe sighed. 'I'm sorry Monsieur, but I've been working almost round the clock. I haven't had time for polishing boots.'

'We've all been working round the clock. That isn't an excuse for letting standards slip; don't forget it. Now sit down, I have a private matter to discuss and I want to do it away from prying eyes or flapping ears.'

Javert stood up and moved towards the door.

'Where do you think you're going, boy?'

Javert stopped and turned. 'Excuse me, Monsieur. You said it was private, so I thought I should go.'

'I'll tell you when I want you to go. Come over here, sit down, and listen.'

He unlocked the drawer in his desk and pulled out a document. He leafed through it for a moment, then turned his attention to Philippe and Javert.

'Right, pay attention, both of you. This is part of a report from Marshall de Stainville, in charge of the garrison in Rennes. He's been investigating the food riots.'

He opened the document and began to read:

'... *The situation continues to be critical. Riots have already occurred in Grenoble, Paris and, Dijon, as well as here in Rennes. Despite these being ruthlessly suppressed, further disorder is expected. The begging population is increasing and becoming more and more aggressive and difficult to control. The dangerous classes are being joined by local peasants, with no previous history of violence or disorder. All grain stores must now be guarded by armed troops. Needless to say, this is a serious drain on our resources.*'

'You're telling me!' muttered Philippe, with feeling. André frowned at him, then continued reading.

'Our intelligence sources tell us that similar riots can be expected elsewhere, accompanied by attacks on the grain stores. If this happens, the troop numbers may be insufficient to defend them.

A number of notorious persons – lawyers and orators known to have been instrumental in sparking the above-mentioned incidents – have been sighted in both Toulon and Marseilles. Seditious pamphlets are being circulated, both there and elsewhere. It is essential that every attempt is made to gather intelligence with regard to these persons, and with regard to their plan of action ...'

André laid down the document.

'That's all that concerns you, now have a look at this.' He picked up a single sheet of paper, which he passed to Philippe. 'This is the kind of thing that's being circulated, they're appearing all over the place – in the inns, café's, streets. Oh, there are numerous written pamphlets as well – every one more seditious than the last.'

Javert leaned over to look at the pamphlet. It was a crudely drawn caricature showing an immensely fat landowner and a clergyman, eating from plates piled high with food. On his knees beside them was a very thin peasant, engaged in scraping grain from his almost empty bowl into their overflowing bowl. Beneath the caricature it said:

YOU SOW – THEY REAP
YOU STARVE – THEY EAT

Philippe sighed. 'The trouble is, there's something in what this says. From what I see and hear, the poor bastards are starving.'

'What poor bastards?'

'The peasants.'

André looked at him sharply. 'You sound as if you're in sympathy with them.'

Philippe shrugged. 'Not exactly, no. But Monsieur André, these peasants really are starving. I've never seen so many beggars – in the country, in the towns, even at the gates of this garrison, where they might know they'll get short shrift. It's hardly justice, is it? They work to harvest the grain, then it all gets taken away and stockpiled for the landowners, the clergy and the richer bourgeoisie who can afford the ridiculous prices.'

André leaned forward threateningly.

'You can cut that out for a start. What's happening to those poor bastards, as you call them, is no concern of yours. Your concern is to do your duty. That means carrying out your orders and upholding the rule of law, not spouting sympathy for the people who break it.'

'I can't help being human, can I?'

'Well, you'd just better start helping it. I tell you, if you let your heart rule your head, you'll not be able to do your job properly. Do we understand each other?'

Philippe had flushed scarlet. 'Yes Monsieur.'

'Well, make sure we do. Now then, pay attention.' He tapped the document on the table. 'If this information is accurate, there's likely to be riots very close to home, most likely in Marseilles because the population there are troublesome enough even without food shortages.'

'Is the information reliable?'

'This source usually is. Bear in mind, riots like that don't just happen, the peasants are just the cannon fodder, not the tinder. We want the tinder - the lawyers, the pamphleteers. We know they're down here. What we don't know - and what we need to know - is what they're planning.' he looked at Philippe. 'And that, my innocent looking young cockerel, is where you come in. I want you to go under-cover. The boy too.'

Philippe's voice rose in protest. 'No! It's too dangerous. He's too young.'

'Nonsense. He's ten years old and it's time he started to earn his keep. The boy's not stupid, he knows how and when to keep his mouth shut, and he knows what to expect from me if he doesn't. He'll go with you as your younger brother, he'll be good cover for you and that's important. Four ears are better than two, and they're more likely to talk in front of him. Who's going to worry about an ignorant little country boy?'

He turned to Javert.

31

'As for you, you just mind yourself. This is serious work, boy - real work. Do what he tells you, keep your ears open, keep your mouth shut. You foul up on this job, you risk your life - and his. Our last under-cover man was found in the river with a knife in his back.'

Javert nodded, giving a sudden shiver at the thought of any action of his putting Philippe's life at risk. He would never let that happen - never! He leaned forward, listening attentively as André briefed them on their forthcoming mission.

Chapter 4

Javert looked around with pleasure and interest as the wagon took the coast road towards Marseille. He felt unusually happy; he was out of the garrison, away from the constantly watchful eye of André, and he was with Philippe. Philippe's good humour and sense of fun had a positive effect on Javert, bringing out the lighter side of the boy's nature. Javert smiled rarely, but when he did it was a sudden gleam of sunlight breaking through a thundercloud, totally transforming his usually sombre expression.

To their left lay the coast, dotted with numerous small bays, surrounded by pine forests that grew right down to sea level. The blue sea shimmered in the sunlight, a sapphire set in jade. On a day like this and in such a setting, it was easy to forget the riots and violence that were sweeping across France – riots motivated by starvation and fuelled by orators and pamphleteers.

Not that Javert and Philippe were likely to forget. They were on their way to the Fleur de Lys, a low class inn on the outskirts of Marseille, known to be the haunt of radicals and political malcontents. Their brief was to mingle with the customers at the inn and find out all they could about the actions – and the plans – of the political activists who were believed to be behind the increasingly organised attacks on food and grain stores. A simple enough task, but a dangerous one. Such men did not take kindly to being spied on. But the dangers of their mission worried the young Javert not at all. To him it was just an adventure, and a chance to escape the confines of the hated garrison.

The wagon driver had given his name as Pierre. He was in his mid–thirties, small and wiry, with quick, darting eyes. The wagon was loaded with chains and shackles of various kinds, for delivery to the port at Marseille for use on the galleys. Philippe and Javert were dressed in peasant garb, in Javert's case little different to his normal clothes. Ostensibly they were brothers who were making their way to Marseille from Beausset. If challenged, their story was that their father had recently died, and Philippe was taking his young brother to Marseille to live with his uncle.

It was approaching dusk when Pierre halted the wagon at a fork in the road, just short of the long downhill drop into Marseille. Ahead of them a huge red sun was sinking into the sea, slowly drowning even as they watched. The area was deserted. Pierre pointed to a narrow track that wound off to the left among the tall pines.

'The Fleur de Lys is down there, about a ten minute walk, where the track crosses the river. I must get a move on, because I need to reach Marseille before dark. Remember we rendezvous back here early tomorrow. I'll leave Marseille half an hour after first light. You need to arrive first and start walking. It's natural enough you should beg a lift from me, but if I sit here and wait for you it could cause attention.

'Make sure you don't leave before it's light. If you're seen walking with a lantern you'll draw attention to yourselves, and if you don't carry a lantern you could very well get yourselves arrested. The police here are very hot on that, especially now with all the strangers and beggars about. And you can't let on who you are or your cover's destroyed.'

He raised his whip in salute, then shook the reins and drove off down the road towards Marseille. Philippe and Javert walked along the track towards the inn, Philippe issuing last minute instructions as they went.

'Don't forget, we're from the country. We're not used to city life and not used to big inns like this one. It'll be expected that you'll be shy and a bit overwhelmed, so say as little and listen as much as you can.'

Javert nodded. That wouldn't be difficult. He had never been encouraged to chatter and he was genuinely ignorant of the realities of life in large cities and towns. With his upbringing, he was as tough as any street urchin that ever roamed Paris, but he was not 'street wise.' His world had been the narrow world of the garrison, his influences the stereotypical views of the guards and police officers.

The inn was situated near the river, so as to catch trade from both water and road. It was very old. The outbuildings looked manifestly unsafe, with crumbling walls and gaping holes in the roof. The battered inn sign hung askew, creaking and groaning even in the light breeze.

Philippe pushed open the heavy door, and the sound hit them in the face. The smell of greasy food and cheap wine was overlaid by the fetid odour of unwashed bodies and the sharp, acrid stink of urine. It was much larger than the garrison mess, but the low roof gave it a claustrophobic feel. Its few windows were filthy and the place was dim and poorly lit.

The place was packed with customers. Most were ordinary peasants, a few looked as if they might be farmers. There was a sprinkling of beggars. Almost everyone looked poor. The majority of the company were men, the few women shabbily dressed and dirty. Most of the women were middle aged, but there were two or three younger women, one of whom immediately importuned Philippe.

'Hello dearie, nice to see a handsome young man in this hovel. Are you going to buy me a drink?'

Philippe smiled at her. She might be useful later, and give him the excuse he needed to leave Javert alone. A very pleasurable excuse too, for Philippe liked women. But not yet, first he had to familiarise himself with the place and find them a good position.

'Perhaps a bit later, darling. Don't go away.'

The woman shrugged. 'Go away? Where would I go dearie?' She turned away from him, her eyes searching for other likely customers.

Philippe gazed around until he located the landlord, then forced his way through to him.

'We're just on our way through to Marseille, but we've been benighted here. Have you a bed for the night?'

The landlord looked doubtful. 'Dunno about that, we're packed out. Only two rooms're taken by the toffs there.' He pointed to the far corner where two men were holding forth to a large audience.

'Anywhere would do, so long as it's out of the weather.' Philippe nodded towards Javert. 'It's cold to sleep out, especially with him.'

The landlord guffawed, showing his blackened teeth.

'Sleep out? Are you crazy? If you sleep out around here you'll find yourselves in the lock–up in no time flat. Tell you what, I can let you have the wagon, in the yard.'

Philippe nodded. 'That'll do very well.'

'You be wanting breakfast as well?'

'No. No thank you, we'll be on our way at first light.'

'Up to you.' He held out a dirty hand. 'That'll be five ecus – each."

Philippe paid him and ordered wine, watering it liberally before handing a cup to Javert. The boy was looking round curiously. He didn't need to pretend to be overcome, he was genuinely disorientated by the noise and press of people, though from his level he could see very little beyond their immediate neighbours.

Philippe surveyed the company, taking particular interest in the two men the landlord had pointed out – the men he had referred to as 'toffs.' Philippe wouldn't have described them in that way - they were quite plainly dressed - but their clothes were certainly of better quality and better cared for than most of the customers. One of the men was now standing on a table, haranguing the crowd around him.

' - and is that right? I ask you citizens, is that right? Why should you have nothing, you who work and sweat all your lives? You have nothing, while your splendid Lord of the Manor sits up there with his acres of good land, that he's never worked for and uses only for the chase, and gets fat on your produce and our taxes!'

There was a subdued muttering from the crowd. Philippe gripped Javert's arm and guided him closer. The speaker paused to accept a cup of wine, then continued, becoming more and more animated as he warmed to his subject.

'Yes citizens, our taxes. Because you and I both pay taxes on what we own and what we produce. But your Lord and his like – what do they pay? Nothing! He, who has everything, doesn't pay a sol. When the taxes make you so poor you can't even afford the tools to work your land, he lends you tools. Then he takes your produce to pay for the hire of them, and grows fat and rich, while you and your families all starve.'

The rumble among the crowd grew as he paused again. The words went to their hearts as they might not have done twelve months before. Last year, the harvest had been good and there had been enough to spare after payment of taxes for farmers to have enough to eat, and a little over to sell.

They were used to no more than that. Making a living off the land was always precarious. A bad harvest meant hardship at best, starvation at worst and this year the harvest had been disastrous. What the orator said was quite true. Even though many of them owned their own land they could not work it without assistance from the Lord of the Manor, or richer farmers. They were obliged to hire tools they could ill afford, or to hire out their own labour when they badly needed the time in order to work their own land.

After a while the man finished speaking and the crowd began to disperse into small groups. Philippe watched them carefully. One of the orators was moving amongst the crowd, distributing pamphlets. These were mostly in the form of cartoon style drawings, more effective than the written word with a population that was largely illiterate.

The second man had moved into a corner, and was sitting at a table with three other men. Their heads were close together and they looked to be talking earnestly and purposefully. The orator was drawing on the back of one of the pamphlets.

Philippe picked up his stool and made his way towards them as casually as possible; a man seeking some breathing space in a corner, out of the main crowd. By the time he got close to them the paper had vanished. One of the men was looking at him in suspicion. He was a big man, with the shoulders of a blacksmith. His long grey hair and beard were filthy, his expression unfriendly to the point of being threatening. The other two men appeared to be slightly better off peasants, reasonably but not well clad. They were also regarding Philippe with caution.

Philippe nodded casually to them, then sat down on his stool. Javert sat on the floor by his side. Philippe took no further notice of the men, but kept swigging copiously from his heavily watered wine. His eyes were straying across the room to the dark haired girl who had accosted him earlier.

Eventually he stood up and lurched over to the three men.

'Scuse me, but I've got a bit of – business – I need to take care of for a few minutes. You couldn't keep an eye on my brother here could you? Buy you a drink!'

The men looked at Javert, who was beginning to nod where he sat, apparently overcome by the effects of the wine. The men followed Philippe's eyes from Javert to the girl, and the older of the two peasants laughed.

'Good bit of business it looks too friend.'

The big man with the beard interrupted. 'You from the country?'

Philippe nodded and repeated his story of taking his little brother to Marseille. The man sneered at him.

'It'll eat you alive, country boy, you and your brother.'

The orator laughed. 'Oh, let him be, Marcel, he seems to be catching on here fast enough. What he's got his eye on looks good to me, I'm sure he'll rise to the occasion all right.' He regarded Philippe more closely. 'Mind you, a pretty boy like you could probably earn a bit on your own account.' He nodded towards Javert. 'Him too. He's a bit young now, but he's got promise.'

There was a burst of ribald laughter. Philippe, keeping to his role, gave a sheepish but confused smile. His obvious lack of understanding led to more laughter.

'You go ahead friend, and good luck with your business. The kid'll be okay – he's nearly asleep anyway.'

Philippe motioned Javert onto the stool, then swayed his way across the room and sat down next to the girl, signalling for more wine as he did so. Shortly afterwards, the two of them left the room. The older peasant laughed again.

'You'll have a long wait for him, boy. Here.'

He handed Javert another cup of wine, unwatered and filled to the brim. The boy thanked him shyly and contrived to tip most of the wine into the rushes on the stone floor; he knew he dare not drink much of the rough, strong liquid. After a while his eyes glazed and his head began to nod again.

The pamphlet re–appeared, and the men began to talk quietly. Javert's attention sharpened and focused. He could see they were sketching some kind of map on the paper, but was unable to see any real detail. He strained his ears, but they were talking too softly for him to hear. He needed to get closer.

A skinny, mangy looking cat stalked across the room, surveyed the scene haughtily, then vanished under the table where the men sat. Javert stumbled off his high stool, almost oversetting it in the process, then crawled across the floor, reaching for the animal. The men paused in their conversation as he knocked clumsily into their table, then shouted with laughter as the cat spat angrily and clawed viciously at the boy's arm, leaving four parallel scratches that oozed blood.

Javert snatched his arm back and looked at the men sheepishly. Then he lay down in the corner by the wall. The orator laughed.

'Boy's nearly out – country bumpkins aren't used to wine like this. Now then Marcel, carry on. What have you to tell us?'

Marcel nudged him and nodded towards Javert.

'Careful!'

The orator looked again at the boy. He was curled up in a ball, back to the wall, head resting on his coat. His eyes were closed. Next to him, the empty wine cup lay on its side. The man laughed scornfully.

'Him! He's out for the count. For goodness sake Marcel, you're seeing spies behind every tree. It's just a little kid from the country who wouldn't understand what we were talking about even if he was awake and sober.'

Marcel nodded.

'All right. They're landing it into Marseille on Thursday. They're ending up here, at the Rue de Mirabelle.' He pointed to the sketch he had drawn. 'This is where it'll be for the night, then they'll take it on up–country. So we need to move Thursday night. I've eight or nine lads lined up just raring to go.'

'What about guards? They'll leave guards, surely.'

'Yes, but only two or three. It's a secret move, don't forget – we're supposed to know nothing about it. We can take it easily, two or three guards are no problem.'

The orator laughed softly. 'So we take it and sell most of it. And then we let the people know what's going on – bringing grain in from outside and taking it up–country while they starve down here. The place'll just erupt.'

Marcel shrugged. 'I don't care about that, just make sure we get our share, that's all.'

'Oh you'll get it – so long as your information is reliable.'

Marcel gave his wolfish grin.

'Oh, it's reliable all right, straight from the horse's mouth, you might say. Those bastards're not the only ones who can use informants, it's the biter bit! I tell you, it'll be like taking a rattle off a baby.'

The men continued to talk quietly whilst Javert ostensibly slumbered on in his corner. His active mind churned over the information he had gleaned. Thursday, Marseille, Rue de Mirabelle. He felt jubilant and excited, he knew this information was valuable. His hard earned control was useful now. He longed to get up and find Philippe, but he kept his eyes shut and his breathing even, still listening attentively to see if he could learn more.

It seemed an age before Philippe returned, and despite his resolve Javert had slipped into a real doze when he was roused by a rough hand shaking his shoulder. He opened his eyes drowsily, for a moment forgetting where he was. The younger peasant was shaking him.

'Come on boy, wake up, your brother's back from his – travels.'

Javert stood up slowly, cold and stiff from lying on the hard stone floor and still half asleep. Philippe was swaying on his feet, reeking of cheap wine and looking definitely the worse for drink.

'Come on boy,' he said drunkenly. 'Time for bed.'

He reeled out with his arm round Javert's shoulders. Outside, they paused while their eyes adjusted to the darkness. It was a moonless night, and the only light was the distant glimmer of the stars. After a few seconds they could see the old wagon standing across the yard. They walked to it cautiously, wary of unseen obstacles, and clambered into the ramshackle vehicle. Once inside, Javert immediately started to speak, but

40

Philippe put his hand across the boy's mouth and whispered into his ear.

'Not yet, not here. Wait until tomorrow, when we're clear of this place.'

They curled up in the wagon, making themselves as comfortable as they could. There was no bedding, and it was cold; the temperature dropped swiftly at this time of year. They slept huddled together for warmth, Javert's back nestled into the curve of Philippe's body. The contact gave him a peace and contentment he had rarely felt before. Exhausted by the unusual events of the day, he slept soon and soundly.

Philippe roused him at first light, whispering quietly into his ear.

'Javert, wake up – we have to go. We must reach the main road before Pierre does. Come on, quietly now.'

They climbed down from the wagon. The yard was deserted and quiet, save for a few scrawny hens pecking in the dust. It was barely light, and the brighter stars were still just visible. The sky, a delicate eggshell blue, looked bright and newly washed.

The air was briskly cool, and they woke up quickly as they made their way up the track towards the main road. At the top of the track they halted. Philippe motioned to Javert.

'You stay here and keep a lookout for that wagon. I'm going down to the river.'

'What for?'

Philippe grimaced. 'To put my head in it, that's what for. You slept like a baby all night, but I didn't. And I shifted too much of that damned wine. Couldn't keep watering it too heavily with the woman watching every move I made, so I drank more than I wanted to, and bad wine at that.'

He looked down at Javert. 'How about you? I saw them giving you wine - I was worried they might get you drunk.'

'I managed to tip mine into the rushes by the wall.' Sunshine broke across his face as he gave his rare grin. 'I can give you some lessons, if you like.'

Philippe laughed in delight. It was rare for Javert to smile like that, even rarer for him to have the confidence to joke and banter. Philippe had sometimes wondered whether the boy had

41

a sense of humour – not that he usually had much to joke about. But today his spirits were up. He was free of the pressures and restraints of the garrison, he was with his friend, and he was frankly pleased with himself. Young as he was, he knew he had done well last night.

Philippe tucked the boy's head under his arm and pretended to punch him, then rumpled the boy's hair.

'Getting cheeky now you're on the payroll, aren't you. Wait here then, since you're the sober one you can be the lookout.'

He made his way towards the river, scrambling over a large fallen tree that lay across the path. Left behind, Javert moved off the track and into the cover of the trees to evacuate his bowels and bladder. He was adjusting his trousers when he heard movement further down the track. He shrank back behind the trees and lay prone, heart hammering loudly.

Two men were coming up the track, talking quietly. Just opposite Javert the footsteps stopped abruptly. The boy held his breath, looking down at the ground as if by not looking at them he could stop them seeing him.

'Hello, what's he doing here?'

'Who?'

'Him. The fellow down by the river – Philippe.'

Javert peeped cautiously through the long grass. The two men were standing with their backs to him. Even so, he had no difficulty in recognising the filthy grey hair, the huge shoulders of one of them. It was unmistakably Marcel, one of the men he had spied on the night before.

They were still talking quietly, but now Marcel's tone sounded ugly.

'You know him?'

'I'll say I know him, he lives at the garrison. Belongs to the *Marechaussee*, same as I do.'

'He's a policeman? You're sure?'

'Of course I'm sure.' The voice grew uneasy. 'He mustn't see me with you! If he does – –'

'He won't!' Marcel's voice was deathly quiet. 'He won't see anybody – ever again.'

His voice sharpened.

'Just a minute – the kid! There was a kid with him last night. About ten, solid build, thick dark hair, dark eyes. Know him?'

There was a pause. 'Could be young Javert, he's thick with Philippe when he gets the chance, but I dunno. Anyway, I can't see any boy with him now.'

Marcel grunted. 'Could just be out of sight. Or maybe he doesn't come from the garrison, could just be a little catamite he's picked up. Just a minute though – he left him with us, and the kid sneaked near enough to hear what we were saying if he – my God, the little bastard was listening – I'll bet my last sol he was. All right, so neither of them get the chance to talk.'

'What are you going to do?' The voice sounded scared now.

'What do you think? I'm not about to let them blow the whistle on us.'

'I want nothing to do with that.'

'I'm sure you don't.' Marcel was sneering now. 'Well, you needn't have, I can handle those two kids all right. Go on, get back to your nice, safe little garrison. Just make sure you keep the news coming. Go on, get out, I'll take care of them.'

Footsteps moved away at a trot, the sound diminishing quickly into the distance. For a few moments Javert stayed flattened to the ground, then he cautiously lifted his head and peeped out. Marcel had moved to the other side of the track and was standing behind the fallen tree, perhaps twenty feet from Javert. He held an open knife in his right hand, and was looking intently down towards the river. Philippe, still stripped to the waist, was on his way back up the path, drying his face and hair on his shirt as he walked. He was very close to Marcel.

Javert drew breath to shout, then choked back the sound. The other man had been moving away quickly, but a loud shout could bring him back.

The boy broke cover and raced straight for Marcel, moving at top speed. The man heard him at the last second and spun to face him as the boy launched himself, all feet and claws and teeth. Marcel staggered backwards at the sheer momentum of Javert's rush, but the boy lacked the weight to bring the big man down. He grabbed for the right arm – the hand that held

43

the knife – and hung on desperately, literally for dear life, his hands too small to get a really solid grip. He felt himself swung off his feet as the man swore.

'You spying little bastard – –'

Javert gasped with pain as iron fingers closed on his arm and twisted viciously, forcing him to release his hold. Marcel easily jerked free of the boy's other hand, then hit out viciously. The blow landed on Javert's shoulder, hurling him backwards to sprawl in the wet grass.

He had held the man for only seconds, but those seconds had been enough. The distraction had enabled Philippe to leap over the fallen tree and pick up a heavy branch. Even as Javert landed heavily on his back, Philippe whacked the branch down hard on Marcel's head. Marcel collapsed dazed to the floor. Before he had time to recover, Philippe's boot thudded solidly into the side of his head. The man crumpled unconscious to the ground.

Philippe bent over him for a moment, then ran to Javert.

'What the hell ...'

'He knew you. There was a man with him who knew you. He was *Marechaussee*, from the garrison.'

'What! Where is he – the other man?'

'Gone, he ran off up the track.' The boy tried to point, then fell back with a gasp as an unexpected pain stabbed his arm. Philippe bent over him quickly.

'What is it? Good God, boy, your arm ...'

Javert looked down in surprise at the blood that was welling from his shoulder; his shirt and coat were already soaked with it. The man hadn't just punched him, he had stabbed him, but in his excitement the boy hadn't felt the pain of the blow.

Pierre suddenly appeared behind Philippe, making both he and the boy jump.

'What's happened?' he demanded.

Philippe explained quickly. Pierre bent over Javert, pulling his coat aside with little regard for the pain it caused. He examined the wound quickly.

44

'All right. He's sliced the skin open, but it's not too deep. We just need to stop the bleeding.' He pulled off his scarf. 'Here, bind this on, tightly.'

While Philippe tied up the wound, Pierre walked down to the unconscious man and bent over him. After a moment he grunted, then picked up the knife and came back.

'He's well out. All right boy, I want to know exactly what these two men said to each other, everything you can remember.'

Javert was leaning back against Philippe, feeling distinctly cold and dizzy. He forced himself to concentrate, repeating all he could remember of the conversation.

'Right. So you've got some useful information, but it won't be useful if these two blow you out of the water.'

Philippe frowned. 'Can't we just arrest them both and get them under lock and key?'

'And have them blab all over the garrison, or the town lock–up, or wherever you put them? No, that's not good enough.' He stood up, pocketed the knife and began to drag Marcel towards the water.

'What are you doing?' Philippe's voice was unusually high pitched.

'Making sure he can't blab on us,' Pierre had reached the river now. He laid Marcel face downwards, then straddled his back and pushed his head firmly beneath the water. After a moment the man's limbs began to twitch spasmodically; unconscious as he was, he was fighting for air. Presently his struggles lessened, then stopped. Pierre held position for a while longer. then released him. Marcel lay unmoving, face downwards, head submerged.

Javert had watched the scene in silent horror. He felt sick. A vivid memory floated into his mind – of being held helpless in thick, viscous mud, of trying desperately not to breath, and eventually being obliged to breath and taking in only liquid and filth. The horror of drowning – he understood that better than most.

Pierre stood up and came back to them.

'That's one. Now for the other. Come on, we have to move quickly, before anyone's about.'

The colour drained from Philippe's face.

'But we can't – '

'We have to; what's the matter with you?' He nodded back towards Marcel. 'He was just pond life, and the other one's a stinking traitor. Come on, get in the back of the wagon, under cover.'

Philippe helped Javert into the wagon and climbed in after him. There was a jerk as the wagon got under way. Javert's face was white, his eyes pools of darkness. Philippe was almost as pale as the boy. He took Javert's hands in his, both their hands were cold.

There was another jerk as the wagon stopped, then Pierre's voice.

'Hello there friend, you're out and about early. Give you a ride?'

'Please, oh yes please,' the voice sounded nervous. 'I'm headed for the garrison at Toulon.'

'Climb aboard.'

'Thank you.' The wagon creaked as the man clambered up. Seconds later there were sounds of a struggle, a strangled scream followed by a dull thud. The wagon rocked and swayed alarmingly. Then Pierre spoke urgently.

'Philippe, get out here, quickly.'

Philippe leapt from the wagon and hurried round to the front. Pierre's voice sounded again.

'Help me with him. Hurry up, I don't want his blood on the ground here.'

The two men came into view a moment later, dragging the third man between them. They bundled him into the back of the wagon. Marcel's knife was buried deep in the man's chest. There was some blood, but not too much. The man's eyes were open, wide with shock and disbelief. They widened even further as he recognised Philippe and Javert. He tried to speak, but could only produce a gurgle. His eyes blanked, his head dropped forward.

'Right, lay him on his back. Leave the knife where it is.'

Pierre hurried to the front of the wagon. He backed the horses up and turned the vehicle, heading back the way they had come. He halted the wagon near the track that led to the inn, then came round to the rear.

'Come on, we'll put him with the other one. It's the other fellow's knife, so hopefully they'll think they had a fight and killed each other.'

He and Philippe manhandled the heavy body out of the wagon and down to the waters edge, negotiating the fallen trees with difficulty and halting a short distance from where Marcel lay face downward in the river. They placed the man on his back, where he lay staring sightlessly at the sky. Pierre immediately began to hurry back to the wagon. Behind him Philippe hesitated, looking down at the two dead men. Pierre looked round impatiently.

'Hurry up, we have to get out of here.'

He was right to urge speed. Day had fully broken now, and the sun had risen above the horizon. It looked down on the still forest, the meandering river, the silence broken only by the chorus of bird song. A peaceful scene! Philippe shuddered and hurried after Pierre.

Pierre hoisted himself into the driving seat, whilst Philippe climbed into the back of the wagon with Javert. He took off his jacket and wrapped it round the boy, trying to avoid touching his injured shoulder. Pierre looked back at them.

'Useful kid you've got there. Got some guts!'

Once again the wagon got underway. Javert lay back against Philippe and closed his eyes. Every bump and jolt sent waves of pain through his shoulder. He was weak, cold, sick and profoundly shaken. But as he slid into an uneasy doze, his predominant emotions were pride and satisfaction.

Chapter 5

1789 opened with considerable public unrest. Another disastrous harvest had brought the poor of France to the point of starvation. A long, hard winter followed. In Paris, the frozen river Seine delayed the shipment of urgently needed food to the capital. Grain rotted in the holds of ships, whilst the people of Paris starved. The mood of the people became increasing ugly. Lawyers such as Camille Desmoulins and Maximilian Robespierre agitated continuously. Driven to desperation by hunger and atrocious living conditions, the common people flocked to support them.

The establishment reacted by extending its network of informants. Police spies, it was said, were everywhere: in the clubs used by the nobility and in the low class 'Tapis Franc' inns frequented by the dregs of Paris; in the Tuileries where the bourgeoisie strolled, and in the gutters. But still the revolutionary movement grew as the people became more hungry and more angry, and the eloquent lawyers fanned the embers of their discontent.

By the summer of 1789 Paris was a smouldering keg, waiting to explode.

Chapter 6
Paris, July 1789

Javert woke suddenly out of an uneasy doze. It was still hot, with a sticky, oppressive heat. The boy could hear the sound of thunder rumbling in the distance, but no rain had yet fallen.

The room's single window stood out as a dim rectangle against the darkness; it was still early, but it was getting light. For a moment he wondered what had woken him, then he realised that the bed next to his was empty. The door of the room stood open, and from outside he could hear the sound of violent retching.

Javert peeled his sweating body off the sheet and pulled on his grubby trousers. He fastened the string that held them and padded over to the door. Even in the street the light was dim - only towards midday did the sun penetrate down into these high sided, narrow alleys. But it looked as if there was little enough chance of sun today; black clouds were gathering overhead and in the distance the thunder growled almost continuously, ominous and threatening.

André was supporting himself against the nearby wall, panting with exhaustion after a bout of sickness. He looked like any other poor Parisian peasant – trousers frayed and dirty, loose smock stained with food and sweat. Both he and his clothing stank. It was a far cry from the obsessively immaculate Lieutenant of the Marechaussee.

Javert approached his guardian cautiously. They had been living in the Paris slums for two months now, working under cover and collecting what intelligence they could. André might accept the discomforts of their present assignment as a necessary evil, but it did not improve his temper. And if he was feeling sick as well -

'Monsieur? Are you ill?'

André turned his head towards him. 'What's it look like, boy? Of course I am, do you think I'm heaving my guts up for fun?'

'What's wrong?'

'How the devil should I know? Bad food I should think - and no wonder, with this weather. Well, don't just stand there, help me.'

Javert hurried over obediently. Sweating with effort, he helped André back inside and onto his bed. André settled back on the bed with an exhausted grunt. 'Now get me some water!'

'The container's empty Monsieur - I'll go to the pump.'

'No, knock up Emil. It's quicker.'

Emil was their landlord, and lived in the room above. Javert hurried up the rickety stairs and knocked on the door. He waited, then banged harder. There was no response. After a moment's hesitation the boy pushed the door open cautiously and went inside.

Emil's room was bigger than theirs, even dirtier and more untidy. The bed stood in the far corner, the single grubby cover thrown carelessly back. A pile of dirty clothing was heaped in the middle of the floor. The water container stood on the ramshackle table, amidst rotting leftovers around which the flies swarmed and buzzed. Emil himself was not there.

Javert paused, then picked up the half full water container and went back to André. The man took the container from him and drank deeply, then leaned back with a sigh of relief.

'That's better! I take it he didn't argue about giving it to you?'

'He wasn't there Monsieur.'

'Wasn't he, by God.' He frowned thoughtfully. 'Now where would he be going at this time of day?'

The thunder was still growling away in the background. It was both louder and closer now, surely it would rain soon. Then something in the quality of the sound caught the boy's attention. He lifted his head and listened more closely. André seemed to realise at the same time. He swore harshly.

'Just a minute - that's not thunder.'

'Then what is it?'

'It's people - a hell of a lot of people.'

He tried to get up, then collapsed back onto the bed, cold sweat running down his face. He swore again under his breath.

'Damn this sickness - today of all days.' He gripped Javert's shoulder. 'Listen boy, we need to find out what's going on. Get

50

out of here and find those people. Find out what's happening, then get back to me. Got it?'

Javert nodded and turned to go, but André pulled him back.

'Wait! I don't like Emil sneaking off like that – I'd trust him about as far as I'd trust a snake.'

'But why Monsieur? I mean, he lets us stay here.'

'Because he's got no choice. He's a ticket-of-leave man.' He scowled at Javert's blank expression. '*Merde* – haven't you learnt anything? He's an ex-convict on parole and it doesn't pay for people like him to upset the authorities. We pay him to stay here, and he lets us because he's greedy and because he's scared. But he's got a bloody good idea who we are and he hates us. He'll kill us or sell us out if he gets half a chance, and don't think he'll care that you're just a boy. Don't come back here - go straight to the Café Gerard. I'll see you there.'

Javert ran swiftly down the alley, skirting the piles of excrement and rubbish and ignoring the half-starved dogs snarling and fighting over the refuse. The alley was narrow, airless and fetid, reeking of rotting food and the stench of sewage. Sometimes there was more than just the stench, after heavy rain these alleys were knee-deep in yellow mud, and it was not unusual for the sewers to overflow into the streets. Last time that had happened was in the spring, during Javert's first week in the city; you could still see the tidemark on the side of the buildings. But after the long dry spell the mud was bone-dry, packed down as hard as rock. Of course the heat made the stink even worse; far worse than it had been in the Toulon garrison.

At the end of the first alley he stopped and listened, glancing up at the thickening clouds. It must be the approaching storm that was giving the air that curious, brooding quality; a feeling of tension that was almost tangible. Early as it was, Javert expected to see some people about, but there was no-one. The alleys were deserted, and curiously quiet except for the snarling of the dogs and that strange, ominous rumbling. As he drew closer, the rumbling changed to a swelling roar.

At the end of the Rue St Denis Javert stopped again, listening and looking about him. Far to the left there was a strange red flickering in the sky, like the glow of a huge fire; the sound seemed to be coming from that direction. He trotted down the road towards it.

As he rounded the corner into the long, straight Rue St Antoine he saw them; a great crowd of people, roaring and shouting and surging their way towards him. The crowd were mainly men, by their dress mostly poor, but there was a smattering of well–dressed bourgeoisie amongst them, and a few women and children. In front were a number of men carrying flags and muskets, accompanied by men dragging a heavy cannon. Others in the crowd were armed with a miscellany of weapons - firearms, axes, knives, pitchforks and pikes. Many of them were waving makeshift flags and other material of blue and red.

Immediately behind the vanguard were half a dozen or so of the National Guard. These were half leading, half supporting a dishevelled man in a grey frock coat. The man looked terrified. His long hair was dirty and matted, his face severely scratched. He was bleeding heavily from a gash on his head, the blood running down his face and onto his already filthy coat.

The crowd approached the La Force prison where Javert was standing. It was impossible to estimate their numbers; they filled the street from wall to wall and back as far as he could see. They were shouting, shoving, swaying from side to side. Many of them appeared drunk, whether with excitement or alcohol he had no way of knowing. Further back, he could hear the splintering of wood and shattering of glass as people smashed shutters and windows and looted the contents of shops. The mob was totally out of control.

In fear of being trampled, Javert drew back against the wall of the prison. As the crowd reached him he was forced back painfully against the stone, then torn away from it. In no time at all he found himself in the thick of the crowd, being pushed to and fro, crushed, kicked and half trampled. Struggling and wriggling, he forced his way towards the front, where he could at least breathe.

When the crowd came opposite the Hotel de Ville there was a disturbance, as the people already gathered in the huge square rushed over to meet the advancing mob. The people at the front were forced to stop and there were curses and shouts as those at the back tried to keep moving. Javert was nearly at the front now, but for the moment he could go no further.

The congestion increased, and with it the noise. But the shrill scream rose even above the din; it was an animal sound - a howl of sheer terror. The man in the grey frock coat was down, writhing about in agony on the ground.

The guards milled about, vainly trying to keep the mob back from him. As Javert watched, a heavy man with greasy black hair snatched a bayonet from one of the guards and drove it into the stomach of the man on the ground. The man shrieked in agony. The bayonet was withdrawn, then thrust in again, and again. The blood jetted fiercely, spattering the clothes of the man wielding the weapon and covering the coarse black hair on his arms with glutinous red. Behind him, Javert heard a hoarse shout.

'Well done Desmot, give it to the bastard!'

Other bayonets were snatched. Then the guards stood back, looking scared and uneasy as they gave up their vain attempt to protect the man on the ground. Javert stood riveted to the spot, numb with shock as the terrible images were etched onto his brain.

He staggered as the mob suddenly started forward again, leaving what had once been a man lying in the gutter. With sick horror Javert saw that the head had been hacked off and was now hoisted aloft on one of the pikes. Next to him another man had collapsed on the ground, hopelessly drunk, throwing up vast quantities of the cheap wine he had consumed.

Like Javert himself, a number of the crowd were barefoot. Their feet slipped in the mess on the stones, leaving a trail of red footprints. To the boy's imagination everything seemed red - red blood, red wine, red ribbons. His first excitement was gone now and he could feel no sympathy with these people; no sense of belonging. Javert had seen some frightening and gruesome sights in his short lifetime, but never had he encountered uncontrollable, feral behaviour on this scale. He felt alienated, isolated, sickened by the spectacle and by the stampeding animals that had once been ordinary, individual men and women.

As they came opposite the Rue St Martin he fought his way to the edge of the mob, determined to break free of them, then stopped suddenly as he saw who was directly ahead of him. It was Emil.

The boy backed away, but was checked by the density of the crowd behind him. At that moment Emil turned and saw him. His face was flushed, his eyes wild. There was blood on his coat.

For a second his eyes widened in surprise, then his arm shot out, grabbing for the boy. Javert ducked under his arm and squirmed away from him. Emil pointed towards him and his high pitched shriek rose above the cries of the mob.

'Filthy police spies! Kill them, kill them all!'

The mob reacted to his cry, shouting and swaying about. Fortunately for Javert they did not know who they were trying to lay hands on. Emil was too drunk to give them coherent information and in any case there was too much noise and general chaos. Instinctively everyone assumed they were looking for an adult, and all around him people were grabbing at each other and cursing. Javert pushed and wormed his way free and raced at top speed for the Café Gerard.

The streets between the Rue St Antoine and the Café Gerard were deserted, presumably everyone was either part of the mob or staying safely indoors. He could hear the sound of the crowd clearly behind him but there seemed to be no pursuit. He stopped running and crouched in a nearby alley, his heart flopping wildly as he tried to recover his breath. Glancing down, he saw that his bare feet and the bottom of his trousers were stained with red, drying now to black. Wine - or blood? He had a sudden vision of the severed head hoisted aloft on the pike, and was sick into the gutter.

After a few minutes his heartbeat steadied and he continued more cautiously. Near the entrance to the Café he checked to ensure he was not followed, then dashed for the door. It was locked. He hammered hard on it, shouting desperately. It was opened almost immediately. Monsieur Gerard pulled him inside, then barred the door again.

'Javert, thank God, boy! You weren't followed?'

Javert shook his head. 'No Monsieur, I checked.'

'Good lad. Come on up.'

He led the boy upstairs. André was there, still looking pale and ill. There was also a younger man who Javert hadn't seen before, by his dress a member of the National Guard. His expression was a mixture of shock and incomprehension, his uniform dishevelled and torn.

Monsieur Gerard led Javert to a chair and pushed a drink into his hand.

'Here boy, drink this down before you talk to us. You look dreadful.'

Javert sipped, choked, then sipped again. The drink was some kind of strong spirit that burned his throat but warmed his insides. After a moment his stomach seemed to unclench. He felt better and more coherent.

'What's happening out there?' demanded André bluntly.

'There's a mob - hundreds of people, I don't know how many. They were coming down the Rue St Antoine. They'd got someone with them, a man they'd taken prisoner I suppose. He was wearing a grey coat - '

The young guard interrupted. 'That was Monsieur de Launay. He's the governor of the Bastille - he surrendered it to them. They took him prisoner then.'

Monsieur Gerard sat down next to Javert.

'This young man is named Henri, he works with us. He was one of the guards at the Bastille; he was there when the mob stormed it. After they took de Launay he managed to get clear of them and come here.'

'They've killed him!' Javert said shakily.

'Killed him. Killed who?'

'The man in the grey coat - Monsieur de Launay. The mob killed him. A man bayoneted him. They all took the guards' bayonets off them and they just kept stabbing and stabbing him, then they put his head on a pike.' He looked at André. 'Then Emil - Emil recognised me. He told the mob we were police spies, told them to kill us.' He looked down at his hand, still holding the glass. It was shaking.

The guard clenched his fists. 'The bastards! He'd done nothing to them, he'd surrendered. Why did they have to kill him?'

Monsieur Gerard spoke dryly. 'You don't ask a mob why - a mob doesn't reason! And I doubt we'll ever know just who killed him. How can we, out of thousands of people?'

Javert looked up. His hands had stopped shaking now and his mind was functioning coolly again, with the strange clarity that often came to him in times of high stress.

'The first man was named Desmot.'

'What?'

'The man who stabbed him first, the one who snatched the bayonet. I heard him called Desmot.'

The young guard leant forward intently.

'What's he look like?'

'About Monsieur André 's age. Heavy. He had long black hair, very greasy, pushed back behind his ears. And his arms were covered in thick black hair - really thick, almost like fur.' Javert shuddered as he remembered that hair, dirty and matted, red with the blood of his victim.

Monsieur Gerard nodded.

'Well, There's nothing to be done now, but at least that's one of them who might face justice one day!' He put his arms around Javert and lifted him to his feet. 'Well done, young man. Now then, you can lie down in the other room and go to sleep. You look half dead for lack of it.'

He led the boy through to the other room and bedded him down on the sofa, closing the shutters to keep out the dimming light. The black clouds had gathered in earnest now and thunder erupted overhead as lightning cleaved the sky repeatedly. The storm that had been threatening all day finally broke. The streets became quiet as water cascaded down, dispersing the mob. Then the thunder moved away and the rain settled down to a steady downpour, cooling the hot sticky air and enabling the city to breathe again. Javert at last slept to the peaceful rhythm of the falling rain.

Chapter 7

Javert slept fitfully and woke feeling restless and edgy, more shaken by the events of the previous day than he cared to admit. He was just ten years old, but already he had seen too much of violent death. First there had been Marcel and the spy, now Monsieur de Launay. But it wasn't only the slaughter of de Launay that stayed in his mind; he couldn't forget the way the mob had behaved, like animals drunk on wine and blood. If Emil had succeeded in catching him, his own head would doubtless have been stuck on a pike and carried through the streets alongside that of the unfortunate de Launay; he knew that his youth would not have saved him.

For the time being he and André stayed under cover at the Café Gerard. It was obviously not safe to return to their lodgings with Emil, the man had already tried to expose Javert and would undoubtedly do the same to André. But they could not remain permanently at the café. It was an ideal rendezvous point - Monsieur Gerard was more than sympathetic to their cause and comings and goings were normal at a café - but André and Javert were supposed to be poor peasants; such people wouldn't be expected to frequent a place like the Café Gerard. It was different for Philippe, the third member of their team of four. Philippe was ostensibly a law student. He was also courting Monsieur Gerard's daughter Adele, so his frequent presence at the café would not be questioned.

Philippe arrived in mid-morning, followed shortly afterwards by Jules, the leader of their team. Jules looked exhausted, as if he had been up all the previous night. Monsieur Gerard handed him a generous measure of spirit, which he accepted gratefully, leaning back in his chair with a weary sigh. He looked across at André and Javert.

'The mob's still on the rampage; they're witch-hunting for anyone they think represents the old regime. They arrested the Intendant of Paris this morning.'

'Monsieur Berthier?'

'That's right. They arrested him and his assistant, and they killed them both this afternoon - beheaded them. They're parading around now with the heads stuck on a pike.'

Javert looked quickly away. In his mind's eye he could see again the bloody bayonets, the grisly head of Monsieur de Launay. Jules leaned forward as if struck by a sudden thought.

'The assistant only came up at the beginning of the year – from Toulon. You may know him. Monsieur Bibet?'

Javert started as André nodded.

'He was my commanding officer down at Toulon, until about six months ago.'

'Oh,' said Jules sympathetically. 'I'm sorry.'

André shrugged. He was just my C.O., not my friend. I've no feelings about him either way.' He smiled sourly. 'The boy might have.'

Jules looked at Javert. 'Was he a friend of yours?'

Javert made no response, he didn't even hear the question. He had taken in nothing since the mention of Bibet, who together with his son had turned Javert's life at Toulon into a hell on earth. In his mind, Javert was no longer in the upstairs room of a Paris café, but on the cliff top outside the Tour Royale prison in Toulon. The stench of pigs clogged his nostrils, the taste of vile, pig–fouled mud filled his mouth -

A hard cuff across the head startled the boy back to the present. André spoke to him sharply.

'Pay attention boy! Jules is talking to you.'

Javert blinked and forced his attention back to Jules.

'I'm sorry Monsieur, what did you say?'

'I asked if Monsieur Bibet was a friend of yours.'

'No Monsieur.'

Javert's voice was toneless, but looking at him Jules saw that his expression was hard and implacable; the sort of look he might have expected to see on the face of an embittered adult, rather than a ten year old boy.

André laughed grimly. 'There was no love lost between Javert and Monsieur Bibet - or Bibet's son. Do you know what happened to him, by the way?'

'The son? I've no idea. I can try to find out for you.'

André shrugged. 'Don't worry. It's not worth the risk of finding out, it's not important. What matters now is the present; the boy and I need a new lodging.'

'I know. Stay here until I find a safe place for you.'

'And me?' queried Philippe. 'Do I need to move?'

Jules shrugged. 'Don't see why you should; you're a respectable law student, after all. You're the perfect messenger; you're courting Monsieur Gerard's daughter, so you've got a genuine reason for coming here.'

André frowned.

'That's all very fine for him, Jules, but don't forget we're supposed to be poor peasants from the slums. This is hardly the sort of place we'd be likely to come.'

'I know that. But Emil's still on the loose somewhere, and if they once suspect you're police agents I wouldn't give a sol for your lives. I'll find you a new cover, André; I think your slum days are over. In the meantime, you need to lie low for a while; it's still a bloodbath out there. Anyway, I must go.'

He put down his glass and walked quickly from the room.

By the beginning of August things seemed to be settling down again. At the end of the month Jules decided it was safe for André and Javert to move out of the café.

'But obviously not back to where you were. We've got a contact who works as a cobbler in the Place Vendome; he's committed to us, much safer than Emil ever was. André, you can work with him. It's a good position because you'll get plenty of customers and customers like to chat while they're waiting.'

'So long as Emil doesn't want his boots mending,' commented André dryly.

'He won't. He doesn't need boots where he's gone.'

André lifted his eyebrows. 'Had an accident, has he?'

'You could say that. We couldn't afford to let him expose you two. In any case he knew what would happen if he failed us. Emil took a gamble too many, now he's paid for it.'

André shrugged.

'Well, he's no loss is he?' He glanced at Javert, noticing his sudden shudder. 'What's the matter with you boy? Don't tell me you're going to lose any sleep over Emil, the man was scum'.

Javert looked back at him, his face expressionless. It wasn't that he regretted Emil's death, but the memory of Marcel was still vivid in his mind. He had little doubt that Emil had been similarly dealt with.

André and Javert moved out of the café and into their new lodgings two days later. Things seemed more settled than they had been since their arrival in Paris. The harvest that year was good, the mood of the populace one of hope. The old regime had been overthrown and the people were looking forward to better times ahead.

As Christmas approached, Javert also looked forward to better times. Their new cover - and the greater status it gave them - enabled them to frequent such places as the Café Gerard. That meant he could see more of Philippe. Javert idolised Philippe. Since his mother's death, Philippe was the only person to show him any affection, and he had become both father and brother to the lonely boy.

Adele, Philippe's future wife, was more reserved, and Javert had mixed feelings about her. It wasn't that he disliked her, but he couldn't feel entirely comfortable with her. She could be very forthright, and although she was kind enough to Javert she did not always encourage his company. She and Philippe were to marry shortly after Christmas, and Javert often felt unwelcome when she was there. There were also times when he resented her presence; Philippe was his only real friend; he didn't want to share him with someone else.

On New Year's Day Javert woke up to an unusual silence, and looked out upon a strange world of white. It had snowed heavily in the night and a six inch carpet lay on the ground, muffling the sound of the traffic. Javert was delighted, never having seen snow before; it had never snowed in Toulon during his short lifetime.

It seemed that the rest of the populace were equally pleased. A holiday mood prevailed and revolution and trouble were, for the moment, forgotten. For that one day, Javert enjoyed the taste of the boyhood he had never really had. He and Philippe pelted each other with snowballs and Philippe rolled him in the snow until, for the first time ever, Javert was helpless with laughter. For many years afterwards he would remember that day as the happiest of his life.

Chapter 8

There was quite an assembly in the upstairs apartment at the Café Gerard. In addition to Monsieur Gerard there were Philippe and Adele, André, Javert and Jules. Completing the party was Philippe's little daughter, Michelle. The gathering was mainly in Michelle's honour - it was August 1792 and the child was two years old today - but for once Javert was also getting his share of the attention. He shared his birthday with Michelle, so it had become a joint celebration. It was the only birthday party Javert had ever been given; his mother had always remembered his birthday, but there had never been any festivities.

As usual, Michelle had clambered up onto Javert's lap. She had conceived a passionate attachment to the boy, and she would shout out 'Vere!' whenever she saw him, toddling about after him on her chubby and still unsteady little legs.

Despite the party atmosphere, the situation in Paris was causing unwelcome undercurrents for them all. During the year following the revolution things had seemed to be improving. The mood amongst the poor of Paris was one of high optimism and towards the end of 1791 Jules considered recommending that André, Javert and Philippe be returned to their normal duties in the South.

Then the euphoria began to die down. The leaders of the revolution had promised a miracle; now the honeymoon was over and the miracle had not yet happened. The poor were still poor, food prices still beyond the means of many people, disease and starvation still rife. As the months went by there was a change in the mood of the populous, at first almost imperceptible but becoming increasingly noticeable. Tension increased and people were once again on the lookout for scapegoats.

Philippe in particular was becoming increasingly concerned by the way in which events were moving. When Adele left the room to fetch more wine he seized the opportunity to pull Jules to one side.

'Have you thought any more about what I said?'

Jules looked uncomfortable. 'Yes, I've thought about it. I've discussed it with my superiors, but they're against it at the moment. The mood out there is getting ugly again, and we need you here. You've built up a good cover over these past three years; You've become more and more trusted and your information is invaluable. We can't afford to pull you out now.'

Overhearing the conversation, André interrupted.

'Pull him out, what are you talking about? What's going on?'

'I've asked to go back to Toulon,' Philippe responded bluntly.

'You never mentioned it to me. What's the matter with you, do you miss the sunshine?'

Philippe sighed. 'Of course I miss the sunshine, don't we all? But that's nothing to do with my wanting to move. It's getting too dangerous here, André. Oh, I don't mean for me, I'll take my chances as I always have. But Adele and Michelle are another matter. You know what the mob is like once the fuse is lit; if they expose me they're just as likely to take it out on my wife and daughter. That's a chance I don't want to take. In any case, I don't see what good we're doing here now. The Ancien Regime is gone; nothing's going to bring it back.'

Jules nodded wearily. 'The old regime has gone, yes, but look what's replaced it. Everyone's fighting for power and the people are being blown here and there like dead leaves. Anyway, so far as I'm concerned, I'm a Royalist. I'll keep on fighting until the king is back in his rightful place on the throne.'

Philippe leaned forward. 'Jules, be realistic. How likely is that now?'

André interrupted again. 'You think too much, both of you. We're representatives of the law and we have a job to do; we stay here until it's done. He scowled at Philippe. 'As for you, I sometimes wonder if you know where your loyalties lie.'

Philippe flushed. 'Yes, I know. Of course my loyalties lie with my job. But I've a duty to my family as well. Can't you see that?'

'And which comes first, tell me that?'

Philippe stared at him steadily. 'If it comes to the crunch, André, then my family comes first.'

'Then you're a damned liability,' snapped André.

Jules interrupted them. 'All right. Calm down, both of you. Philippe, listen and let me finish what I was saying. We can't afford to move you, but we are prepared to move them.'

'Them? You mean, move Adele and Michelle?'

'Yes. We can move them out of Paris, to Neuilly. It's away from potential trouble spots but near enough to visit regularly. Will that help?'

Philippe nodded slowly. 'It's better than nothing, I suppose. I'm sorry Jules, that sounded ungracious. Yes, it will help – it'll help a lot. Thank you.'

Jules shrugged. 'It's not entirely out of consideration for either them or you. To some extent André is right, while half your mind is on their safety you are a liability. I think you'll function better when you know they're safe.'

The party was over and Michelle had long since been put to bed when a late visitor arrived to see Jules. They were surprised to see Henri, the same young guard who had brought the news of the storming of the Bastille, over three years before. Henri greeted them all quickly, then handed a note to Jules. He read it silently, then looked up at Henri.

'You know what this says?'

Henri nodded. 'Yes Monsieur, I do.'

'But the rest of us don't,' prompted Monsieur Gerard.

Jules perched on the edge of the table, scratching his forehead absently as he often did when worried or distracted.

'They've imprisoned the King in the temple!' he said bluntly.

For a moment there was silence, then André spoke.

'He's been virtually a prisoner for years, certainly since last June.'

'Yes, but now it's all out in the open, it's official. I don't like the feel of it, André. They must be supremely confident to do that, or very frightened.'

He turned back to Henri.

'Have you still got your contacts at the Cordeliers' club.'

Henri nodded. 'Yes we have, some of the commune have taken to meeting there recently. Just socially, for drinks, but of course people talk when they drink. In fact I'd better not stay, I want to put in an appearance tonight, just in case. It might be useful to hear what they're saying.'

Monsieur Gerard filled a cup with wine and held it out to their visitor.

'Join us before you go? It's my little grand-daughters birthday celebration, and this young man's as well.' He chuckled. 'I'm afraid you've missed my grand-daughter, but you can still have a drink with young Javert here.'

Henri accepted the wine with a mutter of thanks, running his eyes over Javert. Though as yet nowhere near fully grown, the boy looked set to become a tall, strong man; he was already nearing Philippe's height.

'Well,' commented Henri, 'you've grown up sure enough, young man. How old are you now?'

'Thirteen.'

'That all? I'd have put you as older; fourteen, maybe even fifteen.' He stood up. 'I must go, it's getting late if I'm to stand any chance of catching our friends at the Cordeliers'.'

Monsieur Gerard frowned. 'You're on your own?'

'Today, yes. My usual partner's been taken ill.'

André looked up.

'Take Javert with you. You know it's easier to blend in and listen inconspicuously with two of you. Anyway if you pick up anything useful he can bring it straight back.'

Henri looked doubtful. 'He's a bit young for this sort of thing, and it's not much of a way to celebrate his birthday.'

André snorted. 'Young be damned, he's been doing this sort of thing for years. Anyway you've said yourself he looks older than he is. He won't attract any attention to you.'

He looked sourly at Javert.

'Go with him and keep your mouth shut and your ears open. Make sure you're back at our lodgings by midnight at latest. Got it?'

'Yes Monsieur.'

Henri shrugged. 'As you wish. All right young Javert, come on.'

Henri and Javert stayed in the Cordeliers Club for almost two hours, drinking and ostensibly chatting, but mostly listening. Shortly before midnight Javert stood up.

'Henri, I have to go, I mustn't be late. You stay.'

Henri drained his wine quickly.

'It's all right, I've had about enough of this poison anyway.' He lowered his voice. 'The people I'm interested in won't come now; the place is emptying.'

They left the inn and walked through the dimly lit streets. There was a drizzle in the air and the streets were fairly quiet, save for a few drunks and the inevitable prostitutes. One of the drunks was sitting propped against a wall, shouting and raving at an imaginary opponent. As they passed him the shutter overhead crashed open and a cascade of liquid descended as the householder emptied the contents of his chamber pot onto the drunk's head. Javert and Henri leapt aside just in time to avoid the foul smelling stream. Henri gripped Javert's arm.

'Come on, let's walk back along the river.'

At the river they halted and stood for a few moments, watching the reflection of the lights in the dark water and letting the night air begin to clear their heads. Both of them had drunk a little too much wine.

A voice sounded close by, startling them.

'Henri, hello dearie.'

They turned to see a woman standing behind them. She was very young, little more than a girl, scruffily dressed and not very clean, but attractive in a brash kind of way. She held out her hand to Henri.

'I haven't seen you for weeks, dearie. Come on, why don't you.'

Henri laughed and nodded towards Javert. 'Not tonight Marie.'

'Oh come on.' She smiled meaningfully, 'you know I always give you a good time.'

Henri looked uncertain, then turned to Javert.

'Will you wait for me a few minutes?'

Marie moved closer, swishing her hips as she indicated Javert.

'Friend of yours?'

'A young friend. Little too young, if you see what I mean.'

The woman gave Javert an appraising stare.

'He doesn't look too young to me. Come on Henri, bring him along, he's got to learn sometime. I can find someone for him.'

Henri laughed suddenly.

'Well, I suppose now is as good a time as any; after all, today is his birthday. What about it young Javert, want a very special birthday present? Tell you what, I'll even pay for you.'

The girl moved over to Javert, taking his hand.

'Oh, it's your birthday! What are you, fifteen? Past time you started to learn. Come on, we'll look after you.'

Half reluctantly, Javert allowed himself to be led away. He was by no means naïve and after over three years in the City he was as streetwise as any Parisian urchin. He was well aware what the woman was, and what she meant. He had heard other boys talk about their experiences with women, and was eager to have the status that such experience would bestow on him. At the same time he knew full well that his guardian would not approve. André had warned him about prostitutes such as this and cautioned him against ever going with one. Now he felt excited but guilty, curious but a little afraid.

Marie led them a very short distance along the river, then down under the Pont Neuf. Low moans, gasps and muttered conversations indicated that others were there before them. Marie left them for a moment, then returned with another woman. In the darkness under the bridge Javert could see little of her, just the general details of a slim figure and long dark hair. The woman took his hand.

'Come on dearie, you'll be all right with Maddy. I'll show you what to do. Come on, don't be shy.'

She led him behind the pillar of the bridge, pushed him back against it and deftly unfastened his belt. He submitted passively, his brain still fogged by the wine. He was not sure what to do, what he wanted. He threw back his head and smelled the dampness of the night air, mingled with the stench from the nearby river.

The woman's hands were on him now, touching and handling him. He felt his body begin to react. Soon the

66

powerful physical sensations took him and shook him. The whole thing was happening without his own volition, outside his control. As she moved closer the sweet scent worn by the woman filled his nostrils, over–riding the other odours. Then as she moved right up against him to guide him into her he realised that the river was not the only thing that stank. Strong as it was, the woman's scent failed to mask an unpleasant and rancid body odour.

It was over very quickly. As the woman moved away from him and into the light he saw her properly for the first time. The woman was old! Her face was a painted mask, her hair a harsh, unnatural shade of black with the white roots showing in stark contrast. The slim figure was shrunken and wasted.

Henri's laughing voice roused him.

'Come on young Javert, better get you home before Monsieur André sends out a search party.' He pointed to the boy's trousers. 'Better dress yourself first.'

Javert secured his trousers with shaking fingers, then followed Henri back up to the river bank. Henri chatted happily as they made their way across the hard mud and back into the lights.

'Only just after midnight, so you'll only be a little bit late. Well, how did you like your birthday present? Just think, you're a man now.'

Javert made no response. He was still fuddled from the wine he had drunk and he wasn't sure of his own feelings. On the one hand, he felt a degree of pride and satisfaction; as Henri said, he could now regard himself as a man. But he hadn't liked feeling so out of control and he felt a shiver of shame and disgust when he remembered the smell of the woman, her dyed black hair and wizened body. The woman reminded him of someone, and shock hit him suddenly in the stomach as his mind presented him clearly with the image of the other woman; a woman with a wasted, shrunken form and an ashen face too pale for the thick black hair that framed it. The prostitute reminded him of his mother!

He closed his eyes, finding the similarity unbearable. Bibet's scornful words echoed in his mind; gypsy! whore! Had his mother really been a whore? Had she made her living by doing what this woman had just done?

It was some time after midnight when they arrived back at his lodgings. André greeted them angrily.

'Where the hell have you been? You'd just better have put the time to good use, that's all.'

Henri laughed, still somewhat tipsy.

'Very good use, Monsieur André. Javert isn't a boy any more; he's a man now.'

André turned on him sharply. 'What are you talking about?'

Henri laughed again.

'It is his birthday after all, and he's big for his age so I thought he'd be old enough. He was too! Well, goodnight both.'

He walked away down the street, slightly unsteady. André grabbed Javert's arm, yanked him roughly inside and slammed the door.

'Where have you been?'

The man's voice was deadly quiet, a tone Javert knew only too well. The boy stared back at him but made no immediate answer.

André took a pace nearer to him. 'Where did he take you? Have you been with a woman? Answer me boy!'

Javert looked at the floor and nodded.

'You've been with a prostitute?'

The boy nodded again.

André's buffet took him across the side of the head and knocked him off his feet. He crashed into a chair, overturning it, and skidded across the floor into the table in the corner. The heavy table held, but its contents shot off the top and onto the floor: a pistol André had been cleaning; a bottle of wine that smashed on the hard ground, its contents spilling out onto the stone flags.

'You stupid, filthy little bastard. Haven't I warned you about that? Do you want to get yourself poxed, or worse? I'll flay the skin off your back for this.'

André grabbed his heavy stick and started towards him. Javert snatched up the pistol from the floor and pulled himself up, pointing it towards the advancing man. The weapon was primed and ready to fire.

André stopped short. There was a moment of silent confrontation, then André spoke.

'Go ahead boy, if that's what you want to do. Shoot me and become a murderer like your father. Then run out of here onto the streets and become a vagrant like your mother. Go on, you've got the pistol – all you have to do is pull the trigger.'

He took a pace forward. Javert lifted the pistol slightly.

'Keep back!'

André stopped again, but did not give ground, nor did he appear to be afraid. 'You know you'll be caught sooner or later. Then they'll hang you. Or maybe if you don't manage to kill me you might be lucky and get hard labour for life.'

Javert crouched at bay, backed against the wall, holding the pistol in a hand that shook slightly. André, massive and threatening, was now only three paces away. Javert watched him across the pistol. Already he bitterly regretted picking the weapon up. Over the years, he had learnt the hard way to control his passion and think before acting, but today he had allowed himself to give way to impulse. Although by no means drunk he had taken enough wine to cloud his judgment, and following his encounter with the prostitute he had fancied himself to be almost a man. Now, he realised that there was more to manhood than that.

André was talking again.

'Of course there's another choice you can make; you can put that pistol down and take what's coming to you. You've the makings of a good police officer in you, and it's a pity if you choose to waste it. But no thirteen year old pup calls me out. I'm still leader of this pack, by God!'

Javert took a shaking breath, then laid the pistol on the table and stood upright, head up, meeting the big man eye to eye.

André reached him in two paces. He seized Javert by the chain of his medallion and pulled the boy's head under his left arm, literally ripping the shirt off his back. Then he began to beat him. The stick cut cruelly across his back and shoulders whilst Javert struggled feebly, half choked by the tight chain

69

around his neck. Agony began to scorch through him; he felt as if the heavy blows were breaking his back. Even with his grit and endurance he was eventually unable to restrain himself – he screamed and screamed again. The sound emerged as a strangled gurgle due to the pressure on his throat. It was difficult to breath and he was becoming increasingly dizzy.

By the time André let him go he was close to blacking out completely. He fell onto the floor, coughing and gasping. He tried to stand up but the dizziness and the pain in his back were too great. André was still standing over him, his feet less than a pace away from the boy's head. The man bent down, grasping Javert by the hair and forcing his head up.

'You're not big enough, boy.'

Javert glared back at him, beaten but by no means cowed, his eyes black with anger and pain.

'I will be one day.'

André nodded. 'Oh yes, you will be one day. But not yet, boy, not yet. You challenged too soon.'

He threw the stick on the table next to the pistol and walked out of the room.

Chapter 9

It was several days before Javert was able to move without considerable pain and even longer before he was back to full mobility. A week after his beating he saw Philippe at the café. Philippe immediately beckoned to him and took him through into his private apartment.

'Well, how are you?'

Javert shrugged. 'I'm all right.'

Philippe regarded him closely.

'Never mind "all right", how are you really? Do you need a doctor? Come on, let's have a look at you.'

'No, I'm just a bit bruised, that's all. How did you know what had happened?'

'Oh, André was perfectly open and matter of fact about it, when he told us you were out of action for a few days. I probably shouldn't say this to you, but I'm delighted to say that Jules was furious with him. Gave him a real dressing down.'

'What, because of me?'

Philippe pulled a face.

'Oh, not purely out of concern for you, I'm afraid. He was annoyed because you're a useful member of the team and he doesn't want you out of action just because André can't control his temper.'

Javert looked at him. 'Monsieur André didn't lose his temper, he never does that.'

Philippe sighed. 'Yes, I suppose you're right, I think I'd like him better if he did, rather than being coldly brutal the way he is. Anyway, I suppose I shouldn't be talking about my superior officer like this. Let's just say he showed bad judgment.' He looked at Javert seriously. 'From what I've heard, he's not the only one to do that. He tells me you went with a prostitute?'

'Yes I did.'

'Whatever possessed you to do that? I suppose young Henri took you? Listen Javert, I don't want to lecture you or sound like André, but do you understand why he was so angry with you?'

Javert shrugged again.

'He'd told me never to go with one. He said fornication outside marriage was a sin.'

'Well, yes, that's true of course.' Philippe's tone indicated that it was only a secondary consideration. 'More importantly, it's dangerous. You could get the pox, or some other disease. Are you listening to me?'

Javert nodded, still looking at the floor.

'You did the same once. I remember!'

Philippe looked puzzled. 'What are you talking about?'

'You went with a prostitute. At the inn in Marseille'.

Philippe looked blank for a moment, then recollection dawned.

'Oh, you mean that job we went on. That was different, that was just to give me an excuse to leave you alone. Mind you, I'm not saying it wasn't a welcome excuse.'

He frowned for a moment, then laughed suddenly.

'All right, that's one to you! But seriously Javert, it is dangerous. Listen, if you want to go with a woman that's fair enough, though I think you're still a bit young. But Javert, don't go with a prostitute down by the river again; there are safe, clean women you can have. Look, give it a year, then I'll introduce you to someone who can really show you the ropes when it comes to sex. That's a promise!'

He clapped Javert on the back, then frowned as the boy gave an involuntary gasp of pain.

'Come on, let's have a look at you, take that shirt off.'

He examined Javert's back and gave a grunt of disgust.

'There was no need for this, it's brutal as well as stupid. Just because you let Henri lead you astray.'

Javert pulled his shirt on again, moving carefully.

'It wasn't just that. I held a gun on Monsieur André.'

'You did what?'

'A gun. I knocked it off the table when he first hit me. I'd picked it up before I knew what I was doing.' He shrugged his shoulders. 'I know it was stupid.'

'Did you fire it at him?'

'No, I put it down again.'

Philippe expelled his breath in a soundless whistle.

'I'm not surprised he half killed you! Not that I blame you, but André – anyway, he's been warned now. I suspect he'll think twice before thrashing you again.'

Javert nodded and said nothing. He sometimes wondered why André loathed him so much, and would have been surprised to learn that despite his harsh treatment André did not in fact hate him. To André, Javert was like a pup that needed to be firmly trained and disciplined if he was to become a useful working dog. André had developed a grudging respect for the boy's fortitude. Javert might yell and wriggle with pain under a severe thrashing, but he had never pleaded or whined or snivelled. Even when he had been beaten almost into unconsciousness, he had never begged. And there had been some spirit left in him; as the boy lay helpless on the floor André had seen the fire still in his eyes.

Javert feared and detested André and had good cause for both feelings, but after that last, severe beating he noticed a change in the way André treated him. He no longer called him 'boy', but addressed him by name and generally spoke to him as a fellow adult rather than a child. Javert assumed that it was because he had been warned by Jules, but the real reason was nothing to do with that. André had taken little notice of Jules' warning, but he had been impressed by Javert's behaviour. Not by the challenge the boy had made, he considered that to be rash and impetuous. But he admired the maturity and courage the boy had shown when he realised his own mistake, put down the weapon and accepted the beating he knew would follow.

Javert's growing maturity also had an affect on his relationship with Philippe. It was becoming a friendship of equals, and for the first time in his life Javert felt able to discuss some of his feelings and emotions with another human being. The absence of his family meant that Philippe had more time available to spend with the boy. Javert was pleased, although he secretly missed little Michelle's flattering attentions.

A month after the incident with the prostitute Javert was alone at their lodgings working on a pair of boots when André hurried in, looking unusually flustered.

'Javert, come on, there's trouble!'

Javert put down the boots and jumped up. 'What's wrong?'

'The mob's finally gone on the rampage again. We knew it was coming, of course; the leaders are in a panic, what with the allies practically at the gates of Paris and the constant threat of civil war right here in the City. They've started to round up all and sundry; priests, nobility, anyone suspected of having royalist sympathies. They're all being dragged off to prison at the Cours de Feillants. And that's not the worse of it, we've just had word that Jules is one of them, he was arrested outside the Hotel de Ville about an hour ago. Come on.'

'What are we doing?'

André was throwing things into a canvas bag. 'First we're getting ready to move out at a moment's notice, if we need to. Pack your things quickly and put them in the wagon. Then we're going over to the prison to see what's happening there.'

'Jules won't say anything about us,' said Javert positively.

'Of course he won't, not willingly; but they have ways of loosening people's tongues. Come on, move!'

They packed their few belongings quickly, then headed for the prison at the Cours de Feuillants. The scene there was chaotic. There was a large crowd milling around the prison. Carts full of newly arrested prisoners were arriving constantly, forcing a passage through the excited crowd with difficulty.

André pushed his way to the front of the crowd and approached one of the guards.

'Hello citizen, what's happening here? We were just passing ...'

'We're rounding up filthy Royalist spies, that's what. And we've got the priests and the forgers out of prison. They're being tried for treason, all of them.'

'Tried? When?'

'Straight away – now. In there.' He nodded towards the door that led to the prison.

'Why the rush? In any case the prisons won't hold them all. Surely they're full to bursting already.'

The man laughed harshly.

'From what I hear that's one of the problems. Just think, citizen, what would happen if the prisoners got out and armed themselves? We have to make sure that doesn't happen. So we're putting them on trial and sentencing them now. The innocent go free. The guilty ...'

He laughed and drew a hand graphically across his throat.

'They're going to execute the people they find guilty? When?'

'Right away citizen. Why give the bastards any more time to escape or buy their way out? Go round the back of the prison and see the fun. You're lucky! I can't go, I have to stay on duty here.'

André and Javert exchanged glances, then left the guard and pushed their way round to the courtyard behind the prison. Once within view of the courtyard they both stopped in their tracks. Even the brutalised André seemed shaken by the sight that met their eyes.

The guard had said that the prisoners were to be executed, but this was no execution; this was butchery. The prisoners were being dragged out into the courtyard one after the other. The victims of the revolution were no longer confined to the aristocracy and these prisoners ranged from nobility to peasant; bourgeois to priest. There were so many, being brought out so quickly that the executioners had difficulty in keeping pace with them. The so called executioners were armed with a miscellany of weapons – cutlasses, axes, pikes – and in many cases did not seem to know how to use them. Nor did it appear to matter, so long as the prisoner in question ended up dead. One of the most harrowing sights was that of the next victims – crowded against the windows overlooking the courtyard, or held in the doorway – being made to witness the fate that would soon be theirs.

None of the prisoners were tied and their reactions varied greatly when they found themselves being forced to their knees in front of the bloodstained executioners. Some looked dazed and disbelieving, unable to understand what was happening to them. Others fought like madmen, trying vainly to protect themselves from the slaughter. Javert saw fingers and hands severed, arms severely slashed, before the victims were eventually dispatched. Only a few people seemed to have had time to prepare themselves and these knelt passively on the

75

ground, accepting their fate as inevitable. They were the only ones who died comparatively easily and quickly.

The crowd surrounding the courtyard was shouting and jostling for position, cheering wildly every time a prisoner was slaughtered. Javert glimpsed Philippe nearby, looking white and shaken. He caught Javert's eye for a moment, then turned away. Javert stood still, staring at the massacre in the courtyard. Dislike and contempt of convicts and lawbreakers had been bred in to him; he had witnessed executions before and was used to the harsh justice of the times. But this wasn't justice. This was carnage, anarchy, people gone mad. There was no sense, no order about any of it.

Suddenly they saw Jules, being hauled through the doorway into the courtyard. He looked as though he had been roughly handled, his clothes were torn and his face scratched and bloody. His captors pulled him into the open and dragged him over to the executioners. From where they were it was difficult to make out his expression, but he did not appear to be struggling.

Javert instinctively started towards him, but was restrained by André's hand, tightly gripping the back of his belt. Jules was pushed to his knees on the hard cobbles. He offered no resistance and his particular executioner seemed to know his trade. Jules died quickly, despatched by one skilled blow of an axe.

Javert felt sick. Behind him André tugged hard at his belt.

They pushed their way back through the crowds, only to be stopped by two guards, each wearing the red hats of the commune. Both appeared slightly drunk, whether with wine or slaughter it was difficult to tell.

'What's wrong citizen? Friends of yours out there maybe? Or perhaps you don't like seeing justice done?'

André laughed. 'I've brought the boy here specially to see it, but he's still a bit squeamish. Don't worry citizen, he'll learn.'

The guard narrowed his eyes.

'So maybe he is a bit squeamish, but why are you leaving? Come on citizen, stay and celebrate with us. Have a drink.' He waved his hand towards the nearby inn, where the customers had spilled out onto the square to watch the entertainment.

André hesitated, sensing that the situation could get ugly if he refused. He nodded.

'Thank you citizen, that's generous of you.' He turned to Javert. 'Get off home boy, I'll come along later.' He looked at the boy meaningfully. 'You can make yourself useful finishing off the work we started this morning.'

Javert nodded, guessing that André wanted him to make sure everything was ready for an immediate departure. He pushed his way clear of the throng of people. As he reached the edge of the crowd, he heard a nearby voice speak his name.

'Javert!'

He turned instinctively and his eyes widened in shock. Even after almost four years, he recognised the speaker immediately; a big, shambling youth about fifteen years old, running to fat. It was Bibet!

For a moment they stared at each other, both startled by the encounter. Bibet was dirty and scruffily dressed, wearing a soiled red sash around his waist. He looked a real son of the revolution. He was surrounded by about a dozen youths, similarly dressed and ranging in age from twelve to sixteen. It seemed that Bibet still liked to run with a pack.

Bibet sneered at him.

'Well, well, so you didn't like Toulon then, *gitan*? Decided to run off and try your luck in the big city? You could be about to find out your mistake.'

Javert thought quickly. Bibet had only seen him; he had no way of knowing that Javert was here with André and Philippe, no way of knowing that he was, effectively, working for the old royalist regime. So far as Bibet was concerned, Javert had simply run away from Toulon and André. All he had to do was get himself safely away.

Bibet was looking at him with the familiar sneer. He turned to the youths accompanying him. 'I know this young bastard from a long time ago; we can have some fun with him. Come on, grab him.'

Bibet and his followers closed with Javert. He fought them hard, kicking and lashing out with his fists, but just as in the old days there were too many for him. They dragged him into an alley, out of the crowd.

'Come on.' Bibet's voice was breathless with anticipation. 'Bring him over here – up against the table. That's right. Wait a minute.'

Javert felt hands at his waist. He didn't realise what Bibet was doing until the youth yanked his trousers down round his ankles.

'That's it. Now pull him over the table.'

Javert was forced face down over the table. The wooden top had been full in the blazing sun, and he gasped as the hot wood burnt the flesh of his bare stomach.

'All right, clear off his body, but keep a good grip on him. Watch him – he's tricky.'

They cleared off his back, but held on to his arms and legs, one on each limb, just as Bibet's previous followers had held him years ago when they had pushed his face into the foul mud of the pig pen. Javert's heart hammered wildly. His bruises had scarcely healed from the beating André had given him, and now it looked as if he was to receive another and probably worse thrashing. But that was not what Bibet had in mind.

'I'm going to enjoy this more than you are, *gitan*. You're not quite so little now, and neither am I. Oh no, I'm not going to thrash you, I've a better idea than that. I'm going to shaft you.'

Javert twisted his head to see Bibet unfastening the filthy sash that supported his trousers. He gasped with terror as he realised what the youth intended. Bibet laughed cruelly as he moved up behind Javert, grasping his waist. Javert felt Bibet close with him, felt his hardness as he began to push, trying to gain entry. Javert struggled wildly and desperately. A beating he could have taken, even a threat with a knife or a gun. But this –

Panic swamped him and he began to react instinctively, screaming and shouting for help.

'Philippe! Philippe – help! For Gods sake help! Philippe!

There was a sudden commotion nearby. The table shook, and shook again. Suddenly Bibet was gone and he found himself free, but before he could take advantage of it something heavy crashed into him. The table gave under the impact, then overturned completely, taking Javert with it and pinning him to the ground, trapped between the table and the nearby wall.

For a second Javert stayed where he was, numb with shock. Then he began to fight his way clear of the heavy table. In front of him Bibet and another youth were just picking themselves up. Philippe was confronting the remainder of the gang, who were standing back, looking uncertain; for the moment the youths had given way to the adult. Then Bibet recovered himself as he recognised the man standing there. His arm shot out, pointing towards Philippe. His voice rose to a scream.

'A police spy! He's a filthy police spy!'

The noise had by now attracted a number of other people, who were coming into the alley to see what the commotion was. Philippe took a step backwards but found his escape route blocked. In front of him, Bibet continued to shout, his words tumbling over each other in his haste.

'He's a spy I tell you – a filthy Royalist spy. I knew him before, in Toulon. Get him!'

The mob were already drunk with bloodshed and they needed little urging, They rushed Philippe and grabbed him, handling him roughly. In seconds they had him helpless and were dragging him off into the square. For the moment, Javert was forgotten.

Javert recovered his senses and pushed desperately at the heavy table, eventually managing to wriggle free. He started to race after Philippe but fell sprawling as he tripped over his trousers, still around his ankles. He secured them with shaking fingers and ran out of the alley.

Already the mob dragging Philippe had reached the square. Javert rushed after them, expecting them to take Philippe round to the front where the trials were taking place. But the mob had other ideas, they were headed directly for the courtyard at the back of the prison. Horror struck, Javert realised that they had no intention of even going through the travesty of a trial.

He grabbed a heavy cudgel from one of the guards, taking the man totally by surprise. Before the guard had time to react Javert was across the square and tearing his way through the crowd that surrounded the courtyard. In the dim recesses of his brain he could hear André's voice shouting to him, but he took no notice.

He reached the edge of the courtyard. Philippe was already in the middle, being forced to his knees. Javert shoved through the guards at the front of the crowd and began to race across the courtyard itself. Bibet's face swam before his eyes. He swung his cudgel and the face vanished.

He was close to Philippe now and for a moment that seemed an age their eyes met and held. Philippe was shaking his head desperately, shouting something that was lost in the roar of the crowd, or perhaps the roar was only in the boy's own head. Other faces loomed before him and again he swung his cudgel; then the cudgel was gone, torn from his grasp. Someone tripped him and he found himself rolling on the floor amidst a sea of legs, boots and clogs. Boots and clogs that whammed into him again and again, until something exploded in the side of his head and the world went black.

Chapter 10

A bright light was stabbing at his eyelids. Someone had got inside his head and was alternatively hammering and squeezing mercilessly at the inside of his skull. He tried to reach up and stop them, but found himself unable to move. There was pain everywhere – in his head, in his body. Physical pain, and a mental pain he did not want to admit or recognise. He moaned slightly and began to slide back into the warm darkness.

'Javert. Come on boy, wake up now.'

He allowed himself to float cautiously back towards the light. The pounding in his head was still there, accompanied by a jolting, swaying motion that felt familiar. A wagon! That was it, he was in a wagon, on the way back to Toulon. The man Marcel had stabbed him in the shoulder. They must be nearly there, Philippe was calling him, telling him to wake up.

He forced his eyes open, focusing with some difficulty through the pain in his head. Philippe was not there. Instead Monsieur Gerard was sitting by him, talking to him gently.

Javert tried to move his hand up to his head, then stopped as pain shot through his arm as well. Monsieur Gerard reached over and touched him gently.

'Javert. Can you understand what I'm saying?'

'Yes.' The boy's voice was thready and weak, little more than a whisper.

'Good.' Monsieur Gerard spoke slowly and distinctly. 'Now listen to me, you must try to keep still. You've been hurt. You've been kicked in the head and you've got a broken arm as well. We'll get you some help as soon as we can. In the meantime, try to lie still. All right.'

Javert tried to nod, but winced and gasped as the effort caused another shooting pain to lance through his skull. Monsieur Gerard turned away from him and called out softly.

'André! André, can we stop for a minute? Javert's come round.'

The wagon veered to the side and then halted. A moment later André climbed into the back. For a moment Javert stared at him blankly, then memory returned with a sudden jarring rush. He tried to sit up, but fell back dizzily. The world around him dipped and swayed, then steadied again.

'Philippe! Oh God, where's Philippe?'

Monsieur Gerard took his hand gently. Javert met his eyes and saw the tears shining there; he knew what the man was going to say before he spoke.

'Javert, boy, I'm sorry. I'm so sorry. Your friend – my son – there's nothing I can say ...'

He stopped, too overcome with emotion to continue. Javert forced himself to ask the question to which he already knew the answer.

'They killed him?'

'I'm afraid so. Don't reproach yourself, Javert – there was nothing you could do. God knows you tried hard enough, you nearly got yourself killed trying. Nobody could have done more.'

André interrupted, his voice harsh as usual.

'It was a stupid thing to do. Did you really think you could take on the entire Paris mob single handed? That's what happens when you think with your heart instead of with your head. Philippe too. If he'd stopped to think before rushing to your rescue like a knight in shining armour he might still be here now.'

The words - with their implication that he had contributed to Philippe's death - hit Javert like stones. He stared up at André.

'You were there? You saw what happened?'

'Yes, I saw what happened, right from the beginning when Bibet collared you. You put up a good fight – it attracted quite a bit of attention.'

Javert stared at him. 'But – if you saw what Bibet was doing, why didn't you help me?'

'Help you? If I'd done that Bibet would have thrown me to the mob just as he did Philippe. If I could have been sure of laying Bibet out before he had time to put the finger on me I'd have helped you. Not otherwise.'

For a moment shock and indignation drove out Javert's other feelings.

'You mean you just left me. You were going to let him - '

'Yes. Think straight, Javert. All right, so he was going to shaft you; not pleasant, but you'd have got over it. If I'd tried to help you I'd have been where Philippe is now. I tried to stop the young idiot rushing in, but I couldn't get to him in time. Any more than I could reach you in time to stop you trying to commit bloody suicide as you did.'

Javert stared at him. He could remember chasing after Philippe, but nothing after that.

'How did I get out?'

'I got you out. You'd already knocked Bibet unconscious with that cudgel of yours so there was no risk of him identifying me. You knocked out another man as well, and damaged a few more before they got you down. By the time I reached you they'd hacked Philippe's head off him and kicked you unconscious.'

Javert shuddered and stared into space, trying to fill the gaps in his memory. He remembered Bibet's attack on him, Philippe's rescue, racing across the courtyard towards Philippe as they held him on the ground...

The boy's breathing quickened as another memory suddenly surfaced. When Bibet was holding him, he had screamed out. He had screamed out for Philippe!

He closed his eyes.

'Oh God. Oh no, no!'

Monsieur Gerard laid a hand on his arm.

'Javert!'

'I killed him! I killed Philippe. It was my fault.'

'What are you talking about? You nearly killed yourself trying to save him.'

'No, before that. I shouted for help, shouted for Philippe to help me. If I hadn't – oh God, if I hadn't called out he'd never have come. Bibet would never have seen him.'

André's rough voice interrupted him.

'Rubbish! Do you really think he could hear you call his name above that din? He'd already seen what was happening; he was rushing to your rescue before you'd even opened your mouth.'

It was perhaps the only time in his life that André had said something that was intended to comfort the boy, but Javert –

lost in misery and self blame – didn't comprehend what he was saying. All his life, people had been ruthless with him. Now he was being equally unforgiving with himself, making no allowance for his own youth and natural terror. He had panicked and called for his friend; his friend had responded and died.

The wagon started forward again, moving slowly to spare him too much jolting. Javert lay back and closed his eyes. His thoughts flitted restlessly: the howling mob; the chaos and disorder that had led to the death of the only friend he had ever known; his own lack of control that had helped to cause that death. He thought of his boyhood in Toulon, when only Philippe had shown him kindness; his early days in Paris, and the happiness he had felt as they drove through the sunshine to the inn at Marseille; the genuine camaraderie that had developed between himself and Philippe over the past few weeks.

The pain of his memories was too great. In any case, what good did it do to remember? Resolutely, he tried to suppress his thoughts of Philippe and the affection he had felt for him, burying them deep down, together with the love he had once felt for his mother. André's words echoed in his mind:

'That's what happens when you think with your heart instead of your head.'

He opened his eyes abruptly and lay staring into space. Seeing he was awake, Monsieur Gerard came across to him to see what comfort he could offer. He looked into the boy's eyes, expecting to see there the tears that were still shining in his own. But Javert's eyes were black stones, dry and hard; he hadn't shed a tear.

84

PART TWO

The Hound

Chapter 11
Toulon 1796

The past tugged at Javert as he entered the courtyard of the Tour Royale. Seven years had passed since, as a boy, he had left Toulon for Paris. Since then a revolution had changed France for ever, but the garrison seemed just as he remembered it, only smaller. Familiar sights and sounds were everywhere, but more than anything it was the smells - strong and evocative - that triggered his memories; the odours of horses, horse dung and leather that were peculiar to military establishments such as this.

As he strode across the square, Javert allowed himself a moment of pride. The leather boots snug around his calves felt good after the years of going barefoot, or at the best wearing clogs or canvas. His tall figure looked well in the blue and red uniform, and he knew it. Appearance was important to him, it was part of being a professional representative of the law. In addition, the uniform gave him a welcome sense of identity; a sense of belonging. No one would call him *gitan* now!

The main gates alongside the stable block were already open, the first of the convict carts rumbling its way across the wooden bridge and into the garrison. The children who had followed the carts up from Toulon broke away at the gates and began to scamper back towards the town, still shouting and jeering.

Javert stopped and stood back to let the carts pass; three of them, with twenty four men in each. The men were seated back to back, every neck encircled by an iron collar. A continuous metal chain linked the collars together. Javert wrinkled his nose in disgust as the carts went slowly by. The smell from the nearby stables was strong, but the stench of the convicts overpowered even the stink of the horse dung.

He eyed the occupants more closely as the carts drove past. All of them were lice–ridden and filthy, with matted hair and beards. As yet they were not clad in prison clothing, but their own clothes were little more than rags. They had been on the road for more than a month, exposed to rain, wind and sun for the entire time. Whenever they passed through a town, they had to suffer the curiosity – and often the hostility and ridicule – of the local populace. Now, at the end of their journey, they looked exhausted and apathetic; more animal than human, with no individuality left.

The carts creaked their way towards the prison block and Javert strode away across the courtyard. A guard was walking briskly across the square towards him, wearing a uniform similar to his own. The man was about the same age as Javert, small and thin. Javert frowned thoughtfully as he watched him, there was something familiar about those swift movements; that sharp, weasel-like face. Then, as the man drew nearer, Javert recognised him. Ferrier, who in his boyhood had been one of Bibet's gang. Javert's thoughts flashed back to that never-to-be-forgotten day when they had dragged him into the pig pen and forced his face into the filthy ooze; that nightmare would stay with him all his life. But things were different now. Bibet and his gang were gone, Ferrier no longer posed any threat.

Javert did not particularly want to talk to Ferrier, so he kept his eyes focused on the far corner of the square where the horses were being exercised. But his ploy did not work. Ferrier hesitated for a moment, then approached him.

'Javert? It is you, isn't it?'

Javert nodded briefly.

Ferrier made a move as if to greet him properly, then hung back. He seemed embarrassed.

'I thought so, but you're – very different from how I remember you. Of course it's been a long time. Monsieur André told me you were back and asked me to come and find you. He wants both of us to help supervise the processing of the convicts.'

Javert nodded again and turned back across the square. Ferrier fell into step beside him.

'Javert, listen, I hope you don't still hold a grudge against me. You know what I mean – Bibet – it was a long time ago.'

Javert stopped and looked full at him for the first time. His expression was impassive, his stare cold. Ferrier shifted uncomfortably under that implacable gaze, then tried again.

'Look, we were both young. How old were we? Nine? And Bibet led us, you know that. Oh I know we shouldn't have followed him, but...'

Javert shrugged and looked away.

'As you say, it was a long time ago. It's not important any more.'

Ferrier smiled in relief, then hurried to catch up with Javert, who was already walking on with his longer stride.

'Thank you. After all, it's different now, you're one of us. And Bibet's gone. Did you know his father was killed in Paris?'

'Yes, I heard about that.'

Ferrier chattered on, relieved to have got some response.

'We never heard anything about Bibet though. I don't suppose you know what happened to him?'

Javert stopped again and turned to face him. Ferrier took an involuntary step backwards, half raising his hand as though in self protection. Yet Javert had made no move towards him, nor threatened him in any way. It was just something in his eyes that caused Ferrier to react in sudden, inexplicable fear.

Javert turned away and walked on. On this day of so many reminders, Ferrier's words had triggered other memories long since buried: Bibet's attempted sodomy; Philippe's rescue and death. The recollection had caught Javert unprepared and he was amazed by the pain it still caused.

He forced his mind back to the present, making himself respond to Ferrier's question.

'I saw Bibet just once. He'd become a street thug, the leader of a young Paris gang.' For a moment Javert considered the irony of the strange reversal of fortune that had led Bibet, former son of the Garrison Commander, to become a lawless vagabond; whilst he, the son of a convict and a gypsy, was now an official representative of law and order. The thought caused him a certain wry amusement and he gave a twisted smile.

They had reached the prison block now. The carts were standing in the hot sun, drawn up one behind the other and still laden with men. All the convicts were quiet, even the bravest of them cowed by their first sight of the infamous prison fortress.

André stalked out of the main building. He gave Javert a cursory nod of greeting, then walked round to the front of the carts. For a long moment he gazed at the convicts, his stare hard and appraising.

'This is the end of your journey. You will remain here until you have served your sentence. All of you are here because you have broken the law and so far as I am concerned you have no rights; none whatsoever. If you are obedient and behave well you will be reasonably treated. If you are disobedient or lazy, I promise you'll have cause to regret it.'

He indicated the first cart.

'In a few minutes the men on this cart will be taken into the hall. You will be marked with the Fleur de Lys, your heads and beards will be shaved to get rid of the vermin. Then you'll be given your prison clothing and permitted to go to your quarters for the remainder of the day. Tomorrow you will be allocated to your work details.'

He nodded to the Sergeant to take over, then beckoned to Javert.

'Javert, you stand with Ferrier and watch what's going on. I'll take you across to the Garrison Commander later.'

The convicts in the first cart were unloaded all together, still joined by the chain. Thus hampered, climbing down from the cart was difficult and there were a number of muttered curses as necks were wrenched and toes stamped on. The human caterpillar was led into the large hall, where a number of guards awaited them. Despite the warmth of the spring day a lighted brazier stood at the far end of the room.

The Sergeant walked forward, accompanied by a guard holding a list in his hand.

'You will each respond to your name when it is called out. It's the last time you'll be called by name while you're here, from today onwards you will be referred to by your number. That's all you are from now on – a number!'

He nodded to the guard with the list. The first name was read out.

'Bouvier, Francois.'

The man at the front of the caterpillar raised his hand.

'Here.' He looked at the Sergeant, then added 'Monsieur'.

The guard continued to read from the list.

'Age 20 years. Crime murder. Sentence life imprisonment.'

Two guards approached the convicts. They manacled Bouvier's wrists and pulled the end of the chain through his neck collar, freeing him from the caterpillar. Then they led the man towards the brazier in the corner. He walked passively between them, but stopped short as he suddenly realised the meaning of the brazier and the hot irons protruding from it.

The two big guards dragged him forward to the brazier, then held him whilst the hot iron was pressed to his shoulder, branding the Fleur de Lys for ever into his skin. There was a stench of burning flesh as the man screamed in agony. He struggled involuntarily, but the guards' grip was firm. Moaning with pain, he was pushed on to other guards, who led him out through the door at the far end of the room.

The branding continued throughout the morning, with Javert and Ferrier watching but taking no active part. Each convict was processed as quickly as possible but even so it took almost two hours to deal with the first cart. The remaining carts stood out in the increasingly hot sun, still loaded with chained men. In order to make the administration easier the convicts had been chained in alphabetical order, so those with names at the end of the alphabet were destined for a long wait.

It was well after noon by the time the first two cartloads of men had been put through. As the final cart was unloaded André dismissed the two hefty guards who had been unchaining and holding the prisoners, then turned to Ferrier.

'Ferrier, take over there.' He indicated Javert. 'You too.'

Javert and Ferrier obediently took over the task of unchaining the convicts one by one. Ferrier deftly fastened on the manacles, Javert slipped the chain free and both led that particular convict to the brazier, holding him whilst he was marked.

Javert did not have any sympathy for the convicts, so far as he was concerned they had broken the law and were now paying the just penalty. Nor was he particularly affected by the sight of men being branded, or by their screams of agony. Such sensitivity had been knocked out of him long ago by the sights he had seen in Paris. He did find it slightly disturbing to be actually dragging the men to the brazier and restraining them whilst they were branded. In Paris he had often been a spectator to such macabre activities, but he had never been an active participant. Typically, he remained outwardly impassive. He guessed that this was in part a deliberate test of himself; a way of 'blooding' the guards' newest recruit.

It was approaching evening when they at last reached the last convict of the third cart. Javert was big for his age, but this man made him feel small. Not in height – there was little between them there – but in build. The man was built like a blacksmith, bull-necked, with massive shoulders. He had been chained all day in the hot sun and like the other convicts looked dazed and apathetic, but even so he had a look of power about him. He reminded Javert strongly of someone else. He couldn't immediately recall who, but the memory was not a pleasant one.

The Sergeant tonelessly read out the final name.

'Valjean, Jean.'

The convict made no reply, perhaps feeling that since he was the last man his identity was obvious. The sergeant barked at him angrily.

'Convict, acknowledge. You are Jean Valjean?'

The man raised his head. 'Yes.'

'Age twenty seven. Crime housebreaking and robbery. Sentence five years.'

Ferrier efficiently fastened the manacles onto the man's wrists. Javert pulled the last portion of the chain free of the iron collar. The convict made no move, so Javert seized his upper arm and pulled him forward.

The enormous biceps moved and tensed under his fingers and Javert automatically turned his head to look at the convict. Their eyes met and locked. The convict's former apathy seemed to have vanished and for a second Javert glimpsed a blazing fury in the man's eyes. There was hatred there too; a hot and fierce hatred that seemed to be directed straight at Javert.

Javert let go of Valjean's arm and just stopped himself from actually taking a step backwards. For a moment he felt like a boy again, small and helpless; the way he had felt when he was about to undergo one of André's frequent thrashings, fighting desperately and knowing all the time he was not strong enough. Then he recovered his composure and gestured the man forward.

'Move!'

Valjean remained still, his gaze still locked with that of Javert. He had sensed that moment of fear and Javert could see the knowledge in his eyes. He felt ashamed of his reaction, but even more ashamed that he had allowed this gutter scum to sense it. After all, he wasn't a boy any more; he was a man now, with all the backing of the establishment behind him.

Determinedly he seized Valjean's arm again, dragging him forward. The man's eyes veiled and he allowed himself to be led to the glowing brazier. Javert held on to him firmly, but he made no further resistance; not even when the brand was set into his skin, though he was unable to restrain a low moan of agony.

The branding over, they handed him over to the other guards. As they led him to the door he glanced back over his shoulder at Javert. It was a look full of contempt and smouldering hate.

Chapter 12

Javert had now been at the garrison for nearly a month, during which time André had instigated a number of changes. Discipline amongst the guards had been tightened and uniform standards were far more rigorous. Javert was one of the few not dismayed by the changes. The other guards feared André and groaned under his harshness and severity, but Javert was accustomed to both; they had become his norm.

He quickly settled into the prison routine. The guards on the day shift took the prisoners out at seven o'clock and remained with them until mid–afternoon. The late shift would then relieve them and supervise the prisoners until seven o'clock in the evening, at which time they were permitted to return to their quarters. The guards' work was not difficult, but as he had expected Javert sometimes found it tedious.

There were twelve men on Javert's work detail, including two who wore the green caps of 'lifers'. The man Valjean – now prisoner 24601 – was also on that detail. The breadth of shoulder that Javert had observed proved an accurate indication of the man's strength, his power was proving invaluable on their present task of extending one of the garrison walls.

Hauling and positioning the heavy stones was back–breaking work, particularly in the intense heat of the June days. There was no shelter and in the middle of the day very little shade. The food was adequate, but never plentiful and of poor quality. The mood of the prisoners was often resentful, and therefore dangerous; especially in the case of the lifers, who had little to lose. Javert soon discovered the importance of remaining alert. It was all too easy to be lulled into a false sense of security as day followed day, with little variation. A number of guards had made that mistake in the past. Some, such as the Commander's crippled servant, had cause to regret their lapse of concentration. Others had not lived to regret it.

Javert was working on the day shift, partnered with Ferrier. The convicts had just reached the end of their noon-day break and were gathering up their tools ready to begin work again.

Ferrier suddenly nudged Javert.

'Hey, look at that insolent bastard!'

Javert looked where Ferrier was indicating. The convicts were ready to move off, with one exception. One man was still sitting on the ground beneath a small, twisted tree that provided him with a rare patch of shade.

Javert knew the man – number 25020. He was one of the men serving life sentences and they had already marked him down as potential trouble. He was leaning indolently back against the tree, ostentatiously studying the sky. One or two of the other convicts were looking uneasily in the direction of Javert and Ferrier. One of them said something to the man, who laughed harshly and settled himself more comfortably.

Ferrier swore angrily.

'The bastard – he's doing it deliberately. I'll see to him, you stay back.'

He strode over to the convicts whilst Javert stayed back, watching. That was mandatory procedure and enabled one guard to keep an eye on the other convicts whilst his partner was engaging one of them. If trouble did flare, the second guard could summon help before going to his partner's assistance. Guards had been badly beaten in the past for failing to observe such procedure.

The convict under the tree was now studying the ground between his manacled legs. He looked up at Ferrier's approach, but otherwise did not move.

Ferrier spoke to him briskly. 'Your rest period's over – you should be back at work. Get up!'

The man rose to his feet, not hurrying.

'Now get back to work before I report you.'

The convict stared at him for a moment, then began to walk towards the other convicts, swaggering his shoulders as he went. His slowness was a studied insult, had he not been wearing leg–irons he would have been moving at a saunter. One or two of the other convicts began to snigger at his bravado.

Ferrier flushed, aware that the man was toying with him. Angry and provoked, he suddenly lashed out with his heavy truncheon, taking the convict hard across the back.

The man cried out sharply at the sudden pain and stumbled forward to his knees, overbalanced by the blow and the leg irons that limited his stride. Suddenly he was no longer indolent. He pushed himself back to his feet, twisted like a snake and grabbed the stick from the surprised Ferrier's grasp. Undoubtedly he intended to attack, but two other convicts seized him by the arms and pulled him back.

'Don't be a fool, you'll only make things worse!'

Obeying the procedure for such incidents, Javert had already blown his whistle. Now he came hurtling over to the group, arriving just as Ferrier drew back his fist and struck the now helpless man hard in the face. He was winding up for another blow when Javert pushed his way between them, blocking his access to the convict.

'All right, calm down, everyone.' He indicated the men holding the convict 25020. 'You two, keep hold of him.'

Ferrier stood back, breathing hard. Other guards were arriving now, André amongst them.

'What's going on here? Javert, report!'

Javert related what had happened. In accordance with his training the explanation was brief but accurate, leaving nothing out. Behind him, Ferrier winced unhappily.

André regarded the prisoner coldly.

'Let him go.'

The convicts released the man and stepped back. 25020 was no longer struggling, he was beginning to realise the position he had got himself into.

André considered for a moment.

'Convict 25020, you have committed two offences. First, you failed to instantly obey an order to return to work. Second – and much more seriously – you attacked a member of the garrison staff.'

He walked up to the man, holding his eyes from a distance of less than one pace and speaking very deliberately.

'It's lucky for you these men held you back; normally they add at least two years to a man's sentence for striking a guard. But of course they can't do that with you, can they? They can only give you a long sentence of solitary confinement in the hole. You're already here for life; you're going to die in those chains.'

He paused, letting that message strike home, then continued in the soft, deadly voice that Javert knew only too well.

'As it is – for failing to obey orders, you get a week in double chains. For attacking a guard, you get twenty lashes.' Both sentences were the maximum that André was permitted to give, any greater sentence would need the authorization of the Garrison Commander.

The lash was fetched and the convict, now completely cowed, was securely tied to the back of one of the carts. His back was bared. Work was suspended whilst the remaining men of that work detail were drawn round to witness the punishment, the example being considered good for discipline.

For a moment there was almost total silence. They could hear sounds in the distance as the other details continued with their work, but here there was a hush that could be felt. Then André swung the lash, and the stillness was broken as it whistled through the hot air. It sliced into the man's back, laying open the flesh. The man gave a scream of pure agony. There were subdued gasps from some of the convicts and Javert winced inwardly. He knew – who better – how hard André could hit, and André had never used that kind of a whip on him. His belt or his stick had always sufficed.

By the time the final lash fell the convict was no longer screaming, but was slumped motionless over the cart. André ignored him and turned to Javert.

'Get these men back to work. Ferrier, you come with me.'

André strode away, trailed by an unhappy Ferrier. The fact that he had struck a prisoner would not weigh with André, but he would not be pleased that Ferrier had allowed a convict to relieve him of his weapon. Ferrier knew that the forthcoming interview would not be pleasant.

Watched by the remainder of the convicts, Javert crossed to the man who had just been under the lash and unfastened the ropes that tied him to the cart. The man collapsed to the ground with a low moan. For a moment he lay prone, then tried to rise, using the side of the cart to lever himself up. He got as far as his knees, then collapsed again and lay face down in the dust.

Javert bent over the convict, examining him. His back was criss-crossed with livid weals, many of which were still oozing blood, drying rapidly in the hot sun. Javert lifted the convict's head and looked into a paper white face. The man was conscious, but his gaze was unfocused and he seemed dazed. Despite the heat he was shaking as though with intense cold. He was, Javert realised, in severe shock.

Javert stood up, his face expressionless. He indicated the two convicts nearest to him.

'You two, pick this man up and carry him back to his quarters. See to him, then get back here.'

The men obediently picked up their comrade and began to carry him towards their quarters. Javert turned to the remaining convicts.

'All right, the show's over. Get back to work.'

The men obeyed, picking up their ropes and tools and moving back towards the walls. As Javert moved along the line he caught a muttered remark, uttered by one of the men he had just passed.

'Cold blooded young bastard!'

Javert hesitated for a moment, uncertain whether he should ignore the remark. But if he had heard it, so had the other convicts. He turned and looked back along the line.

'Has one of you something to say to me?'

There was a moment of silence, then Valjean stepped forward.

'I think you heard what I had to say.'

Javert walked over to him. 'Perhaps you'd like to repeat it.'

The man next to Valjean put his hand on his arm.

'Jean, leave it!'

Valjean shook his head. The fire that Javert had marked before was in his eyes.

'Oh no! If the boy didn't hear me properly, I'll repeat it for him. I said you're a cold blooded young bastard, and so you are. How can you do that? Stand there and watch a man almost beaten to death and not even crack your face.'

His companion touched his arm again, but Valjean shook off his hand, the eyes fixed on Javert still sparkling with fury.

'Look at the young whelp! He can't even shave yet, but he stands there swaggering with his tin-pot uniform and his shiny new stick.' He took a step forward, eyes still hot with anger. 'You think we're nothing but thieving scum don't you – dirt under your feet? What do you know about life in the city slums? Most of us had to steal or starve, but you wouldn't understand that. You, with all your advantages and cosseted little existence.'

He turned his head and spat deliberately onto the ground between himself and Javert.

Javert's nostrils flared slightly, for once he had lost his impassive look. He stepped up close to the convict, ignoring the stench that radiated from him.

'And what do you know about my life? Where do you think I grew up? You're not the only one to come from the gutter – my father was a con like you and I was born in this very prison. You made your choices and I made mine, now I'm the one with the stick and you're the one with the chains. And if you don't want to end up with your skin in shreds you'd better remember that'.

The two men were standing very close now, trying to stare each other down and oblivious to everything except each other. The voice that sounded from behind Javert startled them both.

'Javert – what's going on here!'

Javert turned quickly; he had been so intent on his confrontation with Valjean he had not heard any approach. André stood there with Ferrier. Behind them were the late shift guards, here to relieve the day shift.

André continued. 'I believe I saw this convict spit at you?'

The fire left Valjean's eyes and the veil dropped back into place. He shrugged his shoulders.

'I didn't spit *at* him. If I had I'd have hit him, I could hardly miss at this distance.'

André raised his eyebrows. 'Javert?'

Javert was angry with himself for losing his temper. It had not only led him into an unnecessary confrontation, it had made him neglect his duty. With Ferrier absent he had no–one to watch his back, yet he had totally forgotten to keep his senses alert whilst he was talking to Valjean. Anyone could have crept up on him, he was lucky it was only André. What was it about this convict that made him lose his calm so easily?

He took a step back from Valjean and deliberately composed himself, thinking back over the incident and striving for objectivity.

'He didn't exactly spit at me Monsieur, he spat on the ground in front of me.'

'But meaning to insult you?'

'I believe so Monsieur.'

André nodded. 'Very well.' He turned to Valjean. 'Perhaps two days in solitary confinement will teach you manners, 24601. Javert, your relief is here, you can take this convict to the hole on your way back to barracks.'

'Yes Monsieur.'

André beckoned to him and moved out of hearing of the convicts.

'And what do you think you were doing? You were standing right in the middle of them, on your own, with no protection.'

Javert nodded. 'Yes Monsieur, I know. I – lost my concentration a bit.'

'You mean you lost your temper? You let him needle you?'

'Yes Monsieur.'

'Good God Javert, haven't I taught you better than that? If you were still a boy I'd take that whip to you. As it is, you can work a double shift tomorrow. Perhaps that'll teach you to concentrate on your job.'

Javert nodded, remaining impassive. 'Understood Monsieur.'

'All right, dismissed.'

Javert walked back to Valjean, who was being watched by Ferrier. The other convicts had already moved away with their new guards.

Javert glanced at Ferrier. 'Are you coming?'

Ferrier shook his head ruefully. 'No, I'm staying on duty. He's given me a double shift.'

Javert laughed slightly. 'Me too, only mine's tomorrow.'

He turned to Valjean. The man was waiting quietly, eyes veiled, expression unreadable. Javert motioned towards the cell block.

'That way 24601.'

'You know my name, why don't you use it?'

'Not here. You don't have the right to a name here.'

Valjean stared at him, then turned and walked towards the cell block and the stinking hole that awaited him.

Chapter 13

Month followed month with little variation save for the changing seasons. In the world outside the weak Ruling Directory finally fell and Napoleon swept to power, but inside the garrison there was little change, other than the endless paperwork resulting from each change of leadership.

The turn of the century came and went – it was four years since Javert's return to Toulon. Autumn was advancing towards winter, bringing with it the mistral; the cool, strong wind that usually arrived in early autumn. The weather became more changeable, with sudden storms and torrential rain that rarely lasted long but could do considerable damage.

One day in late October 1800 - Brumaire 1X of the Revolutionary calendar - Javert was nearing the end of his tour of duty when André beckoned to him.

'Commander wants you,' he said briefly. 'Wait for your relief, then go.'

'Yes Monsieur.' Javert nodded, feeling his heartbeat increase. He was not precisely alarmed, but he was mystified and slightly concerned. A summons to see the Commander was a rare event.

As soon as his shift was over he hurried to his billet and quickly brushed down his uniform and cleaned his boots. The previous day had brought a prolonged downpour of lashing rain that had turned the hard mud into a quagmire, it was impossible to keep uniforms clean under such conditions. But Javert always started his shift impeccably turned out, his standards had been thrashed into him over the years.

Immaculate once more, Javert strode to the Commander's office and knocked firmly before entering the room. The Commander smiled at him and waved towards the chairs in front of his desk.

'Javert, sit down.'

Javert noted the smile; it was evidently not a discipline matter. He seated himself in one of the two chairs. The other was already occupied by Monsieur Molines, Javert's regular Sergeant.

'So, Javert, you've been here over four years now. How are you liking it?'

'Sufficiently Monsieur.' Trained by André not to waste words, Javert responded with the brief formality he usually used when addressing his superiors.

Monsieur Martin indicated the Sergeant.

'Did you know that Sergeant Molines here is leaving us? He's being transferred to the harbour garrison at Marseille. As a Gendarme, I should add, so it's something of a promotion for him.'

Javert smiled politely but formally.

'Congratulations Sergeant.'

'Thank you Javert.'

The Commander leafed through the file in front of him.

'I hear good reports of your work from both Monsieur André and Sergeant Molines. You're reliable, fair, not afraid to take responsibility.'

He paused for a moment, then continued.

'Sergeant Moline's departure leaves us with a vacancy for a sergeant, so what do you think?'

'About what Monsieur?'

'About taking Sergeant Moline's place. I'm offering you a promotion, Javert.'

Javert's eyes widened in surprise.

'Me?'

The Commander smiled, it was unusual to see Javert at a loss.

'Yes, you. I know you're still full young, but if I didn't think you could handle it I wouldn't be offering it, believe me. So I'll ask you again. What do you think? Can you handle it?'

Javert felt a rare rush of pride and pleasure. He knew that he was one of the more conscientious of the guards, he took his job seriously and always gave total commitment. But André had never been given to compliments and Javert hadn't realised his efforts had been noticed. Certainly he had never expected this. Nonetheless, he didn't hesitate.

'I can handle it, Monsieur. Thank you; thank you very much.'

'Good. Now then, do you remember what I said to you when you first arrived here, about abuse of power?'

'Very clearly Monsieur.'

'You need to bear that in mind again, but this time not just on your own account. Do you understand that? You're no longer responsible just for yourself, you're responsible for the guards under your command. If they break the rules you are expected to report them, or deal with them yourself, according to the severity of the offence. Even if it happens to be your best friend, you deal with them just the same. Understand?'

'Yes Monsieur.'

'The prisoners too. Whereas before you've simply reported any infractions, now you can deal with them yourself, up to a point. You've got additional responsibilities now Javert, I expect you to take them seriously.'

Javert nodded. 'I intend to Monsieur.'

'All right Javert. You can collect your insignia now and put it up tonight. You take up your new rank tomorrow, on the same detail. Is that a problem for you?'

'Not at all Monsieur.'

'Good. Then it only remains to say congratulations.'

He stood up and offered his hand. Javert shook hands with him and Sergeant Molines, then saluted smartly and turned to go. The Sergeant called him back.

'Javert – just a minute. I'm having a farewell drink with the lads tonight. You'll join us, of course.'

'Thank you sergeant, but I'd rather not.'

'But surely you want to celebrate your own promotion?'

'I prefer to celebrate alone.'

The Commander intervened.

'Javert, I know from your reports that you're something of a loner and that you don't like socialising. That's up to you; I don't care, so long as you do your job. But this celebration is a little different and you'll be expected to be there; it's tradition. I'm not ordering you to go, of course; but I think you should.'

Javert looked at him impassively.

'As you wish, Monsieur.'

'All right Javert, you can go.'

Javert saluted, turned on his heel and marched out. The Commander regarded the closed door thoughtfully.

'My goodness, he's a cold fish!'

The sergeant nodded.

'He's always been like that, Monsieur. Not surprising, when you think of his background. I remember him as a young boy, when he first went to live with Monsieur André. But my word, the pup has grown into an impressive hound. He's got the makings of a real pack leader. Don't you think so, Monsieur?'

The Commander shook his head.

'Pack leader? I don't think so. Oh, I don't doubt he could if he wanted to, but – well, you call him a hound; I'd say he's more of a lone wolf. He doesn't want the pack.'

The Sergeant looked thoughtful. 'You could be right; but nonetheless, a useful officer.'

The Commander nodded. 'I think so.'

The following day – his first in his new rank - Javert was on the late shift. The convicts were still working on the extension to the garrison and the walls were nearing completion. The wind was gusting strongly, making work on the high walls doubly precarious. The constant wind frayed tempers and sapped concentration and everyone was tired. The guards were particularly disgruntled. The heavy rain had turned the ground into a quagmire and the thick mud caked on their leather boots and spattered their uniforms. That meant a considerable amount of work during their off duty time, Monsieur André would not lower his standards because of a little mud.

Javert felt slightly nervous at his new status, but typically did not let his concerns show. A few men congratulated him, and even André gave him a lift of the eyebrow and a faint smile. Ferrier positively fawned on him, but then Ferrier had always followed a leader, whoever that might be.

He had wondered whether some of the older men might resent his youth, but if they did they concealed it well. Javert had been shaped by his earlier experiences and by André's training. He was tough and uncompromising and now that he was also in authority over them few people cared to argue with him. In any case, he had always seemed older than his years.

Shortly after commencing duty Javert was standing with André, watching the large stones being hoisted up to the top of the wall.

'Hey, look out! Ware below!'

The shout came from above. Javert looked up, to see a huge lump of stone swinging wildly from one piece of rope, the other rope having broken. The man who had been standing on top of the massive block had lost his balance when the stone swung and was now hanging precariously from the one remaining rope. Even as they watched he lost his grip and hurtled down. He landed on top of André, knocking him to the ground. Almost at the same instant the second rope parted.

Javert hurled himself desperately to one side. He hit the mud and slid helplessly, fortunately further out of the path of the stone. There was an ominous crump and an agonised scream.

Javert rolled over and sat up. His uniform was covered in mud and his cheek hurt him. He put up a hand and it came away wet with blood, where a chip of stone had flown off at high speed and hit him in the face. He realised it had been a close thing, he had been lucky.

He could still hear someone screaming nearby. He picked himself up and turned towards the sound. It was then he realised that others had not been so lucky; the convict and André had been unable to get clear and both were trapped by the fallen block. The convict was almost completely under the stone, with only his head and shoulders sticking out. It was he who was screaming, but already his screams were turning to strangled gurgles as the stone crushed the breath out of him. André was trapped by the legs.

Javert raced over to the stone and put his weight against it, pushing hard. He was quickly joined by others, but all their efforts were in vain. The huge block was firmly anchored in the mud and they were unable to get any real purchase on its almost smooth surface.

Javert turned to the nearest guards.

'You - fetch a lever and a wedge. You - fetch the doctor. Quickly.' He swung round towards the watching convicts. 'You two, get the ropes round this stone; we'll try to drag it off.'

They all obeyed him instantly, racing off in different directions.

The convict's gurgling screams had stopped now and his face was turning livid as the stone continued to crush him. André was silent, his eyes staring into those of Javert. For a moment Javert thought he was too much in shock to even scream, but then André spoke, his voice hoarse but controlled.

'Your wedges will be too late, the stone's sinking.'

Looking at the stone, Javert realised that he was right. The massive block was sinking gradually as it settled into the mud.

Javert walked round the stone, examining it carefully. He noticed a depression beneath one side, just deep enough to take a kneeling man. Perhaps if he tried lifting instead of pushing...

He crouched under the block and wedged his back against it, pushing upwards with all his strength. His muscles cracked with effort and the sweat began to pour down his face, running salty and stinging into his eyes. There was still no movement from the rock. He cautiously eased off the pressure and the rock immediately sank a little further. Javert quickly scrambled clear, in danger of being crushed if he stayed where he was. He had now attained his full height and weight and was as strong as any guard in the garrison; if he couldn't move the stone it was unlikely that anyone else could. The situation appeared hopeless. This view was echoed by a pain filled whisper from André.

'Leave it Javert! It's impossible – too heavy!

Javert had no reason to like André, but he couldn't help admiring the man's courage and composure. He was in a lot of pain and an unpleasant death was only minutes away, but André had not panicked and was still thinking clearly.

A voice spoke behind Javert.

'Let me try. I might be able to move it.'

Javert turned to find Valjean behind him. He started to refuse automatically, then hesitated as he looked at the convict's breadth of shoulder. If anyone could do it, this man could. He nodded.

'All right, try. But be ready to get out quickly - it's sinking.'

Valjean gave him an unfathomable look then got beneath the rock, in the same position as the one Javert had adopted. He too began to push upward. The sweat began to pour down his face. He turned red, then white with the effort and still he held the push. The rock shifted upwards a fraction, then a fraction more.

Javert snapped. 'Get them out of there - quickly.'

A dozen willing hands dragged the victims free. Valjean relaxed his muscles and rolled clear in one movement. He lay prone on the ground, white faced and panting. The rock settled again heavily into the mud.

Javert turned to Ferrier and motioned towards the convict who had been trapped.

'See to him.'

He himself bent over André.

'Are you in pain, Monsieur?'

André shook his head. 'No, but I'm not sure that's necessarily a good sign. Have a look, Javert.'

Javert moved down and examined André's legs. The left one was clearly broken below the knee, a bad fracture with the bone protruding almost at right angles. The right foot was severely crushed, little more than a red mass of tissue. At the moment shock seemed to be holding pain at bay, but once that wore off André was going to be in agony.

'How bad?' queried André.

Javert hesitated, then decided to be truthful. André had never given palliatives and would not expect them from others.

'It's not good, Monsieur. You've one leg broken and the other foot badly crushed. I've already sent for the doctor.'

Ferrier came back and crouched down next to him.

'The convict's dead. The weight was full on his body, it just crushed the life out of him.'

Javert nodded. 'All right, leave me two men here. Get the rest back to work and keep an eye on them. I'll stay here.'

Ferrier indicated Valjean, now beginning to sit up and regain some colour.

'What about him?'

'Leave him where he is.'

The doctor arrived on the run, armed with splints and bandages. He examined André's injuries, then shook his head.

'I think we can set the left leg, but there's no chance of doing anything with the right foot. I'll have to amputate.' He motioned to the two convicts. 'Carry him to the cart, carefully.'

Javert bent over André. 'Shall I come with you?'

'What the devil for, do you want to hold the saw? You'll have to cover for me now in any case. Stay here and do your job.'

André was carried carefully to the cart. The dead convict was loaded aboard and it rumbled away towards the main garrison.

For the next few days Javert had little time to think about the incident. The garrison's other Lieutenant was currently on leave and André's accident meant that Javert and his fellow Sergeant had to take on their duties and responsibilities. After only one day in his new rank, Javert was pitched in right at the deep end.

Three days after the accident he was walking across the square on his way back to his billet. As he walked past the convicts' quarters his attention was caught by a sudden scream, followed by a chorus of shouts and cheers. There was a moment's silence, then another scream.

Javert frowned and hesitated. He was both tired and irritable; it had been another day of wind and lashing rain and he had a good two hours work to do on his uniform if he was to be up to standard for the following day. He didn't want to stop and deal with trouble amongst the convicts; they were often noisy and fights were not uncommon. But there had been something about that scream...

Javert cursed under his breath and turned decisively into the entrance to the convicts' quarters. He gestured the duty guard to accompany him and strode down the dark and narrow stone passage. At the end of the passage he paused, listening. From the cell on his left he heard what sounded like a sob of terror, followed by a chorus of angry shouts.

Javert motioned to the guard to unlock the door, and glanced through the peephole whilst he did so. His view was restricted, but he could see two men – one of them Jean

109

Valjean – apparently struggling violently in the middle of the cell. As Javert watched, Valjean drew back his fist and smashed it into the face of the other man, catapulting him across the small cell to crash into the two-tier bunks opposite the door.

Javert threw the door open, sending it crashing back against the wall. He stalked into the room, curling his mouth in disgust at the stench that met him. There were six men crowded into each small cell, and sanitation was basic to say the least; the convicts' quarters always stank of stale sweat, urine and excrement.

'All right, stay where you are. Nobody move.'

Three men were standing against the wall on his left, mouths still open in surprise at his sudden entrance. Valjean was in the middle of the room, fist still clenched, whilst the man he had struck lay back against the wooden bunks, conscious but dazed.

The sixth occupant was cowering against the far wall. Javert looked at him sharply. He was young – little more than a boy – and he looked terrified out of his wits. His trousers were round his ankles, and as Javert looked at him he fumbled at them with shaking fingers, trying to pull them up.

Javert stared round the room, studying the men one by one. The three in the corner looked sullen, the boy terrified. Valjean just glared back at him, the familiar contempt and hatred in his eyes. The man Valjean had struck looked defiant but scared. After a moment Javert recognised him as 25020, the convict who had been so thoroughly flogged when Javert had first been appointed to the garrison. He knew the man was a trouble-maker and a bully, most of the other convicts were afraid of him. He was also in a state of undress, naked from the waist down.

'All right, what's going on here?"

No–one answered him, he hadn't expected them to. But looking at the terrified boy huddled in the far corner, Javert had little doubt what the man had tried to do – what he would have done, if Valjean hadn't intervened. His mouth twitched as his mind took him back to Paris, eight years ago; the day of the prison massacres, the day of Philippe's death. The hot wood

110

was burning his naked stomach. He could feel Bibet's heat and hardness against him; smell his fetid, animal smell –

Javert's skin crawled. He walked across to the boy, still crouched on the floor, his face streaked with tears. He turned his head away from Javert, unwilling to meet his eyes.

'All right boy, dress yourself. Then get your things together, you're coming with me.'

The boy looked at him then, fresh terror in his eyes.

'You're putting me in the hole?'

'No. I'm moving you to another cell, out of his way.'

The boy stared at him in momentary disbelief, quickly replaced by a look of abject gratitude. Javert shifted uncomfortably; he wasn't accustomed to gratitude from anyone, let alone convicts. He wasn't even sure why he felt compelled to help the boy. Nor did he try to analyse his reasons, Javert was not given to introspection.

'Come on boy! Get your things together and move.'

The boy scrambled to his feet and began fumbling his scant possessions together. Javert turned away, to find Valjean's gaze fixed on him, his expression a curious mixture of surprise and speculation. For the first time since Javert had known him, there was no hostility in his eyes. For a moment Javert looked back at him, his own expression wooden. Then he gestured the boy through the door and followed him out of the cell.

On the following day a new Lieutenant arrived to take up the vacant position left by André's accident. Whatever happened, it was certain that André would never be able to return to full duties. His right foot had been amputated and he was now suffering the fever and infection that were considered an inevitable result of such operations.

Five days after the accident, Javert was walking to his billet at the end of his shift when he heard his name called. Turning, he saw the doctor hurrying toward him. He altered direction and met the doctor halfway across the square.

'How's Monsieur André?'

The doctor shook his head.

'No hope there, I'm afraid. His chances were never good with that injury, but now...'

Javert interrupted. 'What do you mean? Is he dying?'

111

The doctor nodded. 'Yes, he's dying. Gangrene has set in; it's already up past his knee and there's nothing to be done. I'm just going to fetch the priest but I wanted to find you first. He's been asking for you.'

Javert raised his eyebrows, then nodded.

'I'll come, of course.'

'I think you should. He won't be able to talk to you for long; he's conscious, but he's weak and his thoughts keep drifting off. That's largely due to the drugs I'm giving him, I'm trying to keep the pain manageable.'

André was lying on a bed in the garrison hospital. His skin looked ashen and an unbelievable stench came from the blackened bandages around the stump of his right leg. At first Javert thought he was unconscious, but he opened his eyes in response to Javert's 'Monsieur.' His eyes were clouded from pain and the effects of the heavy doses of drugs he had been given, but he still managed to raise a grim smile.

'Well, young Javert, it looks as if you'll never get the chance now.'

'Chance, Monsieur?'

'To call me out. You tried once, do you remember? I told you it was too soon.'

Javert nodded, thinking back to his thirteenth birthday, when he had threatened André with the pistol. It was not a day he cared to remember, and yet it had marked the last beating he had received at André's hands.

He brought his attention back to the present and the dying man in front of him. André was moving restlessly and his gaze was wandering. He seemed to be thinking aloud rather than talking to Javert.

'You grew up on that day. I knew it was the last real thrashing I'd give you.' His eyes focused again on Javert. 'I told you you'd be big enough to beat me one day, but it's too late! Unless you want to take me on now - you'd certainly have no problem.'

Javert shook his head. 'There'd be no satisfaction in that.'

André laughed mirthlessly.

'No, I don't suppose there would. Well, you won't get another chance, I know I don't have long.' He nodded towards his leg and snorted. 'The doctor denies it; he must think I'm a fool. My foot was amputated, not my nose, I haven't lost my sense of smell. It's gangrene isn't it?'

Javert nodded. 'Yes Monsieur.'

'How far has it gone?'

'The doctor says it's up past the knee.'

André nodded in satisfaction, like a man watching his favourite dog perform tricks.

'I knew you'd be straight with me, I've trained you well. You're wasted here. You need to go into the Gendarmerie.'

'I would if I could. I'm too young unless I can afford to buy my way in.'

André nodded. Then his face suddenly contorted and his whole body shook at the sudden onslaught of pain. He was obviously fighting to hold back screams of agony. He spoke again with a visible effort.

'All right, get out now. I don't need an audience.'

Javert hesitated for a moment, but it was evident that there was nothing he could do. He nodded and walked out of the room.

The following day, the garrison was informed that André had died during the night. No one really mourned his passing. André had been feared and in some cases respected, but he had not been liked.

He was buried with full military honours, with the mistral at its worst and torrential rain lashing at the windows of the little chapel. The bleak, dismal day was a fitting epitaph to the man's life.

Chapter 14

Following André's funeral, Javert returned to his billet and changed out of his uniform. Then he left the garrison and walked across the low cliffs to the fishing harbour at Toulon. The rain had stopped and the late sun was struggling out from behind the last of the black clouds, but the wind was still blowing in strong gusts, whipping up the normally placid water. The waves hurled themselves against the walls, wetting the rounded cobblestones on the harbour and forming some sizeable puddles in the depressions between them.

For a while Javert watched the anchored boats rocking restlessly, then he climbed to the top of the harbour wall and settled himself there, ignoring the drenching spray from the waves as he stared out over the stormy ocean. As a boy he had liked to sit and gaze at the sea, particularly when he wanted to think things through. Today he was in an unusually reflective mood and had reverted to his boyhood habit.

André's death had unsettled him more than he expected. The man had been a large part of his life for the past twelve years and his death had made Javert think back over that time, resurrecting painful memories. It was not that he had any affection for André; his guardian would certainly not have welcomed it if he had. Emotion had no part in André's life, he had always been cold and calculating, ruled by his head, never by his heart. It hadn't cost him a momentary qualm to leave Javert to the mercy of Bibet, rather than risk exposing their cover. Not like Philippe - but Philippe had paid with his life for helping Javert.

Javert's thoughts shied away from memories of that day; there was too much pain there, too much guilt. Instead, his mind went back to the scene he had interrupted in the convicts' cell, two days before. He could still picture the boy's face, terrified and ashamed, together with an image of the angry Valjean, fist still clenched from the blow he had struck in the boy's defence. Why had Valjean rescued the boy? For that matter, why had Javert himself been driven to help him? Had he perhaps seen himself lying there?

114

Javert shifted uneasily, trying to shake off the introspective thoughts that caused such confusion in his mind. He was never comfortable trying to cope with emotion, particularly his own, he preferred to keep his feelings suppressed and stick to the hard facts of day to day life - order and disorder, right and wrong. He knew how to deal with those.

The sun was nearly down now and the temperature was beginning to fall rapidly, as it often did at this time of the year. Javert gave a sudden shiver and turned to climb down from the wall. As he did so he noticed a shadowy form hurrying along the harbour.

For a moment he thought it was one of the fishermen, coming out to check his boat before nightfall. Then it struck him that there was something odd about the man's movements. He was moving in quick bursts, staying close in to the walls and darting looks back towards the shore. It was as if he did not wish to be seen. Almost on that thought the man turned his head in a seaward direction and Javert saw his face for the first time. It was the convict Valjean.

Valjean saw him at the same moment and stopped dead in his tracks. For a second both were still, startled by the unexpected encounter. Valjean was still wearing his red prison smock and leg irons, but there was no chain attaching the irons to each other. He must be trying to reach the boats. Javert leapt down off the wall into the path of the convict and grabbed for his whistle to raise the alarm, but his hand encountered nothing save the buttons of his shirt. Being off duty and out of uniform, he had left both whistle and truncheon behind at the garrison.

Valjean seemed to realise this at the same moment. 'So the little tin soldier hasn't got his stick with him. Get out of my way!'

Javert stood his ground and shouted towards the shore.

'Prisoner escaping. Help - prisoner escaping.'

The gusting wind and crashing waves drowned out his shouts. They could not have been heard twenty paces away, let alone on the shore. Valjean bared his teeth in a threatening snarl and advanced towards him.

115

'I'm warning you, get out of my way. You're not strong enough to stop me!'

His voice was a low growl, the familiar fire was in his eyes. Javert remembered the events of the previous week when Valjean had lifted the massive slab of stone and knew that the convict was right; he did not have the strength to beat the convict in a hand to hand fight. He thought back swiftly to his childhood, when he had often been up against impossible odds. Now as then, his best chance lay in surprise.

Javert lashed out viciously with his foot, aiming for the vulnerable area between the convict's legs. Had the kick landed as intended the fight would undoubtedly have ended there and then, but Valjean was fast and he was watching Javert carefully. He twisted like a snake and the savage kick narrowly missed its target. It was still enough to draw a howl of pain, but not enough to incapacitate him.

Javert sprang at him and the two men closed and struggled. For a moment Javert thought he was going to get the better of the convict, his kick had hurt the man. Then Valjean began to recover. He succeeded in breaking Javert's grip on him and swung him round, putting his arm round his neck and pulling Javert back against him.

Held close like that, Javert choked at the sheer stink of the man. He reached back with one foot and raked his heel down the convict's shin, stamping hard on his instep. Valjean swore, but the grip on Javert's throat did not ease. He had Javert down now and was kneeling on his back, pushing his head into one of the puddles of seawater between the stones. Javert could hear the blood pounding in his ears and his vision was beginning to blur; the power that had temporarily saved André was going to end his own life! His senses were fading as he felt himself being dragged roughly across the hard stones...

Suddenly, Javert found he could breathe again. He lay still for a moment, sucking in air and trying to bring himself back to full consciousness. He had almost blacked out, and he still felt weak and dizzy. After a few seconds his vision cleared and he looked up. The convict was a few paces away at the end of the harbour, trying to untie one of the boats.

Javert scrambled up and went for him again. His rush took them both to the ground and his momentum carried him past the convict and almost catapulted him over the edge of the harbour and into the water below. He clawed his way back to safety, but the delay had cost him dearly. Valjean was already on his feet.

'Obstinate young bastard!'

Javert saw Valjean's foot go back. He rolled desperately clear of the edge and tried to scramble out of the way, but the savage kick took him across his cheekbone. There was just a split second of blinding agony, then darkness.

Javert was roused by the sound of a voice calling his name insistently. He could feel water running down his face and thought fuzzily that it must be raining again. His head was pillowed on something soft and warm, but his back felt icy cold.

He opened his eyes, focusing with some difficulty. He was lying on the hard stones, his head pillowed on someone's lap. The new Lieutenant was kneeling above him, gently bathing his head with seawater.

Javert tried to sit up and gave an involuntary groan at the pain in his head. He lay back quietly, waiting for the dizziness to pass. After a few moments the pain subdued to a heavy throbbing, though his cheekbone still felt as though it were on fire. The Lieutenant spoke to him again.

'Don't rush it, he gave you a kick like a mule. I'm surprised you've come round as quickly as you have; I thought you'd be out for an hour at least.'

As Javert looked round he realised that he must have been unconscious for only a few minutes. A few paces away a number of guards were in the process of securely manacling Valjean. The convict was offering no resistance.

Javert looked at the Lieutenant.

'Where did you come from?'

'From the shore. We saw the whole thing from there, but of course it took us time to run along the harbour to help you. I'm afraid we were too late to stop him giving you a kicking.'

'I'm sorry Monsieur. I did try to stop him but he was too strong for me.'

The Lieutenant raised his eyebrows.

'There's certainly no need to apologise for that Javert, we all know how strong Valjean is. You showed a lot of courage in tackling him at all, and you held him long enough to let us get here. If he'd once got to the boats we might have lost him. Come on, can you walk? Ferrier, get the other side and help him'.

Javert stood with difficulty. His balance had gone and he was glad of Ferrier's support. He was severely concussed and his head was throbbing so badly he couldn't see straight. He put a hand to his face and it came away covered with blood; the convict's kick had laid open the skin over his cheekbone.

The Lieutenant turned to the men holding Valjean.

'Take him to the hole. I'll report this to the Commander tomorrow and then the whole thing will be referred to the tribunal.' He glanced at Valjean, now standing passively between the guards. 'I don't doubt they'll add a few years to his sentence for this.'

Javert found sleep elusive that night. The doctor had stitched the wound on his cheek and given him laudanum, but he was running a high fever and the sheet beneath him was soaked with his sweat. His head ached abominably and his cheek felt as if it was on fire. His throat - severely bruised by Valjean's strong fingers - felt like raw sandpaper.

His mind churned endlessly, going back over André's funeral and his fight with Valjean. Valjean's behaviour over the past few days had puzzled Javert. First he had saved André at some risk to himself; that stone could so easily have crushed him as it had André and the convict. Then he had rescued the boy in the cell. Such behaviour was not in keeping with Javert's opinion of the scum he had to guard. But now Valjean's escape attempt had proved him to be just like all the others - a lawless, desperate man. In some ways Javert was relieved, and yet there was also a strange feeling of disappointment.

He moved his head restlessly on the pillow, remembering the man's power and his own feeling of utter helplessness.

Suddenly he knew who Valjean reminded him of; Marcel, who he had encountered on his first mission with Philippe. He had possessed the same massive shoulders and physical strength as Valjean. That had been Javert's first assignment, the one that had started him on the road he was travelling now. He shuddered as he remembered the way Marcel had died, his head held under water until he drowned. Javert knew something about the horrors of drowning; twice now he had almost lost his life in that way. His mouth still tasted of the seawater he had swallowed when Valjean had pushed his head into the puddle on the harbour.

He reached for the water-jug by his side, trying to rid himself of the foul taste. He remembered that he had almost blacked out when he was face down in the water; it was a wonder he hadn't drowned. But he had come round only seconds later to find his head resting on the cold but dry stone. Suddenly he recalled the sensation of being dragged across the hard ground. So Valjean must have pulled him out of the water. But why? Why not leave him to drown?

It was a question to which he had no answer, and just now he was in no condition to grapple with it. The laudanum was beginning to take effect and he felt light-headed and heavy-eyed. He slaked his thirst, then settled back against the pillow and at last slid into sleep.

Chapter 15

Javert had a splitting headache throughout the next day, which ironically was his day off. The following day his head felt somewhat better, though his cheekbone still throbbed and caused an explosion of agony if he touched it. He donned his uniform and reported for duty as usual.

The Lieutenant greeted him with some surprise.

'Well, I must say I didn't expect you back for a day or two. Sure you're well enough?'

'I'm well enough, Monsieur.'

'All right, you know best how you feel. Now then Javert, have you any idea how 24601 managed to get rid of his chains?'

Javert frowned and thought.

'No Monsieur, I haven't. But even he couldn't have freed himself without tools of some kind. So he either got hold of tools from somewhere, or he had help.'

The Lieutenant nodded. 'I agree. And we're usually careful about security of tools, though of course it's possible we were lax and he or another prisoner managed to get hold of them. It's also possible he had help from another source.'

Javert stared at him. 'You mean one of us?'

'Can't rule it out. Either way, we need to know. I want you to try to find out.'

'From Valjean?'

'That's right. The tribunal's decision will be through in another two days; until then he's in the hole. Go down and talk to him.'

'Of course Monsieur. But I'll be very surprised if he tells me anything.'

The Lieutenant smiled. 'There are ways of loosening tongues.'

'You mean torture?'

'Well - let's say persuasion.'

Javert frowned. 'Those methods have been forbidden since the revolution.'

'Oh come on Javert, be your age; who's to either know or care? We have total power over these people.'

Javert's face set. 'With respect Monsieur, I'm not prepared to do that.'

The Lieutenant's eyes narrowed at the flat refusal, then he nodded slowly.

'I see. I've heard people say you do things by the book. Obviously they're right. Very well Javert, do it your way.'

'Yes Monsieur. And can I suggest that we do a thorough search of the convicts' quarters, whilst they're out working.'

'We'll do that. You go and talk to Valjean, though if you're not prepared to use – persuasion - I fear you'll be wasting your time.'

Javert walked over to the cell block and down the steps that led to the oubliettes, the underground cells that were used for punishment. He unhooked an oil lamp and lit it, then pushed open the heavy door and entered Valjean's cell. The stench of urine and excrement almost knocked him backwards.

Valjean was chained to the far wall, his eyes squeezed shut at the sudden light. The glow from the lantern was dim, but it was dazzling to one who had been in total darkness for the past two days. He blinked two or three times, then focused with some difficulty.

Javert walked over to him, holding the lantern high to see his way and frowning as his clean boots squelched through the stinking ooze. As he bent over Valjean the man's eyes focused on the stick Javert carried in his right hand. He flinched involuntarily, then quickly controlled himself. Rules notwithstanding, Javert knew that many of the guards still abused the prisoners.

Javert stood up and took a pace back. For a moment the two men looked at each other, then Valjean spoke.

'What do you want? Have you come to gloat?'

'No,' said Javert flatly. 'I've come to talk to you about your escape - your attempted escape.'

Valjean stared at him in stony silence.

'We want to know how you managed to get rid of your chains. It'll save everyone a lot of trouble if you tell me now.'

The convict still kept his silence.

Javert tried again. 'The tribunal is hearing your case tomorrow. You know you'll get time added to your sentence, probably quite a lot of time. It might help if you co-operated with us.'

Valjean just continued to look at him, saying nothing. Javert sighed in frustration. How could he make the man at least talk to him? He remembered what he had learnt during his time in Paris and changed tack.

'Why did you want to escape?'

Valjean snorted. 'Wouldn't you?'

'No, not under your circumstances. You had less than a year left to serve. You'd have been free soon, now they'll probably double your sentence. And since you resisted arrest they'll almost certainly put "dangerous" on your ticket of leave when you do get out - if you get out.'

Valjean's eyes glittered in the dim light.

'You don't know what you're talking about. You expect men to act normally when you chain them up in places like this? You treat us like animals, that's what we become. Anyway I don't have the advantage of being educated like you. I'm just an ignorant woodcutter.' His eyes clouded for a moment as he thought of his past life. 'At least, that's what I was, once.'

Javert realised he had at least made some contact. 'You want to be educated? Then why don't you get some education? You could start by learning to read.'

Valjean sneered at him. 'What, here?'

'There's a school in Toulon that teaches convicts. You only have to apply.'

Valjean shrugged his shoulders.

'And I suppose you'll put in a good word for me if I co-operate and block me if I don't!'

'I didn't say that.' He hesitated, aware he was making an offer he had no authority to make. 'But I could possibly get you out of this hole. Of course I can't promise you, I don't have that authority. But I can try.'

Valjean shrugged. Javert watched him for a moment, then found himself asking a question he had never intended to ask.

'Why didn't you get rid of me when you had the chance? You could easily have killed me the other day, or just left me to drown. Why didn't you?'

Valjean stared at him. 'I might be a thief, but that doesn't mean I'm a murderer. Can you say the same, Sergeant Javert?'

'We're not discussing me, we're discussing you, and your escape attempt. Who helped you, Valjean?'

Valjean's mouth quirked at the rare use of his name. 'You know I'm not going to answer your questions.' He nodded towards the stick. 'Why don't you use that? I'm surprised you haven't already, especially looking at what I've done to your face. Confound it, aren't you even human enough to want revenge?'

Javert stood up. He had been carrying on the fruitless interview for long enough. His head ached abominably again and the stench and airlessness down here was not helping. Valjean was just a typical convict; a vicious animal that could never be trusted, or even helped.

'It doesn't matter what I want, I do my job. You don't even have the sense to help yourself, do you?'

He turned and squelched his way back to the door, locking it behind him and leaving Valjean alone in the stinking darkness.

The tribunal decision came through two days later and Javert was sent down to fetch Valjean to the Commander's office. In addition to the stench and the darkness it was permanently cold and damp down in the hole. The convict's condition had worsened since Javert had last seen him and he was shivering and shaking with fever. Javert picked his way over to him and unfastened the chain that held him to the wall.

'The decision of the tribunal has come through. I'm taking you to the Commander's office.'

They left the cell and climbed the stairs, slowly because Valjean was too stiff to move quickly. Javert paused in the open air to allow him to gather his strength, then took him across to the Commander's office.

The Commander addressed the convict formally.

'Prisoner 24601, I have to tell you that the tribunal has now added five years to your sentence. Two of those years are for attempting to escape, the remaining three are for assaulting sergeant Javert when you were recaptured. The first two years of your extended sentence will be in double chains.'

He paused for a moment, then continued. 'That is the sentence of the tribunal. In addition, I am adding one month in solitary confinement. I find it hard to blame a man for attempting to escape, however foolish the attempt might be, but I will not tolerate attacks on my guards.' He motioned to Javert. 'Take him down!'

Javert walked Valjean back across the square to the cell block and down the steps that led to the hole. Neither of them broke the silence. Valjean was already weakened by his time in the hole and although he must have been expecting it he still seemed shattered by his new sentence. He walked with Javert passively and allowed him to chain him to the wall. He neither looked at him nor spoke.

Javert left the cell and returned to the Commander's office. The Commander greeted him with a smile and waved to a chair.

'Sit down Javert. How's that face of yours feel? It looks a terrible mess.'

'It's improving Monsieur.' He hesitated, wanting to say something but uncertain how to begin. The Commander looked at him keenly.

'You look as if there's something you want to say?'

'Well, yes Monsieur, there is. It's about the hole - the oubliette. May I ask if you've been down there, Monsieur?'

The Commander frowned. 'Not for many years. Why?'

'The conditions down there are very bad. I don't mean the fact that the prisoners are kept in solitary confinement, or the darkness. The cell is intended for punishment, I have no problem with that. but - '

He paused. The Commander nodded encouragingly. 'Go on, Javert.'

'But I don't see any reason for the stench and the filth down there. I don't think it's been cleaned out in years and it's ankle deep in mud and excrement. Most of the men who go down there catch some disease or other, often they die of it. I don't think that was intended, and it doesn't seem to make sense.'

'In what way?'

'It just deprives us of manpower. Take Valjean - 24601. He has the strength of two men, you heard what he did with that block of stone. Now he's already suffering from fever, and given a month down there he'll most probably die. I've no sympathy with him - or any of them - but it's a waste of a useful worker.'

'So you're saying we should clean up the oubliette?'

'If we want prisoners to survive, yes Monsieur. If we want them to die we might as well sentence them to death and have done with it. As it is, a long spell in solitary usually amounts to the same thing.'

The Commander nodded. 'I can't argue with the sense of what you say Javert. But I do wonder why you're saying it.'

'I've told you Monsieur, it's a waste of manpower. It's not efficient.'

The Commander observed him closely, then nodded.

'All right. I'll take a look at it myself and if the conditions are as bad as you say I'll see about getting the place cleaned up. We can get a convict gang to do that. Is there anything else?'

'No Monsieur.'

'Very well. Thank you Javert; dismissed.'

The news that the oubliette was to be thoroughly cleaned was greeted with surprise. The convicts were - to a man – delighted; there were few of them who had not spent at least a day or two in the filth of 'the hole.' They set about the unpleasant task of cleaning the cell with a better will than they had brought to any previous job.

The reactions of the guards were more mixed. A few welcomed the move as both humanitarian and sensible. Others sneered and felt that the establishment was 'going soft'. Javert made no comment at all and said nothing his part in the decision. He didn't wish his colleagues to think he had any sympathy with the convicts; it was purely a question of common sense not to lose useful men unnecessarily. That was the reason he had given to the Commander and that was what he himself believed.

The Commander was absent for the whole of November, visiting Paris. On his return in early December he immediately summoned Javert to his office.

'Javert, I've something to say to you. I take it you still want to go into the Gendarmerie?'

Javert stared at him in surprise.

'Very much Monsieur, but we talked about that before you went to Paris. I can't afford to buy myself in.'

The Commander leaned back and smiled broadly.

'Yes, you can!'

Javert looked puzzled. 'I don't understand.'

'Monsieur André asked to see me before he died, about the money he was leaving. He hasn't left a great deal, but he asked me to use what there is for you, to get you into the Gendarmerie.'

Javert made no response, merely stared at him in amazement. The Commander laughed; it was rare to see Javert at a loss.

'You look thunderstruck! It makes sense, Javert. I don't say André had any affection for you because I'm afraid he didn't have any affection for anyone; I doubt if he was capable of it. But he had no family and you were the nearest thing he had to a son. In his own way, he was proud of you, and he rated your potential as a police officer highly. You know that.'

Javert nodded.

'As I said, there wasn't a great deal of money, but there was enough for me to pull a few strings.' He leaned back in his chair, smiling at Javert's still stupefied expression. 'You take up your new posting at the beginning of January.'

Javert gave a delighted smile. 'That is good news Monsieur, thank you. Where am I going?'

'To Paris.'

Paris! Javert exhaled slowly as he thought about that, remembering his previous time in the Capital. He had slightly mixed feelings, but pleasure and excitement were predominant.

'I'm sure you'll do well in the Gendarmerie, Javert. I have to say that I find you something of a loner, but that's entirely your own affair; what matters is how you do your job. You're honest and trustworthy and you don't wantonly mistreat the prisoners. I suspect those may be fairly rare qualities in Paris.'

Javert ignored the personal side of the Commander's remarks.

'So I need to travel up at the end of December Monsieur?'

'I'd suggest before that; go as soon as you can. You're due for some leave. You can spend Christmas in Paris. As a matter of fact, I have a message for you.'

'Oh?'

The Commander nodded. 'In the course of my business in Paris I came across someone you know quite well. You remember Monsieur Gerard?'

'I remember him very well Monsieur.' Monsieur Gerard had always been kind to him as a boy, some of his happiest times had been spent at the Café Gerard.

'Well, I told him you'd be starting work up there in January. I must say he was delighted. He suggested you might try to get up there for Christmas and spend it with them. I think it's a good idea Javert, it'll give you a bit of time to look round and get used to the place again. It's been a few years since you were last there.'

Javert hesitated, torn as to whether or not he should accept the invitation. It was almost five years since he had left Paris. It would be good to see Monsieur Gerard again, and Michelle. On the other hand the place would be alive with painful memories. But it would be churlish to refuse. In any case, Monsieur Gerard would be a highly useful contact.

'Thank you Monsieur, I'll be pleased to see Monsieur Gerard again.'

'Good. Then I suggest you get yourself packed and off as quickly as you can. Thank you Javert - and good luck.'

Javert left the office in a daze; for the first time in four years he even forgot to salute. As he crossed the square towards the barracks he felt as though he was walking on air.

Chapter 16

Javert arrived in Paris just before Christmas, after a long, tedious journey over roads that had been turned into quagmires by continuous heavy rain. The City seemed little changed since he had left it almost five years before: the same noise and bustle, the same kaleidoscope of sights and sounds that had once overwhelmed the young country boy from Toulon.

It took some time for the coach to navigate its way across the crowded Pont Neuf; the traffic was even worse than Javert remembered. The din was unbelievable, with hawkers, quacks, artists, traders and letter writers all shouting at once in their harsh, rough accents. Gypsies invited passers by to have their fortunes told. Beggars, looking like bundles of rags, lay inert by the bridge parapet, or slunk among the people walking and riding on the bridge. Javert's mouth curled in disgust at the sight of the prostitutes openly touting for customers.

The short winter day was drawing to its close and dusk was falling by the time he reached the Café Gerard. He entered the Café and climbed the stairs to the first floor, treading in his own ghostly footprints. Monsieur Gerard greeted him enthusiastically.

'Javert - at last! We'd almost given you up. Come in man, come in.'

Javert did so, ducking his head to avoid the low crossbeam over the door.

'Sorry I wasn't here before, it's the roads. Some of them are completely flooded and the ones that are passable are still bad. There were times when I thought I'd be spending Christmas stuck in a coach somewhere.'

Monsieur Gerard laughed. 'Well, never mind, you're here. How long has it been, five years? Stand back and let me look at you.'

For a moment the two men surveyed each other. Monsieur Gerard had changed hardly at all, but it was a different matter for Javert. In the five years since he had left Paris he had grown from youth to man. He was both taller and broader, and Monsieur Gerard saw lines in his face that had not been there before, beginning to impart a look of harshness to otherwise pleasing features. His natural reserve had deepened, and the untouchable quality that he had begun to develop after Philippe's death was more marked now.

Philippe's widow Adele noticed the same thing as she greeted him, cordially enough but with a touch of formality. Not so Michelle, who showed no awe or shyness whatsoever as she hurled herself into his arms with a delighted cry of 'Vere!'

Javert caught her and was betrayed into one of his rare smiles. Evidently the little girl not only remembered him but still retained her old attachment.

Javert was soon installed in the chair in front of the fire. Despite himself, he began to respond to the greeting he had been given. Soon he was more comfortable and relaxed than he had been in a long time, with his shirt collar undone and his feet almost up the chimney. Michelle was curled up next to him. She had pulled his arm round her and her head was resting trustingly in the hollow of his shoulder. Javert felt his heart stir strangely, he had not been close to another human being like this since he was ten years old, cuddling up to Philippe in the wagon at Marseille. For a few moments he indulged himself with wistful thoughts of what might have been, then he gave himself a mental shake. Such things were not for the likes of him and it was a waste of time to hanker after the unattainable. Still, it was the best Christmas he could remember since the time of Philippe's death, and it was with some reluctance that he eventually left the cosy atmosphere of the Café for his cold and modest lodgings.

Javert reported for duty at the Rue Jerusalem on a gusty, snowy day in January. He was greeted by a small, stocky man in his late thirties.

'Welcome to Paris, constable Javert, or perhaps I should say "welcome back?" I'm Inspector Sancé, and you'll be working on my team, with constable Cordel. So, how long is it since you left Paris?'

'Almost five years, Monsieur. I've been working as a prison guard, down in Toulon garrison.'

The Inspector waved him to a chair, sat down behind the large desk and glanced at the dossier in front of him.

'And before that, you were in Paris for what, seven years? And you were living amongst the paupers for most of that time. You understand Argot?

'Pretty well Monsieur.' Argot was an extreme form of slang, the language of the prisons and the gutter.

'Excellent! That will be very useful. And of course you'll be familiar with the ways of the gutter scum: ticket of leave men, paupers, gypsies and whores?'

'Yes Monsieur,' answered Javert tonelessly.

The inspector was still reading the dossier.

'From what this says, you did some good undercover work for us. Well, that's a very useful background, but you'll find this job very different. You need to keep your wits about you in a different way now. When you were here before, the whole idea was to stay invisible. Now you're highly visible, and there are times when you'll find yourself a definite target.'

He leaned forward to emphasise his point.

'Watch out for knives in particular, they're easy to get and easy to hide. A small knife can do a lot of damage.'

Javert nodded. 'I understand that, Monsieur.'

'Well, just make sure you don't forget it. One mistake can be one too many in this job, you might not get a second chance. Your predecessor didn't, that's why you're here on my team.'

Javert looked startled. 'He was killed?'

'Just before Christmas; stabbed by a whore he'd arrested for picking pockets. All right, that's enough of that; come along now and meet your partner. He's an experienced officer so you'll be in good hands.'

Cordel was in his early thirties, scruffy and unshaven, with long greasy hair that looked to be in need of a wash. André had always insisted on a smart turnout, but Javert had soon learnt how unusual that was. It seemed that many Parisians – including uniformed officers - seemed reluctant to wash either themselves or their clothes. Well, there was nothing he could do about that at the moment, but he resolved never to let his own standards slip to that level.

They spent most of that first morning in the Montmartre area of Paris. Despite all the promises of the Revolution, little seemed to have changed since Javert had last been here. The slums were still over-crowded and disease ridden, the children still semi-naked and barefoot despite the harsh winter cold. But at least the smell of the place was not so bad during the cold winter months.

In the afternoon they paid a visit to the gypsy encampment on the far side of the river. The gypsies had been there over the Christmas period, but had already been warned they were to move on before the new year. So far, they had not done so. The Inspector briefed Javert as they walked across the bridge towards the camp.

'I don't expect problems from them today, because I'm only serving them notice to move on. But there could still be trouble; they don't like us any more than we like them. So keep your eyes and ears open and if necessary be ready to get out quickly. We can always come back in force if we have to.'

They had obviously been sighted on their way to the camp because the headman met them at the entrance. Several men were with him, some holding vicious looking dogs on leashes. There were other dogs in the camp, running free and barking at the newcomers, but they kept their distance. Women and children hovered close by, watching silently. There was no overt aggression shown, but the hostility could be felt.

Inspector Sancé opened the proceedings, addressing the headman bluntly.

'You were told to move on after Christmas. Christmas is over.'

The headman regarded him impassively.

'We were here for the winter fair. That only finished yesterday.'

'Then why weren't you gone today?'

'We have to pack up and get ready, and the roads are very bad still. Travelling will be easier in a week or two.'

The Inspector shook his head.

'Out of the question. You must be out of here tomorrow.'

While the two men were talking the children had gradually crept closer, gaining confidence. Now a few of the boldest

131

approached the two police constables standing behind the Inspector. One young boy, aged about eight, sidled right up to Javert and began to tug curiously at the buttons on his uniform. Javert glanced down and felt a strange sensation of shock. It was like looking into a magic mirror that showed his reflection as it had been, many years before; the dark, almost black eyes looking up at him might have been his own.

A sudden howl from nearby caused him to jerk round. Next to him another young boy was sitting on the ground, yelling in pain and holding his leg. Cordel had not appreciated the boy's attentions and had swung his heavy stick at him, cracking him hard across the shins.

A woman ran forward and grabbed up the crying child; another woman pulled the young boy away from Javert. There was a subdued murmur from the men and they moved forward almost imperceptibly. The air sizzled with the heightened tension. Javert glanced around him and took a tighter grip on his stick, but made no overt move.

In front of him, Inspector Sancé concluded the proceedings briskly.

'Very well, you can have two days more, but you must go then. And I don't want to see any of you over the other side of the river.' He glanced at the two men behind him. 'Cordel, Javert. Come on!'

He turned and walked briskly away, accompanied by his two officers. Behind them, Javert could still hear the men muttering, accompanied by the snarling of the dogs. The hairs on the back of his neck prickled at his collar. He resisted the urge to look back, but was relieved to find himself safely out of the camp and approaching the bridge.

Apparently the Inspector felt the same. When they were safely on the bridge he halted and looked around, making sure there was no pursuit. Then he turned angrily on Cordel.

'You idiot, don't you know better than that! I've known them practically riot when one of their kids is hit. What do you think you were doing?'

Cordel looked sullen but wary.

'I'm sorry Monsieur, but the kid had its grubby little hands all over my uniform.'

132

'So tell him to go away, or give him a good shove. But don't make free with your stick in circumstances like that. There were only three of us, Cordel, that could have turned very nasty. As it was, I had to offer them a compromise I didn't want to make. Any repeat of that kind of idiocy, you'll be fined a day's wages. Clear?'

'Yes Monsieur.' Cordel was sullen but cowed.

They walked on across the bridge. The encounter had unsettled Javert, not because of the potential danger but because of the reminder of his own origins. Oblivious to his discomfort, the Inspector was talking to him about the gypsies.

'Never forget, they're all scum, all thieves. That's why we don't want them over the river, or anywhere near the bourgeoisie areas. If you ever have to come to a camp, don't come alone. If Cordel had been alone he'd have been badly beaten, at the very least. Anyway, they'll never tell you anything; they're a law unto themselves.'

He continued to talk disparagingly about the gypsies. Next to him, Javert thought of the medallion he still wore beneath his uniform. He felt a sudden rush of shame, wondering what the Inspector would say if he knew he was patrolling with the son of a gypsy.

Oblivious to the emotions he had aroused in his new officer, the Inspector glanced up at the sky. The sun was still visible, sinking towards the horizon, but immediately overhead slate coloured clouds were gathering. The wind was beginning to rise, cold and biting. A few flakes of snow drifted down. The Inspector grunted.

'This is a good time to check the lodging houses. In the summer vagrants can more or less hide out anywhere, but not in this weather. They'll make for the poorer lodging houses. Come on.'

He led the way to the lodging house by the Pont Marie. Javert had quite often stayed in such places when he was with André; they were commonly used by beggars and the like and could be a good place to pick up information. But it was the first time he had entered one when in uniform and the difference was palpable. Before, he had always been incognito; now he was the focus of instant attention.

133

The keeper looked uneasy the moment they walked in, a fact that did not escape any of the officers. There were several other men in the room, all of whom looked to be from the vagrant class. A man sitting in the corner gave a visible start at sight of the police officers and moved position slightly as if to hide his face.

The Inspector walked over to the keeper, wasting no time on pleasantries.

'All right, who have you got in tonight? Let's see your books.'

The man produced them, still looking uneasy. The Inspector scanned the pages, then jerked his thumb towards the man in the corner.

'Him? Which of these is he?'

The keeper stammered in confusion.

'Well, he - he's only just now arrived, Inspector. He - er - he hasn't registered yet.'

The Inspector closed the book with a snap.

'That's a surprise! Javert, check him out.'

Javert walked over to the man in the corner and stood over him. The man shifted uncomfortably, obviously aware of his presence but deliberately not looking at him.

Javert spoke dryly from behind him.

'No, I won't go away if you ignore me.'

The man gave up the pretence and turned round to face him. His face was bloodless and haggard, his eyes showed his fear. The clothes he wore were little more than rags; despite the cold his feet were bare save for a pair of battered clogs. Javert glanced at the man's ankles; the marks where the manacles had been were clear to see.

'How long have you been out?'

The man dropped his gaze. 'Four days, Monsieur.'

Javert held out his hand. 'Let's see your ticket.'

The man obediently produced his crumpled yellow ticket, which stated that he had just served a period of three years for theft. There were no other notations on the ticket, apparently he had not made any escape attempts or attracted any notice whilst in prison.

'Where are you headed?'

134

'I don't know. I thought I might be able to find work here in Paris, but so far...' He let the sentence tail off.

'Where were you told to go?'

'They told me to head for Fontenay, but I thought - well, that's a country area. There'll be no work there at this time of the year.'

Javert handed him back his ticket.

'Nonetheless, that's where you have to go. You'll have to try to find occasional work until the spring.' He looked the man up and down, knowing that his appearance and the ticket he carried made it unlikely that anyone would employ him. 'You can stay here tonight, but make sure you move on in the morning. Otherwise you'll find yourself arrested again.'

The man nodded, hopelessness and defeat written all over him. Javert turned on his heel and rejoined the Inspector, who nodded his approval then turned back to the keeper.

'If you don't want us to close you down, make sure you register all your customers, not just the ones you want us to see. This is your first warning. You won't get a second.'

He walked out, followed by Javert and Cordel.

Chapter 17
Paris 1810

Javert glanced around to ensure he was alone, then covertly removed his heavy bicorne hat and wiped the sweat from his forehead. It was the middle of June and Paris was sweltering in one of the most intense heat waves for years. Most police officers had taken to carrying their hats except in the actual presence of their senior officers, but not Javert. Javert felt improperly dressed if he was not in full uniform, and the hat was part of that uniform.

He had now been in Paris for nine years, and had fulfilled his early promise as an excellent police officer. He had become well known amongst the criminal fraternity and his mere name was cause for fear. Amongst his colleagues he was considered to be a harsh, uncompromising man who lived only for his job. They respected him, but did not make a friend of him; indeed, he soon rebuffed any overtures of friendship.

Javert replaced his hat and walked out into the open square of the Place des Vosges. His usual beat was the Faubourg St. Antoine and the river, but today he was patrolling one of the better class regions. It was a pleasant change to be away from the slum areas and the fetid stink of the narrow alleys. He walked across the Parc Royal, stopping in the centre to gaze up at the bronze statue of Louis XIII. Javert was always intensely loyal to whoever was in authority, but at heart he was still a Royalist.

A voice suddenly spoke from behind him.

'Vere!'

He swung round in surprise - only one person ever called him that.

'Michelle!'

For a moment they looked at each other in mutual surprise. Michelle and her mother had moved out of Paris eight years before, and he had not seen them since. Michelle recovered from her surprise and put her hand on his arm, looking at him with open pleasure.

'Oh Vere - it is good to see you.'

'You too.' His eyes were running over her as he spoke. Michelle was twenty years old now and had grown into a very attractive young woman. Her wavy black hair – so like her father's - was arranged in ringlets on either side of her face; her features too were reminiscent of Philippe. Javert hesitated for a moment.

'Were you going somewhere special?'

She shook her head.

'Not really, no - just getting out in the air for a little while before I coop myself up in the café. I'd forgotten what Paris was like in the heat.' She wrinkled her nose at him, her laughing eyes reminding him strongly of Philippe. 'Why, were you going to offer me a drink? There's a good café just over there.'

'But Michelle, I'm on duty.'

'Oh come on Vere. You can see what's going on just as well sitting at one of those tables.'

Javert gave his rare smile, it was impossible to remain formal with Michelle. He allowed her to lead him to the café, secretly pleased to remain in her company for a little longer.

'What are you doing in Paris, Michelle? Last I heard you were living out in Neuilly.'

'Yes, we were, but we got back a week ago. We're living back at the apartment above the café. Grandfather's getting on a bit and he needs Mama to help him, in fact she and I are really running it now.' She looked at him accusingly. 'Grandfather says he hasn't seen you for ages.'

'No, I've been busy.'

'But you'll try to come more often now, won't you? It won't be the same if you don't.'

'I'll try, if I have time. And talking of time - I'm sorry Michelle, but I have to go. I need to be back at the Conciergerie in half an hour.'

He raised his hat politely and strode away across the park. Michelle stayed where she was at the café table, her eyes following the tall man until he was out of sight.

The following day Javert commenced night patrol with Inspector Sancé and Cordel. The weather had turned wet during the evening and the streets were comparatively quiet as the three of them headed towards the slum area by the river. This was a favourite time for thieves and robbers; when it was still light enough to see, but dark enough to conceal yourself in the shadows.

As they approached the Pont Marie they heard a sudden shout, followed by a scuffle. They raced out of the alley. A struggle involving three men was taking place just by the bridge. A young boy was perched on the parapet nearby, looking in the direction of the police officers. As they ran into the open he instantly raised the alarm.

'Police - leg it!'

Two of the men immediately sprang up, letting the other man fall to the ground. One man raced away along the river towards the Pont Neuf, the other grabbed the boy and ran away across the Pont Marie.

Inspector Sancé pointed after the two on the bridge.

'Javert!'

Javert immediately gave chase, knowing that Cordel would go after the other man whilst the Inspector looked to the needs of the victim. That was the way they always worked and it made good sense. Not that Inspector Sancé was afraid of a fight - he was prepared to mix in when necessary and could give a good account of himself - but he was older than the other two men and no longer as fast on his feet.

Javert was gaining ground on his quarry; the man was being held back by the boy, who he was evidently reluctant to leave behind. The boy was doing his best, but he was small and his legs were not long enough to out-distance a stride like that of Javert. The man glanced behind him and saw Javert closing fast. He stopped and turned, letting go of the boy. His hand dropped to his belt and Javert caught the glint of metal. He kept going, and the man sprang towards him, stabbing viciously at him in an underarm thrust.

Javert twisted to one side and brought his heavy stick down savagely across the man's collar-bone. There was an ominous crack as the hard wood impacted on bone, followed by a scream of agony from the man. The knife flew from his hand as he slumped to his knees, moaning with pain and clutching at his shoulder.

138

The boy immediately dived for the fallen knife, but Javert grabbed him by the hair and threw him to the ground next to the man, ignoring his screeching. He picked up the knife and put it into his belt as he surveyed his prisoners. Their dress and the jewellery they wore proclaimed both to be gypsies and Javert's lip curled in distaste.

'Over on your faces, both of you! Come on - hurry up.'

The man groaned. 'I can't - you've broken my shoulder.'

Javert hefted his stick threateningly.

'And I'll break the other one if you don't do as I tell you.'

Sullenly the man obeyed him, moaning with pain as he moved his injured arm. Javert glanced at the boy, who was now sitting up, glaring at him. He guessed the boy's age at seven or eight years, no more.

'You too boy - on your face.'

The man growled at the boy.

'Do as he says.'

When they were both prone Javert pulled out his handcuffs and knelt on the man's back, keeping a wary eye on the boy. He fastened the cuffs onto the man's left wrist, then pulled back his right arm to do the same with that wrist. The man screamed at the pull on his shoulder.

'You bastard! Oh, you bastard!'

Javert hesitated for a second, then fastened the second cuff. It was quite likely that the collar bone was broken, in which case the man was probably in agony. On the other hand, he could be exaggerating his injury. Javert was not prepared to risk that, he intended to get both his prisoners back to the lock-up. The man would just have to put up with the pain for a while.

He pulled him onto his feet, ignoring his agonized gasps.

'Don't worry, you'll live! I'll take them off you as soon as we get to the lock-up.'

He grabbed the boy and pulled him up, twisting his right wrist up his back and fitting him easily into the crook of one arm. The man spoke again.

'Please - don't hurt the boy.'

'I'm not and I won't, so long as he doesn't struggle.'

They went back across the bridge, the boy walking passively next to Javert. His arm wasn't quite twisted back enough to be painful, but the policeman's grip was hard and he knew better than to resist. The man was in no condition to struggle even had he not been handcuffed; he was close to fainting with the pain of his shoulder.

Their intended victim was standing now, talking to Inspector Sancé. He looked shaken by the experience but not otherwise injured. The Inspector smiled his approval.

'You got both of them? Well done.' He looked at the man, who was leaning against the bridge, white-faced and groaning. 'Trouble?'

'He went for me with this.' Javert showed him the knife.

'That'll put a year or two on his sentence.'

Cordel appeared out of the near darkness on their left. He was alone.

'Sorry Monsieur, I lost him up by the Pont Neuf. He dived into the alleys.'

'Oh well, not to worry, at least we've got this one. Come on, let's get them back to the lock-up. Javert, bring the man. Cordel, take over the boy.'

Javert handed the boy to Cordel and they all headed back towards the police post, the Inspector and intended victim leading and Cordel bringing up the rear. As they approached the Rue St Denis, Javert heard a sudden scuffle and a cry behind him. He turned just in time to see the boy fleeing into the Rue St Denis. Cordel was bent double, clutching his left hand with his right. Blood was dripping from between his fingers.

'Cordel - what the devil - '

Cordel straightened with an effort, swearing softly. 'Little bastard had a knife!'

Inspector Sancé put his arm round him and helped him to a nearby wall. 'How bad?'

Cordel held out his left hand, which was bleeding heavily.

'Just my hand. He went for my gut but I managed to block him. But we've lost him now, he's well away.'

'Where did he get the knife?'

'Probably taped to his leg – he twisted and bent down. I thought he was just going to try and pull away, but he must have been going for the knife.'

The Inspector started to bind up Cordel's hand, speaking over his shoulder to Javert.

'Did you search that boy?'

Javert's heart turned to ice as he realised his mistake.

'No Monsieur, I didn't.'

Inspector Sancé nodded towards the handcuffed man. 'And him?'

'Well, we've already got his knife -'

'Did you search him?'

Javert looked down. 'No Monsieur.'

'Do it now.'

Javert searched the man thoroughly, finding a wallet in the back of his belt and a small but potentially deadly stiletto in the side of his boot. Shame faced, he handed both to the Inspector.

'All right, let's get him under lock and key while we've still got one left. Cordel, are you all right to walk?'

'Oh yes Monsieur, it's not too serious - just a lot of blood. It was my fault as well Monsieur, I wasn't watching the boy properly.'

'Don't cover for him, Cordel, he's broken a cardinal rule and he knows it.' The Inspector glanced at Javert, his face grim. 'We'll discuss this properly back at the post.'

Javert followed the Inspector. Outwardly he was as composed as ever but inwardly he was fuming; not with the boy, but with himself. He was aware that his mind had not been fully on his job - he had been thinking about his unexpected encounter with Michelle - but that was no excuse for not having searched both man and boy thoroughly.

Back at the police post the handcuffs were removed and the man was consigned to the cells. The Inspector issued his orders briskly.

'Get someone to look at Cordel's hand, then they can check the prisoner's shoulder; the collarbone's probably broken.'

He turned to Javert.

'You, come with me.'

He stalked away to his office, Javert following unhappily. Inspector Sancé had always shown himself to be a good superior officer, both fair and approachable. But he was harsh with any negligence of this sort.

Once in the office, the Inspector rounded angrily on Javert.

'You! I thought better of you than that. What's your excuse?'

Javert regarded him, inwardly quaking but outwardly calm.

'I don't have an excuse Monsieur; what I did isn't excusable.'

The Inspector calmed down slightly.

'Oh, so you realise that much do you? For God's sake Javert, what were you thinking of - not to search either of them. You realise it's only the purest good fortune that you're not lying dead on that bridge?'

'I know that Monsieur. And whatever Cordel says I realise his injury is my fault.'

'Yes it is.' He ran his hand distractedly through his thinning hair. 'Well, it's no use going over it all again, is it. You know what you've done. I'm disappointed in you, Javert. You're fined one week's pay for negligence. All right, you can go!'

Javert hesitated, then left the room quietly. He was still angry, ashamed and bitterly disappointed in himself. The fine bothered him not at all, except for a fleeting thought that it was not enough. Had he been the Inspector and one of his men had done such a thing, Javert would have punished him more harshly. Trained by a brutal man, Javert's standards were exacting and his judgments severe, for himself as well as for others.

Cordel's injury was not too serious and he did not hold it against Javert. He considered him to be a good officer, and he was happy to have him as a partner. Certainly he was never what Cordel would call friendly, but he was civil, and always efficient. Most important, he had shown himself to be brave and trustworthy, useful in a tight corner, and Cordel asked no more than that. As for the incident with the knife, everyone blundered sometimes. The matter was also over and done with

142

so far as the Inspector was concerned. Javert had been punished, and the Inspector did not doubt he had learned his lesson. He was as sure as he could be that Javert would not make that particular mistake again.

Of the three, Javert was the most upset. His shift ended, he left the police post and walked down to the river. He stood for a while, gazing at the water flowing past below him; the river was unusually swollen due to the heavy rain of the previous day, and it was moving faster than usual. Idly he watched the debris being carried under the Pont Royal, whirling in under the arches to reappear again the other side, or else jam up against the bridge supports.

A large rowing boat was approaching him from up-river. For a moment he watched it casually, then gave a sudden frown as his policeman's instinct began to re-assert itself. He had been standing there for some time, watching the driftwood and other rubbish, but he did not remember seeing the boat above the Pont Royal. Yet here it was, now level with him and continuing on its way downstream. He looked at it more closely as it swept past, the oarsmen assisted by the unusually strong flow of the river. There were three men in the boat and from the way it was sitting in the water it appeared to be heavily laden. Some kind of awning covered the stern of the boat, but from this distance he could make out no other details. He filed it in his mind for future reference, then left the river and returned to his lodgings.

On arrival for duty the following night Javert was surprised to see a number of additional officers present, many of whom he did not know. He approached Inspector Sancé, who looked uncharacteristically tired and harassed.

'What's happening Monsieur?

'Special patrols,' said the Inspector briefly.

'Why? Is there a panic on?'

'You could say that. You know the problems we've been having with house burglaries and robberies?'

'Yes Monsieur'.

'Well, last night they really surpassed themselves - they hit the town mayor's house. Fortunately he wasn't there, but they escaped with a lot of property. And they beat his servants very badly, they're both still in hospital. Of course the shit's really flying this time, you can imagine. The mayor's demanding blood!'

Javert raised his eyebrows. 'Well, at least it's not on our area. That's some comfort.'

Inspector Sancé snorted. 'Huh - do you think the mayor cares less whose patch it's on? He wants these men behind bars, and there'll be hell to pay if they're not caught - sooner rather than later.'

Javert frowned thoughtfully. 'Is it the same gang, do you think?'

'Sounds like it. The descriptions are the same - and the brutality. The servants didn't put up any fight at all when they realised they were outnumbered, but they were beaten half to death all the same, just for the fun of it. Listen Javert, we've got plenty of men out there tonight and you've got a nose for these things. I want you to stay here and take a look through this.'

He tapped his finger on the book on the desk in front of him.

'This contains details of all the house robberies for the past four months, which is about how long this particular series has been going on. See if you can come up with something. A pattern, maybe - anything that might help catch these scum. I've already spent most of the day with these and I've tried to group them a bit, but I'm so tired I can hardly see straight, let alone think. It needs a fresh eye.'

Javert seated himself and started to study the book attentively. There were a total of around two hundred and fifty burglaries listed, but only twenty had been grouped by the Inspector. All had taken place at good class bourgeois properties and most had involved violence, whereby the unfortunate householders and their staff had been systematically and brutally beaten.

Javert read through each case carefully, looking for commonalities. Then he sat for a while, thinking deeply. Eventually he looked up from his task.

'Monsieur.'

The Inspector came over to him. 'Got something?'

'One or two possibilities, Monsieur. First of all, all these crimes happened at the dark of the moon, or very near to it. Second, all the houses allow easy access to the river.'

The Inspector took the file from him and scanned quickly. 'Well done. Anything else?'

Javert looked thoughtful. 'Possibly. When I went off duty this morning I went down to the river for a while before I went to bed. I noticed a boat, coming down from the Pont Royal. Heavily laden, contents in the stern covered, three men in it.'

'So? Boats are fairly commonplace objects on a river.'

'But I didn't see this boat above the Pont Royal. It just seemed to appear, between the Pont Royal and the Pont Neuf.'

The Inspector stared at him. 'Could you just not have noticed it earlier?'

Javert shrugged. 'Of course that's possible, but I don't think so. Look Monsieur, this is just a wild idea, I've no real evidence. But it is a possibility. What if a number of men attack good class properties that give them easy access to the river. They take the stuff down to the river and load it into a boat.'

The Inspector nodded. 'Easy enough so far. Go on.'

'They take the boat down the river, but only as far as the Pont Royal. If they try to bring it downriver in the dark they stand a big risk of being checked by us, because there isn't supposed to be any river traffic then without special permission. So they stop under the Pont Royal, and there they stay. Until daylight, when they can bring the stuff downriver and transfer it without anyone giving them a second glance.'

The Inspector nodded slowly.

'As you say, there's no real evidence, except perhaps your mysteriously appearing boat. But it's possible. Javert, the mayor's house was attacked last night. What was the state of the moon?'

'Waning Monsieur - almost gone.'

'And tonight?'

'No moon.'

The Inspector slammed his hand down on the desk.

'Javert, there may be nothing in this, but it's worth a check. Let's go for it. It's an ideal time, with a full shift on. I'll get the men laid on, you do the rest. This is your show.'

Javert raised his eyebrows.

'Mine. What do you mean Monsieur?'

'I mean you organise it. When and where you want the men, the whole thing. It's your idea, you run it.'

Javert blinked, then nodded. For a constable to be given such responsibility was unusual and unexpected. He was delighted at the vote of confidence, and determined that it would not be misplaced.

The small hours of the morning found Javert concealed under the Pont Royal, perched in an uncomfortable and cramped position up on one of the supports. A number of other men were hidden close by, behind the stonework of the bridge and up on each bank.

Despite the warmth of the days it was cold and damp underneath the bridge. After an hour or so Javert began to wonder whether it was such a good idea after all, perhaps he should call it off? Then he gave himself a mental shaking. The idea was good enough, it had simply lost its appeal because he was frozen, cramped and thoroughly uncomfortable. He gritted his teeth and prepared to wait out the long night.

It was still pitch black beneath the bridge when he heard the first sounds; slight noises that might have been no more than the swirl of the river. Then he heard an unmistakeable scraping sound, followed by a muttered curse.

'Careful - watch what you're doing!'

'Watch it yourself, see if you can do any better. It's black as pitch under here.'

'All right, all right. Can you find the rope? Here's the ring - tie her up.'

There was a faint splashing as the boat rocked on the water. Javert strained his eyes, but he could see nothing. As the man in the boat said, it was pitch black. From the conversation it appeared that the men had managed to tie up the boat to a ring set in the bridge support. From the sounds, they were almost directly beneath him.

He eased his position slightly and continued his vigil. It had been agreed that they would make no move until it was light enough to make out what they were doing; there was no point in trying to arrest an enemy they couldn't see. Javert was to give the signal when he felt the time was right.

After what seemed a lifetime the sky began to lighten beyond the bridge arches. The light became slowly brighter until the boat and its occupants could at last be seen, mere shadows in the dimness beneath the bridge.

Javert eased his position again, moving and stretching each limb in turn. His discomfort was forgotten as a tingling excitement took hold of him. He took a deep breath, blew an ear-splitting blast on his whistle and dropped down onto the solid ground beneath him.

There was instant pandemonium. The men in the boat had three choices and only an instant in which to choose. They could jump into the water and swim for safety, but given the time of year and state of the river that was hardly a viable option. They could make for the shore, in which case they would run into Javert and the other men who were already slithering down the steep bank. The only other choice was to untie or cut the rope and make off downriver, but it was already too late for that. Javert had seized the rope and was hauling the boat in to the bank.

There were curses from the boat as the men recovered from their surprise.

'Get him - quickly!' snarled one of them.

Two men leapt out and went for Javert, then checked as other police officers came racing eagerly under the bridge. There was a brief but fruitless struggle; the three men were heavily outnumbered.

The Inspector appeared at the entrance to the cavern beneath the bridge.

'Well done everyone! Bring them out and let's see what kind of fish we've caught.'

The men were pulled one by one out of the shadows of the bridge. As the last one was dragged into the early morning light Javert stiffened in sudden shock. The man was in his mid-thirties, running to fat; a scruffy unkempt individual, with lank, greasy hair. It was over seventeen years since Javert had last seen him, but he had no difficulty in recognising Bibet. Thus far, Bibet had not recognised Javert. He was standing in the grip of two officers, glaring around him with forced bravado.

Javert stepped quietly up to him, standing eye to eye less than a pace away.

'Bibet.'

For a moment Bibet stared at him without comprehension. Then his eyes widened in sudden recognition.

'Javert? Oh God, no. It can't be!'

'Can't it?'

Javert's voice was silky with menace; the seemingly lazy purr of a cat, just before it springs. Everyone else was still, sensing something between these two that they hesitated to interrupt. Those who knew Javert were staring at him in amazement. He was usually so cold, so controlled. In a sense he was cold and controlled now, but they could all sense the hatred and violence lurking behind the façade. This was a Javert they had never seen.

Bibet's expression ran the gamut from confusion, to shock, to fear. Javert could see him thinking back, realising what this encounter meant.

'You remember me, I see. Do you remember our last meeting as well?'

Bibet obviously did, for terror began to replace fear. His face was deathly white. He began to babble.

'No - Javert, listen to me. We were boys together. It was just a bit of fun between boys. I wouldn't really have touched you - I swear I wouldn't.'

'And Philippe?' Javert's voice was a deadly whisper.

Suddenly Bibet's legs gave way. The men holding him relaxed their grip as he fell to his knees on the ground. He who had never shown mercy did not expect any. With the river at his back and Javert in front of him he could see no way out. He expected to die then and there at Javert's hand.

'Javert, no - please. I didn't mean it - I didn't know - Oh God, please Javert.' He clutched at Javert's leg, sobbing and crying for mercy, completely broken.

Javert felt his flesh creep at the contact. His knuckles turned white on the stick he held but he made no other move, not even to kick Bibet away from him. He was afraid to stir, knowing that if he did he would probably kill the man grovelling on the floor in front of him. For a long moment no-one spoke, then the Inspector stepped in.

'Take them up. You two, take him.'

Two constables dragged Bibet away from Javert and pulled him to his feet, still sobbing and totally broken. They handcuffed him and dragged him away up the bank. The Inspector approached Javert.

'Javert. Javert, are you all right?'

Javert turned to face him, his face set and pale.

'Yes Monsieur, I'm sorry. I had - an old score to settle with that man.'

The Inspector waited, but Javert said no more.

'Well, I should think you've settled it. It's thanks to you we've caught him, and he's got a string of charges against him; including robbing the Mayor's house. He'll be lucky if he gets away with twenty years.'

Javert nodded, picturing Bibet on the chain gang down at Toulon. There were a few men still there among the guards who didn't much care for Bibet, and the prisoners would make his life a living hell, once they discovered that he was the son of a former garrison commander. Javert hadn't struck him, hadn't even raised a hand to him, but as he followed the Inspector up onto the bank he felt that his revenge was complete.

Chapter 18

Javert felt unusually nervous as he walked along the street towards the Café Gerard. It was the twenty-sixth of August, and Michelle's twentieth birthday. It was also his own birthday, but that meant little to him. Only once had he ever celebrated his birthday and that had been eighteen years ago, the day of his 'initiation' by the prostitute and his last thrashing at André's hands. The occasion had certainly been memorable, but it was not one he cared to remember.

He put his hand to his pocket to ensure that the small package was still there; it was the first time in his life he had ever given anyone a present. He had seen Michelle a number of times recently, always in the Place des Vosges. He was reluctant to admit to himself that he went there so often in the hope of seeing her, and it never crossed his mind that she was doing exactly the same thing.

Monsieur Gerard welcomed him enthusiastically.

'Javert, what a nice surprise. It's good to see you again, I was beginning to wonder if you'd deserted us for ever. Come on in man. I'm afraid Adele isn't here to greet you. She's ill in bed, nothing serious. But Michelle's upstairs.'

Javert followed him to the apartment above the café. The room was just as he remembered it. A fire was blazing in the large grate, even though it was the end of August it was unseasonably cold.

Michelle greeted him warmly while Monsieur Gerard bustled out to arrange some refreshments. The moment he had left, Javert removed the package from his pocket and proffered it diffidently.

'I - er - I thought you might like this, for your birthday.'

She flushed with pleasure.

'Oh Vere - thank you!'

Impulsively she reached up and kissed him. He returned her embrace a little stiffly, not quite sure what to do in a situation like this, then quickly released her as Monsieur Gerard returned. He seemed to have noticed nothing out of the ordinary as he motioned his visitor to sit down in front of the fire.

'Well, you've timed your visit well this time at any rate, you've remembered it's Michelle's birthday?'

Javert and Michelle exchanged covert glances.

'But of course - it's yours too! Well, in that case - listen, we're dining out tonight in honour of the occasion. You must join us. Come on, I know Adele will be delighted if you do.'

Javert shook his head regretfully.

'I can't. I start night duty today.'

'Come before you start duty, we'll make it an early celebration.'

Javert accepted the invitation somewhat hesitantly. He was not so sure that Adele would share her father's enthusiasm for his company, and that evening he was secretly relieved to hear that although much improved she was still not sufficiently recovered to attend the celebration. The party therefore consisted only of Monsieur Gerard, Michelle and Javert.

Following the meal, the three of them were preparing to leave when the proprietor of the café approached Monsieur Gerard and whispered discreetly into his ear. Monsieur Gerard excused himself and walked away with the man. For a few moments they conversed quietly in a corner, then Monsieur Gerard returned, looking worried.

'Forgive me, both of you, but he wants to discuss a business matter with me. Urgent, he says. Javert, I know you need to go soon. Could you see Michelle home for me, do you think? Obviously she can't walk through the streets alone at this time, and this may take a while.'

Monsieur Gerard exchanged a meaningful look with Javert, who guessed that the 'business' was almost certainly information of a political nature. Many of the café owners were useful in this way, Monsieur Gerard particularly so.

Javert agreed politely and left the café with Michelle. It seemed strange and unfamiliar to be walking through the streets with a young woman as companion. A curious restraint seemed to have arisen between them and there was little conversation. When they reached the Café Gerard, Javert prepared to bid his companion good night, but she detained him with a small hand on his arm.

'No - come up for a few minutes. I know my mother will be pleased to see you.'

Javert hesitated, then complied. When they reached the upper apartment the room was deserted, lit only by the dying glow of the fire. Michelle glanced round the darkened room.

'I suppose mother must have gone back to bed. Wait a minute, I'll light the lamps.'

She moved round the room, lighting the oil lamps, then walked over to Javert, who was still standing in the doorway.

'You don't have to stand out there in the cold, come in and get warm while I make some coffee.'

She put her hands into his and pulled him inside, then led him over to the sofa in front of the fire. He sat down and gazed thoughtfully into the flames. As once before, the peaceful, homely atmosphere began to take hold of him and thoughts of what might have been tugged at his consciousness. This time, he allowed the dream to take shape, trying to imagine a life where he could come home every day to a fireside like this and a woman like Michelle. Could such things happen? Was it possible for a man like him?

Michelle returned carrying a tray of coffee. Javert stood up and took it from her, placing it on the table. Then he turned back to her, looking down into her face. Michelle suddenly moved forward, reaching her hands up to his shoulders and tilting her head back to look intently into his face. She was very small, the top of her head barely reached his shoulder. For a moment she leant against him, then reached up and kissed him gently on the mouth before letting her head fall forward onto his chest. Javert experienced a strange feeling of bewilderment as he realised that he had unthinkingly returned her embrace and was holding her against him.

After a long moment, Michelle stirred in his arms and lifted her head. He found himself kissing her again, this time more enthusiastically. He wondered what she was doing there, what he was doing holding this young woman in his arms. He didn't know quite what to do with her. Javert usually had no involvement with women, except as either prisoners or victims.

152

He stroked her hair, black and glossy like the plumage of a starling lit by the sun. Or like - - -

Abruptly he let her go, pulling his head back. She looked up at him, frowning a little as she tried to interpret his expression.

'What is it - is something wrong? You look so strange. I'm sorry, but I thought - well, I thought perhaps you cared for me as well - just a little.'

Javert shook his head in confusion.

'I don't know. Yes - I suppose I do - or I could do. Michelle...'

He stopped speaking, his mind in a turmoil. Holding Michelle had triggered a memory from his youth; the last time - indeed the only time - he had held a grown woman in his arms; or rather she had held him. He gave a shudder of revulsion as he remembered that day under the Pont Neuf, the stench of the river, the stink of the woman. He could still picture the wizened face, the shrunken body. Her hair had been black too; a harsh, dyed black. Behind that memory was another image; of his own mother, wasted by consumption, her black hair looking stark and unnatural against her waxen skin. The woman under the bridge had been a prostitute. And his mother? All the evidence suggested that she too had been a whore.

He looked at Michelle, standing in front of him with her hands still on his shoulders. He felt his body beginning to harden with desire and moved back from her a little, crushing the feeling ruthlessly. It was unthinkable that he might take advantage of this young woman, Philippe's daughter. But alongside his unmistakable physical response was another sensation, a feeling of gentleness and tenderness such as he had never experienced in the whole of his adult life.

He raised his arms to her again tentatively but made no other move. There was too much emotion, too much feeling. As a boy he had been forced to control and hide his passions, as an adult he had continued to suppress them. Feelings - especially ones such as compassion and kindness - were a nuisance, a weakness that could stop him doing his job efficiently. Now, after years of suppression, he didn't know how to deal with them.

Michelle sighed. She didn't know what was wrong, but she sensed his distress and confusion and realised that she needed to give this uncommunicative man more time. She hugged him again gently, then released him and stepped back. He let her go, feeling a strange mixture of relief and disappointment.

The grandfather clock in the corner began to chime the half-hour. Javert started in surprise, he had forgotten the time. If he didn't hurry he'd be late for work, an unheard of occurrence.

'Michelle, forgive me - I have to go. I'm on duty soon.'

'But you'll come again?'

'Yes, I'll come again.'

For a moment he hesitated, wanting to say more but not knowing how. Abruptly he pulled her into his arms, holding her hard against him and kissing her with a passion that surprised them both. Then he walked out of the room and she heard his footsteps receding rapidly down the stairs.

Immediately his night shift was ended Javert again made his way to the Café Gerard. It was early morning and the place had only just opened its doors. Monsieur Gerard greeted him cordially, but with some surprise.

'Javert, come in. Drink?'

'No. No thank you. I won't stay long.'

Monsieur Gerard looked at him shrewdly.

'I'm always pleased to see you, but I've a feeling this isn't just a social visit.'

Javert smiled slightly. He knew that Monsieur Gerard's outward bonhomie masked a quick and alert mind and he was not surprised at the man's perception.

'No, you're quite right. I wanted to speak to you.'

'About Michelle?'

Javert raised his eyebrows. 'As a matter of fact, yes. How did you know?'

'I guessed. She's been moping around this morning wondering what to do with herself. Then you turn up here straight off a night shift instead of going home to your bed where you belong. What's happened?'

154

'Nothing's happened, not exactly. It's just...'

He stopped, floundering and lost for words. The police officer who was confident in almost any situation was out of his depth in this one, the ground was too unfamiliar to him. He tried again.

'If I wanted to see more of your granddaughter - possibly as more than just a friend - would I have your blessing?'

Monsieur Gerard sat opposite him, looking thoughtful and slightly worried.

'I rather wondered if it was something like that. I'm not sure how to answer you. I know you'd have Michelle's blessing, she's always had a fondness for you. Javert, exactly what are you asking me? Do you want to marry Michelle?'

Javert frowned. 'I don't know, not yet. It's too soon, I'm - a bit out of my depth with this.'

Monsieur Gerard nodded.

'Well, that's honest at least, but then again you've always been that, I'd have expected nothing else from you. Well, Javert, in some ways, I'd be pleased for you to see more of Michelle, you might bring her to her senses before she gets involved in something she shouldn't.'

Javert looked surprised. 'I don't understand. What could she be involved in?'

'Oh, I don't think she is really involved, not yet. But we've been getting quite a few disaffected students visiting the café, and she's been spending a bit too much of her time with them for my piece of mind. Oh, it's nothing like it was back in the 90's; just naive young idealists really. But all the same, I don't like their politics and I don't feel easy about her spending so much time with them.'

'Can't you stop them coming to the café? Or stop her seeing them?

'That's not so easy. I don't want to stop them coming, because at least I know what they're up to when they're under my eye. I suppose old habits die hard. As for stopping Michelle, well, she can be idealistic too, and she's a very determined young woman. I have to say, Javert, I think you'd have your work cut out with her.'

'But have I your blessing to – well – see more of her?'

Monsieur Gerard frowned. 'The thing is, I'm not the only person involved in this. I'm Michelle's grandfather, yes, but there's someone else who's even closer to her.'

'You mean Adele?'

'Precisely. I wouldn't feel I could give you a real answer without knowing her feelings. Listen Javert, let's leave it like this. You go and talk to Adele and see what she says. If she gives you her blessing, I'll give you mine.'

Javert nodded. 'All right. When?'

'Well, she's up now but she's still recuperating. Why not wait a week or so to let her recover and you to get over your night shifts? In the meantime, I'll talk to her and try to prepare the ground for you.'

Javert nodded his agreement and the two men shook hands formally. Javert then made his way back to his lodgings, leaving Monsieur Gerard to his work.

Typically, Javert threw himself into his job, refusing to let himself dwell on his individual problems and worries. It was only at the end of his tour of nights that he allowed his personal thoughts to surface. He was tired out, both physically and mentally, but exhausted as he was he found himself unable to sleep.

At midday he gave it up, dressed and went out. His thoughts were still churning as he walked the familiar streets in a daze, seeing nothing of his surroundings.

He was roused from his reverie by a familiar voice.

'Javert! This is a surprise.'

He blinked and looked up to see Adele and Michelle. Michelle looked delighted to see him. Adele, as always, was a little more reserved.

Michelle smiled up at him and laid a hand on his arm.

'Finished duty for the day? Come on Vere, we were just going to have a drink in here. Come with us.' She indicated a nearby café.

The proprietor hurried forward, greeting them effusively. He knew all of them, though he was surprised to see Javert out of uniform. The policeman did not usually frequent his establishment when off duty. Nor had he ever seen Javert accompanied by anyone else, with the exception - when on duty - of the police officers with whom he worked.

Once seated in the café, Javert looked across at Adele.

'Adele, there's something I'd like to talk to you about - privately.' He glanced towards Michelle, then back at Adele.

Adele looked slightly wary and he guessed that Monsieur Gerard had already broached the subject.

'Well - look Javert, why don't you come for dinner, to our café? After all, I missed the celebrations last week, so we could make up for that. Come tomorrow. Then if you want to talk after dinner, we can do that.'

Javert nodded.

'Thank you, I'd like to. If we can...'

There was a commotion from the direction of the kitchen. A woman's shrill scream, followed by the proprietor's voice.

'Javert - Officer Javert - can you come in here?'

Javert stood up. 'Stay here!'

He strode across the café and into the small kitchen at the back. Michelle and Adele followed, ignoring his order to remain where they were.

The café proprietor was standing against the far door of the kitchen, blocking the exit. In front of him was a small woman, about thirty years of age. She was thin but not actually malnourished, her clothes shabby but reasonably clean.

She turned and saw Javert. Her expression changed from fear to terror. Whether she actually knew him or whether she had heard the proprietor call out the word 'officer', she obviously guessed what he was.

The proprietor nodded in her direction.

'I just caught this woman helping herself in my kitchen.' He pointed to the floor, whereon lay a loaf, a cheese and a hunk of meat.

The woman took a pace forward, then stopped. She looked appealingly at the proprietor.

'Please Monsieur, I'm sorry. I had to do it. I've two children at home - little children, not four years old yet. I've no food in the house, and no money.'

The proprietor frowned at her. 'What about your husband?'

157

'He's just been sent to prison, only last week. There's just me and the children now.'

Javert, who had so far remained in the background, now walked forward and stood in front of the woman. The proprietor stepped back. The woman turned her attention to Javert.

'I've tried to find some work, but it's impossible. I've got to keep the children somehow. I had no choice - it was either starve, sell myself or steal. Please Monsieur - please let me go.'

Javert's expression was cold.

'How would that change your choices? If I let you go, you'll just steal again.'

'Please Monsieur, I won't - I swear it. If I'm arrested they'll send me to prison. What'll happen to my children if I go to prison?'

Javert shrugged. 'Don't you think you should have thought of that before you started stealing?'

The woman began to cry. She turned back to the proprietor.

'Please, I can work for you, work off what I owe you - anything.'

The proprietor looked uneasy. 'Oh, let her go Javert. I won't press charges, so long as she promises to stay away from this café.'

The woman's eyes lit with a momentary hope.

'I'll promise. I'll never come near here again, not ever.'

Javert looked at the woman and shook his head.

'No. It's too late for that now. The law is the law and there are no exceptions. You stand trial.'

Michelle laid her hand on his arm. 'Javert, please...'

He removed her hand courteously, not looking at her.

'Please keep out of this, Michelle; it's a police matter.'

The proprietor spoke quietly. 'Can't you use your discretion, if I don't complain?'

'No. This case is beyond my jurisdiction. She must stand trial.'

The terrified woman had backed right into the far corner. Suddenly, desperately, she snatched a heavy carving knife off the table.

'You're not arresting me - I won't come with you.'

Michelle gasped in horror. Javert snapped at Adele.

'Keep her back - and keep back yourself.'

He considered the woman. The way she was holding the knife showed that she had no idea how to use it, but however weak the hand that held it, the knife was large and sharp. And a cornered animal was always dangerous.

He walked closer, holding her pinned with his eyes. She backed right against the wall until she could go no further. Javert hefted the stick that he still carried, even off duty.

'Listen to me, mistress, you're coming with me one way or the other. My reach is longer than yours and if I have to use this I'm likely to break your arm.'

She stared at him in terror. He allowed her time for his words to sink in, then spoke again, his voice quiet.

'You'll probably get twelve months for the theft. Try to use that on me and I can promise you at least five years. Think about it.'

The woman gave a sudden sob, dropped the weapon and crumpled helplessly to the floor. Javert picked up the knife and put it out of her reach. Then he lifted her, holding her firmly but not roughly. He could feel her small, thin bones under his hands as she leaned helplessly against him, on the verge of collapse.

He spoke to the café owner. 'I suggest you keep your back door locked in future Monsieur, otherwise you might get more unwelcome visitors.' He turned to Michelle and Adele, still standing near the door that led to the café. The two women had their arms around each other. Michelle looked stunned and confused, Adele angry.

'My apologies for leaving you both like this. I'll see you tomorrow evening.'

He nodded to the proprietor, then left the café, half carrying his distraught prisoner.

The following evening Javert went to the Café Gerard for dinner, as arranged. Usually he was more relaxed there than he was anywhere else, but tonight was different. There was an atmosphere of tension in the room and it was an unusually

159

silent meal. Michelle was quiet and subdued; Adele seemed uncomfortable; Javert was never communicative at the best of times. It was left to Monsieur Gerard to try and keep the conversation alive.

After dinner Monsieur Gerard went down to look after the café, taking Michelle with him and leaving Javert alone with Adele. For a few moments Javert continued to stare into the fire, then he looked up at Adele.

'Did your father tell you what I wanted to talk to you about?'

She nodded. 'Yes he has, but before we talk about that, can I talk to you? Personally, I mean?'

Javert sighed and nodded. 'All right, I'm listening to you.'

Adele came and sat down on the hearth in front of him.

'That woman yesterday - the one you arrested at the café - couldn't you have let her go?'

Javert answered her patiently.

'No Adele, that was outside my jurisdiction. I can't make decisions on cases like theft. I can only decide smaller cases, like begging.'

'And if you could have let her go, would you have?'

'No. She broke the law, she had to be arrested.'

'But the poor woman, she was desperate.'

Javert sighed again. 'I know she was desperate - they all are. Listen, do you remember her mentioning three choices?'

Adele nodded. 'Starve, sell herself or steal. Yes, I remember.'

'And if I'd let her go, what choices would she have had then?'

Adele remained silent. Javert answered for her.

'The same three - starve, sell herself or steal. So she'd have stolen again, and again; or she'd have become a whore. She'd have ended up in prison sooner or later, for a certainty. Anyway at least she'll be fed in prison.'

'And her children? What about them?'

Javert shrugged. 'If she had any children. These people are all liars.'

'But you could tell the poor woman was beside herself. Anyway, that's not all. Maybe you did have to arrest her, but

160

you seemed so - so calculating, so cold. You showed no compassion at all. Javert, please listen to me. I'm worried about you - about what you're becoming. Didn't you even feel sorry for that woman?'

'Adele, listen to me, we've both seen what happens without order and justice, we've both suffered through it. Philippe died for lack of it. In any case, my feelings don't come into it. I'm a representative of the law and I have a job to do. '

Adele shook her head.

'A representative of the law; I remember André saying those very words once. You know Javert, when I look at you now, I see a younger version of André.'

Javert's head jerked up and for a moment anger flared in his eyes; her words had at last rattled his composure. Adele pressed home her advantage.

'Oh, I don't mean his cruelty or his viciousness, I've never seen that in you. But I can see his coldness, his lack of anything that might be called feeling or compassion. Don't bury those feelings of yours too deeply, Javert. They might die - as his did.'

There was a moment of silence, then Javert spoke again, his voice tightly controlled.

'All right, you've said what you wanted to say. Now will you listen to me?'

Adele nodded, her expression resigned.

'You said that Monsieur Gerard has already spoken to you, so you know that I want to talk to you about - about Michelle. Your father was prepared to give me his blessing, but he said I needed yours. Do I have it?'

Adele closed her eyes for a second, as if gathering her courage, then looked at him resolutely.

'I'm sorry Javert, but the answer's no.'

Javert's nostrils flared slightly.

'Why?'

'We've just discussed the reasons. I don't want you to court my daughter. I don't want to run the risk of your marrying my daughter. I'm sorry to say it, God only knows how sorry. What makes it worse is that I know she could be just what you need. I feel as if I'm deliberately destroying any hope you have left. But I daren't take the risk; I just daren't.'

161

'Can't you let Michelle make that decision?'

Adele shook her head.

'No! No, because she's besotted with you. What's so ironic is that I might consider the match if she didn't care for you so much. But as it is – oh, Javert, don't you see? If she has to spend her life tied to a man who she loves to distraction but who is incapable of loving her in return, it would destroy her.'

'How do you know I'm incapable of loving her?'

Adele regarded him steadily, her voice suddenly very quiet.

'Are you sure that you can?'

Javert started to speak, then hesitated. His feelings were a jumble. He wanted Michelle physically, he knew that. And he remembered that moment of gentle tenderness he had never felt before, a moment he had wanted to recapture and to keep. But love? That was something outside his experience, something he had never known. Could he really love anyone? Was he capable of it?

Adele spoke again, her voice sad.

'I think you've answered my question. You're not sure, are you? I'm sorry Javert. I know it's always been you for Michelle. When you were both younger I hoped that things might work out between you; but now I know they can't. I've already told you, I don't like what you're becoming - what you've already become. Neither of us are sure if you're capable of love and affection, and I'm not prepared to experiment. Not with my daughter's future happiness.'

For a moment their eyes remained locked, hers shining with tears, his blazing with passion. Then the fire faded from his eyes as he regained control of his feelings. His face resumed its usual cold expression, the mask slipped back into place.

'I see. All right, I understand you. I won't mention the subject again.'

Adele held out her hand towards him, her expression seeming to plead forgiveness, but he turned away from her. She stood abruptly and hurried out of the room. Left behind, Javert continued to gaze into the heart of the fire, watching numbly as the dreams he had scarcely begun to build withered and died among the blazing logs.

PART THREE

The Hunter

Chapter 19
Toulon 1815

Inspector Javert dismissed the coach and strode through the gates of Toulon garrison, followed by his two subordinates. His new, tailor made uniform fitted him snugly, showing his tall figure to good advantage. The black leather of his new calf length boots gleamed in the morning sun.

He walked smartly across the square towards the Commander's office, looking neither to left nor right but nevertheless conscious of the speculative glances that were coming his way. He had been promoted only one month previously and had moved to the district of Toulon on promotion, but this was his first visit to the garrison.

As always, his return stirred old memories; not so much of his time as a garrison guard, but of his boyhood. Maybe it was because those events were more vividly etched on his brain, or perhaps it was the contrast. Certainly the tall officer now striding across the square was a far cry from the young boy who had once padded barefoot across the same stone cobbles.

He entered the Commander's office and saluted smartly.

'Inspector Javert, Monsieur, here to issue convicts' parole tickets.'

The Commander acknowledged the salute, quickly appraising the man before him. The two men had never met, but the Commander had heard about Javert from other officers at the garrison and knew his background. He was impressed by the man's appearance.

'We're all ready for you, Inspector. You can use the Sergeant's office, if that's all right with you. I've detailed him to act as your liaison.' He smiled. 'I don't suppose you need to be shown the way - I understand it was your office once.'

Javert smiled at the memory.

'So it was Monsieur, but only very briefly. I transferred to the Gendarmerie about a month later. I must have been one of the shortest serving Sergeants on record - barring accidents, of course.'

The two men exchanged a few further pleasantries, then Javert saluted again and walked across to the Sergeant's office. The Sergeant stood up as he entered. He started to speak, then broke off, his eyes widening in surprise. Javert recognised Ferrier, who had been his partner on guard duties fifteen years before.

It was evident that Ferrier was not expecting to see Javert and for a moment he was thrown off balance. He recovered quickly, stood to attention and saluted. 'Good morning, Inspector! Won't you sit down?'

Javert nodded, walked round the desk and took the chair Ferrier was indicating.

'Thank you. I understand that you're my liaison officer.'

'Yes Monsieur, I am. There are five convicts being paroled today. I've got the list here, and the yellow tickets are all filled in. They just need your signature.'

'All right, we'll do that in a moment. First of all I'd like to see the list.'

Ferrier handed him the list. Javert scanned it quickly.

'Valjean - he's still here? He should have been out years ago.'

'Yes Monsieur, and he would have been, but he kept trying to escape so they kept adding to his sentence.'

Javert put down the list and pulled out Valjean's file. In addition to his attempt whilst Javert was at the garrison, he had made three further bids to escape. In all, he had served nineteen years, instead of the five to which he had been originally sentenced. Well, it was no more than Javert had expected - the man was just a hot headed fool, forever beyond redemption.

'All right Ferrier, bring them up. One at a time.'

The first four convicts were quickly dealt with. All were men who had been sentenced to short terms of imprisonment and served their time quietly without raising any ripples. They behaved obsequiously towards Javert, not wanting to jeopardise their parole.

Valjean was the last man on the list. Eleven years older than Javert, he was now in his mid-forties. He was still broad and strongly built, but otherwise considerably changed. His hair and beard were long and unkempt, grey with age as well as dirt. His face had an expression typical of many of the convicts; a look of hopelessness, mingled with hatred of the society that had condemned and rejected them.

The convict checked for a moment when he recognised the man seated behind the desk. He said nothing, but his eyes spoke volumes.

Javert addressed him formally.

'24601, I take it you know what today is?'

The convict nodded.

'Yes, it's the day I finally get out of here - the day I'm free!'

'No, it's the day you receive your parole. There's a difference - an important difference. A free man goes where he wishes and does what he wishes, so long as it's within the law. You don't have that freedom. I don't doubt you're familiar with the conditions of your parole - but just to be sure, I'll explain them again to you.'

He held up the yellow ticket in his hand.

'Everywhere you go, you must produce this ticket of leave. And you go only where you've been told to go, and by the way you're told.'

He examined the contents of the ticket.

'In this case you will make your way to Pontarlier. You must go there and only there and you must travel by the route shown here. If you're found anywhere off that route you will be in breach of parole. That means you'll be rearrested and returned to prison. Do you understand?'

Valjean looked at him coldly.

'Yes - Monsieur.'

'Very well. Ferrier, bring this man's property.'

Ferrier walked to the corner of the office and returned with a small canvas bag, a pair of old boots and a coat. He also produced an envelope containing some money. Javert indicated to him to place the canvas bag on the floor and the envelope on the desk.

'This is your property, and here's the money you've earned whilst you've been here.'

He waited for the man to pick up the envelope, expecting him to simply put it into his bag to be checked later. None of the other convicts had opened their envelopes. Typically, Valjean proved to be an exception. He walked over to the desk, emptied the envelope and counted the money inside. His head jerked up.

'There's only a hundred and nine francs here. I've earned more than this! I've kept a tally; I should have a hundred and seventy francs, at least.'

Javert turned to Ferrier. 'Fetch the record book.'

Ferrier gaped at him, the request was unprecedented.

'I'm sorry Monsieur?'

'The record book - the account book where the prisoner's earnings are recorded.'

Ferrier nodded and hurried from the room. Javert turned back to Valjean and surveyed him coldly.

'Have you considered the days when you haven't worked? Feast days, Sundays?'

Valjean looked startled. 'No. But there should still be more than this.'

Javert shrugged. 'We'll see in a moment.'

Ferrier returned with the massive book and turned it to the correct page. Javert scanned it quickly.

'The total is correct, 24601. You've lost twenty four francs for Sundays and feast days, eight francs for replacement clothing and twenty five francs for enforced leisure when you were in solitary confinement.'

Valjean's eyes were ablaze with rage.

'What! You mean as well as shutting me in that foul hole you stopped my earnings as well?'

Javert regarded him stonily.

'You were paid for the work you did. What work did you do in solitary?'

'That's nothing less than robbery. And you've just had me locked up for nineteen years because you say I'm a thief.'

'That's enough! You were locked up for five years for theft. The rest of your sentence was for trying to escape - sometimes with violence. Now, if you want to take your money with you, you sign for it.' He turned the property book round towards the convict. 'Make your mark here.'

The convict glared at him, breathing deeply, then picked up the offered pen. He looked at the property book and regarded the row of 'x's' that adorned the column marked 'signature of prisoner'. Carefully, he wrote the name *Jean Valjean*, then threw the pen onto the desk.

Javert regarded the signature and smiled faintly.

'I see you took my advice.'

'Advice?'

'About learning to read.'

'Yes, I thought it might help me rob people legally, like you do!'

Javert stood up slowly, standing eye to eye with the convict.

'Are you calling me a thief?'

For a moment Valjean glared back at him, then he sighed and stepped back.

'Not you personally. Just the system you represent.'

Javert nodded tightly, back in control of himself and wondering what it was about this man that always seemed to make him lose his composure. He signed the yellow ticket and handed it over to the convict.

'Here. As well as giving your route and destination this also gives details of your crime and sentence. And your behaviour whilst in prison.'

Valjean looked at the ticket.

'Violent and dangerous? You mean I have to show this wherever I go?' He took a step towards Javert. 'You bastard! You've damned me before I set foot out of that gate.'

'You damned yourself when you kept escaping and resisted arrest.'

Valjean looked at him, bitterness and defeat in his face.

'I suppose this is your revenge?'

'Revenge? For what?'

'For the kicking I once gave you - the mess I made of your face.'

Javert shook his head. 'I didn't write out that ticket.'

'You're part of the system that did.'

'Yes, I'm part of the system. And if you've any sense you'll start to conform to the system as well. Otherwise you'll be straight back here. But I don't have much hope, 24601. People like you don't change.'

Valjean started to speak, then stopped.

'Yes? If you've something to say to me, say it.'

Valjean's eyes narrowed.

'All right, I will. I pray that some day I'll have the power over you that you've had over me. If that happens, then God help you. And now I suppose you'll hide yourself behind that uniform and have me put back into solitary for disrespect, or insolence.'

For a moment the two men glared at each other, Valjean's eyes on fire, Javert outwardly cold and controlled. Then Javert shook his head slightly.

'You are now officially on parole. You're only liable to arrest if you break the law, or the terms of that parole. Empty and idle threats don't come into it; your personal opinion of me is of no importance.'

Valjean gave a sour smile, and nodded.

'We'll meet again - Inspector Javert.'

'I've no doubt of it. You're free to go. Ferrier, take him to the gate.'

Valjean stared at him for a moment more, then picked up his canvas bag from the floor. He put his envelope into it and preceded Ferrier through the door.

Javert left the garrison shortly after Valjean and returned to his duties in the district of Toulon. It was October and the days were shortening, soon the mistral would start to blow and the nights would be cold. Still, the air felt wonderful after Paris. The overpowering heat of summer was past and a fresh, clean wind blew off the sea. It was a shame he would only be there for a short time. He knew that his current posting was to be of short duration, probably around twelve months.

A week after his visit to Toulon garrison, one of the Gendarmes from the mounted branch arrived, carrying the messages and news from the region. Javert scanned through them quickly, stopping as he sighted a familiar name.

'Valjean!' he muttered to himself. 'What now?'

He read the message carefully. It was from the Gendarme in the town of Digne, and merely said that the convict Jean Valjean was now in breach of his parole, having committed a robbery on the highway outside Digne and subsequently disappeared. There were no other details.

Javert shook his head, feeling strangely disappointed. And yet he shouldn't be surprised that the convict had broken his parole. Surely he hadn't really expected anything else?

He went to the door and called to the Gendarme, showing him the message.

'Have you any more information about this one?'

The Gendarme shook his head.

'No Monsieur, I'm sorry. I only picked the messages up, I know nothing more than it says. If you wish, I can get the full report for you, next time I'm in Digne.

'And when will that be?'

'Next week Monsieur, and back here the day after that.'

Javert thought for a moment, then checked the message again. The convict had committed the robbery two days previously, so already the trail was cooling. Left another eight days it would certainly be cold.

'Don't worry about it,' he said abruptly. 'I'll go myself, today.'

'Yes Monsieur.' The Gendarme nodded, but looked puzzled. He was probably wondering why the Inspector seemed to regard the message as so important; convicts jumped parole every day, and this was only a very minor highway robbery, with no injuries or excessive violence.

Javert arrived at the old walled town of Digne in mid-afternoon the following day. He tethered his horse and walked into the police post without knocking. The Gendarme on duty was seated in his chair, smoking a pipe. His feet were on the desk in front of him. A bottle of wine and a cup stood within easy reach.

He looked up casually at Javert's entrance. His eyes widened in surprise when he saw the Inspector's uniform and he swung his feet hurriedly to the floor, almost upsetting the chair in his haste to stand up. Javert's reputation had preceded him, and although the Gendarme had never met him he knew who it must be.

'Oh - good afternoon, Inspector. I'm sorry, I wasn't expecting you.'

Javert looked at him. The Gendarme was a big man, almost as tall as himself and considerably fatter. Javert noted his unshaven appearance, grubby shirt and lack of a cravat, the tobacco stains on the uniform. Then he glanced at the desk, observing the half full cup and the half empty bottle.

'So I see! Is this how you usually spend your on duty time?'

'Oh no Monsieur - I was just on my refreshment break.'

'At four o'clock in the afternoon?'

'I've been busy, Monsieur.'

Javert nodded coldly.

'Well, next time we meet I expect you and your uniform to be in a fit state to be seen. The same goes for this office. Now then, tell me more about this.'

He produced the message regarding Jean Valjean.

The Gendarme took it from him, surprised but relieved to have got off so lightly. He leafed through the large book in front of him.

'Ah yes, here we are. Here's the full report Monsieur, on this page.'

Javert took the book from him and read the report through quickly. It was quite brief, stating that the convict Valjean had been checked three days before and found in possession of a quantity of silver from the residence of the Bishop of Digne. When the convict and the silver were taken back to the bishop the man had refused to make any complaint of theft, so the convict had been released.

The following day a young boy had run into the town in tears, saying that a man answering the convict's description had robbed him of forty centimes. The convict had not been seen since.

Javert turned to the Gendarme.

'What have you done about this?'

'Well Monsieur - '

The man stammered, uncertain what to say. Surely the Inspector realised that he had more important things to do than waste his time investigating a theft of forty centimes from a young child.

'Monsieur, it was only a very small amount of money and there was no violence used; no one was hurt. The convict was long gone, so I just recorded it.'

'Where's the boy's address?'

'He didn't have one Monsieur, he was only a young vagrant.'

Javert sighed. 'How long after the theft did the boy report it?'

'I'm not sure Monsieur, quite soon I think.'

'Then the convict hadn't been gone so very long, had he? Perhaps if you'd got your backside off your chair and onto your horse you might even have caught him. Have you spoken to the bishop yourself?'

'Er - no Monsieur.'

Javert scribbled down the address from the book.

'I thought probably not. Right, I'm going to see him myself. Get yourself and this place tidied up and wait here until I get back.'

'But monsieur, I'm off duty in an hour.'

Javert looked at him coldly. 'You'll be here when I get back!'

He left the police post and walked to the Bishop's residence, only a short distance away. The door was opened to him by a middle aged woman, who had the appearance of a housekeeper or some other upper servant. She regarded Javert with some surprise.

'Yes Monsieur, can I help you?'

Javert addressed her abruptly. 'Is the Bishop at home?'

'I'm afraid not, he's out visiting round the town. He always is at this time. We don't expect him home until the evening meal.'

'And what time is that?'

'Around six o'clock.'

Javert thought for a moment. It was now just before five o'clock so it would be no problem to go away and return in an hour's time. On the other hand, he might learn more from this woman than from the Bishop.

'It's possible you can help me yourself. Are you the Bishop's housekeeper?'

The woman raised her head and regarded him with a touch of haughtiness.

'No, Monsieur. I'm the Bishop's sister, Madamoiselle Baptistine.'

Javert bowed slightly, switching his manner of address to what he privately called his 'drawing room style.'

'Please forgive me, Madame, and forgive this intrusion on your privacy. My name is Inspector Javert and I'm making enquiries about a recent guest of yours - a man by the name of Jean Valjean. Do you know the man I mean?'

The woman threw up her hands.

'Oh, him! Yes, I remember him - only too well.' She held the door open and stepped back. 'Please come in, Monsieur.'

Javert entered the house, politely removing his hat as he did so. She indicated a chair.

'Please sit down, Monsieur. What was it you wanted to know about that man?'

Javert noted the disapproval in her voice, Mademoiselle Baptistine at least appeared to have no liking for the convict. He decided to come straight to the point.

'I understand from one of my officers that Valjean lodged here three nights ago. I also understand that he stole some silver from the house.'

The woman nodded, her expression indignant.

'And so he did Monsieur. Oh, he was a terrible looking man, wild looking. I don't think we should even have let him into the house, and I told my brother so at the time.'

'But your brother did invite him in?'

'Yes he did - he would!' She gave a sigh. 'I'm afraid my brother and I don't always agree on things like that, Monsieur Javert. I saw a desperate convict, a dangerous man. He just saw a human being in trouble.'

'And the silver? Can you tell me about that?'

'Oh, he took the silver all right. We had dinner - I have to say I've never seen anyone eat quite like him, he was more like a dog than a human being. Anyway, we had dinner and then my brother told me to prepare a bed for the convict. Then we

174

all went to bed. When we got up in the morning he was gone, and the silver with him. Cups and plates he took. All good, solid silver.'

Javert leaned forward slightly.

'And is it right that the Gendarmes caught him in possession of the silver, and brought him back here?'

'Oh yes, they brought him back, but my brother wouldn't make any complaint. He told the policemen that he had given the silver to this Valjean.'

Her voice rose with indignation.

'And that's not all. Do you know what my brother did next? He gave him two candlesticks as well - solid silver again, worth even more than the plates and cups.'

Javert looked startled.

'Just a minute, Madame. Am I to understand that your brother let this man keep the silver he'd taken?'

'Oh yes.'

'And added two valuable candlesticks as well? My goodness, the man's walked away with a small fortune!' He gave a bark of harsh laughter. 'And to think he still took forty centimes off a young boy. It's unbelievable!'

The woman looked at him in puzzlement.

'I'm sorry, I don't know what you mean?'

'The convict. After he left here - with your silver - he robbed a young boy of forty centimes.'

She looked indignant.

'Well, really! Not that I'm surprised, Monsieur. He looked a desperate man, if ever I saw one.'

'I fear you're right, Madame. Now tell me, do you think the Bishop will make a formal complaint, if I talk to him?'

She shook her head.

'I'm sure he won't. We tried to persuade him - the housekeeper and I - but he wouldn't hear of it. He said that the silver rightly belonged to the poor, and that the convict had as much right to it as him.'

She stood up, looking suddenly agitated.

'Forgive me Inspector, but you'd better leave. My brother will be annoyed if he realises what I've told you. After all, it was his silver, to do with as he liked. But I was so angry at what that convict did, after what my brother had done for him. Please Monsieur, you'd better go before my brother gets home.'

Javert stood up and reached for his hat; he had obtained all the information he was likely to get.

'Just one final question. Did you notice what direction the convict took?'

'Yes I did; be sure I did. I watched him until he was out of sight, I wanted to be sure he didn't come back. He went towards Arnoux.'

Javert bowed politely. 'Thank you Madame, you've been most helpful.'

He left the woman and returned to the police post. The Gendarme was still waiting for him, as ordered. The wine had vanished and both room and man looked considerably more tidy, though neither were at what Javert considered an acceptable standard.

Javert addressed the man abruptly. 'Do you have a change of clothes with you?'

The man gaped at him. 'I'm sorry Monsieur, no I don't. At least, not spare ones. I've got my own ordinary clothes of course, I always change before I go home.'

Javert looked at him distastefully. Judging by the state of his uniform, the man's ordinary clothes would be far from clean.

'All right, fetch them. I'm going to borrow them for a while.'

He removed his uniform and dressed himself in the Gendarme's ordinary clothing. They were not a good fit and as he had feared they were dirty and sweat stained, but he had worn worse than that during his early days in Paris. He turned to the Gendarme.

'I don't know when I'll be back, so you can either wait or go home in your uniform, I don't care which. But you'll be back here by eight o'clock in the morning. Clear?'

The man nodded, still looking bewildered. 'Yes Monsieur.'

It was now past six o'clock and almost dark. Javert lit a lantern and walked back past the Bishop's house and out along the main road towards Arnoux. It was a quiet, lonely road, with

176

only one inn within striking distance of the town. A country inn, with a respectable clientele.

He spent the evening there, making casual but careful enquiries. By the end of the night he was as certain as he could be that the convict Valjean had never visited the place, and there were no similar establishments beyond this one.

Eventually Javert returned to the now deserted police post, frustrated and discouraged. The trail was cold, but like any good hunting dog he would know the scent if he sniffed it again.

Chapter 20
Montreuil-Sur-Mer, 1821

Javert looked around with interest as the coach rumbled slowly through the streets of Montreuil-sur-Mer. He was pleased with his new posting, his role would be very different here. He had spent the past four years in Paris, where he was a very small cog in an extremely large wheel. Montreuil might be a much smaller wheel, but here he would be a much larger cog. That meant he would be able to enforce the law as he felt fit and make the changes he wanted.

His immediate impression was a favourable one. On first sight at least the town appeared to be unusually orderly and prosperous. It was the middle of summer and when he had left the capital the previous day Paris had been sweltering in the heat, but here the proximity of the sea made the air feel much fresher. Javert had always liked the sea, it was one of the things he missed in Paris.

The coachman drew his horses to a halt in the middle of the town. Javert climbed down, accepted his heavy bags with a curt nod of thanks and walked the short distance to the Police Post.

He entered the room without knocking, he did not believe in giving his subordinates warning of his approach. The gendarme on duty immediately stood up at his entrance. Javert was not in uniform but the man was expecting him and knew the arrival time of the Paris coach.

'Good evening Monsieur - might you be Inspector Javert.'

'I am. And you?'

'Officer Dubois, Monsieur.'

Javert deposited his heavy bags with a sigh of relief and looked Dubois up and down. The man was in his late twenties and looked reasonably intelligent and alert. His uniform was creased and grubby and his boots scuffed, but that was fairly typical. Javert would soon change that.

Dubois was also discreetly sizing up his new superior. He saw a tall, military looking man, with something intimidating about him. The dark eyes were bleak and expressionless and there were harsh lines on the face. Not a man to laugh and share a drink with.

Dubois broke the silence.

'Monsieur, you must be tired after your journey down. Can I show you to your lodgings? It's not very far.'

'Presently. First of all, I'd like to look at your incident book.'

Dubois looked surprised, then hurried to do his new superior's bidding. Javert scanned the recent entries swiftly. There was insufficient detail for his liking, but at least the book seemed to be up to date. His first impressions were reasonably favourable, he should be able to put this place in order without too much difficulty. He closed the book, deciding to defer further action until the following day.

'All right, Officer Dubois, I'll go to my lodgings now. Tell me, what time do you start duty tomorrow?'

'Should be six in the evening Monsieur, same as today. My partner Clement is on during the day.' He hesitated. 'I can be here in the morning if you wanted to see us both.'

'And still work your late shift?'

'Of course, Monsieur.'

Javert nodded, giving the man a mental plus for his willingness.

'All right, be here at nine o'clock. I won't keep you too long, but it will save time if I see you both together. And now, if you'll show me my lodgings.'

'Yes Monsieur, this way.' Dubois picked up one of the heavy bags and led the way out of the Post.

The following morning, Javert arrived at the Police Post shortly before nine o'clock. It was the start of another warm day and both door and windows of the Post stood open. As he walked past the window he heard a voice he didn't recognise speaking from within.

'... you think he'll be different to the old man, then?'

Dubois' voice answered.

'I should say so - very dour he was. Civil enough, mind you, but didn't crack his face. Didn't seem to miss much either. I tell you what, I think this one might be a bit of a swine. Better get things tidied up a bit; he said nine o'clock and I'll bet he'll be right on the dot.'

Javert smiled to himself, then spoke dryly from the open doorway.

'He could even be early.'

He walked in, looking even more intimidating in his uniform and enjoying the men's confusion as they leapt to their feet. His position of authority and the greater security that gave him had enabled him to develop something of a sense of humour over the past few years, but it was the humour of the cat that toys with the mouse just before it pounces.

He glanced at Dubois, who looked embarrassed but not particularly worried. Already there was an improvement in his appearance, apparently the man had some initiative. Javert turned towards the other man, who was standing stiffly to attention. He was younger and slighter than Dubois, probably not more than twenty years old.

'I take it you're Clement?'

'Yes Monsieur.'

His tone and expression were apprehensive. Javert gave a slightly twisted smile. He didn't particularly mind being less than popular with his men, provided they did their job and he had their respect.

'All right - don't worry about it. You're quite right, I can be a swine, but only if you warrant it. But I'll tell you here and now that both of you need to smarten up.' He nodded to Dubois. 'I appreciate you've made some effort, but it's not enough.'

Both men nodded dutifully, covertly eyeing Javert's immaculate uniform.

'Dubois, show me round the Post and then get out your record books. I shall want to see details of persons arrested, crimes committed, ticket of leave men in the district, persons checked - for the past three months. Do you have all those?'

'Er - yes Monsieur, I think so.'

'Good. Sort those out for me and we'll go through them later on. You can work a full day shift today and come back on late shift tomorrow.'

Dubois looked surprised. 'Thank you Monsieur, but - who'll do the late shift today?'

'I will, it'll give me a chance to go through things thoroughly.' He saw the two men exchange a swift glance, apparently they didn't care for that idea. Javert turned to the younger Officer.

'Clement, you come with me, I want you to show me round the town; inns, lodging houses and so forth.'

He turned on his heel and walked towards the door. Clement, still looking glum and apprehensive, grabbed up his hat and hurried after his new superior.

The morning confirmed Javert's first impression that the town was generally in good order. Like any town it had its slum areas, but on the whole it appeared to be quite prosperous. After lunch he said as much to Clement.

'Oh yes, Monsieur. It's improved a lot over the past two years or so, mostly because of our new Mayor.' The young man had got over his first apprehension, having discovered that his superior, though tending to be cold and uncommunicative, was at least civil.

Javert glanced at him. 'The new Mayor? How has he helped?'

'Mostly by providing work. He opened a factory a little over two years ago and of course that meant more jobs. The unemployment here is less than most places, or so I'm told. I've only worked here, of course.'

Javert nodded; that explained a great deal. With less unemployment there would be less crime. People with money in their pockets didn't need to steal, and people with work to do had less leisure to fill with undesirable and illegal activities.

'Who is the Mayor? What's his name?'

'Monsieur Madeleine, Monsieur. This is his factory, down here - hello, it sounds as if there's something going on.'

The two Officers stopped and listened. From behind the factory wall they could hear a woman shouting, accompanied by the sound of people jeering. As they watched, the factory gate swung open and a burly man appeared, holding a young woman by the arm. He pushed her out of the gate, then slammed it closed.

181

'There – and stay out! We don't employ sluts like you here!'

The woman rushed back to the bars, shrieking after him.

'You're a load of bloody hypocrites, all of you. You're none of you any better than I am.'

She continued to scream insults through the bars of the factory gate. The young Officer looked uncertainly at Javert, who nodded.

'Move her on. Tell her once; if she doesn't go, arrest her.'

Clement looked slightly taken aback by this uncompromising attitude, then obediently approached the woman and put his hand on her arm.

'You're causing a disturbance - move along!'

The woman swung round at his touch. She was young, probably around her mid-twenties, and quite pretty. Her long blond hair was particularly attractive; freed from the cap she had worn whilst working, it hung loose almost to her waist.

She gripped the Officer by his coat sleeve.

'You don't understand. They've thrown me out - for nothing. Just because they've found out I've got a bastard child. How can I keep her if I'm not working?'

Javert stepped forward quietly and stood immediately behind Clement. She looked at him over the younger Officer's shoulder, taking in the details of his appearance, the cold expression - or rather lack of expression - in his eyes. She fell silent, then turned and walked slowly away down the street. The man who had evicted her now approached the gates, having watched the whole incident with interest.

'Thank you, Inspector; the woman was being a nuisance. We don't want Fantine's sort here, they're decent girls at this factory, not whores like her.'

Javert nodded to him and the man returned to the factory. The two Officers walked on. After a few minutes, Clement broke the silence.

'I wonder what she'll do now.'

'Who?'

'That woman, the one from the factory. What did he call her - Fantine? I wonder what'll happen to her child, if she hasn't any money.'

182

'Why should you worry about what happens to her bastard?'

Clement looked startled.

'Well, I'm not sure why, Monsieur. I just do.'

Javert nodded, his tone ironic.

'I see. Well, that's very caring of you, Clement. Tell me, how long have you been a police Officer?'

'Six months Monsieur, I was - well, I was going to be a lawyer, but I wanted to do this. My father spoke to the Mayor about it, and he helped me.'

'And how old are you?'

'Just twenty-one Monsieur.' He looked at Javert anxiously. 'I know it's a bit young, but...'

Javert shrugged. 'As to that, it's the age I was when I joined, but I came from the prison guards at Toulon. I'm not concerned about your age, Clement, but you'll have to toughen up if you're going to do your job properly. Your duty is to enforce the law; leave the caring to the priests and the philanthropists.'

Clement flushed unhappily. 'Yes Monsieur.'

They continued their patrol, checking lodging houses and inns as they went. As they crossed the main square they saw a number of beggars, congregated near one of the cafés that gave onto the square. Javert indicated them with his stick.

'Move them on, will you?'

'Monsieur?'

'Move them on. Don't you usually do that?'

'Well, no Monsieur, we never have. Not unless they cause trouble. The Mayor often gives them money when he comes by and our last Inspector - well, he liked a quiet life, if you see what I mean.'

'I see. Well, I don't want a quiet life, I want a quiet town. That means beggars and prostitutes stay where they belong, I don't want them up here. We're going to come down hard on these people; that way they'll understand we mean business all the sooner. Now then, tell me more about this Mayor of yours. You say he's in the habit of giving money to beggars?'

'Yes Monsieur. Oh, not just beggars - anyone who needs help. He's a good man, Monsieur; a truly good man.'

Javert reflected that the Mayor might also prove to be something of a damned nuisance, if he encouraged beggars and their like to congregate in the town. However, he did not consider saying anything of that to Clement. The Mayor was in a position of authority, and whatever kind of man he turned out to be, Javert would always respect that.

During the next few days Javert concentrated on finding his way around and getting to know all he could about the town and its people. He heard a great deal in praise of the Mayor, who paid good wages and had the reputation of being generous and open-handed with all comers. Javert quickly discovered that he was also very lenient in the exercise of his powers. On two occasions during that first week, the Mayor released offenders whom Javert would have imprisoned for six months.

Javert was surprised that the Mayor had not yet sent for him, the man must have been notified of his appointment. At the end of the week he decided not to wait any longer, but to initiate contact himself. Accordingly he checked his uniform carefully, then presented himself at the Mayor's office. He was greeted politely by the Mayor's clerk, who enquired as to his business.

'Please tell the Mayor that Inspector Javert is here and would like to pay his respects. At his convenience, of course.'

'Yes Monsieur. Please wait here.'

The man disappeared through the rear door and Javert heard his footsteps on the stairs. He was back in a very short time.

'Monsieur Madeleine says he'll be pleased to make your acquaintance Monsieur, please come this way.'

Javert followed the man up the staircase and into a well decorated, spacious office that overlooked the Town Square. The man behind the desk rose politely as he entered. Something nudged at Javert's consciousness, there was a strange familiarity about the Mayor. He was a big man, not in height but in breadth of chest and shoulder. His curling grey hair was immaculately brushed, his beard neatly trimmed. The Mayor greeted him with quiet dignity and waved towards the chair opposite the desk. For a few moments they chatted about

184

nothing, whilst Javert tried to think why he felt he had met this man before. Suddenly, between one sentence and the next, he made the connection; the man reminded him strongly of the convict Jean Valjean.

Javert started at the memory, then resolutely pushed it away as he looked again at the immaculately turned out man with the quiet, unassuming manner. The man's blue eyes regarded him mildly, with no trace of the fire that had so often appeared in the eyes of the former convict. There was no flicker of recognition in them as they looked at Javert, which surely there would have been. Javert told himself that the whole idea was absurd, but found himself discreetly probing the Mayor about his past.

'Your factory has been a wonderful thing for the town, Monsieur le Mayor. I understand you opened it two years ago?'

The Mayor nodded. 'That's correct, Inspector.'

'And you arrived in the town three years before that? You've done a lot in a short time, Monsieur. May I ask where you were before?'

'I spent some time in Faverolles. I travelled about quite a lot when I was younger, but now I'm older I thought it was time to settle down. And yourself Inspector, that isn't a local accent. Where are you from?'

'Originally Toulon, Monsieur.' He paused, watching the man closely. 'I spent quite some time at the Toulon Garrison, guarding the convicts there.'

'Ah yes, poor souls. Well, Inspector, I really mustn't keep you from your duties any longer. It was kind of you to make yourself known to me. I had intended to send for you, but I'm afraid it slipped my mind.'

So politely but positively dismissed, Javert could think of no excuse to linger. The Mayor's likeness to Valjean disturbed him. He would have liked to question the Mayor further, but the position was somewhat delicate. Of course, the matter would be easily resolved if he could check whether or not Monsieur Madeleine was carrying the brand on his shoulder, but he could hardly ask the Town Mayor to remove his shirt unless he was very certain indeed of his ground. Accordingly he bowed respectfully and left the room.

He was in a thoughtful mood as he descended the stairs and retraced his steps across the square towards the Police Post. The Mayor's eyes had not even flickered at the mention of Toulon, or at Javert's questioning of his past. He had remained polite, dignified, controlled. But Javert's instinct told him that something was not right. He had sensed a deeper level to their conversation; a hidden agenda of which both of them were aware. It was as if the two men had been fencing carefully, testing each other out, with neither of them yet prepared to lay themselves open by risking a direct thrust.

As Javert strode across the square he told himself that the whole thing was ridiculous - but at the same time he knew he would have to learn more about Monsieur Madeleine.

Chapter 21

During the next two years Javert made his mark on the town of Montreuil-sur-Mer. By and large, he was respected by the law abiding community, but hated and feared by those who broke the law. Beggars were forced out of the town centre. Prostitutes plied their trade with greater discretion, and their earnings suffered as a consequence. Accordingly the majority of them left Montreuil to make their living elsewhere.

The Gendarmes under Javert's command soon adjusted to his methods, finding him stern but fair and consistent. They worked much harder than previously, but took more pride in what they did and how they looked. They also noted that Javert put in more hours than either of them; indeed he seemed to live for the job and was rarely off duty. They grew to respect him - they even learnt to appreciate his occasional ironic humour - but they were never allowed close enough to develop any real liking for him.

For his part, Javert was enjoying his time at Montreuil, except for the presence of Monsieur Madeleine. They had crossed swords on several occasions; their differing approaches made such clashes inevitable. The two men were at opposite ends of the spectrum; Javert harsh and severe, the Mayor - by Javert's standards at least - lenient and indulgent.

In addition, the Mayor's similarity to Valjean still haunted Javert. He had enquiries made at Faverolles, but received no useful information. Eventually he took himself severely to task; he couldn't go on hunting for information about the Mayor just because the man reminded him of a convict and had occasionally thwarted him in his duty. He resolved to forget all about the matter.

Early in January 1824 Javert and Clement were patrolling the area around the town square. The first snow of the year had just fallen and a large number of people had turned out to celebrate the event. The cafés around the square were all full and despite the cold a number of revellers were spilling out onto the street.

Javert indicated the far side of the square, where two or three prostitutes were hovering hopefully.

'Keep an eye on them.'

'Yes Monsieur. Do you want them moving on?'

'No, not so long as they just sit there and don't beg or make a nuisance of themselves. Hello - I see she's back again.'

'Who Monsieur?'

'Fantine. You remember - the woman who was thrown out of the factory on my first day here. I've seen her around here a few times, and moved her on twice. Keep an eye on her, Clement. I have to say that foreman was right about her.'

'In what way, Monsieur?'

'About her not being fit to mix with decent women.' Javert motioned with his stick. 'Just look at her.'

Fantine was indeed a sorry sight; she had degenerated steadily since being forced to leave the factory. Her clothes were little more than rags and both they and she looked grimy with dirt. There was now little left of the pretty girl she had once been. Where she had been slim, now she was emaciated. Even the beautiful hair was gone, hacked off close to her scalp.

After a few minutes Javert touched Clement on the arm. 'It seems peaceful enough here just now. Come on - we'll check the inns.'

They turned and walked away from the square, but had only gone a few paces down the nearest street when the noise behind them stopped them in their tracks - a woman's shrill scream, followed by a man's shout of pain. There was a pause, then the sound of voices cheering and shouting. The clamour grew rapidly louder as more people joined in.

Javert looked at Clement.

'What the devil...? Come on!'

They hurried back to the main square. A large crowd of people had gathered in one corner and were shouting and cheering something that seemed to be happening in their midst. The two police officers pushed their way through the crowd. Two people were rolling round on the ground, apparently fighting - a man and a woman. As they approached the man managed to throw the woman off, but she seemed to be beside

188

herself with rage and immediately went for him again, clawing at him savagely.

Javert recognised the woman as Fantine. He strode forward, seized her by the waist of her dress with one hand and plucked her off the man on the ground. He wrinkled his nose in disgust; she was filthy, reeking of stale sweat and gin. She turned on him, clawing for his face. He captured both her thin wrists, holding them easily in one hand.

'That's enough!'

Fantine's eyes rounded as she realised who was holding her. She immediately stopped struggling and he felt her go taut with fear. She began babbling confusedly.

'Oh I'm sorry Monsieur - I didn't know it was you. Please forgive me, I'd never have touched you...'

Javert cut her short. 'Be quiet!'

The woman bit her lip and fell silent.

'That's better. Now then, someone tell me what's going on here.'

The man with whom Fantine had been fighting was on his feet now, straightening his clothes. He looked like a gentleman, albeit something of a dandy. With a sense of shock Javert recognised Monsieur Bamatabois, a Parisian judge who had been spending Christmas with his family in Montreuil. Javert swore under his breath; the thought of so important a personage being assaulted in his town did not please him.

The judge was dabbing his cheek with a lace handkerchief. Scratches from the woman's nails showed clearly.

'Officer, this woman - this whore - attacked me. First she importuned me and demanded money. Then when I'd have none of it she flew at me. Look - look what the cat did with its claws.'

Fantine wriggled in protest. 'No! No, that's a lie! That's not how it was.'

Javert fixed her with his glare.

'Be quiet woman, I'll hear your side of the story in a minute.' He turned to Clement. 'Help this gentleman and find out the full story from him, then talk to the other people who were watching. I want a full report. You, come with me.'

He led the now passive Fantine away across the square. Once inside the police post he released her arm and indicated to her to sit down in the corner of the room, relieved to put some distance between the woman and himself.

'Well - what's your story?'

Fantine huddled down on the bench, shaking. She was prevented from answering him immediately as a severe fit of coughing racked her thin frame. Javert noticed that the dirty rag she held to her mouth came away flecked with blood. The sight evoked a vivid recollection of his mother as he had seen her shortly before she died, lying on the floor of their lodgings coughing into a blood stained rag.

The memory brought pain, together with a totally unexpected wave of sympathy for Fantine. The woman was obviously very ill. Resolutely he over-rode the emotion. He didn't want to feel compassion for this woman, didn't want to see her as an individual with her own fears and sorrows.

Recovered from her coughing fit, Fantine gave him a timorous smile. He noticed with revulsion that both her front teeth were missing.

'He was lying, Monsieur, that's not how it was at all. I didn't bother the gentleman, I was only crossing the street. He'd been pestering me for a little while, calling me names. Then when I ignored him he grabbed me and forced a big lump of wet ice down my back. It was such a shock, I just lost my temper. I'm sorry Monsieur, but that's how it was. I swear it.'

'I've seen you importuning people before. I've moved you on myself twice.'

'Yes, Monsieur. But not this time. I swear it.'

'You're telling me he attacked you. Have you any witnesses?'

Fantine looked confused. 'Well, I don't know Monsieur - perhaps the people in the square...'

The door opened and Clement entered.

'I've spoken to Monsieur Bamatabois Monsieur. His story is just what he told you - the woman asked him for money, then got nasty when he told her to go away.'

'Any other witnesses to that?'

'Well, no Monsieur - at least, no one will admit to seeing anything. You know what they are, not wanting to get involved. They all say the first thing they saw was the man and woman rolling on the ground.'

'I see. What about the other prostitutes? What do they say?'

'Nothing Monsieur, they'd both gone. I suppose they were afraid we'd bring them in as well.'

'Probably. All right Clement, write out a full report.' He turned back to Fantine. 'You wait there while I think what to do with you.'

She looked at him wide-eyed.

'Please Monsieur, I'm telling you the truth.'

'You really expect me to take your word against that of a gentleman?'

The woman's gaze fell, her expression was all the answer he needed.

Javert considered the case before him. To his mind it was clear enough what had happened. He had seen Fantine importuning people before, preying on innocent citizens. The prostitutes and beggars were a nuisance, both could become aggressive when thwarted. He had already warned this one twice, which was one more chance than he usually allowed people.

Clement finished writing and handed the report to Javert, who read it through thoroughly before picking up his pen and writing beneath it. That done, he turned to Fantine.

'All right, young woman; you go to prison for six months.'

Fantine gasped in horror.

'No Monsieur, please - don't send me to prison. What'll happen to my child? It's bad enough now - I can barely earn enough to keep her. If I go to prison, I'll earn almost nothing.'

'At least you'll earn it honestly, instead of selling yourself and robbing innocent citizens.'

The woman began to sob.

'But I'd nothing else left to sell. Look at me - I'd already sold my hair, and my teeth. Please Monsieur, my daughter will die if I've no money to send. They'll throw her out onto the street.'

She threw herself to her knees, wrapping both arms around his legs. Javert was suddenly reminded of Bibet, clinging and pleading for his life. He stood there taut as a wire, restraining himself with difficulty from kicking her away from him.

'Clement, get this woman off me!'

The officer pulled Fantine away from Javert, dragging her across the floor. At that moment there was a brisk knock, followed by the sound of the door opening. Javert turned to berate whoever it was for not waiting for an invitation to enter, but the angry words died on his lips as he realised who the newcomer was. It was the Mayor.

The Mayor advanced into the room and closed the door behind him.

'Forgive this interruption, Inspector, but may I have a word with you.'

'Of course Monsieur - if you wouldn't mind waiting a moment while I finish with this business.' He turned to Clement. 'Take her to the lock-up.'

Clement started to drag Fantine towards the door, then halted as the Mayor deliberately stepped into their path.

'Just a moment officer. Inspector Javert, it was about this woman that I wanted to see you.'

He reached his hand towards Fantine, but she pulled away from him.

'Leave me alone! It's all your fault. It's your fault I've got no job; you made me what I am now.'

The Mayor looked at the woman in confusion.

'I don't understand what you mean.'

'I worked hard at your factory, I earned my money. Until you found out I had a bastard child. Then you just threw me out - or your foreman did, it's the same thing.'

The Mayor looked at her blankly. Fantine was now sobbing hysterically. Suddenly she raised her head and spat full in the man's face.

Both Monsieur Madeleine and Javert recoiled in shock. Javert's blood boiled at the sight of the dirty street slut spitting on someone of the Mayor's status; to him it was symbolic of the scum of the gutters spitting in the face of authority. His latent sympathy with Fantine vanished without a trace. He strode forward and spoke sharply to Clement.

'Get that - woman - out of here!'

Again Clement tried to drag Fantine towards the door, but the Mayor held his position, standing squarely in Clement's way. He produced a handkerchief and wiped the spittle from his face.

'Just a minute - I've still a word to say concerning this woman. Inspector, are you sure you've looked into this case properly?'

Javert took a deep breath. He was irritated by the Mayor's interference, and furious at Fantine's attack on the Mayor. He pushed down hard on his anger, forcing himself to speak calmly.

'I saw the woman fighting in the street and I spoke to the man she assaulted. No-one else came forward to say what happened, so I've used my own judgment. It's what I'm paid for, Monsieur.'

'Inspector Javert, I saw what happened from my office. This woman didn't start the fight, and there are a number of other witnesses out there who are prepared to support what I'm telling you.'

'I asked for witnesses, Monsieur. As I say, no-one came forward.'

The Mayor sighed. 'Forgive me Inspector, but that's because they're afraid of you, especially the other women who were with this one.'

Javert's jaw set, he was becoming increasingly annoyed by Monsieur Madeleine's interference. He kept his tone civil with some difficulty.

'The case has already been dealt with, Monsieur. The woman has been sentenced to six months.' He signalled to Clement. 'Take her out!'

The Mayor shook his head. 'No! I'm sorry to do this, Inspector, but the woman goes free.'

Javert drew himself up to his full impressive height and fixed the Mayor with a stare that had never failed to intimidate.

'I don't believe you have the authority to make that decision, Monsieur Madeleine, and I must respectfully request that you permit me to do my job.'

The Mayor met Javert's gaze steadily.

'If you care to check your books, you'll find I do have the authority. I've explained the matter to you - the woman goes free.'

Javert stood his ground. 'I can't allow that.'

Clement was staring from one to the other in open mouthed amazement. Never had he witnessed a confrontation like this. The air between the two antagonists fairly sparked with tension - he could almost see lightning bolts zig–zagging between them.

The Mayor stepped forward until they were standing face to face. Javert felt a sudden shock as he looked into the Mayor's eyes. The years rolled back and suddenly he was no longer in the Police Post at Montreuil–Sur–Mer. Instead he was in the Sergeant's office at Toulon, looking into the same eyes, with the same fire in them. The Mayor was no longer the calm, controlled Monsieur Madeleine - he was someone else!

The Mayor's voice had become sharp with anger.

'I don't intend to discuss the matter any further. The woman goes free. If you're not prepared to obey my orders and release her then I suggest you leave this room - now!'

Javert hesitated, confused by the strong emotions fighting for mastery of him. He was angry as he had rarely been angry before - at having his authority challenged, at being humiliated like this in front of Clement, at seeing a street slut spit in the face of the Mayor. On top of that, he was suddenly certain that the man in front of him was indeed the convict Jean Valjean.

He made a slight move towards Monsieur Madeleine, then stopped, forcing himself to think what he was doing. To arrest the Town Mayor was a very serious act; one that would most certainly finish off Javert's career if he proved to be wrong. He needed to get control of himself before rushing into actions he might later regret.

Shaking with anger, Javert turned on his heel and walked out of the room, leaving the field to the Mayor.

There was an uncomfortable atmosphere in the Police Post on the day following Javert's confrontation with Monsieur Madeleine. Much to Javert's fury the woman Fantine was now free, and was no doubt telling her tale all over the town. Javert was also enraged that Clement had witnessed the Mayor's treatment of him, but felt unable to discuss the matter with his officer. After all, Monsieur Madeleine was still the Mayor - for the time being at least - and Javert would never openly criticise higher authority to his subordinates.

For his part, Clement felt a great deal of sympathy for his Inspector, but did not know how to say so. By this time he knew Javert well enough to know that he would not welcome pity.

During the afternoon the two men went out on patrol of the town. The weather had turned colder overnight, turning the snow to ice, and the roads were treacherous for both horses and men. As they crossed the main square they saw Monsieur Madeleine leaving his office, heading in their direction. As he passed he nodded stiffly to Javert. Javert bowed slightly, equally rigid. Both men's faces might have been cast from stone.

There was a sudden commotion from the street leading off the square behind them; a rumbling sound, confused cries and shouts of warning, then a shrill scream of pain, mingled with the frenzied neighing of a horse. Javert spun round and ran towards the sound, his boots slipping on the treacherous surface. Just around the corner was an overturned cart, part of its load of coal scattered across the road. The horse, still attached to the traces, was also down, neighing wildly as it tried vainly to free itself. Already several people were gathered around the cart, some vainly trying to free the horse, others to lift the cart. Seeing Javert, one of the men ran towards him.

'Quick Monsieur - help us!   Monsieur Fauchlevent's trapped under the cart.'

Javert ran over to the cart. The man lay partly beneath the cart, trapped by the legs, just as André had once been trapped by the huge block of stone many years before. At the moment the full weight of the cart was not on him because the wall of the café was partly supporting the vehicle, but it looked as if it would not be supporting it for long. Even as they watched the cart slid down a little further, bringing a scream of fear and agony from the trapped man.

Javert looked around quickly for something with which to lever up the cart, but he could see nothing that would be of any use. The Mayor arrived at a run, taking in the situation instantly.

'Come on - we can lift it. Who'll help me?'

No one moved. After a few seconds of silence Javert spoke.

'It's too dangerous, Monsieur. The only way to lift it is to get underneath it, and it could come down at any second. Look at it.'

In proof of his words, the cart slid a little more. The trapped man screamed again.

'Oh God, please - somebody help me!'

The Mayor took off his coat and hat and threw them onto the ground. He walked determinedly across to the cart and crouched beneath the axle, ignoring the protests of the people around him. There was a dead silence as he began to push upwards. Javert signalled to Clement and they moved warily closer to the cart, ready to pull the trapped man clear if it became possible.

Despite the cold, sweat was beginning to trickle down Monsieur Madeleine's face. His muscles were cracking with effort. Slowly the cart moved upwards, a fraction at a time. Silently praying that the Mayor could hold the weight for a moment more, Javert and Clement moved in and took hold of the man. The Mayor made one final effort, raising the cart the additional fraction that was needed. The Police Officers quickly dragged the man from under the vehicle.

'He's clear!' Javert's voice announced their success to the Mayor, who immediately relaxed his muscles and rolled free. The cart settled down with a heavy crunch.

A number of people rushed to the Mayor's assistance, helping him back to his feet. He thanked them politely, then walked over to the man who had been trapped. The man was lying on the ground, supported by Clement, whilst Javert examined his injuries.

196

'I'd say his leg's broken, but it doesn't look like too bad a break. Luckily the full weight of the cart didn't get the chance to settle on him.'

The Mayor nodded. 'Get him taken to the hospital. Tell them I'll pay his fees.'

Javert stood up, looking directly into the Mayor's eyes.

'That was a quite remarkable feat of strength, Monsieur, you undoubtedly saved the man's life.' He paused, then continued. 'I've only ever seen one other man who could have done that.'

The Mayor lifted his eyebrows. 'Oh? And who was that, Inspector?'

'A convict - in Toulon prison.'

The Mayor's eyes flickered, then steadied.

'That's very interesting, Inspector, but hardly relevant. Now if you'll excuse me, I have things to do. Good day.'

He nodded briefly then walked back across the square towards his office. Javert's eyes followed him thoughtfully. He remembered vividly that day at Toulon, when the convict had lifted the heavy stone to free André and the other man trapped beneath it. Today's rescue had been almost identical - the strength, the method of lift, everything. And he had glimpsed that moment of uneasiness in the Mayor's eyes. Already Javert was thinking ahead to his next course of action. This time, he felt certain he was right.

Chapter 22

Javert was in thoughtful mood on the way back to the Police Post. He was now certain in his own mind that Monsieur Madeleine was none other than the convict Valjean, but at the moment the man was still the Mayor. Javert hesitated to arrest someone of such exalted status without higher authority. After some consideration he decided that his best course of action would be to lay his suspicions - or rather his certainties - before his superiors. That meant a trip to Arras.

He checked the time. It was past two o'clock and the Arras coach would already have left. That was of little importance - he had his horse. But in the meantime, the Mayor needed to be watched; it had been a mistake to mention Toulon to him, it had alerted him to Javert's suspicions. He opened the door of his office and called to Clement.

The man hurried in immediately. He had known Javert for over two years and had never known him to be in such a bad humour as he was now.

Javert addressed him abruptly.

'I have to go to Arras immediately. In the meantime I have a job for yourself and Dubois, an important job. I want you to put your ordinary clothes on so you're not so visible, and I want you to keep a permanent watch on the Mayor's residence.'

Clement gaped at him. 'I'm sorry Monsieur?'

'You heard me! I said keep a permanent watch on the Mayor. You can use my lodgings as a vantage point, there's a good view from there.'

'Er - yes Monsieur. But why?'

'I'll tell you that when I get back. Just do it.'

'Well, of course Monsieur, but what if the Mayor does leave his residence?'

Javert hesitated. He could hardly tell the young officer to arrest the Mayor when he was reluctant to take such a responsibility himself.

'Follow him if you can, otherwise try to find out where he's going. At the very least, note the way he goes. I should be back by tomorrow evening.'

He picked up his hat and headed for the door, but was interrupted by Clement.

'Monsieur Javert, when you say permanent watch, you don't mean right through the night as well?'

'I mean especially right through the night.'

'Oh, but - you realise Dubois is away?'

Javert stopped, he had forgotten that. Dubois was absent for the next two days, attending his brother's funeral in Paris. He thought for a moment, then turned back to Clement.

'You'll have to do it on your own. All right, you'll be tired, but you can catch up on your sleep when I get back.' He pointed his stick towards Clement. 'And Clement, this is important. If the Mayor leaves without you seeing him go, you'll be in a lot of trouble. Understand?'

Clement sighed. 'Yes Monsieur, I'll stay awake.'

Javert nodded to him curtly and strode out of the post and into the adjoining stables. Montreuil was a small town and it was rarely necessary to ride, so there was just the one horse between the three of them. Usually the animal was exercised by Clement, the only one of the three who really enjoyed riding.

Javert made good time to Arras, but was still too late to see the Commissaire that evening. He spent a restless night, haunted by visions of Valjean sneaking out of his residence and taking the road, whilst Clement slept. Perhaps he should have arrested the Mayor on his own authority? But he knew there would have been hell to pay had he proved to be wrong.

Early the following morning he presented himself at the Commissaire's office. The Commissaire was surprised to see him, but greeted him cordially.

'Inspector Javert, come in - take a seat. You're very early.'

'I got here last night Monsieur, I was just too late to see you then.'

'So you've caught me as early as you can today? You'd better tell me what the problem is.'

'I have reason to believe that there is an escaped convict in Montreuil-Sur-Mer. A parole breaker, by the name of Jean Valjean.'

The Commissaire looked surprised. 'Well Inspector, if you think that, why don't you arrest the man?'

'Because the man also happens to be the town Mayor.'

The Commissaire gave an incredulous gasp.

'What! Inspector Javert, are you certain of that?'

'Yes Monsieur.' Javert explained the full story to the Commissaire, from his first encounter with the Mayor through to the happenings of the previous day.

'So you see Monsieur, it all fits. Even to the time of the man's arrival in Montreuil, seven years ago.'

The Commissaire expelled his breath soundlessly.

'Well, it certainly seems to fit, but to arrest the town Mayor - You were certainly right to seek guidance on this one.'

He sat and thought for a moment, then stood up decisively.

'The Prefect should be in this morning - I'm going to drop this on his toes. Wait here Inspector, I shouldn't be long.'

He left the room. Javert stood up and paced about moodily, frustrated by the delay.

Half an hour passed before the Commissaire returned. Javert turned eagerly at his entrance, then froze at the expression on his face. The Commissaire looked frankly furious.

'Inspector Javert, you are in a lot of trouble!'

Javert looked at him in confusion.

'I'm sorry Monsieur, I don't understand you.'

'I've just come back from the Prefect's office. He wasn't there, but his aide was. It may interest you to know that the convict Jean Valjean was arrested yesterday. Here, in Arras.'

Javert looked thunderstruck.

'What!'

'Jean Valjean has been arrested. He's in custody now and he'll stand trial the day after tomorrow.'

'But - forgive me Monsieur, but are you sure?'

The Commissaire regarded Javert stonily.

'Oh yes, I'm sure. The man has been identified by no less than three other convicts who knew him personally.'

Javert leaned forward.

'Can I see him Monsieur?'

'No you can't!' the Commissaire exploded. 'For God's sake man, what's the matter with you? You're clutching at straws rather than admit you're in the wrong. What in heavens name do you think you're doing?'

Javert took a deep breath, his thoughts in a turmoil. The Commissaire continued.

'You've behaved in an extremely unprofessional manner, to say the least - coming here and accusing a man of Monsieur Madeleine's status of something like this. It seems to me as if you've let a personal vendetta affect your judgment. I must say I'm extremely disappointed Javert, I'd expected better from you. Are you listening to me?'

'Yes Monsieur.'

The Commissaire seated himself behind his desk and regarded Javert coldly.

'There's a report about this matter waiting on the Prefect's desk. I've no more to say to you, but I suspect that he will have a great deal to say. All right, you can return to your duties - for the time being.'

Javert left the office and walked out into the street in a daze. Automatically his feet carried him to the river. He walked out onto the bridge and stared absently down at the swirling water below. He simply couldn't believe the news he had just heard; he had been so sure.

He considered the interview he had just had with the Commissaire. No less than three people had positively identified the convict Valjean, surely they could not all be mistaken. No, he had to accept that it was he who was wrong. Could the Commissaire be right? Had he allowed his own personal anger and frustration to cloud his judgment to such an extent?

Javert felt a wave of shame wash over him. He, who prided himself on his objectivity, had wrongly accused an innocent man out of pique. It must be so, nothing else could account for what had happened. Had one of his men done such a thing, Javert would have dismissed him on the spot - not for making a mistake, but for lack of integrity in putting his own feelings before his duty.

Javert realised that there was a very real possibility he himself might be dismissed. If so, he deserved no better; but what to do now? There was only one proper course of action -

although it would not undo what had happened. He must go straight to the Mayor, confess what he had done and accept whatever punishment the Mayor thought fit.

His mind made up, Javert left the bridge and proceeded with firm steps to the stables where he had left his horse. With no further delay, he took the road out of Arras.

Javert arrived back at Montreuil-Sur-Mer in the late afternoon. Clement was still on watch at his lodgings.

'The Mayor's in his residence, Monsieur. He hasn't been out at all, except just to walk round the square.'

'All right Clement, you can go.'

'Yes Monsieur. Er - do you still want me to keep doing double shifts?'

Javert looked at him. The man looked exhausted. On the other hand, Javert knew there was a real likelihood that he himself would have to return to Arras within the next day or so, to face an irate Prefect. He could not afford to have no–one on duty during that time.

He nodded curtly. 'Yes, until Dubois gets back.'

He dismissed the man without further explanation. When he had left, Javert cleaned the dust of travel off his uniform and boots and went straight to the Mayor's residence. The Mayor greeted him politely but coldly.

'Yes Inspector, what can I do for you?'

Javert saluted him smartly. Squirming inside with humiliation, he forced himself to come straight to the point.

'Monsieur, I've come to offer you an apology.'

The Mayor looked at him blankly.

'Apology? May I ask what for?'

Javert drew a deep breath.

'Monsieur Madeleine, I fear I've done you a great injustice. When I first met you, you reminded me strongly of a man I once knew. Please forgive me Monsieur; he was a convict, in Toulon prison.'

The Mayor raised his eyebrows. 'Oh?'

'Yes Monsieur. You - resemble him greatly in looks and build, he was a very strong man. He once rescued two men from under a heavy stone slab, very much as you rescued Monsieur Fauchlevent. I was convinced you were him.'

'Well, now you seem to be happy that I'm not. I don't really see there's any harm done.'

'You don't understand Monsieur, I've just returned from Arras. I went there to denounce you to the Prefect and to demand a warrant for your arrest.'

The Mayor's head jerked up and for a second Javert was certain he saw fear in the man's eyes. Javert continued.

'While I was in Arras, I learnt that Valjean had just been re-arrested. I understand he was identified by a number of men who knew him personally, so there's no possibility of a mistake.'

He looked down for a moment, then continued.

'I suppose I must have let personal feelings affect my judgment. I can't undo what I've done, Monsieur - I can only apologise.'

The Mayor stood up and walked over to the window, looking out over the square. He spoke without turning round.

'Tell me, when does - Valjean - come to trial?'

'Thursday morning, Monsieur.'

'And the likely sentence?'

'Well - of course I can't be sure of that, but the outlook isn't good for him. He's wanted for highway robbery, he's broken parole and he's got a history of violence and escape attempts. All those things will go against him. I'll be surprised if he doesn't get life.'

'I see.'

The Mayor turned back from the window and Javert saw that the colour had drained from the man's face. He remembered the fear he had glimpsed a moment before and once again his suspicions flared. He crushed them ruthlessly, angry with himself.

'I'll offer my resignation of course Monsieur.'

The Mayor looked at him with an unfathomable expression.

'There's no need for that, anyone can make a mistake. Sometimes we haven't seen eye to eye, but you've always done your job - efficiently. And now Inspector, I hope you'll forgive me but I have an urgent appointment.'

Javert saluted again and left the office. His emotions as he walked down the stairs were mixed. He felt both irritated and relieved that the Mayor had let him off so lightly; it was typical of the man's clemency. But deep down something was still disturbing him. Try as he might, he still couldn't rid himself of his suspicion that Monsieur Madeleine was not what he seemed.

The next mail coach carried a letter for Javert from the Prefect at Arras, demanding his attendance at noon on the following day. The tone of the letter was curt in the extreme. Javert had been expecting the summons, but all the same his heart sank. The Mayor had not demanded his resignation, but he feared the Prefect might be less forgiving. In any case, he felt compelled to at least offer to resign.

He took the road to Arras at first light on the following morning, arriving at the Prefect's office shortly before midday. The aide ushered him into the Prefect's presence.

The Prefect was pre-occupied with some documents as Javert entered. He looked up briefly and waved towards a chair.

'Inspector Javert, sit down. I won't be a moment.'

Javert sat down stiffly, surprised that he had been invited to do so. After a few minutes the Prefect put aside the documents. He looked across at Javert and smiled.

'Well, Inspector. I must admit that when I first sent for you I had the fire lit and the spit turning, ready to roast you. Now I feel more inclined to give you a commendation. You appear to be the only person who's been seeing things clearly.'

Javert looked at him in amazement.

'I'm sorry Monsieur, I'm afraid I don't understand what you mean.'

'I mean that you were right. The Mayor of Montreuil-Sur-Mer and Jean Valjean are indeed one and the same.'

Javert looked incredulous.

'What! But - I thought Valjean had been arrested in Arras. He'd been positively identified, I was told.'

'Yes. Well, as it turns out he'd also been wrongly identified.'

'Are you sure, Monsieur?'

'Oh yes, we're completely sure. The man who calls himself Monsieur Madeleine turned up at the trial this morning and confessed who he really was. There's absolutely no doubt, he even showed his brand. So you see Javert, you were right all the time.'

Javert was beginning to recover from his shock.

'Where's Valjean now?'

'He left immediately he'd confessed who he was. The place was in uproar, and he just walked out. Before he went, he said we'd be able to find him at his house in Montreuil. I must admit I'll be surprised if he does go back there, but just in case...'

He held out a document. Javert took it and examined the contents, it was a warrant for the arrest of Monsieur Madeleine, alias Jean Valjean.

'You want me to arrest him?'

'If he's there, yes.' He smiled again. 'After what's just happened, I think you deserve the pleasure.'

Javert left the Prefect's office with confusion and triumph struggling for mastery in his mind. Confusion because he could not understand what had prompted the Mayor to confess his real identity, knowing - as he must know - what it would mean. Triumph because he had been proved right after all.

He thought back over his encounters with Valjean. The ignominy of being left sprawled unconscious on the stones of Toulon harbour; the irritations of the past two years when 'Monsieur Madeleine' had constantly frustrated his efforts to deal properly with miscreants; worst of all, the humiliation of the Fantine affair and his self-abasement of the day before.

Still, all that was behind him now. His eight year hunt was up at last, the hound had finally run the fox to earth. Soon he would fulfil his dream of putting Valjean behind bars. Providing of course that the convict was still there.

Javert hurried down to the stable block and ordered his horse to be saddled. Within fifteen minutes of leaving the

Prefect's office he was heading back towards Montreuil-Sur-Mer, travelling at a brisk trot.

Chapter 23

Dusk was falling when Javert arrived back at Montreuil-Sur-Mer and Clement was just preparing to go off duty. Javert stopped him.

'When is Dubois due back?'

'Tomorrow morning Monsieur, quite early.'

'All right. I'm sorry Clement, but I'm afraid it's likely you'll have to stay on tonight. In the meantime I want you to get together an escort of four men.'

'What - now Monsieur?'

'Yes, now. I have to make an arrest, and the man concerned could cause some trouble.'

'Oh - yes Monsieur.'

Clement hurried out to raise the necessary men from amongst the volunteers who formed the town militia when it was necessary to do so. Javert waited impatiently for his return. He still had a vivid memory of the time Valjean had made his escape attempt at Toulon Garrison, and he was taking no chances this time.

When the guards finally arrived Javert briefed them carefully. Two of them were to cover the entrance to the Mayor's residence. The remaining two were to wait at the foot of the stairs, in case assistance was needed in escorting Valjean to the lock-up.

His arrangements made, Javert proceeded to the Mayor's residence. The clerk looked at him in surprise when he entered.

'Can I help you Monsieur?'

'Yes - where's the Mayor?'

'I think he's at the hospital, Monsieur. He's visiting the - er - the lady he saved from - that is, the lady you had a bit of trouble with last week.'

Javert frowned; the man had obviously heard about the confrontation between himself and the Mayor. Probably half the town knew about it. Well, they'd have something more to talk about soon.

He nodded curtly to the clerk, then walked out and called to the men from the escort. The public hospital was only a stone's throw away, on the other side of the square. At the hospital, he positioned two men outside the rear entrance, then walked into the hospital with the other two. The elderly woman who acted as conciergerie greeted him without surprise; she sometimes had cause to call for the police, and Javert was no stranger to her.

'Is the Mayor here?' Javert wasted no time on pleasantries.

'Yes Monsieur, he's with Madamoiselle Fantine.'

'Where?'

'In one of the private rooms Monsieur - upstairs, turn left and it's room three.'

Javert turned to the men from the escort. 'You two, wait here.'

He walked up the stairs. At the entrance to room three he was met by Sister Simplice, one of the nuns who ran the hospital.

'Inspector - can I help you?'

'Thank you sister, but no. I've come to see Monsieur Madeleine.'

"Oh, I'm sorry Monsieur - I'm not sure if the Mayor can see you now. He's with Fantine.'

Javert grunted in disgust at the thought of the prostitute being permitted to stay in the private wing of the hospital, being nursed like royalty. He made to enter the room, but the sister stepped firmly in front of him.

'I'm sorry Monsieur, but the woman is very ill - dying, I fear. I don't think you should go in there Monsieur, but if you'd like to wait a few moments, I'll tell him you're here.'

Javert stopped and regarded her for a moment. She was a representative of the church and as such he had a great deal of respect for her, but he had no intention of letting her balk him now. He spoke to her politely, but in a tone that brooked no argument.

'Please stand aside sister, I'm on official police business.'

He took her arm and led her to one side. Then he pushed open the door and entered quietly.

The room was large and airy, with ornate carvings on the woodwork and an impressive collection of broadswords and rapiers decorating one wall. It was, he thought sourly, probably the best room in the hospital. The woman Fantine was in bed on the far side. Valjean was seated by the bed, talking to her softly. He evidently hadn't heard Javert's silent entrance.

Javert closed the door with a decisive click. The sound caused Valjean to turn.

For a moment he looked startled, then resigned.

'I didn't think it would take you long to get here.'

The woman on the bed tried to sit up, looking to see who was speaking. She gave a gasp of terror when she recognised Javert. Valjean pushed her gently back against the pillows.

'Don't worry, it's all right. He hasn't come for you.'

Javert took a pace forward.

'No - I've come for you!'

Fantine gasped again, clutching at Valjean's hand.

'Monsieur Mayor, what is it? What's wrong?'

Javert looked at her coldly.

'He isn't the Mayor any more, he's a convict named Jean Valjean. I'm afraid you've lost your protector.'

Again the woman tried to sit up, clinging to Valjean in fear.

'I don't understand. Cosette - what about Cosette?'

She looked fearfully from Valjean to Javert. Her voice was thready and weak, little more than a whisper. Valjean held her gently.

'Don't worry, it's all just a misunderstanding. I'll look after Cosette, I promise you.'

Fantine gazed up at him.

'She's at Montfermeil, at the Thénardiers' inn. You'll fetch her? You promise?'

'I swear it to you. I'll take care of her.'

Fantine nodded. Her grip on Valjean tightened for a moment, then her muscles relaxed and her eyes glazed. The familiar rattle sounded in her throat. Valjean laid her back gently against the pillows then swung to face Javert. His expression was one of fury.

'Did you have to do that?'

'Do what?'

'Destroy her peace of mind like that. You could see the woman was dying, couldn't you have waited just a minute or two more? Did your big moment of glory really mean so much to you?'

Javert stepped towards him.

'I'm not arguing with you. Come with me - now!'

Valjean suddenly snatched one of the rapiers off the wall behind him and held it pointed in Javert's direction. Javert halted and stepped back again, watching Valjean warily. A thrust from such a weapon could well prove fatal.

'Killing me won't help you, I'm not so stupid as to try to arrest you on my own. There are men at the foot of the stairs and outside the window.'

'I'm not interested in killing you. Just leave me alone for a moment, that's all.'

He laid the rapier down on the foot of the bed and turned back to Fantine. Gently he closed her eyes and covered her emaciated face with the sheet. Javert stayed where he was, watching. He could have taken Valjean now, but something about the scene before him held him immobile.

After a minute Valjean stood up. His face was calm again. He ignored the sword lying on the bed and walked towards Javert, stopping two paces away.

'I've no intention of resisting arrest, but I'd like to ask a favour of you.'

Javert raised his eyebrows. Valjean continued.

'That woman has left a child behind, a little girl. I promised I'd look after her. I ask you to let me keep that promise.'

Javert shook his head. 'How can you do that now?'

'I want you to let me fetch the child and make arrangements for her to be properly cared for. After that, I'm at your service.'

Javert looked at him in utter disbelief.

'What? You can't be serious. I've hunted you for the past eight years and now you think I'm going to let you walk out of here. You'll come with me now - this minute - or I'll call the guards and have you dragged out.'

For a second the old fire burned in Valjean's eyes. Then he sighed and nodded.

'There's no need for that. I'll come with you.'

He glanced back once at Fantine, then held out his hands towards Javert, wrists together, ready to be manacled.

Javert dropped his hand to the handcuffs at his belt, then hesitated. The sensible thing would be to handcuff the man, but for some obscure reason he was reluctant to do so.

He opened the door and motioned to Valjean.

'Come on.'

Valjean looked surprised, then shrugged. He stepped forward and preceded Javert through the door. As they walked towards the head of the stairs Javert took Valjean's arm in a firm grip.

At the top of the stairs they met Sister Simplice. Valjean halted.

'May I speak to her?'

Javert hesitated, then nodded.

'Very well, just for a moment.'

Valjean spoke to her rapidly.

'Listen sister, Madamoiselle Fantine is dead.'

'Oh, the poor woman. But we expected it, Monsieur. She was too ill to recover.'

'Yes.' He reached into his pocket and took out his money, then hesitated, looking at Javert. Both of them knew that all Valjean's property would soon be seized.

'May I?'

Javert nodded curtly.

Valjean handed the money to Sister Simplice.

'Use what you need for Fantine's burial. Anything left over, do with as you will.'

The woman looked at him in confusion.

'But Monsieur Madeleine - where are you going?'

Again Valjean looked at Javert. 'I don't know.'

'But you will be back?'

'No.'

Javert tightened his grip slightly.

'Come on!' He glanced at the woman. 'Sister, if you want to speak to this man further you can visit him in the town lock-up. He'll be there overnight. Tomorrow he'll be transferred to Arras.'

He nodded stiffly and led Valjean away, leaving the Sister staring after them in stupefaction.

Javert took Valjean to the lock-up and put him in his cell. Then he turned to Clement, who was red-eyed with exhaustion.

'Stay here overnight and keep a close check on this man. I'll be back at eight o'clock in the morning to escort him to Arras. Dubois should be back by then, so you can go off duty.'

Clement looked bewildered. 'But Monsieur, he's already behind bars. He's not going anywhere.'

'Don't argue with me, just do as you're told.'

'Yes Monsieur.' Clement agreed without further argument. He already knew that his superior was verging on obsession regarding this particular prisoner. Javert himself was not aware of this, just as he was unaware how his own behaviour had changed over the past few days.

Javert returned to his lodgings, wondering why he did not feel as delighted as he had expected to feel. He kept thinking about the woman Fantine and the manner of her death, so like the death of his mother. But his mother had at least died with her mind at rest, reassured by the priest's promise that her son would be cared for. Had Fantine also died in peace, or had Javert's words and actions destroyed her serenity of mind at the moment of her death? Valjean's accusing words sounded in his mind.

'Did you have to do that - destroy her peace of mind like that? Did your big moment of glory really mean so much to you?'

His thoughts turned to Valjean. His long hunt was up at last and tomorrow he would take his quarry to Arras. He remembered the other occasions when he had escorted Valjean: to be branded with the mark that made him forever as an outcast; to spells of solitary confinement in the hole; to the Commander's office to receive the news of his extended sentence. Tomorrow he would be escorting him for the last time, to be sentenced to prison for the rest of his life.

Javert shook himself angrily. Whatever was he thinking of? He had been on the verge of feeling sympathy for these people. The man was a convict and the woman was a whore, both were the sweepings of the gutter. It was ridiculous to waste any pity over either of them.

The following morning Javert arrived at the Police Post shortly before eight o'clock. Dubois was there, and much to Javert's surprise so was Clement. Javert nodded to Dubois then spoke brusquely to Clement.

'What are you doing here? You're supposed to be looking after the lock-up.'

Clement made no immediate answer. Javert regarded him more closely. The man was pale and exhausted, but there was something more than that. He also appeared agitated to the point of fear.

Javert's tone sharpened. 'What's wrong?'

Clement looked around as if seeking a way of escape.

'Monsieur, I ...'

'Speak out man. What's wrong?'

Clement stammered for a moment, then regained control of himself.

'I'm sorry Monsieur, but the Mayor - I mean Valjean - he's escaped.'

'What!'

'He's escaped Monsieur. I checked this morning and the cell was empty. There are two bars pulled out of the mortar in the window, he must have got out that way.'

Javert rounded on him furiously.

'You were told to watch him! When did he go?'

'Well - I don't know Monsieur. I checked just a few minutes ago, and he wasn't there.'

'And before that? When was the last time you checked him?'

If it were possible, Clement looked even more unhappy.

'Around - two o'clock, Monsieur.'

Javert's voice dropped to a quiet, deadly tone.

'Are you telling me you didn't check this man for almost six hours?'

'Yes Monsieur. I'm sorry - I fell asleep.'

Javert stepped towards him. His dark eyes had a hypnotic quality, like a snake about to strike. Clement stood frozen, his face now paper white. Losing a prisoner was bad at any time, but to lose this particular prisoner! He knew that his career was at an end, Javert would undoubtedly dismiss him on the spot.

Dubois' voice interrupted the silent drama.

'Monsieur, please may I speak with you? Privately.'

'Wait!' The word was no more than a hiss.

'Now Monsieur. It's urgent!'

The tone was peremptory, verging on insubordination. Javert turned in angry surprise.

'Please forgive me, Monsieur, but it is important.'

Javert took a deep breath as he regained the self-control that he had so nearly lost. He turned back to Clement.

'You wait here. I'll deal with you in a moment.'

He walked over to his office. Dubois followed him, closing the door as he entered.

Javert folded his arms.

'Well? This'd better be important.'

'I think it is Monsieur, but first - I don't think you're going to like what I have to say. Will you listen to me, please?'

Javert nodded. 'I'll listen to you, but make it quick.'

'Yes Monsieur. It's about Clement. Are you going to dismiss him?'

Javert frowned.

'What do you think? He's just lost a prisoner through sheer neglect of duty, quite literally sleeping on the job. There's no excuse for that.'

'Forgive me Monsieur, but I think there is.'

Javert drew a breath to order Dubois out of the office, then bit his lip. He had promised the man he would listen to him.

'What excuse can there be?'

'Clement was telling me the hours he's been working. He said he spent the whole of Tuesday night and most of Wednesday watching the Mayor's residence. He worked a double shift yesterday, then he was expected to stay up all last night as well. It's too much to expect of anyone, Monsieur.'

'Are you telling me it's my fault he fell asleep?'

Dubois looked at him steadily, outwardly calm but inwardly quaking. 'Yes Monsieur, I am.'

Javert's eyes blazed at him. Dubois waited for the explosion, but it never came. Instead Javert turned away and walked over to the window. He leant his hands on the sill,

214

staring at but not seeing the street outside as he strove for the objectivity that he usually found so easy. Was Dubois right? Had Javert pushed his subordinate beyond reasonable limits, and thus contributed to his lapse? He thought back over the past three days and realised that one thing at least was true. Clement could have had almost no sleep during that time.

The street outside came into focus. The Paris coach was just halting outside the inn. On the far side of the square two prostitutes were leaning against the wall, on the lookout for any early customers. The women made him think again about Fantine.

Javert stiffened suddenly. Fantine!

His brain presented him with an image of the dying woman, lying in bed and looking up at Valjean. Her words sounded clearly in his mind's ear.

'Cosette - she's at Montfermeil, at the Thénardiers' inn.'

Javert swung back from the window and addressed Dubois.

'Go to the stables, check if the Mayor's horse is still there. Then get straight back here. And on your way out tell Clement to come in.'

Dubois started to speak, then decided not to chance it. He had already taken a grave risk saying what he had and was surprised that he had not been severely upbraided, at the very least. He hurried out to do as he had been told.

Clement entered the office quietly. He still looked drawn with fatigue, but resignation had taken over from fear.

Javert spoke to him abruptly.

'What made you fall asleep?'

'I was just so tired Monsieur, I'd had almost no sleep for three days. I suppose that and the warm room - '

'You're telling me you were exhausted because of the hours I'd made you work?'

'Well – yes, Monsieur.'

Javert took a deep breath. His mind was already leaping ahead to his plans for the re-capture of Valjean and he was finding it hard to concentrate on anything else. He forced his attention back to Clement.

'All right. I'm finding it hard to be objective towards you at present, I'll decide later exactly what to do with you. You can go.'

Clement hesitated.

'Monsieur, I know it's a bit late to say I'm sorry, but - well, anyone can make a mistake. It'll never happen again, I swear. Is there any chance you might - you might let me keep my job?'

Javert hesitated. He was back on balance now and realised that Dubois was right in what he had said, Javert himself must bear at least some of the responsibility for what had happened.

'I'm not considering dismissal, Clement, but I may well fine you. You should have told me the state you were in.'

He paused, then continued quietly.

'And I should have noticed it, so some of the responsibility is mine. You owe a lot to Dubois for having the courage to point that out to me. Now get yourself home and go to bed. Your job's safe.'

Clement flushed with relief.

'Thank you, Monsieur.'

He looked as though he wanted to say more, but thought better of it and left the office. Despite his physical exhaustion his step had considerably more spring than when he had entered.

Dubois returned shortly afterwards.

'The Mayor's horse is gone Monsieur, the ostler says it was missing when he arrived this morning. He didn't really think anything of it; Monsieur Madeleine often used to go for an early morning ride, before he started the day's business.'

'Right, go to the stables and hire an extra horse. Get your musket. Get back here. We leave in half an hour.'

'Where are we going, Monsieur?'

'Montfermeil. I'll explain as we go.'

'Yes Monsieur.' He hesitated, then continued. 'Where's Clement, Monsieur?'

'I sent him home to bed.'

'Oh! Er - have you dismissed him, Monsieur?'

Javert's tone was dry.

'No, I haven't dismissed him, and I've told him he owes that to you. You were right, some of the fault is mine. But Dubois - '

'Monsieur?'

'Don't push your luck, I won't make a habit of accepting that kind of insubordination from you. Now then, get moving and do as I've told you.'

The two officers pushed their horses hard and managed to get within four leagues of Montfermeil before halting for the night. By the time they stopped Dubois was tired out, he had already been travelling for the whole of the previous two days. Javert scarcely noticed his own fatigue. He would have preferred not to stop at all, but to go further that night would have been to risk killing the horses.

They reached Montfermeil shortly before noon on the following day. The Thénardiers' inn stood about half a league from the village, surrounded by woodland. The place looked dirty, dismal and depressing.

He trotted his horse across the muddy yard. Two little girls were playing outside the inn door; when the men dismounted the older girl walked up to them, looking up boldly into Javert's face.

'Do you want my papa?'

Javert regarded her thoughtfully. The girl looked healthy enough. Her clothes were crumpled and dirty, but perfectly adequate. She was around eight years old, the right age for Fantine's child.

'Who is your daddy?'

'He's the innkeeper,' she announced proudly.

'I see. And what's your name?'

' 'Ponine.'

Javert considered for a moment - that wasn't the name Fantine had mentioned.

'Tell me 'Ponine, do you know a little girl called Cosette?'

She wrinkled her nose at him.

'She's gone. My daddy says she's not coming back here any more.' She beamed suddenly, as if reminded of something.

'And he says I can have a new doll, because the man gave him a lot of money for her.'

Javert continued to question the little girl. The child called Cosette had apparently left the inn that very morning, with a man. He could get no further detail from the child, and eventually lost patience with her and went into the inn. As he had expected, the place was filthy, stinking of cheap wine and urine.

The innkeeper came forward to greet them. He was a small, unprepossessing individual with a face like a weasel. He smiled ingratiatingly when he saw their uniforms.

'Yes Monsieur, how can I help you?'

'With information,' responded Javert briefly. 'About the child Cosette. I want to know the exact circumstances under which she left here. What time, who with, what he gave you for her - everything.'

The man looked doubtful.

'Cosette? I don't know anyone named Cosette.'

Javert stepped up close to him, looking down from his superior height. His eyes bored into those of the innkeeper as he spoke slowly and quietly.

'Let's be clear about this, shall we? I know Cosette was living here until this morning, I know she left with a man. If you don't tell me the rest, and quickly, I promise you you'll have cause to regret it. You're a ticket of leave man, aren't you?'

The man looked uneasy, then nodded.

'Yes Monsieur, but the local police know I'm here. They let me run this inn.'

'They won't let you run it for much longer unless you cooperate with me.'

The man nodded again, now obsequiously eager to please.

'Yes, Monsieur. Well, a man came here early this morning for Cosette. He said her mother was dead, and he'd promised to take the child. So we let her go.' He looked at Javert doubtfully. 'Why, is something wrong? He seemed a proper gent.'

Javert ignored the question. 'How much did he give you?'

218

'Give me? You don't think I'd sell a child, do you?' He paused at the expression on Javert's face, then spoke again hurriedly.

'Fifteen hundred francs, Monsieur.'

Javert raised his eyebrows, wondering where Valjean had laid his hands on that kind of money. He must have stolen it from somewhere; unless of course he had secreted money away in his lodgings, in case he ever had to flee. That was the more likely option.

'What did he look like?'

'He was big. Not as tall as you, but very thick across the shoulders.'

'Age?'

'Oh, I don't know, Monsieur. About fifty I suppose, perhaps a bit more.'

Javert nodded. He had heard enough to establish that the man was indeed Jean Valjean.

'When did they leave? And how?'

'Oh, early Monsieur. He got here just after ten o'clock and he was gone again by half past. He had a horse.'

'Which way did they go.'

'Towards Paris.'

Javert turned to go, then swung back towards Thénardier.

'If we meet again, don't waste my time playing games. And if you ever see or hear of that man again, you get word to the police immediately. Understand?'

'Yes Monsieur. But - who is he?'

'He's an ex-convict named Valjean, and he's wanted for robbery and parole breaking.'

The innkeeper looked amazed.

'Well, who'd have thought it - he acted like such a toff. Had a bit of money about him too. I'll report it straight away if I see him, Monsieur.'

The innkeeper suddenly found he was talking to the air. Javert and Dubois had already mounted their horses and were cantering in the direction of Paris. At the pace they were travelling, the city was less than a two hour ride from Montfermeil. Given the start Valjean had, Javert did not really expect to catch up with him.

Nor did he. They checked every inn, every passer by who might conceivably have seen the man and the child, riding double on one horse. They received two positive sightings between Montfermeil and Paris, but when they reached the capital their luck ran out. Valjean and the child had disappeared without trace, swallowed up by the huge city. Once again, the trail was cold.

Chapter 24
Paris 1832

Javert stopped and wiped the sweat from his forehead, feeling hot and sticky in his heavy uniform. He had been in Paris for only two days, and already he missed the sea breezes of Montreuil.

Javert had been recalled to the capital at the request of the new Prefect of Paris, Monsieur Gisquet. Less than two years ago, yet another revolution had removed King Charles X and replaced him with Louis-Philippe, but the change did not appear to have affected either the running of the country or the ugly mood of the populace. Now cholera was sweeping through the slums of the City, making the people even more restless. Monsieur Gisquet wanted a strong police presence.

Javert glanced at the large clock on the front of the Chatelet, he still had an hour before he needed to report for duty. Impulsively he turned away and headed down the road that led to the Café Gerard. He half expected to see Michelle, but the young woman in charge was a stranger to him.

'Good morning Monsieur, what can I get for you.'

'Nothing, thank you, I was wondering if Monsieur Gerard still lived here.'

'Well, no Monsieur. It still belongs to his family, to his grand-daughter. But Monsieur Gerard, I'm afraid he died two months ago.'

For a moment Javert felt shocked; yet the news should not have come as a surprise. After all, Monsieur Gerard had been getting on in years, he must have been well over seventy.

The young woman asked him to wait, then disappeared through the door that led to the stairs. A few moments later she returned, accompanied by Michelle.

Michelle looked momentarily astonished, then came forward quickly.

'Vere, this is a surprise! I didn't know you were back in Paris.'

'Only just. I've been here two days.'

Michelle took his arm.

221

'Come and sit down outside, it's too stuffy in here. I'll get you a drink, then you can tell me all your news. If you've got time of course.'

Javert sat down and accepted the offered drink. He hadn't seen Michelle for many years, not since his request to pay court to her had been unequivocally rejected by her mother. He was surprised at the turmoil of emotion he felt at seeing her again.

'I'm afraid I haven't long, I have to be at work soon.' He hesitated. 'I've just heard about your grandfather - I'm very sorry.'

She shook her head. 'He was nearly eighty, Vere, and he hadn't been getting about so well lately. He wasn't ill, just old. He died peacefully enough, in his sleep. That's all any of us can hope for.'

Javert nodded and looked down at the table, swirling his wine round the cup.

'And you? How are you?'

'I'm all right.' She hesitated, then continued. 'It's been a long time, Vere.'

'Almost eleven years.'

'Yes.'

'Michelle, are you – did you ever marry?'

'Yes, Vere. I have a son now, he's almost eight years old.' She smiled sadly. 'I called him Philippe, after his grandfather.'

For a moment they sat in silence, their thoughts on the original Philippe. Then Michelle spoke again.

'And you Vere? How long have you been back in Paris?'

'Just two days. They're increasing the manpower here, to deal with these darned insurrectionists.'

Michelle was silent for a moment, then she threw back her head and looked him squarely in the eye.

'Vere, you might as well know that I have every sympathy with these insurrectionists, as you call them. And they're not all young students, a lot of older people support them as well. My own husband fought with the commune in the last uprising.'

'Well, if you don't want to be a widow you'd better tell him to keep out of it this time - and to keep his views to himself.'

Michelle shrugged. 'I can't ask him to be less than he is, and in any case I agree with him. Things'll never change unless

222

some people have the courage to challenge the status quo. You say he should lose those views, but I think we need more people like him, willing to stand up and fight for what they believe in.'

Javert stared at her, this was a different Michelle. She might have changed comparatively little outwardly, but the frivolous girl had vanished, to be replaced by a serious and mature woman. But she was, apparently, still as strong-minded and determined as ever. Javert felt a tremor of unease at what might happen if she allowed herself to become involved in the rebellion. He leaned forward.

'Michelle, listen to me. I remember when I first came to Paris as a youngster - the filth, the starvation, the disease. I lived amongst it, remember? You go to the slums now and look at the conditions, tell me what's changed! Things are no different now.'

Michelle looked bewildered. 'So you're agreeing with me?'

Javert grunted in irritation.

'No, I'm not agreeing with you. Look around you - things are following just the same pattern now as they did forty years ago. The same blind belief that everything is going to be different, and soon there'll be the same disillusionment when they realise nothing's changed. Nothing will ever change. The ordinary people can't help themselves, they're just not capable of it. What do you want, a bloodbath like the one we lived through when I was a boy? What did all the deaths and the bloodshed achieve? Come on Michelle, try to face reality.'

His tone had become increasingly irate. Michelle looked at him in surprise, this was a side of Javert that she had never seen. Her mother had been wrong about Javert's lack of feeling; she had just glimpsed a little of the passion he kept hidden below the surface, and her instincts told her that there was a great deal more. She suddenly had another thought - was it possible that some of that anger was born of concern for her?

'You really think it's dangerous, supporting the commune?'

'I know it is. Listen Michelle, this time the commune can't win. The National Guard are a strong force, and the new prefect's a man to be reckoned with. Any rebellion will be crushed, ruthlessly. Keep out of it, and tell your husband to do the same.'

Michelle looked doubtful.

'Well, I'll talk to him, but I'm afraid he won't listen. He's very idealistic, and I must say I think - '

She broke off suddenly, leaping up from her chair.

'Hey, you little devil, stop that!'

Javert spun round, in time to see a young street urchin jumping back from the fruit stall where he had been helping himself. Michelle's shout had startled him into dropping the ripe peach he was holding: it landed on the pavement with a juicy squelch.

Javert leapt up and the boy turned to run. His foot came down on the slippery fruit and he skidded precariously, almost overbalancing. He recovered quickly, but the slip had cost him his chance of escape. He had gone only a few paces when Javert's hand closed on the back of his collar, lifting him off his feet.

Holding the boy by the collar and one arm, he dragged him back to the café where Michelle stood waiting. She looked at him uneasily, wishing she hadn't drawn his attention to the boy. She knew how inflexible Javert was when it came to his job, and she didn't want the child to go to prison for stealing a few pieces of fruit.

Javert had started to question the boy.

'What's your name?'

'Gavroche.'

Javert regarded him grimly. He was just another Paris street urchin, about ten years old, wearing a pair of men's trousers cut short and tied up with string and a tattered canvas coat that fell down almost to his feet. The boy looked boldly back at Javert. There was no fear in his eyes, only a roguish twinkle.

'Right then Gavroche, you can come with me - '

He broke off with a gasp of pain as the urchin suddenly reached his free hand between Javert's legs and squeezed as hard and sharply as he could. For a vital second Javert relaxed his grip on the boy's arm. The next moment he found himself holding nothing but the tattered coat, whilst Gavroche raced away at top speed.

Javert made a move to chase the boy, then stopped. Gavroche was already at the corner, and once he had reached the maze of alleys that lay beyond, pursuit was a waste of time.

Javert leaned against the table for a moment, the sudden pain had brought beads of sweat out on his forehead. Michelle approached him uncertainly.

'Are you all right?'

Javert swore under his breath, looking at the empty coat in his hand. Then, unexpectedly, he gave a bark of laughter.

'Well, fancy letting myself get caught with that trick - I must be getting old. Sorry Michelle, I'm afraid he's well gone.'

She shook her head.

'I didn't want you to arrest him anyway, not just for a few pieces of fruit. Are you sure you're all right?'

He nodded and straightened up.

'Yes. But Michelle, I must go - I'm on duty soon.'

For a moment they looked at each other, each wanting to say more, but not knowing the words. Then he touched his hat in salute and strode away down the street.

Javert reported for duty, then headed back towards the river. The meeting with Michelle had left him feeling uncharacteristically unsettled; it had reminded him of times gone by and dreams he thought had died long ago. Suddenly his future seemed lonely and uninviting. All his adult life he had lived only for his job; it was all he had, his reason for existence. But he was getting older, sooner or later he would no longer have the job. What would he do then?

He leaned his elbows on the parapet and gazed down at the concentric circles of light and shade that were peculiar to this river. Memories of Philippe and Michelle haunted his mind. It was perhaps not surprising that he should remember them so vividly; they and his mother were the only people in his life who had ever shown him love and affection. But his mother had died when he was very young. His mental picture of her had blurred over the years, whereas the images of Michelle and Philippe were still sharp and clear.

The sound of running footsteps accompanied by a sudden shout jerked him back to the present. He turned towards the sound and his heart jolted in sudden shock - he seemed to be face to face with Philippe.

For a moment Javert thought he was in the midst of a waking dream. Then his heartbeat steadied and he looked more closely at the young man before him. Of course it wasn't Philippe, but there was a strong resemblance. The young man in front of him was about twenty years old, the age Philippe had been when he was killed. He had the same build, the same eyes; allowing for changes in fashion, even the same style of dress. The hair was perhaps a little lighter than Philippe's.

Javert pulled himself together. The young man seemed agitated about something, he was badly out of breath and speaking as rapidly as he could. The result was an almost incoherent jumble of words. Javert held up his hand.

'Slow down young man, I can't understand you when you gabble on so fast; one thing at a time. Now then, who are you?'

'Marius. Marius Pontmercy.'

'And what's the problem, Marius?'

'Robbery! There's going to be a robbery. I heard them planning it.'

'Where and when?'

'This afternoon. Soon – now! At the Gorbeau Tenement. That's in – '

'I know where it is! Come on – we'll collect some men from the Chatelet and you can tell me the rest as we go.'

Javert's cool and matter of fact approach seemed to have a calming effect on Marius. He took a deep breath and began to speak more coherently.

I'm a law student and I have rooms at the Gorbeau Tenement. The man in the room next to me is the one setting up this robbery.'

'Who is he? What's his name?'

Marius shook his head. 'I don't know. He lives there with his wife and two daughters, but we don't have anything to do with each other. He's a skinny, dirty little man with a face like a rat. His wife's a big woman – she'd make two of him - with a real bird's nest of ginger hair. He's got a gang he runs about with. I don't know all of them, but there's a man called Brujon

- big man, running to fat - and a little dandy named Montparnesse.'

'I know them!' said Javert shortly. He did indeed know them, as two of the biggest villains in the city. If this neighbour of Marius's was mixed up with them, Javert very much wanted to meet him. He quickened his pace, now more inclined to take the young student's story seriously. 'Keep talking.'

'Well, this neighbour of mine seems to make a living from swindling people out of money. His daughter dropped a pile of letters this morning and I found them on the stairs. I was taking them back to him, but when I got near the door I heard him talking to his gang, about tricking some old man into coming to the house this afternoon. He said something like 'that old bastard's got money and I'm due a good share of it. We'll invite him in nicely, but he won't get out so easy!' And he said to make sure there was a good fire and to get his knife ready. They mean him some harm, Monsieur Javert, I think they mean to torture him for money!'

They had reached the Chatelet. Javert signed Marius to wait and disappeared into the building, to emerge some ten minutes later accompanied by two sergeants armed with swords and eight police officers with heavy sticks. They set off once more for the Gorbeau Tenement.

'How did this neighbour of yours persuade the victim to present himself so conveniently?' asked Javert. 'The area around the Gorbeau tenement is notoriously bad – I wouldn't have thought anyone with any sense would have gone there on his own.'

'The letters,' said Marius. 'When I looked at them they were all begging letters. Addressed to different people, signed with a different name, but all the same writing. From what my neighbour said, the old man has been to the address before, bringing money.'

The streets were becoming increasingly mean and run down; it was an area Javert knew only too well, from his boyhood in Paris. Little seemed to have changed; the buildings were derelict hovels and there was still an all pervading stink of rotting refuse and sewage.

'What are you doing here?' asked Javert abruptly.

227

Marius looked confused. 'I beg your pardon?'

'Why are you living here, in a slum like this? You might be a student, but you're no bourgeois; you were raised a gentleman!'

'Yes, well, this gentleman's family have disowned him.' Marius's tone was bitter.

They were now nearing the Gorbeau tenement. Javert held up his hand to halt the accompanying men, then divided them up.

'You two, go round the block and come in from the other side. You four, get round the back but keep out of sight. Give us five minutes, then show yourselves cautiously. That will give us time to get into position. Marius? You'd better stay here, in case it gets rough.'

'I'm not afraid.' Marius's tone was both aggrieved and defiant.

Javert shrugged. 'Just as you like, but keep out of the way.'

They moved cautiously down the street, keeping close to the walls of the buildings. Marius touched Javert's arm.

'Third window along – the pane is broken.'

Javert stopped short of the window. There was a murmur of voices from within the room, but nothing intelligible. Then came a cry from the back of the building.

'Police – quick, leg it.'

There were incoherent shouts from within the room. A man's leg appeared over the nearby window sill, only to vanish again as he was apparently pulled back.

'Wait your hurry!'

'Why the devil should you go first? We all need to scarper – '

'Maybe you'd like to draw lots – I'll put them in my bloody hat!'

A predatory smile spread over Javert's face; the mice were neatly caught in the trap.

'You're welcome to borrow my hat!' he offered.

He strolled into the room, followed by his men. In the far corner he caught a glimpse of an elderly, white haired individual – presumably Marius's 'old man' - who was tied to some kind of truckle bed. Kneeling next to him and tugging

228

vainly at the ropes was a woman, young and well dressed. There were three other men in the room – Brujon and two others who he hadn't seen before – and a big, red haired woman.

'Stay where you are, and keep calm,' suggested Javert. 'You're well out-numbered, believe me.'

He glanced around. Marius had followed him into the room and was now by the bed, apparently comforting the young woman and helping her to free the old man. Another police officer came in, dragging a sullen young woman with him.

'This one tried to raise the alarm, sir.'

A shout of 'ware' from one of his men caused Javert to swing round and duck, just in time to avoid a chunk of broken paving slab, which flew over his head and shattered against the wall. He found himself facing the red haired woman. She was indeed formidable, large and muscular, her hair a tangled mane. Having heaved the slab, she had snatched up a cudgel dropped by one of the gang and was squaring up to Javert with bared teeth - the snarl of a vixen defending its mate.

He moved towards her and she swung the cudgel wildly at his head. He ducked and closed with her, getting under her guard. He caught her wrist and wrenched it violently. She gave a scream of pain, dropped the cudgel, then turned and clawed for his face; she was a strong woman and he controlled her with some difficulty. He forced her down onto the dirt floor, pulling her arms behind her and kneeling on her back. She finally seemed to realise the hopelessness of further resistance and allowed him to handcuff her with sullen passivity.

Javert pulled her up and turned to survey the other prisoners, all of whom were now standing in a line, handcuffed to each other. He stiffened in sudden recognition.

Small and thin, with a face like a rat; Marius's description had been a good one. Javert's mind took him back nine years to the inn at Montfermeil, where the prostitute Fantine's daughter had been living. This man was the former innkeeper, Thénardier.

Thénardier recognised him at the same time. His eyes widened. He began to gabble.

229

'Oh - it's you! Listen Monsieur, I ...'

Javert cut him short. 'Be quiet!'

'But Monsieur, you said ...'

'Be quiet! You'll get your chance to speak soon.'

One of the officers nudged Thénardier with his stick, not gently. The man lapsed into sullen silence.

Javert turned to Marius.

'Can you identify these men?'

Marius pointed to Thénardier.

'Him, certainly, he's the one I was telling you about. The big man is Brujon and the other man I've seen with him before; the red haired woman's his wife.'

He nodded towards the woman whom the police officer had caught, the one who had raised the alarm. She was quite young, certainly less than twenty years old.

'That one's his daughter Eponine, I don't think she was involved in it.'

Javert looked at her more closely. Of course, 'Ponine, the young girl he had questioned at the inn when he was looking for the child Cosette. He grunted.

'She was on guard, she raised the alarm. I call that being involved.'

He turned round to speak to the victim of the robbery, then stopped in surprise. The man was nowhere to be seen. He looked at Marius.

'Where has he gone? Did you see?'

Marius looked equally surprised.

'No. He was here a minute ago. I was talking to his daughter, at least I suppose that's who she was.'

Javert looked round in puzzlement, wondering why the victim had left so abruptly. Something was niggling at the back of his mind; it had been there ever since he walked into the room and saw the old man tied to the bed; the set of the head, the breadth of shoulder. He had already guessed the terrible truth, even before Thénardier began to speak again.

'You won't see him for dust! He's a ticket of leave man, same as I am, he's not about to hang around. I've been trying to tell you, but you wouldn't listen. He's the one who took Cosette away that morning, before you come to the inn.'

230

Javert swore under his breath, then motioned to his officers.

'You four, take these men and women and get them under lock and key. The rest of you, come with me.'

Four of the men led the line of prisoners away, whilst the others obediently accompanied Javert. He hurried back towards the heart of Paris, questioning passers-by as they went. The first person he asked had seen the big man and the girl. People he asked subsequently had not.

Javert divided his men and instructed them as to what areas they should search, whilst he himself began to check the maze of alleys where he had once lived with André. He knew from bitter experience how quickly a man could disappear in a city like Paris, and he had little real hope that they would find Valjean.

Nor did they. Eventually Javert was forced to acknowledge the hopelessness of the task and call off the search. Once again he had lost his quarry. Maybe Thenardier knew where he lived, but Javert was under no illusions about that. Valjean was pre-warned now; he would leave his lodgings and go on the run. Javert was choked with frustration at having been so close, but at least he knew the man was still in Paris. He set his mouth grimly; sooner or later he was determined to run the fox to earth. Once more, the hunt was on.

Chapter 25

Following his latest encounter with Valjean, Javert returned to the Conciergerie in an ill humour. He was angry and frustrated, not with the ex-convict, but with himself. To think he had actually had his hand on the man, and still lost him.

He became even more irritated on the following day, when he discovered that he had lost not only the victim, but also the witness. Javert had been too involved in his hunt for Valjean to make proper arrangements with Marius. He enquired for him at the Gorbeau tenement, only to be told that Marius had moved out that very morning.

Javert's thoughts were gloomy as he walked slowly back to his lodgings that night. Marius had probably bolted because he feared repercussions from Thénardier and his gang. That was understandable enough, but it left Javert with neither a victim of the robbery nor a witness to the planning of it. He reflected morosely that he had little hope of proving his case under such circumstances.

His fears proved to be well founded on the following day when Thénardier and his gang appeared in court. The case of robbery was swiftly dismissed, leaving only the charge resisting arrest against Madame Thénardier. She received a sentence of one month's imprisonment. The remainder of the gang escaped with two weeks, instead of the five years Javert felt they deserved. The girl Eponine had not been involved in the actual brawl, and was released immediately. Her saucy smile and elaborate curtsy to Javert did nothing to improve his humour.

The following day, Javert commenced a spell of late duties. In the late evening he and his two subordinates crossed the river to check on the gypsy encampment that had taken up residence there in preparation for the summer fair. The headman was waiting for them at the entrance to the camp. He was a big, sombre looking individual, a few years older than Javert; the same man who had met them on Javert's first visit to the camp, more than thirty years ago. Three other men accompanied him. Javert addressed him brusquely.

'How long were you planning to stay?'

The headman regarded him impassively.

'The fair starts in a few day's time. We shall stay until the end of that, and a few weeks more. Perhaps until the end of the summer.'

Javert frowned. 'There's no question of your staying until the end of summer. Once the fair's ended, on you go.'

'We need time to pack up our wagons and dismantle the camp.'

'You can have two days, after the fair finishes. No more than that.' He pointed his stick at the headman. 'And I don't want to see you or any of your people on the other side of the river after dark - there's nothing for you there.'

The man made no reply. Javert frowned at him.

'Do you understand me?'

The headman spoke to his companions in his own language, then turned back to Javert.

'Yes inspector, I understand you perfectly.' His tone was not precisely hostile, but it was decidedly frosty. There was little love lost on either side between the police and the gypsies.

Javert gave him a curt nod, then turned on his heel and stalked away, followed by his two subordinates. It annoyed Javert that he was unable to move the gypsies on immediately, but the summer fair was a long-standing tradition, and popular with the people of Paris.

Javert paid a brief visit to the Conciergerie, then headed back for the right bank. They were crossing the Pont de Notre Dame when they saw what looked like a disturbance on the bridge, apparently involving a number of people. As they hurried closer he realised that there were two men, a woman and a young boy. The men were struggling to subdue the woman. She was fighting hard, but had no chance against two much stronger assailants. Already they had her down on her back and one of them was straddling her, whilst the other man pinned her upper body. The boy hurled himself at one of the men, but was brushed aside with ease.

Javert and his two officers raced onto the bridge. The man holding down the woman's upper body turned and saw them. He leapt up immediately, grabbing his companion by his jacket.

'Police - scarper!'

He made to run away across the bridge, but was hindered by the boy, who made a futile attempt to stop him. The man swore, picked up the boy and hurled him violently at the parapet of the bridge. The boy's legs struck the stonework, then he somersaulted head first over the side. His scream of terror was echoed by the woman.

The two men were already racing for the far side of the bridge. Without needing to be told, Javert's young officers sprinted after them, whilst Javert ran to the parapet and looked over. The boy was a few feet below him, clinging like a limpet to one of the pieces of statuary that decorated the bridge. One foot had found the narrow ledge that ran below the statuary, his other foot dangled in space. Terrified eyes looked into Javert's, pleading desperately but silently for help.

Javert swiftly examined the bridge. The stonework above the boy's head was smooth, he had no chance of climbing up unaided. Nor could he remain where he was for long, already his fingers were slipping from their precarious hold.

Javert leaned over and called down to him.

'Get your other foot on the ledge, it'll take your weight off your arms.'

The boy gazed back at him with eyes full of terror. His reply was no more than a low gasp, barely audible above the sound of the river.

'Can't - my leg - I can't move it!'

Javert swore softly, remembering the thud with which the boy had struck the stonework before plunging over the top. Next to him, the woman had regained her feet. Now she threw one leg over the parapet, obviously bent on climbing down to the boy.

Javert dragged her back.

'No! You'd have no chance. I'll get him.'

He hastily pulled off his coat and hooked one sleeve over the protrusion on the lamp-post, allowing the rest of the garment to dangle over the parapet. It should at least give him some purchase where the stone was too smooth to afford a handhold. He straddled the parapet, then gripped the coat and lowered himself cautiously down until his feet found the ledge next to the boy.

'Try to get yourself onto my back, boy. Quickly, I can't hold on like this for long.'

He heard the boy's foot scuff on the stonework, then a hand grasped his shirt by the back of the collar. Next second the boy's full weight came onto him. He felt rather than heard the coat tear, and slid helplessly further down the wall. His shirt collar yanked tight against his neck, choking him. A second later the boy's other hand closed on his hair.

Javert gasped, half strangled and with his head feeling as if his hair was being torn out by the roots. One hand lost its precious grip on the coat and he scrabbled desperately at the wall in front of him, striving to find a hold. A cold sweat broke out on his body. Javert could swim - it had been one of his rare pleasures during his boyhood in Toulon - but this particular stretch of the river was notorious for its currents. Anyone who fell in the river here rarely emerged alive.

The front of his shirt tore, relieving the strangling pressure and enabling him to speak hoarsely to the boy.

'For God's sake boy, grab my shoulders, not my hair. You'll have us both off.'

The hand let go his hair and grasped his shoulder. The fingers clutched convulsively at both the material and the skin beneath, pinching painfully. Javert managed to regain his grip on the coat and began to climb. Under their combined weight his arms felt as though they were being torn from their sockets.

Slowly but doggedly he continued to drag himself upwards, feeling like a spider hauling itself up the thread of its web. The boy was light, but his weight still tugged Javert backwards, threatening to pull both of them off the bridge. Then the weight suddenly vanished as they came within the woman's reach and she plucked the boy to safety. Javert pulled himself back onto the bridge with a gasp of thankfulness and collapsed against the parapet, recovering his breath and waiting for his heartbeat to return to something resembling normality.

After a few minutes he stood upright, examining himself ruefully. His boots were badly scuffed, his uniform coat and shirt badly torn and dusty. The nails on one hand were broken and the ends of his fingers bruised and bleeding where he had clawed at the rough stonework. His long hair blew loose about his face, the tie that had held it back lost when the boy clutched at his head.

He turned to the woman, who was leaning against the parapet, holding the boy to her. Her brightly coloured skirt was ripped and filthy and her blouse was in tatters. Seeing Javert's look, she tried to cover herself, but the blouse was too badly torn to be of any use.

To save her embarrassment, Javert turned his attention to the boy. He examined the dark eyes and hair, then looked back at the woman, noticing the style and colours of the garments she was vainly trying to piece together. With a slight sense of shock, he realised that both of them were from the gypsy encampment. The woman was watching him warily, regarding him with as much suspicion as he did her.

Javert hesitated. He did not regret his rescue, he could hardly have left her to be raped or the boy to be drowned; but he was uncertain what to do next. Had she been a lady he would have put his jacket round her and taken her home; but she was not a lady, she was only a gypsy. In any case, he was conscious of his own highly dishevelled state. Javert always liked to appear immaculate, and he wanted to change as quickly as possible.

He turned to leave, then stopped as the woman swayed unsteadily against the parapet. Her face was badly bruised where she had been hit and there were livid finger-marks on her almost bare breasts. She looked to be in a state of shock. The boy was now seated on the ground next to her, trying to ease his injured leg. The knee was swollen to twice its normal size.

With sudden decision Javert walked back to her and wrapped his torn coat round her shoulders. Then he picked up the boy.

'Come on - I'll take you back to your camp.'

She looked surprised but made no effort to refuse his help. The boy clung to his neck as they walked across the bridge. Javert felt a strange stirring of emotion. The only children he was used to holding were young street urchins and vagabonds - children he was arresting, or restraining. He was not accustomed to holding children - or indeed anyone - in a compassionate way. Last time he had carried a child like this it had been Michelle, many years ago.

He supported the woman across the bridge and down to the nearby gypsy camp that he had visited only an hour before. They were again met by the headman and a number of other men, all of whom looked wary and suspicious. A few women were also approaching. Javert felt a moment of unease; he hoped they would give the woman time to explain before they jumped to wrong and possibly dangerous conclusions.

The gypsies clustered round him. One of them took the boy from Javert's arms, whilst another wrapped the woman in a concealing shawl. She was speaking to the headman rapidly in their own language. The headman nodded, but he seemed to be only half listening. He was staring curiously at Javert.

When the woman had finished speaking she and the boy were taken to a nearby wagon. Some of the women went with them. The remainder dispersed, leaving Javert surrounded by the men. There was a feeling in the air that puzzled him. Given their past encounters he had not expected to be welcomed with open arms, but he had expected at least some show of gratitude, not this strange wariness and tension.

The headman stepped forward so he was standing within a pace of Javert. He pointed to Javert's chest.

'Where did you get that?'

For a moment Javert looked at him blankly, then looked where the headman was pointing. His torn shirt lay open almost to his waist and the medallion that was usually hidden by his clothing was clearly visible. Of course! The headman must have recognised it as a gypsy symbol.

Javert made no immediate response. The sense of threat heightened as he felt the group of men close around him.

'Did you take that medallion from one of our people?'

'I didn't take it from anyone. This belongs to me.'

'And how would a *gavver* - a policeman - come to possess such a thing?' The headman's voice was dry with disbelief.

Javert felt a spurt of anger; was this vagabond accusing him of theft? He knew that some of his colleagues were not above helping themselves to property from prisoners, but Javert prided himself on his honesty.

'If you mean did I steal it from one of you, no I didn't! This belonged to my mother; she gave it to me when she died.'

There was a subdued murmur from the gypsies as they tightened the circle round Javert, crowding him. The headman spoke to them sharply, then stepped right up to the policeman. He looked at him intently, examining his features, his hair, his eyes. Returning his stare, Javert felt the strange dislocation of time he had experienced years before, when he had visited the camp with Inspector Sancé. He seemed to be looking into the same magic mirror - only this time the mirror reflected his face not as it used to be, but as it might be in a few years time. The gypsy's eyes were identical to his own.

For what seemed like an age the headman stood stock-still, his eyes still locked on Javert. When he spoke again, his voice had lost its hostile tone.

'Your mother was a gypsy?'

Javert lifted his head defiantly as he told the headman what he had never voluntarily revealed to anyone else.

'Yes.'

The headman held out his hand.

'May I see the medallion?'

Javert closed his hand round it defensively. These people were all thieves - they weren't about to get the medallion from him without a struggle!

The headman again spoke sharply to the men clustered around them. Javert tensed himself for an attack, but instead they stepped back from him, then turned and walked away. Javert was left alone with the headman.

The gypsy spoke to him again.

'May I look at it?'

Javert unclasped his hand. The headman stepped forward and lifted the medallion, examining it closely before letting it fall back on Javert's chest.

'You say your mother gave this to you when she died. When did she die?'

'When I was nine years old, the year before the revolution. I mean the big revolution. She died of consumption.'

'Where?'

'Toulon Garrison. We lived there then.'

The headman nodded.

'I see. And your father - is he still alive?'

Javert frowned, wondering at the personal nature of the questions. But for some reason he felt compelled to answer them.

'I don't know, but I should think it unlikely. I never knew my father. He was a convict who was sentenced to the galleys before I was born.'

The headman nodded slowly.

'And now you're a police inspector. You've done well for the son of a gypsy and a convict.' He continued to scrutinise Javert closely. 'We have reason to be suspicious of the police here; we're not used to receiving help from them. My daughter tells me you saved her from rape and her son from death. For that, you have my gratitude.'

He paused, then continued.

'Your uniform will never be welcome here. Without that uniform, you will always be welcome. We owe you a blood debt. And whatever you may feel about us, you are still gypsy. No doubt you are ashamed of that, but we are proud of what we are. Never forget that, policeman.'

He looked long and hard at Javert, then turned and walked away without another word.

Javert walked slowly back to the Pont de Notre Dame. Halfway across the bridge he stopped, leaning on the parapet and gazing down into the dark shadows as he thought back over his encounter with the headman. The conversation had awakened images long forgotten, or at least suppressed. In his mind's eye, he could see his mother on her deathbed, meeting the priest's eyes above the cross he held as she begged him to look after her son. Afterwards, she had received a pauper's burial; but it had been a Christian ceremony, so she must have converted to Christianity on her deathbed. Why had she done that? Of course! She had done it for him. She had adopted the Christian faith as the price of his safety; possibly his very survival.

Javert stared down at the river with unseeing eyes. What else had she done for him? He remembered André's comments about his mother; remarks cruelly echoed by the other boys.

They had called his mother a whore. But why had she sold herself in that way?

An image of the woman Fantine drifted into his mind; Fantine on her deathbed, her death in many ways so like his mother's. She had sold herself for the sake of her daughter. Had his mother sold herself for his sake?

'Monsieur. Monsieur!'

Javert jerked his mind back to the present as he realised that someone was speaking to him. His two subordinates were standing there, both sweating and panting for breath. The older of the two was speaking to him.

'Sorry Monsieur - they got away from us.'

He was covertly looking Javert up and down, obviously noting his dishevelled state. Javert addressed him brusquely.

'They'd thrown the boy over the bridge, but he managed to hold on the statuary. I had to fetch him up.'

'Oh - yes Monsieur.' He looked around him. 'Where are they now, Monsieur?'

'I took them home.'

The man looked surprised.

'Oh. But - I thought they were gypsies.'

'So they were. I could hardly leave them lying on the bridge, could I? All right, you two continue your patrol. I'm going to change.'

He strode away across the bridge, leaving his subordinates staring after him in amazement.

Chapter 26

Javert flapped irritably at the flies that swarmed and buzzed around his head, taking his concentration from the dossier in front of him. Screams and shouts floated up from the tenement below, adding to his annoyance. This neighbourhood was both poorer and more noisy than his usual lodgings, though he had certainly lived in far worse places. It was also disease-ridden, and with the cholera again on the increase it was not where he would have chosen to live.

In some ways Javert felt as if he had been transported back in time, to the Paris of 1789. There was the same feeling of tension, the same gatherings on street corners - even the oppressive heat was the same. And once again Javert was operating under cover, with orders to find and infiltrate the gang of students who were believed to be responsible for much of the present unrest.

Javert determinedly shut out the noise and other distractions, focusing his attention on the dossier in front of him; a dossier that contained all the information they had collected on the insurrectionists. Their prime meeting place was the Café Musain, their leader believed to be a man by the name of Enjolras. A well educated man from a good family, Enjolras was described as being both idealistic and highly intelligent; a combination which in Javert's view made the man doubly dangerous. Javert had already spent a full day studying the dossier, and he intended to spend at least one more before making any other moves. He wanted to know as much as possible about the organisation he was to infiltrate, and the individuals within it. Hard experience had taught him to do his homework thoroughly.

It was well into the following evening before he felt sufficiently well informed to leave his new lodgings and head for the Rue de Charonne, on a mission similar to the ones he had undertaken so often forty years previously. As he tied back his hair the ghost of a small, excited boy looked back at him from the mirror. But this time he would not be gathering his information in the *Tapis–Franc* and other low class taverns.

Today he would be visiting the haunts of the students and fledgling lawyers – as Philippe had done, all those years ago.

Once in the area, he began to visit the taverns and cafés, getting the feel of the places, listening carefully to the conversations and watching for men who seemed likely contacts. For the first week he learned very little, except to confirm the Prefect's belief that Paris was once again a cauldron waiting to boil over. The population was angry and restless – just as in the first revolution, miracles had been promised, but not performed.

In the middle of the second week his attention was caught by a small group of men, sitting at a table playing dominos. One of them had been drinking steadily all evening and was beginning to show the effects in the increased volume of his voice. With a sudden sharpening of concentration Javert recognised him as Grantaire; described in the dossier as a potential rebel. He was also described as irresponsible, and a heavy drinker, which made him a potential weak link for the rebels.

Javert stayed in his corner, casually drinking and chatting whilst he kept one eye on the group. Twice he caught the name of "Enjolras". After a while the game broke up and most of the men left. Grantaire ordered a fresh jug of wine and stayed at his table, continuing to drink on his own.

Javert wandered over past the table, knocking into it clumsily as he did so. The jug wobbled precariously as if about to topple over. Grantaire made a grab for it, but his reflexes had been slowed by the wine he had drunk. He only succeeded in fetching the jug a swipe that speeded it on its journey to the floor, where it smashed on the hard surface. Its contents gurgled out onto the stones.

Javert swore in chagrin. 'Oh, I'm sorry. Here - let me replace it for you.'

The man shrugged, blinking at him owlishly.

'Doesn't matter - nearly empty anyway'.

'No, there was quite a bit left in it - I must buy you some more.'

He called to the landlord and ordered another jug of wine, then turned back to the man.

'Can I join you? It's lonely drinking alone.'

The man mumbled acceptance, already engaged in pouring himself more wine. Javert sat down next to him.

'The name's Jacques. You?'

The drinker suddenly seemed to remember his manners, and held out a hand.

'Grantaire,' he mumbled.

During the next hour they drank their way steadily through two flasks of wine - or rather, Grantaire did. By now he was too drunk to notice that Javert was nowhere near emptying his cup, he was merely sipping occasionally and keeping it topped up. Grantaire, on the other hand, was emptying his cup completely prior to each refill.

Towards midnight two men entered the tavern and noisily demanded wine. They looked around with condescending amusement as they drank, making disparaging comments about the other people in the tavern. They were richly but foppishly dressed - noblemen by their speech - amusing themselves by "slumming it" in the students' quarter.

Javert gave a grunt of disgust and jerked his thumb in their direction.

'Look at them! Look at the contempt on their faces. They think they're so much better than the rest of us. They've probably got a coach and four waiting outside to take them home, while some of the poor kids up the road haven't even got shoes for their feet!'

Grantaire blinked at him. 'That what you think?'

'Don't you?'

Grantaire considered him with owlish care.

'D'you think we ought to do something about it.'

Javert's expression became cautious; the look of a man who had spoken his mind without thinking and was now debating the wisdom of his words. Grantaire leaned forward.

'S'all right, I'm with you. Don't worry - we're going to do something about it. Soon now.'

Javert shook his head. 'I'm sorry, I've said too much I think - you never know who's listening in these places. I'd better go.'

He started to stand up. Grantaire reached up a hand and tugged at his coat.

'No - wait. I mean what I say. You sound like you want the same things we do. Let me introduce you.'

'Who to?'

Grantaire dropped his voice to a slurred whisper.

'To my friends - to Enjolras.'

Javert stood up decisively. He sensed he had a good bite here and he had no intention of losing his catch by trying to land the fish too soon.

'Perhaps, but not tonight. I'm - not sure I want to get that involved.'

Grantaire let go of the coat and slumped back in his chair. For a moment he seemed to lose the focus of his thoughts, then he looked back up at Javert.

'Another time. If you want to help us, come to the Café Musain. That's where they'll be, most nights anyway - ' His voice tailed off as he slipped into a drunken doze.

Javert felt pleased as he left the tavern and walked home. At worse, the drunken Grantaire promised to be a good source of information. At best, he might provide Javert with an introduction to the real leaders of the commune - particularly Enjolras. He waited two days - the actions of a man needing time to think - then made his way to the Café Musain.

He arrived there in the early evening. A number of people were gathered together in the far corner of the café, including Grantaire. The man was drinking again, but was nowhere near as drunk as he had been on the previous occasion. He saw Javert enter the café, and immediately hurried over to him.

'I wondered if you'd come.'

He pulled Javert over to the corner.

'Enjolras. Enjolras! This is the man I was telling you about.'

The man thus addressed turned to face Javert. He was young, quite small and slim in build, with classic features, fair hair and blue eyes. Thus far, he fitted the description in his file perfectly. But what struck Javert immediately - and what the file had not conveyed - was the man's presence, the tremendous force of his personality.

For a moment the two men regarded each other. If Javert was impressed by Enjolras, the student leader was equally impressed by the tall, forceful looking man facing him. He was not like the usual hangers-on produced by Grantaire.

Enjolras broke the silence, waving towards a table in the far corner of the café.

'Join me for a drink?'

Javert nodded, still cautious. Enjolras ordered wine for them both, then sat down next to Javert.

'Grantaire tells me you were quite outspoken the other day, in criticism of this regime.'

Javert looked down.

'I only said what an awful lot of people are thinking. But I probably said more than was wise - you have to be careful nowadays.'

'What do you mean?'

Javert lowered his voice. 'I mean you don't know who might be listening; even here. There's a lot of unrest about, and they're not happy about it.'

'Who aren't?'

'Them - the establishment. Listen, Monsieur Enjolras, I was a soldier for years, down in Toulon, then up here in Paris. I still have contacts - old friends I've kept in touch with. I tell you, the establishment are worried. And when they get worried they start witch-hunting. Take my word for it, you need to be careful what you say - and who you say it to.'

Enjolras nodded. 'Fair enough. We're safe enough here, there's no one within earshot and we won't be disturbed. So tell me about yourself, Monsieur - Jacques, wasn't it?'

Javert nodded. For the next hour he talked to Enjolras, responding with apparent openness to the man's questions. Wherever possible, he told the truth, substituting the soldier for the police officer and giving a viewpoint sympathetic to the students' cause.

In his heart of hearts, Javert took little pleasure in this kind of undercover work; he prided himself on his truthfulness and integrity and did not like the falsehood and prevarication involved. However, he accepted that there were times when such jobs were necessary. When he did lie, he did it well and convincingly, aided by a personality that, though severe, exuded honesty and rectitude.

By the end of their meeting, Javert sensed that Enjolras was beginning to trust him, albeit cautiously. Javert knew better than to push too far or seem too eager. He returned to the café two days later and thereafter continued to attend regularly.

As the days passed he gradually became more accepted by Enjolras and his followers, though as yet they had not discussed any concrete plans in his presence. If anyone started to do so someone else would quickly change the subject, often with a quick flick of the eyes in Javert's direction. Such behaviour did not concern him; he had expected that it would take a little while to gain their confidence. He occupied his time picking up what snippets he could and getting to know the men better.

The drunken Grantaire he already knew, and regarded him as a pathetic creature. The man had a dogged devotion to Enjolras, and fawned on him constantly. For his part, Enjolras seemed to regard Grantaire much as Javert did. He tolerated his attentions, but there were times when he treated him with little more than contempt.

Of Enjolras' remaining followers, two in particular stood out as being in stark contrast to each other. Courfeyrac was a fire eater, angry and impetuous. Had it been left to him they would have stormed the Conciergerie with no further delay, and undoubtedly been shot to pieces for their pains.

Combeferre, on the other hand, was vehemently opposed to violence so long as there was any other choice they could make. In his way he was as idealistic as Enjolras, but with a much gentler personality. He constantly advocated attempting to negotiate, to discuss. Javert reflected that with more people like him there would be less chance of a bloody insurrection, with its inevitable loss of life. At the same time, he knew in his heart of hearts that the establishment would never listen to the students' demands unless their hand was forced.

Against his will, he was beginning to have considerable respect for Enjolras. Of course he was a naïve young idealist, but he seemed to be a man of integrity. Certainly he was no common rabble rouser. Still, this particular rebellion was doomed to fail; if indeed it ever really started. And at the end of the day that's all these people were - just another bunch of rebels, however well intentioned they might be.

Javert thought back to the revolution, and the horrors he had witnessed as a boy. No doubt many of the leaders of that revolution had also meant well. That hadn't stopped the mindless behaviour of the mob, the disorder, the sickening violence. Javert had been through all too much of that. An image of Philippe flashed into his mind, held helpless on his knees by the mob before they hacked his head from his shoulders. Javert had not witnessed Philippe's actual death, but he saw it all too often in his mind's eye.

Javert had been attending the café for just over two weeks when he received the first sign of genuine trust. When he walked in the students were clustered around a map, spread out on one of the tables. They glanced up at his entrance, but this time they made no attempt to hide the map. There were no nudges, no meaningful glances directed towards Javert.

Javert's heartbeat quickened, this could only mean that they had discussed him amongst themselves and decided to accept his presence. He gave no visible sign, but his attention sharpened and focused. They made way for him as he approached the table. Courfeyrac was speaking.

'I tell you Enjolras, we're ready to move right now - today, if we have to.'

Enjolras shook his head. 'Not yet!'

'But why wait? We've got the guns ready, and the ammunition.' He tapped the map in front of him. 'And we know where we're going to barricade.'

Enjolras held up a hand to check the flow of words.

'But the people aren't ready yet. We can't do this on our own, Courfeyrac, there aren't enough of us. We've guns enough, yes - but we can only fire one at a time.'

Courfeyrac shrugged. 'All right, have it your way. But when will the people be ready?'

'They will - just wait. They're behind us all right, it only needs a spark to set them alight. Wait, Courfeyrac, or it'll all be for nothing. In any case, I don't want to move until I know a bit more about the opposition.'

Javert had occupied his time openly studying the map, the natural thing to do. Thick strokes were marked on the map at two points - on the Rue de la Chanvrerie and on the Rue Mondetour. Now Enjolras turned to him and tapped the map as Courfeyrac had done.

'What do you think?'

'You mean the positioning of your barricades? I think you've chosen well. They won't be able to come up against you unseen, that's for certain.' He leaned over and indicated the junction of the two streets. 'That's the most dangerous place, they can come at both barricades together there.'

'Not if we block the alley - we can do that easily enough.'

Javert nodded, looking slightly doubtful.

'Don't forget they can call on a lot of firepower.'

Enjolras nodded. 'I know it, never think I don't. Jacques, can you help us?'

'Depends what you want. I'm no orator.'

'I'm not asking that of you. But - '

He was interrupted by a shout from Grantaire.

'Marius - at last! Where the devil've you been?'

The students clustered round the table swung round. Javert instinctively spun with them, then immediately turned back to the table. The man who had just entered was young, aged about twenty, with dark hair and laughing eyes - even in that quick glimpse Javert was again struck by his uncanny resemblance to Philippe. This Marius was the same young man who had told him of the Thénardiers intended robbery.

Javert's heart had leapt into his mouth and was still hammering wildly. This encounter was potentially disastrous for him. If Marius recognised him - and he almost certainly would - Javert would immediately be exposed as a spy, with all that entailed. It was likely that it would entail his life, especially now that he knew so much. Enjolras was no street thug, but he was highly committed to his cause. He might not want to kill Javert, but Javert had little doubt that he would do so, in order to protect their plans.

He eased himself back onto his chair, casually studying the map whilst the excited chatter went on above his head. Marius had evidently been absent from the café for some time; from

Javert's point of view it was a pity he hadn't stayed away just a little longer.

Marius was speaking now.

'I know I've not been here for a few days, I'm sorry. But I've been busy.'

Grantaire laughed. 'Oh yes, we know. Cosette, isn't it?'

'Well - yes, it is. I would have been here before, but - damn it all, I've only just met her. I just had to see something of her.'

Enjolras spoke to him sharply. 'Listen Marius, we need you here. You need to make up your mind just how committed you are to us. I know it's wonderful that you're in love, but can't it wait until after this business is finished with? '

Despite his danger, Javert was listening intently. Cosette! Surely that was the name of the prostitute Fantine's daughter - the child Valjean had fetched from the inn at Montfermeil, nine years before. Suddenly he thought of the young woman who had been with Valjean during the attempted robbery by Thénardier, and the way in which Marius had been talking to her. So Valjean had kept his promise to Fantine, and the girl was still with him. Javert had failed to run Valjean to earth, but apparently Marius had been more fortunate with Cosette. If only Javert could have talked to Marius, he would at last have been able to lay his hands on Valjean. But he couldn't talk to Marius now; if he did, his own life would soon be forfeit. A terrible feeling of frustration rose up in him, so strong it almost displaced his present fear for his life.

Marius was speaking again.

'I am committed to you, Enjolras - you should know that. That's why I've come back now. This business could be over sooner than you think - I've just heard that General Lamarque is dead!'

The students lapsed into a stunned silence. Sounds from outside drifted in through the open doorway - birdsong, voices of passers-by, an occasional burst of laughter - but for the moment the interior of the Café Musain was enclosed in its own little bubble of stillness.

The hush was broken by Enjolras.

'All right, listen, all of you. This could be it - this could be just the spark we need. Lamarque was the only man who fought for the people, this is really going to stir them up.'

Courfeyrac was on his feet.

'So we move now?'

'No!' Enjolras voice was sharp. 'We need to pick our moment. We need a time when the people are all together - when we can talk to them in a body and get them behind us.'

There was a moment of silence. Then Combeferre spoke.

'Of course - the day of his funeral. They'll turn out in their thousands.'

'Right. And that's the day we move. Marius, go back and find out just when and where that will be. Courfeyrac, go and check on the guns; we need them available, quickly. Prouvaire, Combeferre - go to the Tavern in the Rue Mondetour and start making preparations for the barricade. And all of you, go carefully! The last thing we want to do is to alert the authorities at this stage.'

Everyone scattered to do Enjolras' bidding. Javert heaved a silent sigh of relief as Marius hurried out; that had been too close for comfort.

Enjolras sat down next to Javert.

'You asked how you could help. When we first met you said you had contacts amongst the soldiers. How good are they - how reliable?'

Javert shrugged. 'They're reliable enough. They're not informers, you understand. They're just friends of mine, who sometimes talk more than they should.'

'Are they high enough to know what contingency plans the establishment are making against us?'

Javert considered. 'Most of them are sergeants, as I was. They won't be involved in the initial planning, but they'll probably be consulted regarding the practicalities.' He smiled grimly. 'Some of the higher ranks don't know the first thing; they've just paid for their commissions, not earned them. They have to consult us.'

Enjolras nodded. His blue eyes bored directly into those of Javert.

'Jacques, I need information. I need to know how much they know about us. I need to know their strength. I need to know their contingency plans. Can you find out - and quickly?'

Javert looked thoughtful, then nodded.

'Yes, I think so. I should be able to contact at least two of my friends tonight.' He stood up decisively. 'See you back here?'

'No, we'll be busy making preparations now. It doesn't give us long, but it's just too good an opportunity to miss. Come to the barricade - but for God's sake be careful how you approach, we don't want to shoot you! Call out first. Good luck.'

Javert nodded, reflecting grimly that if Enjolras knew the truth he would most certainly want to shoot him, with no further delay. He left the Café, checked he was not being followed, then walked away with his long, purposeful stride; heading for the Place des Vosges and the private address of Eugène-Francois Vidocq, head of the Brigade de Sûreté.

Chapter 27

Javert arrived in the Place de Vosges shortly before midnight. The servant who greeted him looked at him in some surprise.

'I'm sorry, but Monsieur Vidocq has just gone to bed.'

'Would you tell him I'm here please - the name's Javert.'

The servant looked at him doubtfully. 'I don't think he'd thank me for getting him out of bed.'

'On the contrary - he won't thank you if you don't. Come on man, this is important. If he's annoyed you can blame me.'

The man grunted. 'Huh, that's what you think! All right - I'll risk it. For both our sakes I hope you know what you're doing.'

He disappeared from view, but returned in a few minutes, looking relieved. His tone when he addressed Javert was considerably more respectful.

'You're to come straight up, if you please. This way Monsieur.'

Monsieur Vidocq was in his dressing gown, but looked fully awake and alert. Javert ducked his head respectfully.

'Forgive me for disturbing you at this time Monsieur, but I felt it was important.'

'What's happened?'

'First of all Monsieur, did you know General Lamarque was dead?'

Vidocq gave a soundless whistle.

'No, I didn't! I knew he was dying of course, but you say he's dead? When?'

'I got the news about an hour ago - and so did Enjolras and his followers.'

Vidocq raised his eyebrows.

'And?'

'They're planning to go to the barricades on the day of the funeral - whenever that is.'

Vidocq rang for his servant, ordered coffee for both of them, then sat down again.

'All right Inspector. Take me through all you know, stage by stage.'

Javert talked for some time, explaining what he knew of the students' plans. Vidocq nodded.

'You've done well, Javert. That barricade won't be easy to take. I told you Enjolras was an intelligent man - he's chosen a good position. Easy to defend, dangerous to attack.'

'Why wait for them to build the barricade Monsieur? We know who the leaders are, why not round them up straight away?'

Vidocq shook his head.

'No. If we do that, they'll just become a focus of discontent. In any case it won't be so easy to prove what they're up to. Better let them build their barricade. That way we get both them and their followers in the net together; with no doubts and no argument. Tell me, do you think they'll surrender when they realise what they're up against?'

'Enjolras? I doubt it. I think he'd rather die fighting - and most of his men will follow him, unless I'm much mistaken.'

Vidocq shrugged. 'So be it, let them die fighting. All the better for us, they won't trouble us again and they'll serve as an example. All the same, I fear that barricade won't fall without some losses on our side as well.'

Javert stood up and moved over to the window. He was deep in thought as he stared out over the Parc Royal. It was likely that Marius would be at the barricade, and Marius knew who he was. That made it highly dangerous for Javert to return. On the other hand, he wouldn't need very long for what he had in mind.

His decision made, he turned back to Vidocq.

'We could keep our losses minimal Monsieur, if the barricade could be destroyed from within.'

Vidocq leaned forward intently. 'Just what do you have in mind?'

'As far as they're concerned I'm one of them. They're expecting me to join them when I've got some information. I can wait until the barricade is built, then go back. It'll only take me moments to plant some explosives under the barricade and light a match.'

Vidocq shook his head.

'No Javert! I expect my men to take risks, but that's too much. For one thing, you've already said one of these students can identify you. For another, you could well go up with the barricade.'

'It's not such a risk, I only need to avoid Marius for a short time. If he's actually there when I arrive then it's curtains, but I'm prepared to take a chance on that. And I'm not about to stay sitting on the barricade once I've lit that match!'

'And after you've lit the match - when it blows?'

'They'll be in utter chaos - totally confused. We can mop them up before they even get around to realising what's happened.'

Vidocq still looked dubious.

'Bullets don't discriminate, Inspector. You could just as easily get shot, together with the defenders.'

'I won't wait around for that. I'll plant the explosive then get straight round to the smaller barricade. The moment it blows, I'll just walk out during the confusion.'

Vidocq sat down again, turning the matter over in his mind. Eventually he looked up at Javert and nodded reluctantly.

'All right. I wouldn't ask this of you, but if you're willing to try, heaven knows it could save a few lives on our side. I'll make sure the men watching the small barricade are ordered to take anyone who surrenders alive, so make it obvious you're unarmed. Meantime, go back to your lodgings and get some rest while you can. We can't do anything until we know when the funeral is. And Javert - '

'Yes Monsieur.'

'If you change your mind about this, I'll think none the worse of you. You'll be taking one hell of a chance.'

Javert nodded. 'Thank you Monsieur, but I won't change my mind.'

He gave a formal bow, then left Vidocq's residence to return to his own more modest lodgings.

The day of General Lamarque's funeral started off sunny and hot, but it was a sultry heat and humidity was high. Black clouds were banked to the far west, and an occasional rumble of distant thunder could be heard. As expected, a lot of people seemed to be taking to the streets. The City Guard was also out in considerable numbers, providing a highly visible show of force which it was hoped would deter all but the bravest or most foolhardy.

It was mid–afternoon when Javert arrived at the scene of the barricade, a canvas bag slung casually over his shoulder. The Guard were massed near the junction with Les Halles, within easy distance of the barricade but out of sight of it. Their present orders were that they should not approach until the barricade exploded, at which time they would attack hard and fast, before the defenders had time to gather their wits.

Javert hesitated before showing himself. This was a dangerous moment - if just one of the students lost his head and started shooting prematurely Javert would never reach the barricade alive. Steeling himself, he walked boldly round the corner and into view of the barricade. Then he shouted down the street.

'Ho there - you at the barricade! I'm coming in. All right?'

For a moment there was no response, then Enjolras himself appeared, standing boldly on top of the barricade.

'All right Jacques, come on.'

Javert walked down to the barricade and clambered over it, not without some difficulty. A quick glance around assured him that Marius was not there. Javert heaved a silent sigh of relief.

Enjolras helped him down onto the inside of the barricade.

'Any news?'

Javert nodded. 'Some. There's no immediate rush, they don't intend to attack you before nightfall. If you can find me a map, I'll try to explain what I can. But you understand, this is all second hand information.'

Enjolras nodded. 'Second hand is better than none. Stay here a minute - I'll find a map.'

He vanished into the interior of the tavern just behind the barricade. Javert immediately unslung his canvas bag, pulled out the explosives and pushed them well under the barricade. Despite himself, his hands were shaking a little. He pulled out his matches prior to lighting the short fuse, then froze as something hard was pushed into the small of his back. At the same time a chirpy young voice spoke behind him.

'Hello Inspector - how's your balls?'

For an instant Javert made no move, then he cautiously turned his head. The urchin Gavroche was standing there, grinning from ear to ear. Next to him was Courfeyrac. It was his rifle that was grinding into Javert's back.

Javert forced a puzzled frown onto his face.

'What's all this about? Get that gun out of my back.'

Courfeyrac shook his head. 'Not before you've answered a few questions.' He turned to the boy by his side. 'Gavroche?'

The boy nodded. 'He's the one all right. Only about three weeks ago, I saw him - he was in a police uniform, real posh he looked. He nabbed me for stealing some fruit but he let me go quick enough when I twisted his balls for him.'

He took a step towards Javert, making a grab for between his legs and grinning roguishly when Javert flinched instinctively.

Courfeyrac yanked Gavroche back.

'This is no time for fooling about!' He looked at Javert. 'Well?'

'The boy's either a fool or a liar - I've never seen him before in my life!'

Courfeyrac frowned. He stepped back a pace, but kept the gun carefully trained on Javert as he shouted.

'Enjolras. Enjolras - come out here!'

Javert regarded his captor calmly as he waited for Enjolras. The situation was highly dangerous, but all might not yet be lost. Gavroche was after all only a young boy, he might yet be able to talk himself into the clear. But within a few moments he realised that any chance of bluffing his way out was gone. Enjolras was hurrying out of the Tavern in response to Courfeyrac's shout. With him was Marius.

Javert's thoughts raced. In a moment Marius would confirm Gavroche's story, and any hope of carrying out his mission would be gone. These few seconds were all he had. The matches were in his hand, if he could just get to the fuse -

On the thought, he turned and dived for the foot of the barricade, striking the match even as he landed on the ground.

But his desperate attempt was doomed to failure. Courfeyrac's boot came down hard, extinguishing the match and almost breaking Javert's hand in the process.

'I think you've just confirmed what the boy says. Get over on your stomach - spread your arms wide. Quickly, or you die now.'

Javert shrugged and obeyed the command. It seemed strange to be lying face down on the ground like this, in the very position which he had made many of his own prisoners adopt. The barrel of Courfeyrac's rifle ground painfully into his back, just above his kidneys. A number of boots were clustered round him now, as the defenders of the barricade arrived and demanded to know what was happening. Enjolras' voice spoke from above him.

'All right, search him thoroughly - then we'll see what he's got to say for himself.'

Javert was searched roughly, then dragged to his feet. Enjolras regarded him sternly, Marius in amazement.

'I know this man! He's the one I talked to about the robbery - you remember, I told you about that.'

Enjolras nodded, his eyes still on Javert.

'So - what young Gavroche says is true. You're a spy!'

'If you like. I'm a police officer.'

'Your name?'

'Javert. Inspector Javert.'

Courfeyrac put in. 'He was poking about down under the barricade, trying to light a match. Probably trying to set it on fire.'

Enjolras' eyes narrowed.

'Or maybe worse than that. Have a look.'

Courfeyrac ferreted about under the barricade, then emerged, cautiously holding two of the sticks of explosive. There were exclamations of anger from the watching students. Courfeyrac's expression was savage.

'Bastard was going to blow it sky high - and us with it if we happened to be in the way. I say we hang him, right now!'

His words were greeted with shouts of agreement. Javert was jostled to and fro as some of the students tried to get hold of him, whilst others tried to protect him. Foremost amongst his protectors were Marius and Combeferre. Enjolras shouted for order, and the students released him and stepped back.

Enjolras regarded them all coldly.

'That's better. There'll be no hanging or anything else without a hearing. Inspector Javert, have you anything to say?'

Javert shrugged his shoulders, making no reply. Enjolras continued.

'I take it you've informed against us already? The authorities know the exact position of these barricades, our strength, everything?'

Courfeyrac pushed his rifle roughly into Javert's stomach, forcing an involuntary gasp of pain.

'Give him to me - I'll soon have the truth out of him.'

Javert still made no response. He had little doubt that his life was due to end shortly - if Courfeyrac had his way it would also end painfully. His stomach was knotting with fear, but long practice enabled him to keep his expression impassive as he met Enjolras eye to eye. The student leader stared back at him bleakly, but with no animosity that Javert could see.

'There'll be none of that here, we're not thugs or murderers. Take him into the tavern and tie him up, then we'll discuss what to do.'

Javert was bundled into the tavern and lashed securely to one of the pillars. They left him there and went back outside to talk over their plan of action. His position opposite the door gave a good view of part of the barricade, but he was unable to hear what was being said. Still, he was sure that the discussion could only have one outcome so far as he was concerned.

After a few minutes Enjolras returned, accompanied by Marius and Combeferre. Enjolras approached Javert.

'By your own admission, you're a spy,' he said bluntly. 'You will be shot before this barricade falls.'

'Why wait? Why not shoot me now?'

'We're saving our ammunition. But shot you will be, trust me for that.'

'So you recognise that the barricade will fall?'

Enjolras shrugged. 'I think you've helped to make certain of that.'

'Then why don't you give it up? Why throw your lives away?'

'Are you trying to bargain for yours?'

Javert shook his head.

'I don't bargain with criminals. And that's all you are, whatever your high-sounding ideals.'

Enjolras looked at him coldly. 'Is there anything else you want to say?'

'Nothing at all. Most of you will be going on ahead of me, the rest of you won't be far behind.'

Enjolras shrugged again. 'You're probably right. Take comfort from that, if you can.'

He turned and walked out of the tavern, accompanied by Marius. Combeferre stayed behind, regarding Javert fixedly. Something seemed to be troubling him. Eventually he spoke to Javert abruptly.

'Did you say your name was Javert?'

'That's right. Why?'

'It doesn't matter! Look, I'd save you if I could - I did my best for you. But they're all set on shooting you. I'm sorry.'

Javert looked at him in curiosity.

'Why should you be sorry? Don't you think we'd do the same to you, if you were caught spying on us?'

Combeferre shook his head, a strange expression of sadness and defeat on his face. He seemed about to say more, but apparently thought better of it. He turned away abruptly and walked out of the tavern.

The night that followed was one of the most uncomfortable of Javert's life, both physically and mentally. The ropes holding him did not restrict his circulation, but were still tight enough to be painful, and lashed as he was to the wooden pillar he was unable to ease the pressure on his legs, which began to ache and throb intolerably as the night wore on. The way in which his arms were pulled back forced his shoulders into an unnatural position, causing initial discomfort that soon became intense pain. At last they simply went numb, but he knew that he was going to suffer agonies when he was eventually untied.

259

If he ever was untied - they would probably shoot him where he stood.

However hard he tried to keep his thoughts off the subject they inevitably strayed to his imminent death. His mouth was becoming increasingly dry, partly from sheer thirst and partly from fear. Physically, Javert was a brave man, but to be tied up like this with nothing to do but wait for death was stretching even his nerves. In his time he had seen many men condemned to die, he had even escorted them to their deaths. Now he knew how it felt. He hoped he would be able to retain his mask of composure to the very end; he was almost more afraid of showing fear before these people than he was of dying.

For most of the night Javert was alone, with the exception of Grantaire. But he was no company. The man spent his time drinking steadily, trying to drown his fear in alcohol until he lapsed into a drunken stupor.

Shortly before dawn Enjolras entered the tavern. He looked tired and drawn as he approached Javert.

'Well, so you lied to us about the night attack? I suppose you'd arranged for them to give you time to blow up the barricade, and make it easy for them to just walk in?'

Javert looked at him impassively. Enjolras' suspicion was in fact correct. The plan was to allow Javert the night to destroy the barricade, then launch a dawn attack in the event of his failure. Enjolras watched him for a moment, then nodded.

'All right, I don't really expect you to answer me - not even if Courfeyrac had his way with you.'

He turned to go, but stopped as Javert spoke to him. His tone was ironic, but his voice was hoarse with thirst.

'I don't suppose you could find time to give me something to drink before you go back to your barricade?'

Enjolras turned back to him. Javert expected only a curt refusal, but instead the Student Leader looked mortified. He fetched a mug from a nearby table, filled it with water and held it to Javert's mouth, then repeated the process.

'Enough?'

Javert nodded. 'Thank you.'

'We should have thought of that - I'm sorry.' He hesitated. 'Do you want anything else? I mean, anything stronger?'

Javert glanced over at the slumbering Grantaire, then met Enjolras' eyes. 'You're offering me the chance to drink my way to oblivion? I appreciate the courtesy, but no thank you.'

Enjolras nodded 'I didn't think you would. I'm sorry we're on different sides, Javert; you could have been an invaluable asset to us.'

Javert smiled faintly at the intended compliment, then jerked his head up as a sudden volley of gunfire sounded outside. The dawn attack had started.

Enjolras swore softly and hurried out. The gunfire continued for some half an hour, then stopped. There was a ragged cheer from the students. Inside the tavern, Javert smiled faintly. These people were deluding themselves if they thought they had driven off the attack. The first foray had been planned merely to assess their firepower, the next attack would be less easy to repel.

There was a further commotion outside, and two shots rang out. From his position in the tavern Javert saw a young boy appear on top of the barricade. He managed to clamber down to the ground, then collapsed. Apparently he had been hit by one of the two shots; even from here Javert could see the blood on his grubby shirt. Then the students clustered round and he lost his view.

For a few minutes there was silence outside. Then the group around the boy dispersed. Two of the students entered the tavern, bearing the body of the boy between them. Marius was with them, looking distraught.

They laid the body on the table just in front of Javert. He glanced down at it without much interest, then stiffened. This was no boy - this was a young woman, dressed in boys' clothes. Javert had seen her somewhere before. For a moment the memory nagged at him, then suddenly he had it. The girl was Thénardier's daughter, Eponine. He remembered the arrest at the attempted robbery on Valjean, the brief trial, her saucy smile and ironic curtsy when she walked free from the court. Ironic indeed - had she not been released she might still be in prison. Not free, but at least alive.

Marius stayed by her side for a few moments, then gently drew the table cover up over her face. He turned to Javert, his face grief-stricken.

' She never had any real life - and now she's dead, shot for nothing! She only came to the barricade to see me. She was nothing to do with all this - not really!'

He was addressing Javert, but it was as if he did not really see him. He was just someone to talk to - someone who happened to be there. Javert made no response, there was nothing he could say.

Enjolras hurried in. He glanced at the body on the table and regarded Marius compassionately, then laid a hand on his arm.

'Marius, I want you to take some men round to the small barricade and relieve the women there, they've been on watch all night.'

Marius nodded and went out. Javert heard him calling to some of the other students, before they all vanished in the direction of the smaller barricade. Shortly afterwards he heard the sound of voices outside, then five women appeared in the doorway. As the first one entered the tavern, Javert stiffened in shock. For the first time in many hours he totally forgot both his physical discomfort and his predicament. The woman was Michelle!

Michelle saw him at the same time. Her eyes widened, and her face assumed an expression of stunned disbelief. For a moment she stood stock still, then suddenly she rushed forward to his side.

'Vere! Oh my God, Vere - what are you doing here?'

From behind her came Courfeyrac's harsh voice.

'He's waiting to be shot! He's a spy. Do you know him?'

Michelle ignored the question, but had obviously taken in the information.

'Oh God, no! No, you can't do that.' She threw her arms round the man lashed to the pillar, as if protecting him with her own body. 'Vere, they can't shoot you - they just can't!'

Combeferre had entered with Courfeyrac. He came over and put his hands on Michelle's shoulders, pulling her back and turning her round to face him.

262

'Michelle. Michelle, come away! There's nothing to be done. I've already tried, believe me.'

Over Michelle's shoulder he was regarding Javert with the same look of sadness and defeat that he had worn before. Javert looked at him in sudden comprehension.

'You're her husband?'

Combeferre nodded.

'That's right. I knew who you must be when you said your name was Javert - she used to talk about you quite a bit. That's why I tried to get Enjolras to let you go, or at least not to shoot you.' He turned back to Michelle. 'I'm sorry, there's nothing I can do to help him.'

'Yes there is!' Javert's voice was suddenly angry. 'You can help me by getting her out of here! Do you want her to die with all of you?'

Michelle turned to face him. Tears were streaming down her face, but her head was up, her expression suddenly proud and passionate. Javert had always thought of Michelle as wholly Philippe's daughter, now he suddenly saw Adele in her.

'Do you really think I'd go? You think I'd skulk at home, while my husband dies on the barricade, and you - '

She stopped, as if afraid to say any more, then turned and rushed out of the tavern. Combeferre gave Javert an uneasy look before following her out.

The endless day wore on, with only spasmodic firing from the barricade. With his inside information, Javert could guess the reason for the delay. They were almost certainly fetching up the cannon, to blow the barricade apart.

Early in the afternoon Michelle suddenly appeared in the doorway again, an expression of determination on her face. She glanced cautiously at Grantaire, but the man was fast asleep, still in his drunken stupor. Michelle walked over to the table, picked up a sharp knife, then approached Javert. He felt the knife sawing at the bonds of his wrists.

For a moment Javert hesitated. Obviously she intended to cut him free, come what may. If she did free him, it was quite possible he could go through to the back of the tavern and get clear of the barricade. The temptation to escape his inevitable death was almost overwhelming. But at what price would she buy his life?

He whispered to her desperately.

'Michelle, do you know what you're doing? If they catch you –'

'I don't care! They're not going to shoot you!'

'Then you'll have to come with me - you can't stay here.'

Michelle continued to saw at the ropes, cursing in frustration at her slow progress.

'I can't come with you, Vere. I have to stay with my husband. And I've a young son at home, as well.'

'Then what the devil are you doing here? For God's sake, Michelle, don't be a fool! If they find out you've let me go they'll probably shoot you instead!'

'They probably would!'

Both Michelle and Javert froze at the caustic voice, then looked up. Enjolras stood in the doorway, with Combeferre behind him. Combeferre hurried over and took the knife from an unresisting Michelle, then turned back to Enjolras.

'Enjolras, please, you can't blame her. They were friends way back, you can't expect her to just let him die.'

Enjolras came forward, looking suddenly unutterably weary.

'I'm not blaming her, but she doesn't stay here any longer! We've enough to do watching the barricade, without having to mount a permanent guard on the prisoner as well. Get her out of here - quickly.'

Combeferre nodded and dragged the protesting woman to the door. Enjolras checked Javert's bonds, ensured that he was still secured, then hurried out. Javert had mixed feelings as he watched them go. Michelle was safe, but once again he had to resign himself to death.

Chapter 28

It was late afternoon, and very quiet. Javert's physical discomfort was now extreme. His legs would no longer support his weight and he was sagging forward more and more - but when he did that it only increased the painful pull on his shoulders and the chafing of the ropes. It was more than thirty two hours since he had last slept. He had now reached the stage where his exhaustion was beginning to overcome his discomfort, and had lapsed into a state of torpor.

He was roused by the sound of a voice, calling loudly and clearly.

'Hello the barricade! Can I come through? I'm not armed.'

There was a pause, then Enjolras' voice.

'All right, come on - but keep your hands above your head, where we can see them.'

There was a pause, then the sound of people speaking more quietly just outside the door. One voice was certainly that of Enjolras, the other presumably that of the newcomer. Javert could not immediately place the second voice, but there was something familiar about it.

With an effort Javert sharpened his concentration and began to listen. Enjolras was speaking.

'Courfeyrac, search him - thoroughly.'

There was a pause, then Courfeyrac's voice.

'Nothing. He's not armed.'

Enjolras spoke again. 'All right, why have you come here?'

'I'm here to help you, if I can.'

'Wearing a soldier's uniform? Are you sure you're on the right side of the barricade?'

'How else could I get through to you? Surely you need all the help you can get!'

There was another pause, then Enjolras spoke dryly.

'All right Monsieur, we'll accept your help. But you must forgive us if we're slow to trust you, we've already got one spy on our hands. Come on, you can start by sorting out the ammunition for us.'

He led the way into the tavern. Javert started in amazement. The newcomer was a big man, not in height but in breadth of shoulder. His hair and beard were almost white, carefully cut and groomed. It was the former convict, Jean Valjean.

Valjean recognised Javert at the same instant. For a long moment they stared at each other without speaking, then Enjolras led Valjean to the corner of the room and showed him the pile of ammunition. Valjean began to sort through it as Enjolras walked out of the tavern.

For a short time there was silence, then Valjean left the table and walked over to Javert.

'What are you doing here?'

Javert smiled faintly.

'I'm the spy he was telling you about. Don't worry, they're going to shoot me soon. You'll be able to watch - if you're still alive, that is. But tell me, why are you here? These people aren't rich, there are no pickings for you.'

Valjean sighed softly. 'You still can't think of me as anything other than a thief, can you?'

'That's because I've never seen you as anything but a thief.'

'Have you ever looked? You knew me for years as the Mayor of Montreuil; I didn't steal then.'

Javert tried to shrug, but winced at the pain that shot through his stiff shoulders.

'Perhaps not - but you didn't need money then, did you? You'd made your pile. Mind you, that didn't stop you from robbing that little Savoyard boy in Digne.'

Valjean's face clouded.

'You're right, Javert, that was shameful. I think in its way it was one of the worse things I've done. But I swear to you, I've never stolen a thing since that day.'

'Nor needed to! You must have got a fair amount for that silver and candlesticks.'

'I've never sold the candlesticks, and I never will. That's one thing I'll never part with.'

Javert smiled cynically. Valjean shook his head and turned back to his work. Javert watched him for a moment. He preferred to talk to Valjean rather than be left alone in silence, at least the man was diverting him from his own gloomy thoughts.

'You'd sell them if you got a good enough offer! Come on, Valjean, you don't really expect me to believe anything else.'

Valjean regarded him thoughtfully. 'Listen Javert, that man trusted me, and welcomed me to his house. I repaid him by stealing his silver in the night, and even after that he trusted me again, when he gave me those candlesticks. Don't you see? Those candlesticks were more than a gift, they were a symbol. Oh, I can understand where you're coming from, Javert; you're right about what I was then. But you're wrong about what I am now.'

Javert shook his head.

'People like you can't change, any more than I can.'

'People can change. Even me - even you! But - oh, I don't know, I suppose I couldn't have done it on my own. But after all I'd done, that man still believed in me - in what I could be. No-one had ever believed in me before.' Valjean was no longer looking at Javert, but staring into the middle distance, lost in his past. 'And then there was Cosette. If the Bishop taught me how to forgive, Cosette taught me how to love.'

'Ah yes, the whore's daughter - I'm sure she did! Does she keep your bed warm for you Valjean?'

The comment jerked Valjean from his memories. He was across the room in an instant, eyes blazing with the fury and passion Javert had seen several times before. He grasped the policeman by his shirt-collar and shook him violently. Javert jerked his head back instinctively, banging it painfully on the pillar behind him. Valjean held him for a few seconds more, breathing hard, then regained control of himself and let Javert go as abruptly as he had seized him. He turned away and walked back to the ammunition table.

Javert watched him for a moment. His head hurt where he had banged it on the pillar and Valjean's strong fingers had left livid marks on his neck. He felt curiously ashamed of himself; what had made him say what he had? But Valjean had got under his skin, as somehow he always did. Javert had wanted to needle him.

Valjean spoke without turning round, his voice still shaking with anger.

'Cosette is my daughter - my adopted daughter. I've never laid a finger on her in the way you suggest.'

Javert made no response. He did not for a moment believe his own accusation, in fact he now regretted the gibe, but somehow he couldn't bring himself to apologise to Valjean. The man was still just a common convict!

Valjean suddenly put down the ammunition he was sorting and walked back to the bound man. 'Tell me Javert, have you ever cared for another human being? Or has anyone ever cared for you?'

Javert stared at him as images flooded into his mind. In the forefront was Michelle, behind her the shadowy figures of his mother, and Philippe. For an instant his emotional barriers were down, then he regained control of himself. Whatever was he doing, letting this convict glimpse feelings he rarely admitted even to himself? He banished the images and set his mouth determinedly.

Valjean sighed in frustration as he watched the impassive mask slip back into place. 'How can I make you see - '

He was interrupted by warning shouts from outside the tavern, followed by a volley of gunfire. The attack was picking up again. Valjean broke off in mid-sentence, scooped up the ammunition and hurried out, leaving Javert alone with his thoughts.

The latest attack on the barricade lasted for less than half an hour. At the end of that time Enjolras entered the tavern, accompanied by Marius and Valjean. They walked over to the table and surveyed the small store of ammunition. Marius shook his head.

'We're getting low.'

Enjolras nodded calmly.

'I know it. That's what they've been up to all day - just drawing our fire and getting us to exhaust our ammunition. They've probably got some idea of how much we started with, thanks to our friend over there.' He nodded towards Javert.

Marius frowned. 'We'll have to get some more. Listen, there's plenty out in the streets, all the fallen soldiers have got ammunition pouches with them. I'll go out and get them in here.'

Enjolras shook his head.

'No Marius, it's too risky. They've got men planted on the rooftops and in some of the buildings. If you show your head over the barricade, you'll just get yourself shot.'

Gavroche wandered into the tavern. He ignored the three men, but came over and stood in front of Javert. He held his hand in front of Javert's crutch and clenched his fingers suggestively, giving his impish grin. Javert glared at him.

'If I were free, boy, I'd give you such a thrashing - '

'You'd have to catch me first Mister - you didn't do very well last time.'

He abandoned his game and danced over to the three men. Valjean had now entered the argument.

'Let me go. Look, I'm an old man now - I've lived my life.'

Gavroche piped up in his chirpy, cheeky voice.

'I'll go! They'll never get me!'

On the word, he suddenly raced out of the tavern and leapt up the barricade with extreme agility. Enjolras recovered from his surprise and ran after him, but he was too late. Gavroche was already on top of the barricade and clambering down on the other side.

Javert heard some spasmodic gunfire, followed by bantering shouts from Gavroche. In his mind's eye he could see the boy, darting about the street with his impish grin. A chorus of calls came from the defenders on the barricade.

'Gavroche - give it up! Get back here while you can.'

Gavroche's voice sounded again, still cheerful and defiant. There was a further shot, then an ominous silence.

Enjolras and Marius came into the tavern, accompanied by two young boys. All of them looked stricken. Marius was beside himself.

'I should have gone - he was only a little kid.'

'Then you'd have been lying where he is.'

Javert interjected. 'He's dead?'

'Yes. Your friends shot him.' Enjolras gave him a sharp look, but there was no triumph in Javert's face. Despite the trouble Gavroche had caused him there had been something likeable about him. The boy reminded Javert of the girl, Eponine. It hadn't been his fight, any more than it had been hers - but now both of them were dead, caught in the crossfire between the adults.

Valjean walked slowly into the room. Enjolras nodded to him.

'Monsieur, thank you for your help - you're a good marksman.'

Valjean ignored the comment and walked over to the ammunition table.

'We're almost out.'

'I know, we'll be lucky if we last out another attack. Sort out what you can. Marius, come on, let's see what the lookouts have to say.'

He and Marius hurried out, leaving Valjean and the two boys in the tavern. The boys were both young, only around thirteen years old. Both looked pale and afraid. They glanced at each other, then one of them suddenly threw himself to the floor. For a moment he gave way to despair, wrapping his arms around one of the wooden pillars and sobbing in abject fear.

Javert looked at him, expecting to feel contempt for the boy's weakness. Instead - to his own surprise - he felt an unexpected sympathy, verging on compassion. It was as if the closed shutters in his mind slid back and he saw the young boy he had once been himself, peeping out.

Valjean glanced at Javert. Their eyes met and for a moment there was a strange feeling of empathy between them. Valjean crossed over to the boy, picking him up and talking to him gently. After a few minutes he seemed to recover from his fright. He gave Valjean a sheepish smile and went out with his friend.

Enjolras hurried into the room, accompanied by a number of the defenders. Enjolras looked pale and drawn, even more so than usual. His followers were abnormally silent. Some wore a look of shock. A few minutes later Marius came in with a number of men who had been watching from the smaller barricade.

Enjolras addressed the gathering.

'Listen, all of you, we have a decision to make. We're very low on ammunition, and it was always unlikely we'd survive another attack. Now it's nigh on certain we won't - they've just brought up a cannon!'

Shocked exclamations came from the defenders of the small barricade. The rest were silent, Enjolras' tidings were not news to them.

Enjolras looked round at his followers, then continued.

'Anyone who wishes to can surrender now. Of course there's no way I can say what they'll do with you if you do.' He turned to Javert. 'Do you know?'

'I don't know, but I can guess. I presume there've been a number of soldiers shot trying to take the barricade?'

Enjolras nodded, tight-lipped.

'Yes.'

'Then I'd expect them to either shoot you or hang you.'

'Without a trial?'

'Probably. We're talking about soldiers here, not police officers. To them, this is a state of war, and you're the enemy.'

Enjolras nodded, then turned back to his followers.

'Well, the option is still there, though it doesn't sound a very hopeful one. Or you can try to get out through the small barricade - they may not be watching that one so carefully. If we can hold on until dark you might have a chance.'

Marius spoke.

'What are you doing?'

'I'm staying here - I fall with the barricade.'

'Then so do we!'

There was a chorus of agreement. Not for the first time, Javert felt a stirring of reluctant admiration for Enjolras. The man was a fool, of course, but he was a committed fool - and a natural leader.

Enjolras continued.

'Prouvaire is upstairs keeping an eye on the cannon. He'll warn us when they're about to fire. When that happens, get back in here, quickly. We can fire at them from here once they reach the barricade. When they take the barricade, we retreat to the back room.'

He hesitated, then continued.

'Once we're in there, that's it! We can't retreat any further. When our ammunition is gone - '

He shrugged. Everyone knew the score by now, there was no need to spell it out further.

Enjolras walked over to Javert. For a moment he hesitated, as if reluctant to follow through on his decided course. Then he placed a pistol on the table in front of him.

'Courfeyrac, when they take the barricade, shoot this man. If Courfeyrac falls, the last man out do it.'

Javert's guts twisted, but he kept his face impassive as he gazed back at Enjolras. In a way he was glad it was almost over - he was utterly exhausted, and the long wait was fraying his nerves to breaking point.

Valjean stepped forward.

'Enjolras, may I ask a favour of you?'

'Of course Monsieur, we owe you a great deal. Without your help we'd have lost a lot more men than we have.'

Valjean nodded towards Javert.

'Let me settle with this man.'

Enjolras lifted his eyebrows.

'Why?'

'We go back a long way. He was a prison guard in Toulon, where I was a prisoner. He paroled me when I left there. Since then, he's hunted me for years.'

Enjolras thought about it, then nodded.

'As you wish.'

'Can I have him now? It's possible I won't survive to do it later. And - can I take him out of here? I'd like to talk to him privately - first.'

Enjolras frowned.

'All right. But listen Monsieur, whatever else he is, he's shown himself to be a brave man. He deserves a quick death.'

Valjean nodded. Enjolras and the defenders left the room to return to their duties at the barricade. Combeferre and Marius both hesitated in the doorway, looking back uncertainly at the condemned man. Then they too vanished. Javert was alone with Valjean.

Valjean approached Javert and cut the rope binding him to the pillar. Javert promptly collapsed onto the floor. He had been standing for over twenty four hours now and his stiff and throbbing legs could no longer bear his weight.

He managed a bitter laugh as he lay helpless at Valjean's feet.

'Well, you've got your wish now, sure enough.'

'What wish?'

'When I paroled you, you prayed you'd have this kind of power over me one day. Well, enjoy it while you can; you won't be far behind me.'

Valjean made no reply. Instead he bent down, lifted the big man as if he had been a child, and put him into one of the large chairs. Javert flexed his legs, trying to ease some of the stiffness in the joints. Both knees and ankles were extremely painful and the ankles were badly swollen. Still, that wouldn't be bothering him for long!

After a few moments Valjean addressed him gravely.

'Can you walk now? I'll help you.'

Javert gave his ironic smile.

'I'll do my best; I don't want to keep you waiting longer than necessary!'

They walked slowly out of the tavern and round to the smaller barricade. Javert's legs were beginning to loosen up, but they were still very stiff. Without Valjean's initial support he would probably have collapsed again, but by the time they reached the barricade he was walking on his own.

Valjean led him to the side of the barricade, out of sight of both students and soldiers. Valjean leant his rifle against the barricade and pulled out a knife.

Javert glanced down at the weapon.

'I suppose that's more appropriate for you!'

Valjean pulled him round so Javert was facing the barricade, with Valjean behind him. Javert felt the blade touch his back. Despite his resolve he flinched slightly, then steadied himself again as he waited for the thrust that would finally end his life. He wished the man would hurry up about it! There was no way Javert would plead for his life, but he was afraid he might start to shake. He would rather die than betray his fear to Valjean.

He felt the cold blade touch his arm and something fell at his feet. He stared down stupidly, then realised it was the ropes that had bound his wrists. Valjean had cut him free.

He turned round, trying to move his arms, but after so long they were solidly locked in position. Valjean put the knife in his pocket, put one hand on Javert's right shoulder, then eased his arm forward. He did the same with his left arm. Javert gritted his teeth. He was breathing hard, and the pain had brought him out in a cold sweat.

He sat back against the barricade, massaging the feeling back into his arms and shoulders.

'Now what?'

'Now go!'

Javert frowned. 'What?'

'Get away from here. Quickly - before they find out what I've done.'

Javert stared at him in shock.

'You're letting me go? Why?'

'I don't want your life, Javert - you've only done your job. Can't you believe me, even now?'

Javert shook his head. 'How can I? You vowed vengeance on me once, and I've been hounding you for the past seventeen years. You must hate my guts!'

Valjean shook his head. He looked suddenly very tired.

'I used to hate you - God knows I did. But now - now I just feel sorry for you.'

Javert stared at him. 'You'd do better to feel sorry for yourself. I don't want your pity.'

'No, I don't suppose you do. Now get out of here, while you've got the chance.'

Javert shook his head in disbelief. Did Valjean realise what he was doing? He stood up to go, but something compelled him to turn back.

'Valjean, listen to me, I'm making you no deals - no promises. You're an escaped convict. If you let me go now, I'll still hunt you down.'

The two men stared at each other and for a moment Javert glimpsed something of the old passion in Valjean's eyes. Then the fire died and a look of sad resignation took its place.

'Let me save you the trouble. I live at number seven, Rue de l'homme Arme. If I survive this, that's where I'll be.'

'You're going back to the barricade?'

'Yes.'

'But why? You know they can't survive the cannon - you'll just die with them.'

'Javert, we haven't time for this. Just go!'

Javert stared at him, utterly confused. Then he scrambled over the small barricade and walked away from it, holding his arms well away from his sides for the benefit of any soldiers who might be watching. He was not out of the wood yet, the soldiers could still shoot him and he half expected a bullet in the back from Valjean. He reached the corner with a deep feeling of relief. Behind him he heard the sound of a single shot - presumably fired by Valjean, for the benefit of the students.

As he rounded the corner Javert was met by two soldiers. Both of them appeared to know who he was, presumably his description had been circulated.

'Inspector Javert?'

He nodded wearily. 'Yes.'

'We're delighted to see you, Monsieur. We've been watching for you all day - we thought you were probably dead. If you'll come with me, I'll take you straight to Monsieur de Lobau.' He looked doubtfully at the obviously exhausted man before him. 'Can I help you, Monsieur?'

Javert shook his head.

'No need - I can manage.'

The soldier fell in next to him, and they walked slowly away towards the safety of the Rue des Precheurs.

Chapter 29

Monsieur de Lobau, head of the National Guard, was surprised but delighted to see Javert.

'When the barricade didn't go up and you didn't get out before the first attack we thought you'd been caught. We'd about given you up for dead!'

'I very nearly was!'

Monsieur de Lobau looked at him more closely.

'Good Lord, man, you look exhausted!'

'I am. They've had me tied to a pillar for the past twenty four hours, waiting to be shot.'

'How'd you get out?'

'They didn't shoot me straight away because they wanted to save their ammunition. Then - one of them let me go.'

De Lobau raised his eyebrows. 'Another of our agents?'

'No. I don't know why he did what he did. I'll probably never know. So, what's happening with the barricade?'

'We're just about to fire the cannon, it'll soon be all over after that. Do you want to see the finish, or had you better get yourself home and get some rest? You look about ready to drop.'

Javert shook his head. 'I'll see it through.'

They made their way to Les Halles by a roundabout route. As they approached the junction with the Rue de la Chanvrerie they heard the steady crump of the cannon, accompanied by rapid gunfire. Then the cannon fire stopped. The gunfire slowed, became spasmodic; then there was silence. The barricade had fallen.

By the time Javert and Monsieur de Lobau reached the scene it was all over. They passed the body of Gavroche, sprawled amongst the dead soldiers, and approached what remained of the barricade. Men – both soldiers and students - lay amongst the wreckage. In some cases there were only parts of men; a legless torso, a severed hand still wearing its gold wedding ring. Combeferre lay a little beyond the barricade. He was dead, but unmarked save for a little blood around his nose and ears. He must have been killed by the concussion of the explosions. Javert thought of Michelle, a widow now, left to raise her child alone like her mother before her.

He walked away from Combeferre and swiftly checked the other bodies. He knew most of them, but none was the man he was looking for.

There was a commotion nearby and he turned to see Enjolras and Grantaire being led out of the tavern. For a moment he was surprised that Enjolras had been taken alive, then he looked more closely at him. The man had a dazed look, and a deep cut on his forehead. He had probably been knocked unconscious during the final attack.

Javert glanced at Grantaire. He looked unusually sober, and to Javert's surprise no longer appeared to be afraid. He was going to die side by side with the man he idolised, and in the final moments of his life he seemed to have discovered a courage he had never had before.

The soldiers pushed the two men up against the wall. Enjolras glanced across towards the tattered barricade, then saw Javert. He looked surprised, then smiled slightly.

'How did you manage that? I thought you were dead.'

'So did I!' Javert responded briefly.

'He let you go? Why?'

Javert shook his head. 'I don't know why.'

'Ah well, I can't really say I'm sorry. I didn't like the idea of killing you, but under the circumstances there wasn't any choice. I wish you'd been on our side!'

The soldiers had walked back and formed a line, leaving Enjolras and Grantaire against the wall. Javert glanced round and saw them readying their weapons. He left Enjolras and walked across to Monsieur de Lobau.

'Don't they get a trial?'

'I'm sorry Inspector - they've had one. I've lost a lot of my men to these people. In any case, what difference would it make? They'd be sentenced to death anyway, and probably hanged instead of shot.'

Javert nodded, recognising the truth of that statement. Enjolras would undoubtedly prefer to die now, beside the barricade he had tried to defend.

'Are there any other survivors?'

Monsieur de Lobau shook his head. 'No. Just these two.'

Javert walked away slowly and went into the tavern. Behind him, a fusillade of shots announced the execution of Enjolras and Grantaire.

Most of the dead students were still inside the tavern where they had made their last stand, although the bodies were even now being brought out. Javert checked each one, then went into the back room and checked those. Courfeyrac was there, lying close to the bodies of the two young boys. There was no sign of Valjean, and Javert suddenly realised that he hadn't seen Marius either. He went out of the tavern and approached one of the Sergeants.

'Tell me, was there still a guard on the small barricade?'

'Yes Monsieur. A few of them tried to get out that way; none of them made it.'

Javert frowned, then walked round to the small barricade to check the bodies there. At first he thought the place was deserted, then movement caught his eye in the shadow of the barricade. Someone was bending over one of the corpses. Javert realised what the man was doing at the same moment as he recognised him. It was Thénardier, and he was robbing the corpse.

Javert headed for him at a run. Thénardier saw him coming, leapt aside, and literally seemed to disappear into the ground. Javert swore with surprise, then realised that the man had simply vanished down a manhole that led into the sewers.

Javert tried vainly to prise up the lid, but was unable to move it. Thénardier was either hanging on from underneath or he had secured it in some other way. Well, he couldn't stay in there forever.

Javert straightened and called to the Sergeant.

'Listen, there's a criminal just gone down into the sewers - he was robbing the corpses.'

The Sergeant swore angrily.

'Filthy bastard! We'll get him for you Monsieur.'

He called over two soldiers. They also tried to lift the manhole cover, but failed.

Javert considered for a moment.

'Can you lend me a few of your men?'

'No problem Monsieur - but what for?'

'I'd like a couple of them to stay here by this manhole, in case he decides to come back up. I'll put two men at one of the other entrances, and take the third entrance myself.'

The Sergeant nodded and swiftly assigned the men Javert had asked for. Like any good officer, Javert knew the sewer outlets, Thénardier was not the first man to use them as a refuge. Javert sent two soldiers to cover the nearest exit, then headed for the second one at a trot, accompanied by the remaining soldier.

He arrived out of breath, but certain Thénardier could not have got there before him. Thénardier couldn't travel as fast in the darkness, mud and slime as Javert could in the light.

Half an hour crawled by, and Javert was almost ready to believe that Thénardier had chosen the alternative exit when he heard the scrape of the manhole cover. He drew back into the shadows, signalling the soldier to do the same.

He heard Thénardier's whisper.

'This is it. This comes out just below the Pont Marie.'

Two shadowy forms emerged from the sewer, one apparently dragging the other. Thénardier was probably robbing yet another corpse. But why drag it all the way up here? Why not leave it in the sewers?

There was a scraping sound as the manhole cover was replaced, then the first of the shadowy forms laid the second on the ground. He knelt down and cradled the head on his knees.

Javert stepped forward.

'Thénardier!'

The kneeling shadow spun round at his voice. Not Thénardier, but Valjean!

For a moment the two men stared at each other; it was difficult to say which of them was the most surprised. Then Valjean sighed and seemed to sag in defeat.

'You were waiting for me?'

Javert recovered himself and shook his head.

'No, I was waiting for Thénardier. I saw him go into the sewers by the barricade - I thought he might come out here.'

'He knew you were waiting for him?'

'I suppose he could have guessed that I might be.'

Valjean nodded wearily.

'He guessed all right, he led me straight to you.' He laughed bitterly. 'He offered to show me the way out, I might have known there was something odd about him being so helpful all of a sudden.'

Javert walked forward. For an instant Valjean put up his hand as though to ward him off, then let his arm drop back to his side. He again bent over the man whose head he was supporting.

Javert looked down and drew a quick breath. The man on the ground was Marius. His face was like that of a corpse. Blood stained the sleeve and front of his white shirt.

'Is he dead?'

Valjean shook his head. He too looked pale, his voice hoarse with weariness. He had been concussed by the explosions at the barricade, and it had been no easy matter carrying Marius through the sewers.

'Not yet, but he's badly hurt. Javert, please listen to me. I accept that I'm your prisoner - I accepted that when I let you go and gave you my address. But before you lock me up again, please let me get this boy to a doctor.'

Javert's mouth twisted. He knelt down next to Valjean and examined Marius, then gave a non-committal grunt. He stood up and called to the soldier.

'Go and fetch a doctor. Bring him to seven Rue de l'homme Arme, as soon as you can.'

The soldier immediately ran off into the darkness. Valjean and Javert swiftly improvised a stretcher from their coats, then carried the unconscious Marius the short distance to Valjean's house, putting him on the couch in the downstairs room.

A young woman hurried in, looking distraught. She seemed not to notice Javert, but ran straight to Marius.

'Papa, what's happened? Oh God – he's not dead!'

Valjean put his arms round the distressed girl.

'No, he's not dead, but he is badly hurt. We've sent for a doctor, he'll be here soon. Cosette, listen to me, I want you to look after Marius. You must wait here with him until the doctor arrives.'

Cosette stared at him in confusion.

'But papa, aren't you going to stay? I don't understand. Where are you going?'

Valjean turned to Javert.

'Please - can you let me have a few minutes to explain to her?'

Javert had been watching in an abstracted silence, not really taking in the scene before him. He gave a sudden jerk and turned to Valjean.

'I'm sorry - what did you say?'

Valjean looked at him in puzzlement.

'I asked you if you'd let me explain what's happening to Cosette.'

Javert nodded, the same faraway expression on his face.

'Very well. I'll wait for you outside.'

He walked out of the room, closing the door quietly behind him. Valjean stared after him in surprise. It was unusual for Javert to take such a risk of losing his prisoner, the man was behaving very unlike his usual self. Then he remembered all that Javert had been through on the barricade; it was really no wonder if he was acting a little oddly.

Javert left Valjean's house and walked out into the street. He did not stop there, but kept on walking. Never in his life had he felt so exhausted and so confused. Never had his emotions been in such a jumble as they were now.

He walked across the Pont Neuf and entered the Conciergerie, where he wrote a brief report on the happenings at the barricade. For a reason he dare not yet examine, he made no mention of Valjean.

When he left the Conciergerie an hour later it had begun to rain heavily. He threw his heavy coat on over his clothes and walked slowly along the street until he reached the Pont de Notre Dame. For a while he leaned on the parapet of the bridge. On his left he could see the gypsy encampment, on his right the imposing bulk of the Conciergerie. It was like looking at two facets of himself - what he was now, and what he had come from. He felt torn apart between the two.

He made no move for a long time. The shadows lengthened as evening moved towards night. Lamps began to appear on the left bank and the island and still he stood there, unconsciously clasping the medallion and gazing unseeingly at the river below.

It was late now, approaching midnight. Javert was at breaking point; he had been through too much trauma in the past two days. The hours spent waiting for death, the unexpected reprieve from Valjean that had only thrown him into more confusion; and now this!

He, who lived only for his job, had just blatantly failed in his duty. Helping young Marius had been bad enough, but to let Valjean go, that was unforgivable; it made him as bad as the convicts! In his mind, he could hear André's voice.

Your father was a convict and your mother was a whore! You've got bad blood in you, boy.

It must be true! Why else had he let Valjean go, after a lifetime of hunting him? And why couldn't he just go back and arrest Valjean now? But when he tried to move his feet refused to obey him. He was a man divided against himself. His duty demanded that he immediately go and arrest Valjean. But his latent humanity - buried for so long - would not allow him to do so. It was as if his brain could no longer control his actions.

His thoughts were really jumbling now, out of control. His head felt like the inside of a volcano, his emotions the white hot lava. More and more lava was pouring out of the cracks as the feelings he had suppressed for so many years forced their way to the surface. The cracks were widening and it was now impossible to contain the pressure within. The destructive force that had been building for years was finally loose and the volcano was bubbling, ready to erupt.

Javert released the medallion he was holding, letting it drop back onto his chest. He could see little of the actual water - just pools of darkness - but the river drew him strangely. Its cool depths spoke of peace, and an end to the inner conflict and turmoil that were tearing him apart.

He stood upright and stepped over the parapet, standing balanced on the ledge that ran just below it on the river side of the bridge. For a long moment he stood there, gazing down, then he swayed forward and plummeted into the river below.

He felt a cold shock as he hit the water. For a few seconds he floated, held up by the coat that had been open when he fell and was now acting as a buoy. Then the heavy coat became waterlogged and dragged him down instead. He had let himself fall quite deliberately, but now his survival instincts took over. He automatically tried to swim, fighting vainly to get his head back above the surface. He tried not to breathe, but his body's instinctive demand for oxygen forced him to do so. Just as when he was a boy in the pigpen he gasped for air, but took in only liquid and filth. He was starting to black out now.

With his last vestiges of consciousness he felt the river begin to take him. Something heavy struck him in the back, the current seemed to seize his coat and drag him sideways. Then the darkness claimed him, and there was nothing.

Chapter 30

Javert was in a confused nightmare. Traumatic events from the past replayed themselves in his head, vivid as the day they had happened. He was a boy again, back in Toulon; numbly watching his mother as she lay dying. He was in Paris, seeing Philippe held helplessly on his knees prior to his execution. He was tied to the pillar at the barricade, his nerves fraying as he waited for death. He was in the water, desperately trying to breathe, but choking and dying. Faces rose up to haunt him, some living, some long dead - his mother, Philippe, Michelle, Valjean.

Once he thought he was awake, but even then he did not know if he was really conscious or in a waking dream. Everything seemed to be out of focus, the colours heightened and garish. He let himself slip back into the darkness and the nightmares.

Next time he opened his eyes he knew he was truly awake. He felt weak and ill, but fully aware. He was lying in bed in a dimly lit room. For a moment he thought it was night, then realised that the curtains were drawn almost across the windows. The room was very small, but cosy, furnished in warm, glowing colours.

Javert turned his head. Michelle was seated a short distance away, looking down at the embroidery in her hands. Her expression was sad and abstracted.

'Michelle.'

His own voice surprised him, it was little more than a croak. Even so, the effect on Michelle was dramatic. Her head snapped up and a wave of colour flushed up her face. She was beside him in an instant, her embroidery falling unheeded to the floor.

'Vere! Oh thank God!' She peered at him anxiously. 'Vere, are you really awake? Can you understand what I'm saying?'

He moved his head restlessly on the pillow.

'Is there anything to drink? I'm thirsty.'

Michelle hurriedly fetched him some water and lifted his head while he drank. The water had a strangely bitter taste, as if herbs or drugs had been mixed with it, but Javert was too thirsty to care. He lay back again and looked at Michelle, feeling better after his drink.

'Michelle, what am I doing here? Have I been ill?'

She nodded. 'Yes, you have. Don't you remember?'

He frowned and tried to think. Suddenly memory flooded back to him. The barricade; Valjean; the bridge. He remembered standing on the parapet staring down at the river, then jumping down into the water. After that, there was nothing.

He turned his head away, staring upwards. The ceiling looked strange; low and curved, made of wood decorated with ornate carving.

'Where am I?'

'You're in a caravan, in the gypsy encampment.'

'What?' He tried to sit up. Michelle pushed him back gently.

'It's all right Vere, you're safe. Just lie still.'

Reluctantly he lay back.

'Michelle, what happened to me? 'The last thing I remember is jumping in the river. Or am I dreaming that? Did I jump?'

'Yes, you did. You most certainly did.'

Javert stared abstractedly at the wooden carving, his brain sluggish and his thought processes slower than normal. If he'd jumped into the river, why wasn't he dead?

He turned back towards Michelle.

'How did I get here?'

She looked at him, observing his high colour and slightly glazed eyes.

'Later, Vere. All that matters for now is that you are here. Just stay quiet, you've been ill for a long time. I'll explain everything to you soon.'

'How long have I been here?'

'Two weeks.'

Two weeks! No wonder he felt so frail. His mind flitted to and fro; there was so much he needed to ask Michelle. But she was right; he was too tired to think clearly yet. Wearily he closed his eyes and slipped back into his uneasy sleep.

The next time he woke he felt much better, though still weak. The drugs he had been given were wearing off and the high fever had left him.

Slowly and with difficulty he got out of bed. His back hurt a great deal and his legs felt like soft rubber, but he gritted his teeth and persisted, searching around until he found his clothes. He was astonished at how his shirt hung on him, he had evidently lost a great deal of weight while he had been ill.

Michelle came into the van, carrying a tray. She seemed surprised to see him up and dressed.

'Vere! Oh, you shouldn't have - it's too soon.'

She helped him to the bed, then pulled the curtains back, letting in the sunlight. He squinted at the unaccustomed brightness, then looked at Michelle.

'From what I can remember, I should be dead. Are you going to tell me how I got here?'

She sat down next to him.

'All right. I suppose you'll only fret until I do.'

She looked away, her eyes losing focus as her mind took her back.

'That evening - the day it all happened - I heard the cannon fire. I knew it must be the barricade, knew it must have fallen. I couldn't just stay at home, not knowing, I had to go and see. When I reached the barricade, the soldiers wouldn't let me pass at first. Then when they understood why I was there - that I was looking for my husband - they let me through.'

She looked up for a moment, her eyes bright with tears. Not thinking about it, Javert took her hand. She let it remain in his as she continued her story.

'Of course, I saw my husband - and all the others. But I couldn't find you. I thought they'd shot you and the soldiers had taken you away; they wouldn't have left you with the rebels, would they? I was just beside myself, Vere - I thought I'd go mad! To lose my husband and my - and you - on the same day.

'I left the barricade and walked for a long time, not really thinking where I was going. I ended up by the river. It was very late by that time. Suddenly I saw you there, on the bridge. At first I thought I'd finally gone mad. After all, I thought you

286

were dead, and you were standing so still for such a long time. Then you stepped over the parapet and I suddenly realised what you were going to do. I started to shout and scream at you like a mad woman.' She looked at him. 'Did you hear me?'

'No. I didn't hear anything.'

Javert unconsciously tightened his hand on hers as he thought back to that moment on the bridge. Nothing could have penetrated the black fog that had surrounded him then. Michelle continued.

'I slid down the bank to the edge of the river. It was a useless thing to do really, or it should have been. I couldn't reach you, and I can't even swim. I got there just as you jumped. I saw you hit the water and go under. Then a boat came under the bridge; quite a big boat, going fast. It hit you hard and knocked you sideways towards me, and I managed to get hold of your coat.'

She shivered as the memories rose vividly before her.

'I pulled! My God, how I pulled! But the current was too strong and you were so heavy. I was already up to my waist and being pulled deeper; I thought you were going to take me with you. I started shouting again, calling for help - I was just about hysterical by that time. Then suddenly two men were there. Two gypsies.'

Javert frowned. 'Gypsies? From the encampment over the river?'

'From this encampment, yes. They'd heard me screaming the first time and come to see what was going on. They helped me get you out and up the bank, then they picked you up and carried you here. They talked for a bit in their own language, but I heard one of them say "Javert," so they must have known who you were.'

Javert nodded. 'Yes, they would.'

Michelle looked at him wonderingly.

'I know gypsies don't like the police. I was surprised they helped you, knowing who you were, and what you were.'

Javert touched his medallion.

'This is why - or it's one of the reasons.'

She looked at it wonderingly. 'I know. When we'd got you back here, I asked the headman why they'd helped me. He lifted the medallion – it was almost reverent, the way he held it – and he said that you belonged to them.'

Javert frowned. 'He said that the medallion belonged to them?'

'No Vere. He said that you belonged to them. Vere, you always wear this medallion, I've never seen you without it. Where did it come from?'

'It belonged to my mother, she gave it to me when she died.' He hesitated, he had never discussed his gypsy background with Michelle, or indeed with anyone.

'I think you know I was born in Toulon garrison. Well, to be more exact, I was born in Toulon prison. I'm the son of a convicted murderer and a gypsy. My mother was the gypsy.'

'Ah.' Michelle nodded as if she also understood a lot that he had left unsaid. 'And how did you come to be with Monsieur André?'

'He was my guardian. I never knew my father and my mother died when I was nine. André took me in then.'

She picked up the medallion, regarding it thoughtfully. 'And this? Why does this mean so much to these gypsies? Is it just because it's a gypsy symbol, or is this particular medallion special for a different reason? Vere, I think you need to find out.'

He shrugged. 'Why? I know my mother was a gypsy. What more is there to find out?'

'I don't know, Vere. And you'll never know either, will you? Unless you ask.'

Javert grunted and turned the subject. 'Why have I been here for so long? What's been the matter with me?'

'I don't know exactly, but you've been very ill. At first I thought you were dead, and it had all been for nothing. You must have been half drowned, but it wasn't just that, you've had some kind of fever as well. For a time you were completely delirious. At first they were terrified that it might be the cholera, but thank God, it wasn't. Anyway, we fetched a doctor, but he didn't want to risk moving you. Your back looked an awful mess where the boat had hit you and we didn't know how badly you'd been hurt. So you stayed here. This van belongs to the headman's son; he and his family have moved in

288

with other families, so you could be looked after. And that's it - you know the rest.'

'And you? Where have you been staying?'

She flushed. 'Here, with you. My son's with his grandparents - my husband's family.'

She looked at him closely, noting his pallor and look of exhaustion. It was enough for one day, what he needed now was rest. She freed the hand he didn't know he was holding, and left the van.

The following day, the doctor paid him a visit, accompanied by the headman. He was gratified to find his patient awake and fully aware, and even more pleased to learn that he had full movement, albeit not without considerable pain.

'You're very lucky,' he said. 'When I first saw the state of your back, I was afraid you might have serious damage to your spine, but the impact seems to have been mostly to the right hand side of your back. It was impossible to tell, with such extensive bruising. You should make a full recovery, Monsieur, but you must be patient. Your back muscles were damaged too, it will be some time before you can move without pain. But all the same, you must exercise; a little more each day.'

He closed his bag with a decisive snap and turned to Michelle. 'Monsieur Javert can be safely moved now, Madame.' He looked disapprovingly around the caravan. 'I won't call again, unless you send for me. Goodbye Madame, Monsieur.'

He gave a stiff nod to the headman and left the van. The headman, however, remained behind. For a moment there was an uncomfortable silence, broken by Javert.

'I have to thank you for saving my life,' he said stiffly. 'And for allowing me to stay here. I'm still not entirely sure why you did so, but I'm grateful.'

The headman inclined his head. 'We take care of our own.'

'I'm not your own.'

'You are. You won't admit it, policeman; you're ashamed of it. But you can't escape your past, or your *karma*.'

He looked into Javert's eyes, as if waiting for his response. Javert fingered the medallion round his neck.

'This medallion, it's obviously very special to you. Why?'

The headman nodded slowly, as if he had been expecting the question. He sat on a stool by Javert's bed.

'I'll answer you, but first you must know something of the past. My past, and yours.'

Michelle stood up to leave, but he imperiously motioned her back.

'You're his woman, you should stay.'

Michelle sat down again, looking a little embarrassed. Javert kept his expression wooden. For a moment the headman was silent, apparently marshalling his thoughts, then he began to speak.

'One day a long time ago, when I was just a *chavvie*, we were camped here for the Easter fair. My grandfather was headman then. I was in our caravan, with my grandfather. There was a commotion, so we went to see. It was my *dat* and *dai* — my mother and father. Both of them were covered in blood. My mother's blouse was almost torn off. I remember how I ran to them, and how I was afraid.'

He paused, muttered something in his own cant, then continued.

'So much I remember. The rest, my grandfather told me later, when I was grown more. My mother had been to the market over the river, to buy fresh food. When she was late back, my father went to look. She was heavy with her second child, and he was afraid for her. He found her on the bridge, fighting against three men. She had defended herself with her knife and stabbed one of them in his arm, but they had her down, and one of them was already astride her - raping her; even though they must have seen she was carrying an unborn child. They didn't see my father until it was too late. He tore the man off my mother, and he slid his knife between the man's ribs. The other two ran for it then. Both of them got away.

'My father tipped the body into the river and brought my mother home. She was shaken and had many bruises, but not too badly hurt. The baby inside her had taken no harm. But my father had killed a man; he had to flee.'

Michelle butted in. 'But surely — he was defending his wife from rape. He couldn't have been blamed for that.'

The headman regarded her coldly.

'That's *sheka,* woman. Two men got away. Do you think they would tell the truth? Would they admit that the three of them had been raping a woman, a pregnant woman? They would lie, they would back each other up. We're gypsies, remember? Who would the police and the courts believe? And those three weren't ordinary men, they were *gavver* - police officers.'

'Oh God,' breathed Michelle.

The headman nodded grimly, then turned back to Javert.

'Well, *gavver*? Who would you have believed?'

Javert shook his head, unable to bring himself to give the obvious answer. Of course he would have believed the police officers. After all, weren't all gypsies thieves, rogues, liars? And yet he knew – somehow he knew – that this gypsy was telling him the truth.

The headman nodded as if Javert had spoken aloud, and continued his story.

'My father had to go, and quickly. My mother too, since she had stabbed one of them. They took what provision they could and a little money, and they left the camp together. And that's the last anyone here knew of them; until the day you walked into camp, wearing this.' He flicked the medallion.

Javert frowned. 'But why ...'

'That medallion was worn always by the tribe's leader; the headman. Then it was my grandfather. It would have passed to my father, so my grandfather gave it to him before he left. My father must have given it to my mother.'

He looked at Javert.

'And when my mother died, she gave it to her son.'

Michelle gasped aloud. She and Javert stared at the headman, who nodded slowly.

'Yes, policeman. I'm your brother.'

Chapter 31

Javert left the camp the following morning, not for his own lodgings, but for Michelle's home at the Café Gerard. Physically at least, Javert was on the mend, but it would be some time before he regained his full strength. Meanwhile, he had a great deal to think about. The gypsies had moved on now, and Javert was glad of it; at least it gave him a breathing space. They would be back the following spring, time enough then to decide whether or not he would seek out his newly discovered brother.

Already aware of his gypsy heritage, the revelation that both his parents had been gypsies didn't bother him unduly; but the circumstances under which his father had fled from Paris troubled him a great deal. True, his father had killed a man; but Javert knew that under the circumstances his act would usually have been considered justified; had he not been a gypsy, and had his victim not been a police officer. He was obliged to admit the truth of Michelle's recent comments; law and justice didn't always march together. And in his father's case, it seemed that justice had not been done.

As his recovery progressed Michelle's young son Philippe became a constant visitor. Like Michelle when she was a child, he seemed instantly able to engage with the taciturn man. It may have been that Javert's presence filled at least some of the void left by his father's death. For some reason, Javert had expected the boy to resemble the original Philippe, but in looks at least he took after Combeferre. In one way Javert was glad of it; at least Michelle would have something left of her dead husband.

Mentally, he felt drained, but calm; the terrible destructive force was spent, at least for the time being. He knew that there were still decisions he had to make - about his future, his job, his newly discovered brother - but they could wait. For now, he was content to take each day as it came.

It was Michelle who forced him to make one decision. She raised the subject abruptly, as they were sitting together after dinner.

'Vere, listen, I have to talk to you - about Jean Valjean.'

Javert's head jerked round.

'What do you know about him?'

'Quite a lot. Don't forget my husband was one of Enjolras' followers. I knew Enjolras well, and Marius. Marius came to see me yesterday. He told me everything that had happened on the barricade, and afterwards.'

'So young Marius recovered? I must admit I didn't think he would, he was badly hurt.'

'Marius recovered, yes. But Valjean - he's still very ill.'

Javert looked surprised. 'I didn't know that.'

'No, of course, how could you? Well, he's been ill since the night of the barricade, and he's getting worse.'

She paused, looking at him intently.

'Marius said Valjean was expecting you to arrest him, but you just walked away?'

Javert frowned. 'Yes.'

'Vere, listen, Valjean is still waiting for you; still expecting you to arrest him. Marius says he can't believe it, that you'd actually let him go. He thinks you left because you were just too exhausted to think straight.'

Javert gave a hollow laugh. 'He's not far wrong about that.'

Michelle regarded him curiously.

'Why did you let him go?'

Javert shrugged and looked away from her. It wasn't a subject he wanted to think about, whenever he tried to get to grips with it his mental confusion returned. Michelle leaned forward and took his hand.

'Vere, for God's sake talk to me! You can't just keep everything locked up inside you all the time.'

For a few moments Javert sat silently. He had always found it difficult to share his emotions; a long time ago he had begun to do so with Philippe, but then Philippe had died. Since that day, Javert had never discussed his innermost feelings with anyone.

'I'm not sure myself,' he said at last. 'I just couldn't do it; couldn't make myself arrest him. I wanted to - I'd told him I would. But then when it came to it - '

He looked up at her, his face tormented.

'Michelle, that man had every reason to want me dead. I've hunted him for years - ever since he jumped parole, back in 1815. Even at the barricade I told him I'd hunt him down; and yet he still let me go free. I just couldn't bring myself to condemn to death the man who'd saved my life.'

'But Vere, what's wrong with that? Surely it's natural to want to repay a man who's saved your life. Why are you torturing yourself so?'

'Because I should have arrested him - I still should. Michelle, don't you see? It was my sworn duty to take him in, and I couldn't do it. Oh, I've made mistakes before - everyone has - but to deliberately fail in my duty like that! The man's a thief and a parole breaker. How could I let him go?'

Michelle looked confused.

'But Vere, that was a long time ago. He's not a thief now - he's a good man.'

Javert shook his head in confusion.

'I didn't think a man like that could ever change, but it seems he has. But I should still have arrested him - that was my job. I let my heart rule my head.'

'And you really feel that's wrong? Listen Vere, you think it was the biggest failure of your life when you showed mercy to this man. I think you took the biggest step forward of your life. Don't you see that? Don't you see what you've gained?'

Javert looked at her in confusion. He had been immersed in the system for so long, his entire life had been ruled by it. It had wrapped itself around him like bindweed, gradually strangling the flower of his humanity until it had so nearly died. And the bindweed was still there, wrapping its tendrils around him; it wasn't easy to shake off the habits and beliefs of a lifetime.

'Vere, what are you going to do now? About Valjean?'

So there it was; he was facing the same dilemma he had faced on the bridge. In a sudden flash of clarity, he realised that his decision was already made; he had made it that night on the bridge, when he had jumped into the river rather than go back and arrest Valjean.

He turned abruptly to Michelle.

'So far as I'm concerned, Jean Valjean died at the barricade. I've no intention of trying to arrest him - not now, not ever. I can't do it! Tell Marius that.'

For a moment Michelle stared at him in apparent astonishment, then she came over and put her arms around him.

'Vere, I'm so glad!'

'For Valjean?'

'For him of course. But mostly for you.'

Javert returned her embrace, feeling a stirring of the same desire he had experienced all those years ago. She hugged him hard and he felt her tremble against him, then she freed herself quickly and hurried out.

It was the end of October. Physically Javert had recovered his old strength, mentally he was still in limbo, content to live in the present, and let the future take care of itself.

The days were shortening as the autumn waned. It was not yet six o'clock, but already the light was fading. Javert was standing by the window, gazing out at the last of the sunset. The door opened and Michelle came quietly in. Her expression was unusually solemn.

'Vere, you've got some visitors.'

She stood aside. Marius walked into the room. There was a young woman with him, around eighteen years old, slim and attractive. He had glimpsed her briefly twice before; when he unwittingly rescued Valjean from Thénardier, and when they had taken Marius home. This must be Valjean's adopted daughter, Cosette; as he looked at her more closely, her likeness to Fantine was apparent.

He remembered Fantine as he had last seen her - toothless, emaciated, dying of consumption - and compared her to the healthy, well-to-do young bourgeoise in front of him. Valjean had done that for her. For a moment the three of them gazed at each other in an awkward silence, then Marius stepped forward.

'Monsieur Javert, forgive us bursting in on you like this, but I thought you should know. Jean Valjean died late last night.'

Javert stared at him in shock, belatedly noticing the young man's sombre expression, the tears shining in the girl's eyes. Memories both good and bad flooded his mind, but uppermost was an unexpected sadness. Somehow he had thought that he and Valjean would meet again; this time not as enemies, but as free men. Now they never would.

Cosette moved forward and laid a hand on his arm.

'I wanted to say thank you, Monsieur. Papa at least died happy, because of you.'

Javert shook his head.

'I'm sorry - I don't understand.'

'That day you brought Marius home, Papa told me about his past - about being a convict and breaking his parole. He said you'd have to come back and arrest him, it was your job. I don't think he was worried so much about himself as he was about me - the scandal, you understand. As if I cared about that!

'Then one day Marius came home and told us you'd let Papa go; that you weren't going to arrest him after all. He was really free for the first time in his life.'

Javert's mouth twisted, his words unintentionally harsh.

'He didn't have much time to enjoy his freedom.'

'Perhaps not, but he died a free man. I don't think you can understand what that meant for him.'

Marius stepped forward.

'Monsieur Javert, we won't stay - I know you've been ill yourself. But before we go I've something for you. Before he died, Jean Valjean asked me to give you these.'

He opened the bag he carried, took out two candlesticks and placed them on the table. The silver gleamed almost golden in the late sun.

Javert stared at them. In his mind's eye he could see Valjean, standing in the tavern by the barricade, whilst Javert was bound to the pillar. Valjean's words sounded clearly in his brain.

Those candlesticks were more than a gift, they were a symbol. That man believed in me, he believed in what I could be. '

Javert turned away and walked over to the window. Behind him Marius was speaking again.

'He wanted you to have them; he said you'd understand.'

Javert nodded. He understood Valjean's message. But at the moment he couldn't turn round or respond to Marius' words. He didn't want anyone to see that the first tears for forty years were coursing down his cheeks.

The visitors had left. A subdued buzz of voices came from the café downstairs, where Michelle was working. It was getting late, Javert suddenly realised that the room was almost in darkness.

He stood up carefully and moved across to light the oil lamps. Then he stopped as his eyes fell on the candlesticks, standing on the table where Marius had left them. The white candles that had last been lit by Valjean showed pale in the shadows.

Javert gazed at them, then he replaced the oil lamp without lighting it and walked over to the table. He struck a match, his hand shaking a little as he applied it first to one candle, then the other. The flames flickered in the draught. For a moment they almost died, then they brightened and the shadows retreated.

He heard a sound behind him and turned to see Michelle standing in the doorway. He held out his arms to her, and she came into them without a word. Behind them the candles burnt steadily - their warm glow dispelling the darkness.

Afterword

I am indebted to the late Victor Hugo, whose novel Les Misérables provided the characters, and some of the plot, for this book. However, it would be untrue to say that this is a retelling of Les Misérables; only a relatively small percentage parallels the events in Victor Hugo's novel, most notably the later encounters between Javert and Valjean, and the student Barricades of 1832.

First and foremost, this is the story of Javert. From my first reading of Les Misérables, I was fascinated by Javert; in some ways the most tragic character in Victor Hugo's novel. Victor Hugo doesn't give much detail about him; we know he was born in prison, the son of a convict; that his character is unyielding; that he has an inflexible view of right and wrong. What I have principally done is try to put some meat on the skeleton of Javert's story and character.

Where we overlap, I have tried so far as possible to be true to Victor Hugo's story; but if you have read both books you will know that I took considerable poetic licence by continuing the story past Victor Hugo's original ending. My apologies to Les Misérables purists, and I hope Mr Hugo isn't turning in his grave too much.

Printed in Great Britain
by Amazon.co.uk, Ltd.,
Marston Gate.